P9-DVD-683

Ace Books by Dawn Cook

FIRST TRUTH
HIDDEN TRUTH
FORGOTTEN TRUTH

forgotten
truth

dawn cook

ACE BOOKS, NEW YORK

FORGOTTEN TRUTH

An Ace Book / published by arrangement with
the author

PRINTING HISTORY
Ace mass market edition / December 2003

For information address: The Berkley Publishing Group,
a division of Penguin Group (USA) Inc.,
375 Hudson Street, New York, New York 10014.

ISBN: 0-441-01117-9

ACE®
Ace Books are published by The Berkley Publishing Group,
a division of Penguin Group (USA) Inc.,
375 Hudson Street, New York, New York 10014.
ACE and the "A" design
are trademarks belonging to Penguin Group (USA) Inc.

PRINTED IN THE UNITED STATES OF AMERICA

10 9 8 7 6 5 4 3 2 1

For Tim

I

Alissa's throat tightened at the sight of the updraft, a deeper blue against the washed-out autumn sky. It rose like a column of shimmering heat from the open field of grass. Beneath her was the icy cool of the surrounding forest. Tops of individual trees were lost in a blur of damp pine smell from her speed. The wind slipping over her felt and sounded like gray silk, but instead of her usual pleasure, she felt only a coming dread.

"*See it?*" Beast said in her thoughts. "*What's going to happen when we find it?*"

"We go up," Alissa thought back, swallowing nervously. "*The sun's setting, and I have a lesson tonight. Perhaps we should stop. It's getting hard to see the updrafts.*"

"*It is not. We've been at this since sun-high. It's not that hard, Alissa.*" The voice in her thoughts gave the impression of an aggravated sigh. "*We're almost there. What do you do when you reach it?*"

"*I—uh—cup my wings about it and turn into a rising curve?*"

"*Yes.*"

Alissa's long tail made an exasperated twitch. She was sure Beast had done it. Alissa wouldn't have minded, but it shifted their momentum, and Alissa gasped. Beast said nothing as she impatiently abandoned this pass and angled Alissa back to the forest. Beside her came a faint chitter as Talon, Alissa's pet kestrel, protested at the sharp shift of direction.

The bird had accompanied her all afternoon as if in encouragement.

"Beast," Alissa asked, *"why are we bothering? I don't care you do all the flying."*

"I've seen your teacher watch you when we fly. He knows something is wrong. Someday he might realize it isn't you who is flying but me." Beast turned Alissa back to the updraft. *"Look sharp. I'm not going to help you this time."*

"Beast?" Alissa thought, concerned as she took control over the gentle glide Beast had left her in, but the voice didn't answer. Alissa eyed the approaching updraft, knowing from countless passes she had a moment to gather her courage. She glanced forward to the Hold. The nearly abandoned fortress nestled into the rock of the mountain. Behind the peak was a steep drop. The setting sun had beaten upon the sheer rock face all afternoon until the wave of heat streaming from it was so strong, it was almost purple to her raku eyes.

Beast had sported them in the windy violence earlier, showing Alissa the glorious possibilities to be found in updrafts before settling down to try to teach Alissa to fly on her own. The heavy upwelling of energy behind the Hold made the updraft over the fallow fields look like a washbasin in comparison to the sea, but even so it scared Alissa silly, making her long fingers tingle down to the tips of her savage claws.

Cup my wings and ease into it, she thought, her lips pulling back from her long canines as she felt Beast's thoughts turn impatient.

"Not so stiff, Alissa," her feral consciousness complained. *"Tear my dame's wings to shreds, why don't you trust the wind? It's more faithful than the most loyal mate."*

"Mate?" Alissa thought, embarrassed. Distracted, she slammed into the updraft unprepared. The wheat-scented wind caught her wings, shocking her with the force behind it. Alissa overcompensated. Feeling herself stall, she tried to flap her wings. It was a mistake. Pain shot through her back as she sought to find lift from a standstill.

"Alissa!" Beast shrieked. *"You can't rise that way! Cup your wings!"*

Alissa's tail whipped wildly as she tried to find her center of balance. It smacked painfully into a treetop. She was out of the updraft and back over the trees. Without the help of the rising air, she fell. A massive hemlock loomed before her. *"Beast!"* she cried.

Beast tried to snatch control, but panicked, Alissa wouldn't let go. Wings flailing, Alissa crashed through the canopy. Branches as thick as her arm snapped. Pain raked her wings. Frantic, Alissa struggled to fold them. There was no time to even gasp as the ground came at her.

She hit hard. In an uncontrolled barrel roll, she tumbled along the ground. Undergrowth and small trees cracked. End over end she spun until slamming into a tree. Her long neck flung out, and her jaw smacked into the earth. The tree shivered, sending dead needles to the ground and birds into the air. Blood filled her mouth. She had bitten her tongue.

"Oh, Ashes," she moaned aloud, her words coming out as a pained, guttural groan. Talon fluttered down to perch on her head, the bird's nails digging painlessly into Alissa's bare scalp. Alissa waved a nastily clawed hand at her bird to get her to leave. It was so undignified when Talon perched on her head like that. The kestrel made an insulted squawk and flew away.

"Alissa?" came a dry, disgusted thought from the depths of her mind. *"You are the only raku I know who can fall down in an updraft."*

"Ow," Alissa groaned aloud, her thick rumble carrying more pain than her human voice ever could. She slowly picked herself up, settling into a suffering, hunched crouch. Red-rimmed scratches marred her golden hide, and she was sore with what would probably be bruises.

"Look at your wing," Beast demanded. *"I think you tore it."*

Stomach turning, Alissa extended her left wing, being careful to not hit any of the remaining trees in the clearing she had made. Her neck snaked to look behind her. *"Burn it to ash,"* she thought. A panel close to her body had been punctured, making a tear almost as long as a man was tall. She looked to the ground, trying not to pass out or vomit. What would Useless, her teacher, say? He would ground her for a week.

"A week?" Beast thought sourly. *"It's going to take twice that long to heal."*

Alissa said nothing, relieved when her feral consciousness seemed to disappear. There was little to interest Beast on the ground. Only anger or the promise of flight would bring Beast to the forefront of Alissa's thoughts again.

She carefully folded her wing, holding it from her side as it was still oozing blood. The faint sound of someone calling her name filtered through the woods. It sounded muffled, as her hearing was now more attuned to deep tones her human ears couldn't discern. Her pulse quickened as she recognized Strell's voice. He had probably seen her fall. A second voice joined Strell's, and she grimaced. Lodesh was with him. Better and better.

Having the always-composed, self-assured, onetime ghost find her hurt and foolish was the last thing she wanted. Alissa sighed. Not really a ghost. Not anymore. The ancient Warden of Ese'Nawoer said he was as living as any man. It was a claim she tended to believe, as Lodesh's hands were warm when he pulled her into a dance, and his frequent, overly expressive looks often brought a blush to her face.

There was a faint tug upon her awareness. Recognizing Lodesh trying to reach her thoughts, she set up a block so he couldn't find her. And she could shift back to her human form to hide the tear. What her hurt wing would turn into was a question she had hoped she would never have to answer.

"Alissa?" came Strell's low-pitched voice, close and worried, and she sat up with a surprisingly quiet shuffle of leaves.

"Ali-i-i-i-issa?" called Lodesh, his careful pronunciation sounding concerned as well. Then, softer, clearly to Strell. "I know she came down here somewhere. I hope she's not unconscious. I can't reach even her thoughts."

She felt wicked, but the shame of her torn wing kept her mouth shut and her mind closed. Lodesh would shake his head, then tease her until her teacher found out about the tear. Strell would tactfully ignore the situation—providing she seemed all right—knowing she would be embarrassed for having fallen out of the sky. If she was going to shift, it would have to be now.

With three slow breaths, Alissa unfocused her attention. Quick from practice, she set up the proper pathways in her mind to work the ward. Cool, silver force flowed from her source to fill her tracings, deep in her awareness. The heavy smell of bracken and sap vanished as she broke herself down to a thought, shifted that thought to the body she had been born with, then made that thought real. At the last moment, she remembered to clothe herself, and a new pattern joined the one already resonating in her mind.

Alissa coalesced into existence wearing a Keeper's traditional garb of long tunic and short vest bound about her small waist with a black scarf. A skirt hemmed in green ribbon finished the outfit, edging her toes. Her feet were bare but for a pair of thin stockings with holes, and her face warmed for the lack of shoes. At least she had stockings on. She may as well be naked if she hadn't had those.

Useless hated her Keeper attire, saying as a Master, she ought to dress as such. But she hadn't yet taken the time to learn how to craft anything else with her thoughts. The task was tedious, and she would learn how to make shoes before more clothes. Alissa ran a hand over her skirt to reassure herself it was there. The one time she had forgotten had been mortifying.

The stark savagery of hide, claw, and primitive strength had been replaced by sun-darkened skin and horridly straight fair hair that went halfway to her elbows. Her eyes had retained their odd gray color; it was something she wished she could change. Scratches marred her arms when she pushed up her long sleeves to see, and her jaw was tender. A new soreness ran down her back, and she stretched painfully to test her limits. Something was torn inside her. By feel she decided her back was whole and unmarked. The damage was hidden inside.

Heart pounding, she lurched her way through the shattered branches and ducked behind a tree. If she planned it right, she might get a moment with Strell alone.

"By the Navigator's Hounds!" she heard Lodesh exclaim, and she knew they had found her clearing. "Look what she did!"

Alissa peered around her tree. Strell and Lodesh stood with their feet edging the new destruction in the setting sun. Talon was perched on Lodesh's wrist. The canny bird swiveled her head and looked directly at Alissa. She winced as Strell cupped his hands and shouted, "Ali-i-issa-a-a!"

Strell shivered and ran a hand over his brown hair, ending the motion with gripping the hair clip at the back of his neck in a tight fist. The action was clearly one of worry. Strell was from the desert and probably felt the chill of the coming night as much as she did—though she had yet to hear him complain about it. He was surprisingly tall, almost gaunt despite the plates of food he ate. Dressed in his simple brown shirt and trousers, he looked like a poor cousin next to Lodesh's extravagant clothes.

Lodesh was the only Keeper the Hold could boast of right now, and he was admittedly faster with his wards than she, despite his lower standing. Nearly four centuries ago he had been the Warden of the nearby abandoned city, Ese'Nawoer. Now, the revived ghost spent much of his time helping her practice her wards.

He was dressed in Keeper attire cut from a rich, dark green fabric befitting his Wardenship. Around his neck was a silver pendant in the shape of a mirth flower. It was the symbol of his city and was repeated on his heavy ring. He, too, kept his cheeks clear of even the hint of a beard, knowing Alissa liked it that way. The Keeper cut a startling figure with his blond hair, green eyes, and confident poise, but it was upon Strell her gaze lingered.

Alissa sighed in frustration. Strell, who had saved her life, who had freed Useless from his cell, who had returned her mind to her when she went feral—who could never be a Keeper, forever unable to perform even the simplest ward, and thus forbidden to her. It was Strell she loved. Strell and the smile he reserved for her when they were alone.

The two men picked their way through the ruin, clearly awed. Even from behind her tree, she could see Strell's worry. "Can you reach her thoughts yet?" he asked Lodesh after finding her blood on the leaves. It was a rare question, proving how concerned Strell was. She knew Strell's aversion to bringing up Lodesh's Keeper abilities. It only pointed out Strell's lack.

"No." Lodesh confidently put his hands on his hips and shook his head. "She's ignoring me, so she must be all right. Obviously she isn't in her raku shape anymore."

Loosely unfocusing her attention, Alissa modulated her thoughts so Strell could hear her in his mind. By rights she shouldn't be able to reach any but another Master, but Alissa never listened to impossibilities, managing to speak with not only Masters and Keepers, but Strell as well. Useless said it was from having started life as a human instead of a raku, thereby forcing her mind to develop human strategies for verbal language. She didn't care.

"Strell?" she thought, knowing he wouldn't be able to answer. *"Don't tell Lodesh. I'm over here."*

She smiled at the faint rush of emotion she could sense from him: relief tinged with anticipation. Her smile deepened as he turned to Lodesh. "Obviously she isn't here," Strell said, the fallacy falling from him as convincingly as one of his numerous tales. "Why don't we split up? I'll check the woods. You see if she's gone back to the Hold."

"Good idea." Shaking his head at the devastation, Lodesh walked the length of the new clearing and vanished under the trees. From his wrist came Talon's chitter. The bird clearly knew he was going the wrong way.

"Alissa?" Strell whispered as soon as Lodesh was gone.

"Here, Strell," she called, coming out from behind the tree.

He beamed, his shoulders relaxing as he saw she was all right. He crossed the clearing in eager, long strides.

"Wait," she said in alarm. She held up a hand before he

could sweep her into an embrace and show the world her lack of footwear. "I lost my shoes."

Strell jerked to a stop. His brow furrowed, and he took her shoulders in his hands. "Are you all right?" he asked, his brown eyes intent on hers.

Her breath caught at his tight grip, and she dropped her gaze, flustered. "Yes. I'm fine. But I left my shoes this side of the garden's wall. Come with me to get them?"

"Ashes, Alissa," he said, reddening as he released her shoulders. "Would you hurry up and learn how to make them?" Taking advantage of the rare opportunity of having no eyes upon them, Strell cupped her hand in his as he helped her over the upturned earth.

"Thanks." Eyes lowered, she paced beside him, keeping her steps slow to prolong their walk, as much as from the pain in her lower back. His hand was warm, and rough from his work at keeping the Hold's few fires lit. She ran her fingertips to the ends of his fingers and back, feeling the calluses from his twin professions of musician and potter. His other hand lacked a full pinkie, and she knew he had shifted to her right side so as to hide it.

Alissa's mood went soft. It was foolish, and she knew it meant little, but Strell so rarely felt free to show his feelings for her that even the smallest gesture was a treasure. It didn't help that he had been raised in the stiff-necked culture of the desert, either. Useless would be annoyed if he found out she had been alone with Strell in the woods.

It had been made very plain to her that Strell would never be allowed to formally court her. Part of the bargain to bend the rules and let Strell remain at the Hold had been based on the understanding that he would keep his thoughts—and hands—from Alissa. Useless made it no secret that he hoped with time Alissa would turn her fancy to a match more suitable to her Master standing.

And time stretched forward for her in abundance. As a Master, she now had a life span ten times Strell's. Again, she didn't care, or at least that's what she told herself.

"Play a tune for me tonight?" she asked, already knowing the answer.

"M-m-m," he sighed, holding a branch for her as they passed into the shadow of the trees.

A familiar fluttering brought a groan of dismay from both of them. Talon hovered in a noisy complaint, waiting for Alissa to offer her a perch. The robin-sized bird's chatters were accusing, and Alissa drew her hand from Strell's with a guilty swiftness. If she didn't, Talon's protests would turn physical. And though it wouldn't be hard to fight off the small bird, it would be difficult explaining to Useless why Strell was scratched.

Annoyed, she held out a wrist for the kestrel. "Hush," Alissa soothed as she brought Talon close and tried to cover her head. Talon would have nothing to do with the pacification, worrying Alissa's fingers with her sharp beak until Alissa gave up and put Talon on her shoulder. The bird's harangue never slowed, but it at least grew softer, turning into a muttering complaint.

Alissa looked at Strell and winced. Lodesh had probably flown the bird, knowing she would seek out her mistress. Strell took a reluctant step from her, clearly coming to the same conclusion. "You really should teach that bird to wear a hood and jesses," he grumbled. Cupping his hands, he looked in the direction Talon had come from. "Lodesh!" he shouted before the Keeper found them and guessed he had been manipulated. "She's over here!"

"Is she all right?" came Lodesh's distinct call.

"I'm fine," she said as the outline of Lodesh became obvious, quashing her guilt for not having answered his silent hail earlier.

"Are you sure?" he asked as he came even with them in a crackling of undergrowth. His gaze ran over her from head to toe, and she flushed. The hint of amusement dancing over him made Alissa wonder if he had known her plan all along, letting her and Strell think they had gotten away with something, but not giving them enough time alone to get into trouble. It was hard to remember the man had a lifetime of experience to draw upon when he looked like—Alissa glanced up at him and away—like a young, handsome, carefree nobleman's son.

"I'm fine," she said again, slouching so her skirt hid her feet. Her back gave a deeper twinge, and she forced her brow smooth so as to not show it. "But I have to fetch my shoes—again."

Lodesh brightened. "I'll make you a pair," he said cheerfully.

Alissa and Strell exchanged wondering looks. Lodesh had never offered to before. She hadn't known he could make shoes from his thoughts. "But it takes years for a Keeper to learn how to craft something," Alissa said. "I didn't know you had been practicing."

Lodesh put a finger to his nose. His eyes glinted roguishly. "Years is what I've had, yes? And you aren't the only one who has small, dainty feet, Alissa."

She took a breath to speak, then shut her mouth, embarrassed. It had been vain to assume he had fixed a new form in his thoughts solely for her. There was a tug on her awareness as Lodesh worked his ward. Curiosity prompted her to unfocus her attention to see the pattern of tracings he used. When she was close enough, the creation of a ward set up a resonance within her own tracings, setting her dormant pathways to faintly glow. It was how wards were taught to students.

A pair of soft, gray slippers ghosted into existence, cradled in Lodesh's hands. Alissa accepted them gratefully. Both men looked away. Strell's back was stiff as he turned. She wanted to think it was to give her some privacy, but she knew it was because he hated Lodesh using his Keeper skills. Alissa wedged her feet into the gray slippers and shook her skirt out to cover them. "Thank you, Lodesh," she said softly, not liking how he had made Strell feel.

Strell was unable to hide his sliver of frustration. Lodesh held an arm out to help her back to the Hold, and Alissa miserably declined it. Undeterred, Lodesh gave her a good-natured smile. "Let me escort you back to the Hold, Alissa. If I remember correctly, you have a lesson in the garden tonight. You're late."

Alissa's eyes widened, and her gaze darted to the Hold's tower showing beyond the pines. "Ashes," she exclaimed softly, tensing in worry. "Is it after six already? Last week the sun wasn't much higher at six," she complained. "How am I supposed to be on time if it changes that fast!" Then another thought pushed her concern to alarm. She glanced over her shoulder toward her clearing. "You don't think Useless saw that, do you?"

Lodesh shook his head, grinning mischievously. "If he had, I'm sure you would have known it by now."

Reassured, she took a quick step toward the Hold, then hesitated, knowing she ought not leave her other shoes outside the garden wall just because she had a new pair.

"I'll get your shoes," Strell volunteered, apparently knowing where her thoughts lay. "You go ahead with Lodesh."

Alissa dropped her gaze. An uncomfortable silence fell between them. Preoccupied with his thoughts, Strell gave her only a wave before stomping off in a direction that was nowhere near the garden wall. She allowed herself a small sigh as she turned to Lodesh and accepted his arm. They silently made their way to the Hold. Talon's complaining finally stopped.

It was obvious Strell loved her. Lodesh had also made it clear with intent looks and uncommon courtesies that he cared for her, too. Lately, Alissa had come to believe Lodesh was biding his time, betting Strell would eventually make a mistake that couldn't be overlooked and find himself banished from the Hold, leaving Alissa all to Lodesh. But for now, he seemed content to be a friend to them both, knowing until he absolved his curse, he would remain in existence for as long as Alissa did—in some form or another. He need only to wait.

The situation put Alissa in a foul mood when she thought about it too long. But it was hard not to like Lodesh, with his quick wit and cheerful disposition. She also appreciated his steadfast tolerance of her. She was putting all three of them through the Navigator's hell as she refused to abandon what her heart wanted over what she knew was right, proper, and inevitable.

Alissa glanced up at Lodesh's firm profile. The handsome Keeper was clearly a better match for her, seeing as there were no Masters left to choose from. With Lodesh, her children might make the jump to Master as she had; with Strell, they likely wouldn't even make Keeper. And she did like Lodesh. . . . But there had to be a way to get what she wanted. She just hadn't found it yet.

Squinting, Alissa brought them to a halt as they found the edge of the trees and the setting sun. The Hold stood before them, gray in the shadowy light. Her breath slipped from her in a sigh as she tried to imagine what the Hold had been like when it was full of Keepers, Masters, and students. It was easy this time of day, the few moments between sunset and the lamps being lit. She could pretend the stillness hard upon her ears and eyes was from grace being said, not twenty years of near abandonment.

Lodesh stirred, and she flashed him a quick smile. The sun was almost down. Useless would have undoubtedly spent the interim planning out a fine lecture as to the proper use of time.

"Thank you, Lodesh," she said as she flung Talon into the air and they moved forward. "If it weren't for you, I would have completely forgotten. How late am I?"

"You have no idea, Alissa," he said mysteriously, but if his look of alarm was contrived or not, she couldn't tell.

2

Lodesh met Alissa's quickening stride as they entered the smaller of the Hold's two kitchens. "Why," she complained, "did Useless get it into his head to hold class at night, anyway?"

"You really should call Master Talo-Toecan by his given name, Alissa."

She shifted her shoulders. "He told me I could call him that, and at the time, he was."

"A Master of the Hold is anything but useless," Lodesh insisted.

"Perhaps," she muttered. "Unless bound by his word or her lack of skill."

Lodesh put out a hand and stopped her. Ashamed, she dropped her gaze. "You," he said gently, "are not useless." The clean scent of mirth wood filled her senses, and his hand lifted her chin. She went still as their gazes met. When she had first made his acquaintance, he had diligently striven with subtle words and sly looks to get her to blush. Repeated exposure and a comfortable friendship had made her immune to his considerable charms—for the most part. That, and her slow awareness of the old grief he hid behind his eyes.

His eyes were old. In them was the pain Lodesh had endured as his beloved, cursed city faltered and fell: watching his people leave family by family, seeing the prosperous streets go empty and silent, knowing it was his fault and his fault alone. Uncomfortable, she looked away.

"Even in the best of circumstances a Master takes the better part of two centuries to become proficient," he continued, clearly not knowing she could see. "Be patient."

"Now you sound like Useless," she said.

"Just so." He smiled. "And you should call him Talo-Toecan. Besides," he said as he picked up a cloth and moved a kettle from the flames, "your schooling is going frighteningly quickly. I imagine he's currently deep into the theory of line tripping."

"How—how did you know?" she asked.

He looked up from filling a teapot with the lukewarm water from the hearth. There was a flash of resonance across her tracings as he used a warming ward and the teapot began to steam. "Your evening lesson gave it away," he said. "Tripping the lines of time to view the past is complicated. It would be unlike Talo-Toecan to allow you to sleep on half the lesson, risking you would figure the rest out on your own and get yourself into trouble."

Alissa winced, knowing Useless had cause to worry. "Ah, yes."

Smiling, Lodesh found a soft cloth and dabbed at her jawline. It came away with a red smear, and she reached up to touch her jaw. "Did you fall because of Beast?" he asked lightly.

Her breath seemed to freeze. Taking the towel from his hands, she turned away. "No," she said, too embarrassed to tell him she couldn't yet fly on her own.

He hesitated. "I'm concerned, Alissa. Masters always destroy the second, feral consciousness that evolves when learning how to shift from raku to human. None have ever agreed to live with it. Perhaps this is why?" His green eyes went worried. "Is Beast—trying to take over?"

"No. She isn't," Alissa said defensively, not liking to talk of Beast so openly. If Useless realized Alissa had retained her feral conscious, he would make her destroy Beast. Even Strell didn't know. How Lodesh had guessed was beyond her.

Lodesh's head tilted, his worried stance saying more than words that he wasn't convinced. "Here," he finally said, extending the brewing pot. "You're late, but if you bring him tea, he will most likely overlook your tardiness." Alissa's brow pinched at the reminder. "You had better run," he said, leading her by the elbow to the door.

With a final, extravagant gesture, Lodesh opened the garden door. The sound of crickets slipped in to pool behind her, urging her to be out among them in the dew-ridden darkness of a night with no moon. Alissa gathered her skirts in one hand, the pot of tea in the other. Her back protested as she started down the weed-lined path to the large, sunken firepit that often served as her schoolroom. Behind her, the door shut with a gentle thump.

Talking of Beast had tightened Alissa's sense of unease. Her lower back gave a strong twinge, and she slowed, wishing she knew how to tell time. It didn't make sense that the hours shifted independent of the sun. Moving as fast as her back would allow, she turned a corner and came to a dismayed halt. Not only was Useless at the firepit, but he had already lit the fire.

The Master straightened at the sound of her approach, his white eyebrows rising in question. Alissa tossed her tangled hair from her eyes and sedately continued down the path with a false nonchalance. At least he was in his human shift. Trying to reason with him when he was a raku was impossible.

"Alissa?" came his clipped accent. He sounded puzzled, not annoyed as she had feared.

"Good evening, Useless," she said meekly.

"You're early tonight."

"Early?" Her head came up. "Lodesh said I was late!"

Her teacher's expression went from amusement to bother. "Then you probably are," he amended, frowning in what she recognized as irritation at himself, not her. Apparently Useless had the same problem as she when it came to time. Perhaps, she mused, stepping down into the bench-lined pit surrounding the fire, it had something to do with how their minds were laid out.

Useless held his comments to a grimace as he took in her Keeper attire. He made a great show of shaking out his long Master's vest. It was the color of ripe wheat and went all the way to the ground, giving her the impression of a sleeveless robe. Having it bound tightly about his waist with a black scarf only strengthened the image. Peeping from under the vest were trousers and a wide-sleeved tunic. Though of a simple cut and pattern, the fabric was of a quality that had never made it to her foothills home, being tight of weave and even of color.

The Master had no beard and kept his hair cropped close to his skull—to hide the whiteness of it, Lodesh had once said in jest. He was as tall as Strell and nearly as dark, with a ramrod stiffness about him whether he was sitting or standing. Since he was quick to anger and even quicker to admit to a mistake, keeping abreast of his moods was often a losing battle.

Though in his human shift, his eyes retained the unreal golden color characteristic of all Masters. His hands, too, couldn't hide his raku origins and were abnormally long. Each finger had four segments instead of the usual three. Alissa had long ago adjusted her thinking to see them as normal, but tonight her gaze lingered on them as he reached for the teapot. Her fingers looked as they always had. Alissa exhaled heavily. Even as a Master, she didn't quite fit in.

The stone benches built into the surrounding earth still held the day's warmth, and she settled to his right, glad the night was dark enough to hide the scrape on her chin. She winced when she realized she had forgotten the cups. Seeing it, Useless sighed, and with a tug on her awareness and a flash of resonance across her tracings, two cups glazed a hideous brown materialized on the bench between them. He silently poured the tea and handed her the first cup. Taking a sip, he grimaced and set it down. "Lodesh's tea?" he asserted sourly.

Blinking, Alissa nodded. "How did you know?"

"He always wards the water to boiling. The kettle never warms sufficiently, so the leaves don't brew properly."

She took a cautious sip. It tasted fine to her, but then, she wasn't over eight centuries old.

Holding the cup to warm her hands, Alissa sat and tried not

to fidget. As soon as she had stopped moving, her back had begun to throb, all the way down to her rear. Clearly some of the mass for wings came from that area, and she wondered what sort of mischief had managed that. She glanced nervously at her teacher. How was she going to hide the tear until it healed?

Useless shook his head at some private thought and drained his cup. Lodesh's brew or not, he was still apparently going to drink it. He adjusted his vest over his spare frame, and his slippered feet withdrew underneath him to sit cross-legged upon the bench. Alissa's breath quickened. He was ready to teach.

"This morning," he began, "I explained the theory behind line tripping. Tell it to me."

She sat straighter, frowning at the ache in her back. The stone bench wasn't helping. "Sending your thoughts to the past is reexperiencing a memory, be it yours or someone else's gifted to you. There's no way to change it because the threads have already been tightened. You're not so much reliving the past as seeing one person's view of it."

"Excellent," Useless praised. "The difference is subtle but tantamount to success."

"You mean you're going to let me try tonight!"

Useless chuckled, hiding his smile behind a hastily raised cup. "No-o-o," he drawled, and she collapsed against the back of the bench, straightening as a rush of pain shot through her. It was getting worse. "But I'll explain how it's done," he continued. "You should be decades along in your studies before learning this, not years. Seeing as you've been among the lines last fall, it would be prudent to present it to you now." He frowned. "Before you decide you can figure it out by yourself."

Grimacing at the slight jibe, Alissa shifted uncomfortably and sipped her tea. Perhaps she could risk complaining of a minor pain. Useless might run a ward of healing for her, clearing everything up with him never knowing the difference. She would have done it herself, but she hadn't been given permission to work the complex ward without supervision.

"Finding and fixing a memory in your thoughts is the first step," Useless said. "But it's an important one. Engage the ward before that, and you'll slip into a long, unproductive sleep. There're several methods to fix a memory. The easiest is to use one of your own." He looked up as she fidgeted. "The second is to be gifted one by another. The third is to use a *septhama* point." He leaned to top off his cup.

She thought about that. The word *septhama* was familiar, but she couldn't see how it related. Septhamas were a blessedly rare group of individuals whose tracings were almost complex enough to make Keeper but had been malformed. Usually stemming from Keeper parents, they had the ability to do one thing, and one thing only. And even that was rather pointless. "I give up," she finally said.

Useless didn't even try to hide his smile. "You're aware septhamas can modify the pattern—the flow of psychic energy imprinted after a tragedy—so as to make the corresponding physical manifestation of such energy more pleasing to the general populace?"

Alissa nodded, finding slight relief as she leaned to adjust the fire. Why didn't he just say they got rid of ghosts?

"Well, a septhama point is that stored energy, which in this case functions like a memory residing in a place or a thing." He hesitated. "Or more rarely, a person."

Her gaze went distant, recalling that Strell's broken pipe had such a memory on it. Rising, she went to the opposite side of the fire to nudge back a stick she had intentionally pushed out.

"What are you doing?" Useless asked in wonder. "I've never seen anyone so reluctant to sit still since I—" His voice cut off. Arms clasped about herself, Alissa glanced up to find her teacher's lips pursed and his eyes knowing. "You damaged your tail," he said.

Panic mixed with shame, and she looked away. He would be so angry! "Uh, no," she warbled.

"Your wing, then?" he guessed, and she nodded, cringing at his heavy sigh.

"I'm fine," she said, returning to her spot and sitting on the edge of the bench. The pain swelled, and she reluctantly got to her feet.

"You were sporting in the heavy updrafts behind the Hold again, weren't you," he said, though it really wasn't a question. "I told you to be careful. Do you know how many young rakus have ended up at the bottom of that rock face?"

She said nothing, content to let him believe what he wanted.

"You're the only one left, Alissa," he lectured gently. "You must be more careful. Why do you think I've been teaching you what only an experienced Master should know? I'm not going to last much longer, and I won't let a millennium of study die with me."

"Useless," she cajoled, not liking to hear him speak like that. His eyes meeting hers were full of a patient understanding, surprising her.

"Shift and show me what you did," he demanded in a soft voice. "It can't be worse than anything I've done. I'll run a ward of healing on it, or better yet, you can. The practice will do you good." He shook his head and fussed with the fire, his long fingers perilously close to the low flames. "Though I ought not to have taught it to you in the first place," he finished.

Alissa's excitement at having been granted permission to practice the tricky ward was blunted by worry. Perhaps his understanding attitude would become anger after seeing what she had done. Still, she hurt, and having a three-day acceleration of healing would be a relief.

The sun had since vanished, and feeling a chill, she stepped awkwardly up onto the stone bench and from there to the long, neglected grass. Making no comment, she removed her slippers so as not to break them down to nothing with the rest of her clothes when she shifted. Useless didn't care if she wore shoes or not, but her foothills upbringing made her uncomfortable without them. The loud pop as they hit the bench made her jump.

Despising disorder, Useless arranged her slippers neatly. "You should be more careful with your footwear until you can fashion them yourself," he said, clearly recognizing they weren't the shoes she had on when she left the Hold that morning.

"Useless?" she asked, curious. "Why is it my hurt shifts with me? I would think that since I was in a completely different form, it wouldn't show at all."

Useless sipped his tea. "You shift to your idea of yourself, and your mind knows you're hurt. Oddly enough, that's one of the reasons we live so long. You are," he said, "literally as young as you think, or in this case, as your thoughts remember you to be."

Her brow puckered in disbelief. This was far beyond her original question, but she fastened upon it greedily. "So if I shifted thinking I was ten years old, I would coalesce as that?"

The warm sound of her teacher's laugh slipped like a sunbeam about the weedy shrubs and overgrown grasses of his expansive garden. "No. You would show up as your rightful age, but your youthful appearance will persist for ten times longer than you might imagine. Your mind can't be fooled, but it's slow to accept change. Pain, though, makes a very strong impression, which is why it shifts with you."

She nodded in acceptance. It made sense, as much as any of it ever did.

Knowing Useless would take the chance to evaluate her skill at shifting, Alissa went through the preparatory steps with a measured slowness. Eyes open, she visualized her source with her mind's eye. Deep in her awareness was a sphere of white so stark as to be possible only in her imagination, a gift from her papa before he died. It was bound by silvery gold threads, glittering like glory itself. She had never been able to see what lay past the threads. Useless had once told her it was because limit-bound thoughts had a hard time with infinity.

Surrounding her source, but seeming to be twisted half an angle away, sprawled her tracings. The bluish black lines spread out in all directions, connecting and fracturing into a maze of astounding proportions, looping back at the limits of her mind. Being empty of all but the smallest energy, they were hard to see. Only the gold tracing they were shot through with gave evidence that they were there. That would change.

Alissa slipped a thought into her source. A glowing ribbon darted from it to make the curving jump to her tracings. From there it circled back, crossing against itself to make a twisted loop before returning to her source, leaving a humming circle of energy running through her mind. It was the beginnings of everything. She didn't care that Useless called her tracings her neural net and the first loop the primary circuit. She only knew together they made wards.

From here it was simple to direct the force into the proper pathways. Chosen tracings burst into light as the energy filled them, making the far-flung, complicated pattern needed to hold her soul together as she destroyed her body and fashioned mass about it again.

There was a familiar feeling of perfect disconnection as the chill, dark garden winked out of existence. She knew from watching Useless that she had vanished into a mist that grew as she pulled energy from her source to make the additional mass for her larger form. In a moment the garden was back, but she was viewing it from a perspective two man lengths higher.

"Very nice," Useless grumbled, clearly pleased at the quickness of her shift. In his opinion, she spent far too much time existing as only a thought. "Now, show me what you did to yourself. Skin your wing on a cliff, did you?"

"No," she said into his mind, being incapable of verbal speech now. Twin feelings of wanting sympathy and wanting to be left alone warred within her as she extended her wing.

"Oh, Alissa," Useless breathed as the rip came to light. A pattern resonated across her tracings and held steady as Useless made a ward of illumination. The globe rested in his long fingers to show the bone and blood within them. "You should have come to me right away."

She said nothing, thinking the reason she hadn't was obvious.

"How did you ever get back up to the top of the cliff with a rip like this?"

Her shoulders shifted in a shrug. She couldn't look at him, wishing he had gotten angry instead of sympathetic. Lies of omission were still lies.

Brow furrowed, he went to stand under her wing. The glow from his light shone through the rip. She snaked her neck under her wing to see, lifting it out of his reach as he threatened to run a finger along the cut. "Put your wing down," he said dryly. "I'm not going to touch it." She heard his sigh. "It would have been better had you run a healing ward before shifting," he said. "Human back muscle heals differently than wing canvas."

"You told me not to run a healing ward alone," she said, feeling her shoulder ache from holding her wing extended for so long.

"That I did." He came out from under her wing, his features sharp in his light. "I suppose if you're brave enough to chance the rock face's updrafts, you're ready to run a healing ward on your own." He grimaced. "Lay your wing on the ground. I'll hold the ends together the best I can as you run it. Even so, you're going to have a scar. I imagine the indignity of having to explain it to your future students will be punishment enough."

Surprised at his attitude, she sent a docile thought into his. *"You aren't angry?"*

Useless gave her an unfathomable look. "Accidents happen. Especially when playing in an updraft that strong. Tell me next time you want to try the rock face. You should have a spotter."

"Yes, Useless," she said, relieved he was taking it so well.

"Go on," he encouraged gruffly. "Put your wing where I can reach it."

She crouched, angling her wing around the overgrown

shrubs. Useless drew his light closer and left it to hang in midair. Her breath escaped in a pained hiss as Useless pushed the torn edges together. His long fingers were gentle, but her nausea rose. She closed her eyes, not wanting to watch her flesh knit together.

The sight of her mindscape eased her sick feeling. She set up the proper pattern, holding it steady when she felt a light, familiar touch on her thoughts as Useless checked it. Almost she could feel his satisfaction. Only now did Alissa release the ward, and her tracings went dark.

It was like bathing in sunshine. Warmth eased through her, the ward pulling behind it a sensation of tingling whispers, soothing away the pain from her scrapes and the headache she hadn't realized she had. The sensation back-washed at the limits of her body, then returned to her wing, slipping through her like water through hot sand.

Alissa drooped as the throbbing pain in her wing turned to the mild ache of a three-day-old wound. All too soon the ward had spent itself. She sighed, reluctant to move, only now realizing she had slumped to an undignified, foolish-looking sprawl on the damp ground.

"Feel better?" Useless said sourly, jerking her back to awareness.

"Rather." Embarrassed, she sat up and looked at her wing. The tear had been replaced with a long, raw-looking scar, black from the fire behind it. Alissa sighed. It was ugly, but at least it didn't hurt as much.

"No flying until at least one more healing ward," he said as his light went out and he returned to his spot at the fire. "And you will wait the required three days between them. It takes that long for your body to recover its reserves. Trying sooner will do more damage than good. That will give you a total of nine days of healing in five days: three days accelerated, three days unassisted, and another three days accelerated. Understand?"

"Yes," she thought as she settled herself on the grass. They had been over this before, but now his words had a practical meaning. She found herself more comfortable in her

raku form, so she stayed where she was, not caring that the earth was damp with dew. Crouching, she rested her chin on her forearms to stare into the fire, watching with her more sensitive eyes the patterns of heat shift and stream upward, rolling along the ground to backwash against the benches.

"Now, where were we?" Useless prompted. Alissa could tell he wanted to join her in raku form, but there wasn't enough space around the firepit for two such hulking beasts. Besides, someone had to finish Lodesh's tea.

3

Strell kept his features impassive as he sat before his wheel and worked his cold, gritty clay. It was too dark to be spinning clay; the shadows were thick in the Hold's second, unused kitchen, and he didn't have a candle. But he had been born with clay beneath his fingernails and could throw a pot by feel alone. Though having made his way as a musician and storyteller for the last seven years, this was his first craft, the one he turned to when his thoughts were heavy.

Strell's gaze lifted to the shadowed lump of Alissa's shoes upon the nearby drying table. He had found them outside the garden wall where she had shifted and abandoned the earth. Her shoes and he seemed alike in that way: dusty and worn, set aside while she learned new limits that he could never see. Tomorrow, he would return them to her. He would like to put them next to his, under his bed, someday. Strell straightened, feeling his back crack all the way up.

He had been so worried, especially after finding her bruised and scraped in the middle of a new clearing. Flying was a learned skill, and she had only a few months to practice it. Thankfully, it seemed only her pride had been hurt. Even so, he had wanted to lift her up and carry her back to soft cushions and warm compresses. But he knew she would be embarrassed and so had contented himself with holding her hand. He might have done more if that cursed bird hadn't shown up.

Sighing, he kicked the wheel up to speed and formed a pleasingly proportioned bowl. Talon or Lodesh. Someone always interfered, leaving him frustrated and out of sorts but still in Talo-Toecan's good graces. It didn't help that Lodesh was so blessedly charismatic. Alissa would be inhuman if she didn't like Lodesh.

With a rough savageness, Strell forced the bowl into a tall vase. It was not a move that lent itself to a smooth transition, and only the base stood firm as the vase wobbled. All Lodesh had to do was wait, Strell brooded. And wait was exactly what the Warden of Ese'Nawoer was doing. Neither commenting on or ignoring Strell and Alissa's stymied relationship, Lodesh waited, content to be a friend to both of them, knowing if he forced his hand he might alienate Alissa. Time was Lodesh's guarantee he would win Alissa's affection, and the cursed man seemed to rest easy in the knowledge.

Nearly four centuries ago, while the Warden of Ese'Nawoer, Lodesh had built a wall about his city. Wisdom had prompted its construction, but fear kept the gates closed against the women and children who desperately sought sanctuary there against a plague of madness. The inhabitants of the city turned a deaf ear to their locked gates, even when the pleas for mercy turned to a mindless, savage rage, and mothers beat their children to death before turning on themselves.

The city remained untouched by plague, but the blood on their doorstep cursed the people to eternal unrest until making amends for their crimes against humanity. Alissa had since freed them, but Lodesh, the builder of the walls and the holder of the blame, remained cursed.

It seemed unfair to Strell that the clever man could turn something as damning as a curse to his favor, allowing Lodesh to accompany Alissa in her recently expanded life span as Strell couldn't.

Strell, though, had his own guarantee. Alissa loved him, not Lodesh. All Strell had to do was convince her teacher to bend the rules again. And after having kept Alissa alive last winter while biding with an insane Keeper, changing the mores of a raku seemed an easy task.

Strell and Lodesh had evolved a strange, competitive friendship, each sublimely confident they would ultimately win Alissa and therefore not threatened by each other's presence. That Lodesh thought he would gain Alissa meant nothing to Strell. He knew the Keeper was mistaken.

The wheel creaked and complained in the chill silence as it slowed. Eyeing his vase, Strell ran a cord under it to loosen it from the wheel. Fingers spread wide, he lifted it free and tossed it to the barrel of waste clay. It hit with a solid slap, collapsing into an unusable shape.

Cleanup was quick from long practice, and before it became much darker, he found himself in the Hold's upper rooms. A soft fluttering over his head as he passed through the dark great hall pulled his fist up, and Talon lighted upon it. "Hello, old one," he murmured, running his fingers over the bird's markings, gray with age. He and Talon got along quite well as long as he kept his distance from Alissa. Humming the bird a soothing lullaby, he went into the Hold's smaller kitchen. If Alissa was with Talo-Toecan, then he and Lodesh would prepare the evening meal alone. But it was late. Lodesh had probably already finished.

Quiet in the soft-soled shoes Alissa insisted Strell wear inside the Hold, he found Lodesh sitting unawares as he often did, legs stretched out to the hearth, slumped on one of the kitchen's hard chairs. The Keeper's fine clothes looked startlingly out of place, yet he evoked a feeling that here, of all places, was where he felt most comfortable. Lodesh was waiting, simply waiting.

"What's for dinner tonight?" Strell asked quietly so as not to startle him.

Grunting, Lodesh straightened and turned. A wisp of a mischievous smile was about him, clear even in the shadow light from the hearth. "What would you say to roast duck?"

Strell started in surprise, then grinned. "M-m-m," he sighed, tossing Talon to the thick rafters. "With the skin crispy . . . cooked so the meat falls off the bone, begging to be eaten." Gaze unfocused, he collapsed into a chair across from Lodesh.

"Stuffed with small new potatoes and onions," Lodesh said dreamily.

"Or a piglet, roasted all day over a spitting fire, flaring up as the juice drips out," Strell said, his mouth watering. He put his elbows on the table and rested his chin on a fist.

"Or venison cooked over an open fire . . ."

"Or a haunch of sheep, rolled in crushed mint and pastry."

"Or even—even a goat," Lodesh finished longingly.

Together, they heaved a wistful sigh. Strell stirred first, breaking out of their dream as he sat back. "What are we really having?"

"Vegetable stew and biscuits."

They sighed once more.

"I'll never eat meat again," Strell lamented, leaning his chair precariously back on two legs. "It's not that I can't do without it, but every once in a while . . ."

Lodesh rose and went to the oven. "Alissa would take us flying if she caught us cooking meat in her kitchen."

"Maybe she could get lost in the garden one night," Strell said, "and we could have a real dinner."

With a scrape of the metal latch, the oven opened and seemed to fill the warm space with the smell of Alissa's stew. "Maybe she could at that," Lodesh said into the desert heat billowing out. He turned with a tray of biscuits. "Do you want to call them, or should I?" he asked brightly.

"I'll do it." The legs of his chair hit the floor with a thump as Strell levered himself up. Striding eagerly to the door leading to the Hold's walled garden, he went into the night, weaving his way through the tangled paths. The way curved and turned so sharply that he could hear Talo-Toecan's voice before he was even close.

"The pattern of tracings used for finding a septhama point is really just a looser form," the Master was saying. "Once a strong enough thread is found, you narrow your concentration."

A faint whisper of thought touched Strell's, and he smiled. Alissa must be in her raku form and was forced to speak silently. He could hear her only when she directed her thoughts specifically at him. It should be impossible, but Alissa never listened to impossibilities.

"Correct," came Talo-Toecan's rumble. "The smaller the pattern, the less time spent unconscious while reexperiencing the memory."

Strell jerked to a halt as he nearly ran into a low-hanging limb in the dark.

"Try finding one," Talo-Toecan said. "There're numerous septhama points in the garden, especially at the firepit. Keep the energy flow below the threshold of invocation. I don't want you tripping the lines without me."

Coming around the last turn, Strell paused. Nestled at the foot of the Hold's wall was a circular, sunken firepit large enough to hold eight people comfortably. Stone benches were built into the earthen walls, lending it a sense of permanence. Overgrown bushes, tall weeds, and untidy scrub circled it, creating a private space. Tonight it was occupied by a man, more old than young, with yellow eyes. The Master looked up at Strell's approach, his sharp, angular features acknowledging him with a simple, respectful nod.

Pressing an oval of grass flat behind him was his sweet Alissa. Her petite figure was gone, replaced by a lithe but large, sinuous shape. The only thing familiar about her was her gray eyes, and they widened, noting his arrival and his besotted smile. Oh, yes; she had wings, too. Great, glorious things that blocked the sun when she flew.

In a flurry she stood and vanished in a swirl of pearly white glowing from more than the nearby fire. Alissa knew her hulking size made him uneasy, a reminder of that horrible morning when she had been entirely a beast and none of Alissa, and she had tried to kill him.

Useless watched the thought of Alissa swirl and coalesce. "She had better remember to clothe herself," he said, and Strell grinned. That had been a sight, but no one knew he'd seen it.

The mist that was Alissa continued to swirl, and Strell's smile faltered. Useless, too, paused. She was taking a long time to shift, even for her. Together they watched in horror as her misty shape blurred, shrank, and continued to shrink until with a slight pop, it vanished completely.

Useless blinked in the stunned silence, rising to his feet, his hand outstretched.

"Alissa?" Strell breathed. "Alissa!" he called again, fear slicing icily between his soul and reason. Even the light trace of her thought he had never recognized before, lying still and warm within his, was gone.

"Alissa!"

And the elegantly dressed figure of Lodesh, hearing Strell's cry even from that distance, stood, his eyes bright and knowing, waiting no longer.

4

Strell! Alissa thought, catching sight of him on the path. She didn't want him to see her like this! Not, she admitted, that he ever said he didn't like her as a winged monstrosity. Energy slipped coolly into the proper mental channels to maintain her existence as she began her shift. Beast awoke, watching in undisguised boredom. *"Why,"* she asked, *"the extra lines this time?"*

"Extra?" Embarrassed, Alissa realized that in her rush, she had forgotten to shut down the pattern used for tripping the lines. It stood silver and quick against the darkness of her mind. She left it, afraid to take anything down until her neural net was a reality again, not just a thought. In fact, she mused, she was nothing but thought.

"One who had better clothe herself," Beast said drowsily.

"I remembered, thanks," Alissa said dryly, eyeing the third pattern. She swirled back into reality and blinked in bewilderment. The fire was out. Then she smiled. Useless had probably snuffed it, concerned she might forget her clothes again. Before he had the chance, she formed a containment field about the wood and put within it the proper ward to set the wood alight. The amount of energy she had to use was more than she expected. It was as if the wood was stone cold, not still warm from its recent extinguishment. But her fire snapped to life with a satisfying whoosh, throwing back the dark.

She was alone. The teapot and her cup were gone. Even Lodesh's slippers. "Strell?" she called, stepping down onto the bench, then, "Useless?" There was no answer. Concerned, she sent a thought to find them. Her breath seemed to catch in her. The Hold was full of people.

Alissa sat down rather hard on the bench.

"I must have tripped the lines with no memory fixed," she whispered, "and as Useless warned, I fell asleep and missed their arrival." The pattern for tripping the lines had been set when she shifted. Perhaps she had engaged it unwittingly. Her confusion slowed, but a whisper of unease lingered, fluttering at the edge of her awareness. Pushing it aside, she sent a silent call to Useless. Who knew how long she had been asleep?

Again, there was no answer. *"Strell?"* she called, twisting her thought so he could hear. *"Lodesh?"* Almost panicking, she tried again. A faint response touched her mind, and her shoulders drooped relief. *"Lodesh,"* Alissa thought with a sigh, then hesitated. *"What are you doing out on the road? And where are Strell and Useless?"*

"Who?" came his somewhat garbled reply.

"Sorry. Talo-Toecan." Alissa frowned. Lodesh was always so blessedly formal.

"No." It was stronger now. *"Who is this?"*

"It's Alissa," she blurted in a stunned surprise.

"You're in the Hold's garden?"

She nodded, forgetting for a moment he couldn't see the gesture. Her unease returned full force, settling into an immovable lump.

"Odd." His thoughts slipping into Alissa's were tinged with confusion. *"I should be under the Hold's ward of silence by now."* He hesitated. *"Wait. I'll be right there."*

Alissa's knees came up to her chin, and she waited on the hard bench, just her and the crickets, in the cloudy, warm night. Lodesh was on the road between his abandoned city of Ese'Nawoer and the Hold. What was he doing there? And he was moving fast. Too fast for running. And why, she wondered, worrying at the hole in her stocking, had he mentioned the Hold's ward of silence? He knew it didn't bind her, only Keepers.

A log slipped, threatening to roll out of the fire, and she

twisted to find a stick in the brush behind her to shove it back. Her eyes widened. The grass was trimmed! She rose, afraid to make a light to see clearly. But even in the hazy glow from the cresting moon she could see the bushes had been pruned and the flowerbeds weeded. She spun about, her heart pounding. "That tree," she whispered, pointing with a trembling finger. "I don't remember that tree." There was a scuffling on the path. Alarmed, she turned to see Lodesh striding towards her, his boots crunching on the gravel path.

Tall and lithesome, he moved with the grace of a dancer. His head was bare, and his blond waves were in an unusual disarray. There was a pair of gloves in his hand, which, even as she watched, he slapped together and tucked away in a back pocket.

Riding gloves? Alissa questioned, realizing how he had gotten here so fast. Where did Lodesh get a horse?

Catching sight of her, he paused. "Alissa?" he called.

"Here," she breathed, and held her hands out to draw him into the firepit. "Thank the Navigator's Hounds. I was beginning to think I had lost my mind. What's happened?"

Lodesh took her hands and stepped down. "I don't know, but trust me to find out."

Alissa felt his eyes travel from her mussed-up hair to the hem of her skirt. Used to his warm, inviting gazes, she smiled back. His hands exerted a warm pressure, drawing her gaze to his. He was trying to make her blush! "Where did all the people come from?" she asked, neither recognizing or dismissing his invitation. "They're all over, even the old annex dorms."

"Old annex dorms?" His eyes smoldering, he drew her hand to his lips, hesitating as she stiffened. His fingers were bare.

Her eyes went to his shoulder and then his chest. "Lodesh?" She dragged her hand from his. "Where are your city's ring and pendant?"

His smile vanished. "All right. Who put you up to this?"

Feeling her face go cold, Alissa backed away. This wasn't Lodesh. He didn't know her.

Lodesh took her wrist. "Was it Earan?"

"Uh," she stammered, suddenly frightened.

"I hope he didn't promise you one of the Keepers' private quarters for this performance."

"I—uh . . ."

"How dare he mock me by telling you I was the Warden."

"But that's who you are," she said, taking a ragged breath. It sounded harsh against the crickets. "You're Lodesh Stryska, the last Warden of Ese'Nawoer."

"That," he snapped, his face going hard, "is enough."

Alissa gasped as he yanked her off balance and out of the firepit. "Lodesh! What are you doing?" she cried. "Lodesh!"

"We're going to find Earan." He halted, eyes vacant with the familiar look of someone running a search. "The Keepers' dining hall." He frowned. "Cards, most likely." And their pace resumed.

Alissa stumbled after him, stunned into complacency, dazed, confused, and very frightened as she stared at the moon. It was supposed to be new, not a waxing crescent. Lodesh didn't know her. The Hold was full of people. Useless and Strell were gone!

Lodesh's boots found the path, crunching determinedly forward. Alissa bit back a cry as her foot found a sharp stone. "Ow! Lodesh, stop!" she demanded, tugging free.

He squinted down at her stockings in disbelief. "Where are your shoes?"

She looked blankly at him. "I can't make shoes, yet," she said, her voice cracking.

"Yet?" he repeated. Then his face cleared. "Come on," he said.

"No, wait," she pleaded as he dragged her forward. "Lodesh, please. Something is wrong. Just—let me figure it out." Ignoring her fingers prying at his grip about her wrist, he pulled her to the kitchen. The door was painted; she could see it in the moonlight. Stunned, she stumbled past it, feeling a tingle of a ward shiver through her. More atrocities met her increasingly panicked eyes.

All three kitchen hearths were in use; they were banked for the night, but they were in use. There were four pitchers and two stacks of plates stretching unsettlingly high, waiting for breakfast. The overhead rack where she hung her wash held more herbs than she could use in a year. An acidic, unfamiliar scent hung in the air, and she stiffened, realizing it was the odor of cooked meat. All this she saw and despaired over in a moment. Then the angry voices coming through the open archway from the dining hall drew her attention.

"You're cheating, Ren!" came a harsh accusation. "No one has such good luck."

"Am not!" asserted a higher pitched, indignant voice. "Ask Connen-Neute. That's what he's here for."

"Connen-Neute!" Alissa gasped, yanking herself free. Connen-Neute was a Master who had gone feral almost four hundred years ago. *Ashes!* Her stomach tightened, and with a sick feeling, she knew she wasn't viewing the past. This was nothing like reliving a memory. She was conscious, interacting, an active participant. What had she done?

Lodesh's fingers resumed their grip, and despite her efforts, he pulled her stumbling into the brightly lit hall. Silence greeted their arrival as five people looked up from the far end of one of the familiar black tables. Three were garbed in Keeper fashion, one in commoner, and the last, sitting apart by the hearth, was in the clothes of a Master.

Alissa returned his stare, her heart pounding. He was young, with a long, solemn face, dark of skin and hair. It was cut obscenely short as she remembered her father liking his. Even without the black Master's vest and red sash about his waist, she would have known he was a Master; his eyes were as golden as Useless's and his fingers had that extra segment. Seeing her gaze on them, he hid them in his wide gray sleeves.

The largest Keeper cleared his throat, making it into an insult. "Really, Lodesh. Don't be stupid." His thin lips pressed together disapprovingly. "Dressing your latest conquest up as a Keeper to sneak her in? Common folk aren't allowed after sunset." Running a hand over his neatly trimmed, reddish beard, he returned his attention to the cards in his hand, giving her presence as much consideration as he would a stray dog. "Take her out," he muttered.

Lodesh drew back a step, leaving her alone under unfriendly eyes. "I thought she was one of your jests, Earan. You don't know her?"

His flat face unreadable, Earan looked up from his cards. "No."

"Nisi?" Lodesh turned to a young woman, who, with her fair features, had to be from the foothills like Alissa.

The woman shook her head seriously, the tips of her hair brushing her ears.

"I've never seen her either," volunteered the youngest. He wasn't a Keeper, for he lacked the proper attire. Actually, he wasn't dressed well at all. Ankles showed above mismatched shoes, and there were patches in the huge shirt he kept tugging straight. He was growing too fast to justify better was Alissa's guess, seeing as he had the thin, awkward look of adolescence.

"What about you, Breve?" Lodesh turned to a dour-looking man whose beard was shot with gray and whose face was leathered from the sun.

"Never seen her," he said as he crossed his arms and leaned back from the table in mistrust. His words were startlingly rich for his gloomy demeanor. He was, Alissa realized, a voice musician. That voice was too cultured not to have been schooled. It was similar in timbre to Strell's, and she felt a stab of loss.

"I found her in the garden," Lodesh said.

The mismatched adolescent tilted his chair back on two legs to look under the table. "In her stockings?" he said, and everyone but Connen-Neute leaned to look.

"Shut up, Ren."

Alissa flushed, scrunching down to hide them. Even her mentally crafted stockings had holes. Useless said it was because her fundamental concept of stockings included them.

Earan collapsed the fan of cards in his thick hands. "Who are you, girl?"

"Alissa Meson," she heard come out of her. "Student

Ma—" Eyes wide, she clasped her hands over her mouth to keep the rest of her title from slipping forth. It was the Hold's truth ward, demanding an answer. That's what that tingle as she passed the kitchen's threshold had been! While under it, she couldn't lie, but she could stretch the truth or refuse to answer by walking away, or even stall for time, hoping to divert his attention. Her father had lost his life breaking the ward almost a decade ago, yet here it was.

The cards in Earan's hand hit the table in a soft hush. "I don't know you," he threatened, eyes narrowed. Alissa took a step back, feeling her face go cold.

"Well, somebody knows her," Lodesh said. "They told her I was the Warden."

Earan laughed, sending the patronizing sound into the rafters. "That's rich!" he said, making the table thump with a heavy fist. "My little brother, made Warden ahead of me."

"Be that as it may, she believes it," Lodesh said stiffly.

Abruptly loosing his mirth, Earan leaned back with his thick arms crossed before him. "Enough," he said impatiently. "Who are you?"

"I already told you," Alissa said, sidestepping the truth ward. Telling them she was a Master would only label her insane. She jumped when Lodesh put a comforting hand on her shoulder. The faint smell of mirth wood came to her, and her pulse quickened. This was all wrong. What had she done?

Earan leaned across the table. "How did you get into the garden in your stocking feet?"

"I walked," she said, feeling her stomach tighten.

Ren and Breve chuckled. Earan gave them a dark look, clearly not liking to be made the fool. "Sorry little snippet," he said as he placed his hands upon the table and levered his bulk up.

"Earan . . ." Nisi warned, her voice carrying a hint of fear. "Sit down. Let's just find out who she is and let Redal-Stan handle it."

"That's what I'm doing." Out from behind the table, Earan was a huge, red bear of a man, tall as a plainsman but thick as a foothills farmer. Alissa's eyes widened. Earan carried his mass easily, gliding to stand before the table with a masterful grace, which he spoiled with a spiteful expression. "Who told you Lodesh was the Warden?" he demanded.

"Useless," she whispered, knowing he would take it as defiance, not truth. Frightened, she felt Beast stir. Alissa wanted nothing more than to leave, but there was nowhere to go.

Earan's face went red under his beard.

There was a slight pressure upon Alissa's awareness as someone tried to edge into her thoughts. Already unnerved, she sent a blistering response out and slapped it away. Much to her surprise, Connen-Neute jumped. He slipped from the room in a hush of black and gray fabric. No one else saw him go. Beast was fully awake, and Alissa turned their attention back to Earan.

"Who," the heavy Keeper snarled, "brought you to the Hold?"

Alissa knees turned to wet rags. Feeling the beginnings of panic, she took a gasping breath and held it as she fought the Hold's truth ward.

"Earan, leave off." Nisi had stood; her thin face was pinched.

Earan shook off Breve's restraining hand. "Who dressed you in Keeper garb?"

"That's enough," Breve commanded.

"Don't tell me what to do!" Earan shouted. He turned to her. "Who's your Master, girl!"

Alissa's pulse pounded. She was trapped in a nightmare. He had to stop!

"Tell me!" Earan demanded, and she felt a buildup of energy about her source caused by her fright. She was about to loose an unconscious pulse of force, and in the state she was in, it was likely to do someone considerable damage. "Tell me now!" Earan thundered, and the level reached its threshold and very quietly passed it.

Time seemed to slow as Alissa felt her sphere of will form about Earan. She despaired as she found enough force in it to burn his tracings to slag. It was too late to draw it back. But she could harness the energy before it did any damage. Immediately she formed a containment field above Earan and set a ward of illumination in it. There was barely enough energy in it to keep it running; it was unnoticed. But it wouldn't be for long.

Alissa closed her eyes against the coming flash. Her wildly released energy slipped into the ward instead of Earan's tracings, drawn by the promise of an easier path. The soundless boom was red against her eyelids. There were cries of surprise. Lodesh's hand fell away.

Heart thudding wildly, she found herself leaping toward Earan. In her concentration to save Earan's tracings, Beast had taken control.

Alissa crashed into Earan, her knees landing on his chest to pin him against the table. "She doesn't want to answer," Beast snarled through her. "And if you don't stop, I will rip your throat out." Her lips were a finger's width from his face. His eyes had glazed with fear.

"Beast!" Alissa admonished in her thoughts. With a jolt, her alter consciousness realized what she had done and hid herself in the deepest corner of Alissa's mind, mortified. The ferocity disappeared from Alissa. "I—I'm sorry," Alissa stammered, sliding from his chest and to the floor. Uncertain and afraid, she backed up almost into the fire, her arms clasped about her. Everyone was staring at her in wide-eyed shock.

"The Wolves take you," Earan whispered hoarsely, covering his fright with anger as he straightened. "You have a source. The foothills squatter has a source. You're a rogue Keeper!"

Nisi gasped, going white. Alissa stiffened. Rogue Keepers had their tracings burned to an unusable ash when found.

"It fits," Earan said into the frightened silence. "It explains her clothes and why she was dumped in the garden with no boots. I think not only is she rogue, but insane!"

"Mad?" Breve glanced at Alissa and away.

"I say she was drawn to a Master when he or she stayed too long in one spot, much as Keepers did before the Hold was made," Earan said, his words loud and harsh. "And realizing she was mad, the Master instructed her in the old school, alone and unchaperoned, until she knew enough to persuade the rest from burning her tracings to a commoner."

There was a deathly silence. Alissa tried to still her fright. They wouldn't burn her tracings. She would talk to someone, convince them who she was, but if she did, they certainly would think she was mad. How could she convince anyone she wasn't when she thought she might be?

"I will see her tried as a rogue Keeper and her tracings burned to ash!" Earan shouted. He stomped out into the unseen great hall, leaving a cold in Alissa no fire could drive away.

Nisi cleared her throat, and seeing Alissa standing with her arms clenched about her, the young woman held out her hands in a formal gesture of greeting. "Leave it to the men to foul a simple introduction." She sighed. "I'm Nisi Tak, Keeper." Her hands were light and cool on Alissa's hastily proffered palms. "I apologize for Earan—"

"You're from the foothills," Alissa blurted, then winced. She hadn't told Nisi her name yet. "Alissa Meson," she said.

"Also from the foothills?" Nisi asked gently, and Alissa nodded, conscious of her scandalous mix of plains and hills features for the first time in months. "I'm afraid your welcome hasn't been one of our best efforts," Nisi continued.

"But it will be the best remembered," Ren said, and Alissa smiled thinly. Her knees still felt weak, but at least no one was shouting at her. This wasn't right. None of it. She felt ill.

Nisi turned. "Alissa? This is Ren. He's a student."

Ren waved a distant greeting. Having seen Earan pinned to the table, the young man looked none too eager to get close. "No last name?" Alissa asked.

Breve stepped forward. "Ren wandered in when he was five," he said. "He has no name but the one he gave himself." Alissa nodded, and Breve engulfed her hand in his. "Breve," he said in his somber voice. "Keeper. I need no woman to make my introductions."

Nisi cleared her throat with a hint of warning. "And you already know Lodesh?"

Alissa's unease rushed back. "Apparently not," she said, and the tension in the room visibly relaxed.

"Then allow me," Nisi said. "Alissa, this is Lodesh. He's a Keeper."

Lodesh stepped before her. His green eyes were eager, and his smile was as familiar and comforting as the morning sun. "I'm glad to properly make your acquaintance, milady." Taking her hand in his, he exerted a small pressure, a question to the possibility of more than the friendship he now offered. And where once she would have been disconcerted, she was now only comforted. This was her Lodesh. He was the only thing that hadn't changed, the only person who was familiar, and her shattered soul grasped and held on to that, bracing her sanity upon his immutability.

"A pleasure," she murmured, meeting his ardent gaze with her own as she often did when they teased each other. Much to her surprise, Lodesh dropped her hand, clearly taken aback.

"By the Wolves," Ren breathed. "She didn't blush!"

"No, but Lodesh did," Breve said with a snort.

Nisi, too, was smiling. "That leaves Connen-Neute," and she turned to the empty hearth to make a small sound of dismay. "Oh, well. You will undoubtedly make his acquaintance on his terms, anyway. We've lost our spotter, gentlemen. Perhaps we should call it a night."

"Aw, come on, Nisi," Ren complained. "Just one more hand."

Her eyebrows arched. "Don't imagine I didn't see you stacking the deck."

"Nisi!" the youth cried, his eyes wide in an overdone hurt. "I'm too good to cheat."

Nisi frowned. "The first is a queen," she said, sounding bored. "The next, a beggar."

"Maybe you're right," he said, his gaze dropping. "It's late, and I pulled field duty again."

"Will you do me a favor then?" Nisi said, and Ren froze, hand outstretched to his cards. "Redal-Stan should make Alissa's acquaintance now, before previous commitments move it to a ridiculous point of his day. She needs a place to bunk, and much as I hate to admit it, Earan's accusations should be headed off before he has time to bandy them about."

"What does that have to do with me?" Ren said as he nervously shuffled the cards.

"Someone needs to wake him up if Connen-Neute hasn't already."

"No." Ren backed from the table. "The last time someone did that, they were—"

"I'm sure he will apologize," Nisi continued as if that would make all the difference.

"Uh-uh." White-faced, Ren continued to shake his head.

"The third card was a page," Nisi said lightly. "And you were going to give me a wolf."

"All right. I'll go."

Breve clapped Ren across the shoulders. "I'll go with you. With two of us, he won't know who to get angry at, and we'll be able to explain before he does any serious damage."

"Ashes, thanks." It was possibly the most relieved voice Alissa had ever heard. Ren was hardly old enough to be out from under his mother's apron strings.

Breve laughed, his musical voice pushing out the last vestiges of Earan's ugly scene. With a gesture of farewell, they left, the old lightly supporting the young.

Nisi watched them go. Her eyes still held a smile as she turned to Alissa, but they widened upon seeing Alissa's dread. "Oh, Alissa," she said. "Redal-Stan isn't as bad as they make out. Of all the Masters, he's the most approachable. And by the time he gets down here, he will be fully awake. He's quite nice then." Brow furrowed, she bit her lip.

Lodesh found Alissa's hands. "She's right," he said. "Redal-Stan is my teacher, and I've found he has a soft spot for handsome, comely women such as yourself."

Nisi shook her head in exasperation and turned away.

"Thank you, Lodesh." Alissa acknowledged his compliment with a preoccupied smile. He hesitated, clearly unused to such a graceful acceptance from someone just met.

"Why don't you sit down?" Nisi interrupted. "Redal-Stan

appreciates his tea. Lodesh?" She grimaced as he was making eyes at Alissa. "Would you help me in the kitchen?"

"You know how to make tea, Nisi," he said, not looking away from Alissa.

"I want the nice teapot. The one Keribdis made." Nisi put a hand on her hip and pursed her lips, waiting. "It's too high for me to reach," she finished pointedly.

Lodesh sighed, then executed a dramatic, extravagant bow. "I will return," he said. Spinning upon a heel, he strode dramatically into the kitchen, his head held high.

Nisi and Alissa exchanged knowing looks. "Don't mind Lodesh," Nisi whispered as he disappeared. "He's a confirmed bachelor. He means nothing by all his words."

"Yes. I know."

"Well, you would be the first to recognize it so quickly," she said, turning away as Lodesh's voice came filtering back in.

"Which one *is* it, Nisi?"

5

Alone at last, Alissa inspected the dining hall. It wasn't much different, eerily so. The drapes were the wrong color, but they still shifted in the night breeze, ushering in the scent of chives and sage from the kitchen garden. The long, black tables were the same, as were the high-backed chairs. There was no picture above the mantel, and the space looked barren without the large canvas done in swirling blues she had found in storage last winter. A woven mat had replaced the rug she and Strell had lugged up from the annexes.

Strell, she thought miserably. What had she done? Feeling disconnected, she sank into her her chair, the only thing comfortable in the room to sit on. And it was her chair. The colors were brighter and the stuffing was distributed evenly, but it smelled right: clover and book paste.

She curled up and anxiously waited for the daunting presence of Redal-Stan. The fire was warm and soothing, and the soft, give-and-take of high and low murmurs of Nisi and Lodesh in the kitchen brought back memories of before her papa left home and he and her mother would talk long into the night. Alissa's eyes closed, and she must have fallen asleep, for suddenly the acidic smell of tea washed over her, and a new, masculine voice said, "She called you what?"

"The last Warden of Ese'Nawoer," Lodesh said, his voice hushed so as not to wake her. Obligingly, Alissa kept her eyes shut and her ears open, wondering if it was Redal-Stan.

"But you aren't in line for the title," the voice said. His accent hinted at plains, and her interest sharpened. "It would go to your uncle's children first, then your father, or even your brothers or sister if necessary. No offense, Lodesh, but you aren't even under consideration."

"None taken," Lodesh said in obvious relief.

There was a hiss of fabric, and the warmth of the fire was eclipsed. "So who is she?" came the voice so close Alissa's eyes nearly flew open.

Lodesh sighed. "I don't know. I found her in the garden."

"In her stockings?"

There was a pause, and Alissa could almost see Lodesh grin. "She sounds like she is from Ese'Nawoer, but I don't know her."

"You know all the pretty girls in the city, eh?" the voice teased.

"I know all the girls, pretty or not," Lodesh shot back, sounding wounded. "And Redal-Stan, despite what you may hear tomorrow, she isn't insane."

There was the sound of the fire being rearranged, and a flush of heat soothed her sudden angst. It *was* Redal-Stan. She cracked her lids, finding the room's shadowed lumps lit by the fire.

"Mad?" the Master breathed from the hearth. "Is that the general consensus?"

"Earan," Lodesh nearly spat the name, "is demanding she be tried as rogue."

"Harrumph?" It was a rumble of disbelief, and she shut her eyes.

"She nearly burnt his tracings with an unconscious pulse," Lodesh said. "It was too strong to be unsupplemented. She has a source."

"In possession of a source and lacking control? This isn't good," Redal-Stan said flatly. Alissa felt him lean forward, and she fought to keep her breathing slow. "I can tell you disagree," he said. There was a hesitation. "Please," Redal-Stan insisted. "If it impacts my decision over the small problem before us, you should tell me."

"Alissa is anything but careless with her restraint," Lodesh said reluctantly. "At the risk of bearing witness against my brother, you should know he goaded her, using the truth ward to go beyond what a student is capable of withstanding."

"He has done this before?" Redal-Stan interrupted icily.

"She let slip a pulse," Lodesh said. "But she recognized it and put up a ward of illumination to draw it in before it finished coalescing. The flash was bright enough to stun my eyes!" he whispered fiercely. "When I could see again, she was pinning him to the table!"

"She has a Keeper's skills," Redal-Stan muttered, "a Keeper's strength, and possibly a Keeper's restraint." He sighed. "But no Master claiming responsibility. We have a very large problem before us. Any ideas who has made it so?"

"I'd rather not say." Lodesh sounded miserable. "She mentioned someone, but . . ."

"Talo-Toecan?" Redal-Stan guessed, and a wash of alarm tensed Alissa.

"You know?" Lodesh exclaimed, but clearly Redal-Stan wasn't listening.

"I have to call him back," the Master said. "This is a grievous claim. It must be settled."

Panic filled her, and she couldn't believe they didn't see her stiffen. She would get home, she had to, but she couldn't let Useless see her in the interim. He hadn't known her when she met him. She couldn't let him see her now! *"No!"* she sent wordlessly to Redal-Stan, and she heard him grunt in surprise. *"Don't tell him!"*

"But my summons can wait until morning," Redal-Stan finished smoothly. "It's late, Lodesh. Why don't you go to bed?"

"I, um, would like to see Alissa to her room, if that's agreeable."

Redal-Stan snorted. "She looks comfortable enough where she is."

"In your chair?" Lodesh whispered urgently. "You never let anyone sit in your chair, much less *sleep* in it!"

"I don't know where to put her," Redal-Stan said patiently. "Once I know if she is a Keeper or student, I will assign her a bunk. I just hope she's a student. There're no acceptable empty rooms in the Keepers' halls."

"I'll stay with her here, then," Lodesh valiantly persisted.

"Go to bed." It wasn't a request anymore. "We don't know if Meson is her maiden name or matron. It would be unseemly for you to accompany her alone, especially at rest."

Alissa's heart beat six times into the silence. "Of course," Lodesh agreed, clearly unhappy.

"Good night, Lodesh," Redal-Stan said dryly as there was a soft rustle and the sound of Lodesh's footsteps went faint. Only the hiss of the fire on damp wood remained. It was joined by the tinkle of tea filling a cup.

"It's also unseemly," Redal-Stan said sourly, "to feign sleep, when one isn't."

Chagrined, Alissa opened her eyes. Sitting on the hearthstones, soaking up the warmth and light, was Redal-Stan. Her astonishment grew as she took in his brown eyes—rakus invariably retained their gold eyes when in their human shift—and the telltale marks the desert instilled, marks even his brown Master's vest and black sash couldn't hide. His creased, shaven face had the wind-scarred look of one who has seen too many springs spent in want, but it had been tempered by years of abundance. His probing gaze was gentled by wisdom, tamed by the lack of concern. Redal-Stan was at peace with himself, and this she instinctively felt she could trust.

"So," he drawled, sending a hand across his bald head. "How is it a Keeper has learned to speak soundlessly to both Keeper *and* Master?" He proffered Alissa a cup of tea.

Her eyes widened as she accepted it. His hand encircling the cup was like hers! "You must have been Talo-Toecan's teacher," she blurted. "He never told me you were born human!"

"What do you mean, *have been* Talo-Toecan's teacher," he said. Then his mouth fell open and he blinked. He set his cup on the flagstones with a sharp crack and shook the tea from his hand. "By my Master's Wolves!" he exclaimed. "How do you know that?" His eyes hardened. "Who are you?" he demanded. "Name, title, and responsibilities."

The truth ward took her, but she wanted to tell him. Useless's teacher was possibly the only one who could help her. "I'm Alissa Meson, born to the same," she stated, making her marital status clear. "And my responsibilities are to myself and the freedom of one other soul." Whether he knew it or not, Lodesh's future self looked to her to free him from his curse.

"One other soul?" he questioned. "Go on."

"I'm a student—and Master of the Hold," she finished, her chin raised defiantly as it was obvious he didn't believe her.

Redal-Stan topped off his cup, replacing what he had spilled. "You can't be. Your eyes are," he squinted in the firelight, "gray? Anyway, they aren't gold, and your fingers are short."

"So are yours," she said. He thought her insane, deluded into believing she was a Master.

"Regardless . . . you aren't."

"Yes, I am." Frustrated, she snuffed out the fire with an impervious field. Redal-Stan grunted in the new darkness. Keepers knew permeable fields, but only Masters knew of the potentially deadly impervious ones capable of smothering flames and anything else in them. "And as for my fingers, it's amazing what a good book can do," she said, speaking of the *First Truth*, the book that had made her jump from Keeper to Master possible. Demonstration complete, she relit the fire with a satisfied thought.

Redal-Stan's eyes meeting hers were wide. "Talo-Toecan taught you impervious fields?" he whispered hoarsely. "But even worse, told you of my *First Truth*! How else could you know that it's possible for a Master to come from a human?"

"It's *my* book," Alissa muttered with a flush of possessiveness, but he wasn't listening, having lurched from the flagstones to his full, narrow height.

"Talo-Toecan," he whispered as his gaze went distant. "Your rebellious tendencies have lifted you far beyond the limits this time."

Useless a rebel? Alissa thought. *Do tell?* She stiffened as her gaze fell on Redal-Stan standing with one hand on the mantel, the other on his head.

"I have to call him back," he muttered. A thin arm was flung dramatically into the air. "I'll have to call them all back! Burn him to ash, there will have to be a trial. A Bone and Ash, spit-in-the-wind quorum . . . What the Wolves was he thinking!" he exclaimed.

Trial! she thought, fear slicing cleanly through her. She had made a mistake. She should have kept quiet! "Wait!" she cried. "It wasn't his fault! Let me explain."

Alissa leaned forward and grasped his sleeve. He jerked free, staring down at her as if she had the plague. "One—ash-ridden, wind-shredded—reason."

And this was the sticky part. The truth ward wasn't reliable when insanity figured into it. Alissa placed her cup on the nearby footstool and clasped her hands together. "I— uh . . . He . . . Talo-Toecan doesn't know me yet?" she said, feeling sheepish.

The silence was rather long, but true to his Master standing, Redal-Stan's anger eased in the presence of a conundrum. He pulled Lodesh's abandoned chair closer. Sitting down, he hunched so as to look her eye to eye. "Yet? I thought he was teaching you."

Cringing, Alissa decided if worse came to worst, she would drag him into the great hall and shift to prove her Master standing. It was hard to argue with a room full of sharp teeth and wings. She took a deep breath. "The Hold has been my home for nearly a year. Before that, the foothills." His forehead wrinkled in disbelief, and she noticed he'd lost even the hair on his eyebrows. "The Hold," she asserted, and at his derisive snort, she added, "My Hold, not yours."

Redal-Stan pursed his lips. "You will have to explain."

"Well," she hid behind her cup, sneaking glances at him, "we were in the garden, Talo-Toecan and I—"

"You said he doesn't know you."

"He doesn't—yet," she said, then winced as Redal-Stan frowned. "Anyway, I was practicing to set up the pattern for tripping the lines using a septhama point. Strell was coming, so I shifted back from my—my raku form. I didn't want to forget my clothes, so it took a long time." Her eyes flicked up, but she saw interest, not amusement. "I-I'm not that good yet. The lines were set for a septhama point. I never meant to actually use it," she continued, going desperate for answers. "Only compare it to what I had seen already. I think it was an accident!"

"I see," Redal-Stan breathed, his gaze distant. "You were in transition and got pulled into it." His focus sharpened, and he blinked. "Wolves. Do you know what you've done?"

"I didn't mean to—"

"Your entire being was thought, so you sent yourself where only thoughts could go! How?" he barked, his eyes wondering. "The patterns don't cross. You can't use them together!" It was almost an accusation, and she stared helplessly at him. Then his face went slack. "You are a Master!" Reaching out, he grasped her hand and stared at it, cradled against his rough skin. "Wolves, tears, and sorrow. You're the next Bone and Ash transeunt!"

"I just want to go home," she cried, tugging from his grip. She could stand no more. She had mislaid herself only to be found by a stranger wearing a dear friend's face, been taken to a place she had made her own now strange and foreign, been threatened with being burned to commoner status, called a liar and a rogue, and all she wanted was to go home.

Miserable, she stared fiercely at the fire, but it was no use. A tear slipped down as she sat stiffly in her chair that wasn't even her chair anymore. "Nothing is right," she whispered as an overwhelming sense of loss broke over her. "I can't find Strell. . . ."

There was a tug on her awareness, and Redal-Stan handed her a soft cloth. At his show of compassion, she allowed herself one gasping sob, then held her breath, refusing more. She felt another ward, and the edge of her sorrow inexplicably blunted. The tightness in her chest loosened, and she took a deep breath as her grip on her cup eased. "Sorry," she mumbled, dabbing her eyes. Obviously it was a ward. She hated being manipulated, but she hated crying in front of people even more. "What kind of a ward was that?"

"Talo-Toecan is teaching you to trip the lines before a ward of calming?" he said, aghast.

"That's what that was?" Glad for the distraction, she sniffed back her tears and set the pattern up to glow in her thoughts. "Do I have it right?" She glanced at him, looking for approval and finding a startled alarm.

"M-m-m, yes. You do, actually." Stiff fingers ran over his nonexistent hair in a gesture she was rapidly equating with worry. "Here." He topped off her cup. "Have more of Nisi's tea. She makes an excellent brew." He hesitated. "Strell is your—ah—suitor? Is that short for something?"

"No," she said shortly.

Seeing her eyes pinched in heartache, he added, "Best tell me now, while the ward lasts." He froze in his reach for the fire irons. "Ah—Strell isn't the name of a Master."

"No. Strell is from the plains," she said, suddenly wary.

"They're letting a Keeper court you?" he said, brown eyes wide.

"They aren't *letting* me do anything of the sort," she said, and Redal-Stan knelt before the fire with a satisfied sound. "Strell is a commoner," she finished.

"A what!"

"There's no one left to choose from," she said, "but feral beasts and dimming memories."

He said nothing as he took that in. Brow furrowed, he looked away to stir the fire. For a time there was no sound but the dry rattle of coals. "Is that why Keribdis isn't teaching you?" he asked. "Did she . . ." He took on an uncomfortable look. "Does she go feral?"

Alissa's eyes widened with a sudden thought, and her pulse leapt. With a few words, she could change the path the Hold would take. Ese'Nawoer wouldn't be cursed! Lodesh wouldn't be condemned to an eternity of servitude. The Masters wouldn't drown while trying to find a mythical island. The Hold would be strong and standing when she found it.

She took an eager breath only to have it slip from her in

dismay. If the city wasn't cursed, who would destroy Bailic? Perhaps he would do worse than he had. Perhaps he would marry her mother, and she wouldn't even be born! Ashamed for her cowardice, she dropped her gaze to her tea. "I don't think I should say anything," she said.

Redal-Stan set the fire iron away with an excessive clang. Alissa thought he might insist, but then he sighed and returned to slouch in his chair in an unmasterly sprawl. "Perhaps you're right," he said. "No telling what your words might change, and I think you would prefer to return to find the Hold as you left it, fallen though it is."

"I never said the Hold fell!" she exclaimed, meeting his knowing expression.

"But it has, hasn't it," he said. "Talo-Toecan would never be allowed to instruct you if there was any choice. He isn't trained for it." The Master frowned. "Obviously."

Alissa bit her lip, resolving to watch her mouth.

"So," the Master said firmly, "Lodesh will be unhappy when he finds you gone, but Earan will be pleased. You should leave directly. Talo-Toecan always comes back early from his too-infrequent leaves. He shouldn't make your acquaintance for another—six hundred years?"

"Closer to four hundred, I think," Alissa corrected, her thoughts very relieved in that he seemed sure he could get her back home.

Redal-Stan went still. "Four hundred," he repeated. "It happens so soon?"

Her eyes widened, and he smiled a sad, uncomfortable smile. "No worry, Squirrel," he said as he watched the amber depth of his tea. "I can keep my mouth shut. Let's just get you back. And I'm anxious to see this new ward of yours."

He settled in his uncomfortable chair, set his cup aside, and waited. She stared at him, a sick feeling slipping through her. "I thought you would know how to get me home," she said.

Astonishment filled him. "Isn't this a new ward?"

"I told you," she whispered, her stomach clenching. "It was an accident. I don't even know how to trip the lines."

Redal-Stan stared at her "You're jesting."

Alissa shook her head, her throat going tight. Redal-Stan opened his mouth but nothing came out. He pursed his lips and rubbed his head. Miserable, Alissa's gaze drifted to her empty cup. She would never get home.

"Well," Redal-Stan said, "I can see no help for it. I'll simply have to teach you how to trip the lines so we can piece together how you got here and then how to get you back."

Alissa's head snapped up. "You will?" she cried, relieved.

Redal-Stan's eyes crinkled at the edges. "Yes, I'll teach you the entirety of line tripping. It's my specialty. Everyone learns it from me. No reason you shouldn't as well. It might take as long as a week. Can you keep your mouth shut and your wards to yourself that long?"

"Yes," she said, not caring that her voice trembled. "As long as Talo-Toecan doesn't see me."

"Ashes," he muttered. "You're only worried about Talo-Toecan? What about everyone else? Do we all go Bone and Ash feral?" he said crossly.

Alissa dropped her gaze, refusing to explain, and he sighed. "Fine," he said dryly. "Be in my chambers at the top of the sixth hour tomorrow."

"Yes, Redal-Stan." She eased back in relief, glad he had dropped the issue. She was determined not to ask what the sixth hour was and make herself look foolish. Lodesh would know. He'd know which one of the tower's rooms was Redal-Stan's as well.

"The only thing left is to decide if you will pose as Keeper or Master." He grimaced as he weighed the teapot and set it back down. "The way I see it, you can either confine yourself to your human form and be the mad rogue student, who because of her innocence won't be burned into commoner status, or you can be a Master refugee from the fabled lost colony over the sea."

"Lost colony!" she exclaimed, horrified.

"We have to explain you somehow." He drained his cup and looked at the empty teapot.

"No." Alissa shook her head vehemently. "Not a lost

colony of Masters." She wouldn't start the rumors. She wouldn't.

"Really?" He watched her suspiciously. "Is that how we're all done in?"

Her mouth dropped open. Frowning, she shut it, refusing to say anything. He had guessed almost everything, and she had hardly said a word. Useless's teacher was more clever than he looked. "I'll be a mad Keeper, thank you," she said stiffly.

"Be sure," he warned. "Once decided, it can't be reversed."

"Beast?" Alissa whispered into her thoughts. *"Can we do this?"*

"It will be my punishment for attacking the arrogant one," Beast whispered forlornly, hiding herself all the deeper.

"Oh, Beast," Alissa thought gently. But Beast didn't answer, and so Alissa nodded.

"Keeper, then," he said, clearly pleased he had wormed so much out of her. "Someone will have to double up. Being mad as you are, you rate a private room. Who knows what you will do next after pinning Earan to the table."

"Sorry," Alissa mumbled, feeling herself warm.

"From what I heard, he had it coming."

"Maybe." Alissa looked away. "But it shouldn't have happened."

"We all slip now and again," he whispered, his eyes on the dying fire. It was almost to coals. There was the faintest tug on her awareness as a ward of sleep sifted over her. She tried to fight it, but the ward was too fast, and she slipped into an unwanted, troubled sleep.

6

His slippered feet ghosted on the rug in the great hall as Lodesh strode through the dark to the mouth of the first annex tunnel. The white glow of a sprig of asters peeped from his shirt pocket, having been pulled from the display at the foot of the stairs earlier. Entering the tunnel's more certain gray, he smiled at the comforting smell of leather and horse. Redal-Stan had told him to go to bed, but he was of no mind for sleep. He had a favor to ask someone in the city.

Soon the sound of grinding teeth on hay reached him. Someone was always awake in the stables, though more often than not it was the horses and not the students assigned to care for them. As expected, he found two girls asleep on cloth-covered bales of straw. He crouched and shook one awake. Blinking in the torchlight, she rubbed her eyes. Upon seeing whom it was, she sat up and reached for her friend.

"Sh-h-h . . ." Lodesh said. "Go back to sleep, Coren. I just wanted to tell you I'm taking my horse."

"I'll get him," she whispered urgently. "I should have been awake." Her face was pinched, making her all the more comely.

"No, you shouldn't. It's the middle of the night. Only madmen and fools in love are up at this hour."

She opened her mouth to protest, and Lodesh presented her with the asters. Just as he had hoped, she blushed. "Now go back to sleep and dream of that lad I saw you eyeing in the streets last week." Lodesh sat back on his heels. "He's apprenticed to the weaver guild, isn't he?"

She nodded, eyes lowered as she twirled the stem in embarrassment.

"He would make a fine match," Lodesh said. "Give him a few years to grow up." He stood, winked, and humming softly, located his boots and tack, filling a cup with grain in passing.

"G'd evening, Nightshade," he murmured, stroking the nose of the beautiful black animal who had woken and come forward at the sound of sliding grain. After offering her a quick handful, he moved on.

"Tempest," he whispered. "You're looking better." Sidled against the back of a box stall was a new arrival. His ears went back at Lodesh's approach. The stink of rakus was unfamiliar to the gelding, and Lodesh knew he reeked of it. There would be no attempt at taming him. As soon as his leg was sound, he would return to the wild, but managed, herd.

Smiling, he came to a tall gray. There was no hesitation here, and the smooth-limbed beast nuzzled him aggressively for the grain. "Easy, Tidbit." He laughed. "Do you like the stables, or would you prefer the open field as would I?" Lodesh gave her a handful of grain and stepped away.

"Good evening, Frightful," he breathed, and a long-nosed, awkwardly formed horse hesitated at his dinner, flicking a tattered ear before resuming his grinding. Lodesh hung his bit and pad on the hook and slipped on his boots. "I know you just got here and were undoubtedly planning on regaling Tidbit with your tales of the field, but I need to return to the city."

As if understanding, the horse shifted his hindquarters, nearly pinning Lodesh against the wall. Dancing clear, Lodesh shoved him back over. "Please, Frightful. No horse here is as fast and steady as you. I can't trust anyone else."

An ear flicked back, then forward. The grinding teeth stilled, and a clear eye focused on him, black in the almost nonexistent light. Encouraged, Lodesh scratched the tender skin where the flies knew a horse's tail couldn't reach. "I go to see Sati," he whispered into a soft ear, and Frightful snatched a last mouthful of hay and sighed.

Grinning, Lodesh fastened the pad he used for a saddle and

slipped the rope bit in place. The clops echoing off the low roof seemed inordinately loud, and it was with relief that he unlocked the thick stable doors and went into the moonlit yard. He turned as he mounted to wave at the two stable hands standing by the door. They waved back before scampering inside, undoubtedly to compare whispered notes until they fell asleep again.

Lodesh relaxed, glad he could let Frightful find his way. His mind was swirling, returning time and again to the mystery of Alissa. She was as irritating as a splinter and equally hard to ignore. And rogue, he thought, taking a quick breath. Who knew what she could do? Honesty forced him to admit a portion of his interest was sighted along that line. But it was more than that. He had chased the dangerous and won the unwinnable before. No. It was almost as if he was smitten with her.

How, he wondered as he slipped under the trees, had that happened? He wasn't a dewy-eyed goat herder to moon over a pretty face, even if that pretty face sheltered an indomitable will and intelligent spirit. She hadn't even noticed his charms but saw right through them, treating him with an easy friendship he hadn't had in—in years. He wouldn't allow himself to be open to that kind of pain again.

Yet it seemed he had.

As he traveled the road to Ese'Nawoer, the moon slipped from behind the clouds. Before it had moved a hand's width, the sound of Frightful's steps echoed between houses and walls. His mount slowed, and at Lodesh's subtle suggestions, he wove his way to a house surrounded by an unusually large yard, made more so by bordering one of the city's open tracts.

To his surprise, light still flickered against the curtains. Lodesh softly found the ground. There was an eager blowing from behind the house, and Frightful tossed his head, nearly knocking Lodesh over in his awkward haste to greet a one-time stablemate. Satisfied Frightful wouldn't stray, Lodesh turned to the wide, cracked steps leading to the door. He stepped over the squeaky boards and dodged the pots of cat-grass Sati kept to entice the feral cats to stay. He boldly raised his hand to knock only to hesitate before contact.

They hadn't parted on the best of terms. They hadn't parted on any terms. Others had told him to go.

Lodesh grimaced at his guilt. Taking a deep breath, he knocked. There was movement within, and the door opened, mixing the dim light of a candle with the moonlight.

"Lodesh." Her eyes were haunted. "You're here for my horse."

Taken aback at her firmness, Lodesh blinked. "No," he said, then slumped. Sati was the best shaduf the city ever had. It was obvious she not only knew what his question was, but probably already had his answer. The horse was an excuse to evade answering him.

Standing before him in her nightclothes, Sati looked like a child, but her eyes were old, having seen death a thousand times. "You promised next time Beauty was in season . . ." She gestured to Frightful energetically stomping, pushing against the fence.

"It's fall, Sati. You can't be serious," Lodesh protested, willing to play her game.

"Yes." It was low and insistent.

Lodesh looked askance at his mount with an unmistakable disgust. "But he's so—"

"Ugly? Yes. But his coat is very soft."

"It's that horrid splotchy brown! He looks like he has had the mange." Lodesh winced as the two horses began twining their necks.

"He is very tall," Sati whispered, her gaze upon them.

"Too tall." Lodesh grimaced. "He's all bones and sinew."

"It makes him very fast and even of gait."

Lodesh hesitated. "It does at that," he admitted, "but there must be some other horse."

"If I can't have the man," she snapped, "my mare will have his steed."

Lodesh slumped. "Sati. . . ."

They stood awkwardly, he on the porch, she in the threshold, neither reaching out though it was obvious they wanted to. They knew better. She was a shaduf. The smallest touch from her would set his Keeper tracings on half-resonance, filling Lodesh with an unbearable nausea. It hadn't always been so.

"Let Beauty out before you come in," she finally said, listless. "They'll get to the field with no problem. Everyone knows Frightful; no one will deter them. Besides, no one is up at this hour but madmen and—" Biting her lip, she spun inside, leaving the door open.

Telling himself he had every right to be here, Lodesh went to the horses. It was a challenge to remove the tack from the excited animal. He had to shove Frightful aside to untie the gate. With a squeal and toss of her head, Beauty was away. Frightful followed, agitated and quick. In a heartbeat, they were gone. Lodesh hung the bit and pad on the fence.

Lodesh paused as he shut the gate, picking at the latch. It was still broken. He had tried to fix it once, but Sati hadn't let him. "Why?" she had said, giving him that empty stare that pained him. "The rope works. Just because it wasn't meant for that purpose doesn't mean you should change it."

Depressed, he looped the gate shut. With steps slow and reluctant, he mounted the stairs, hitting every squeak and groan. He shut the door behind him, giving it that extra kick it needed to latch. He looked about in the fresh brightness of a newly stirred fire. There had been changes.

Once this had been an expansive kitchen belonging to Sati's mother, a contented chaos of sly, youthful cleverness, tempered with firm, aged wisdom; the heart of the home. Now it was a sitting room, far more useful in Sati's profession of shaduf. She only needed a small space to prepare her solitary meals.

Sati's parents and siblings had been granted quarters in the citadel. It was supposed to have been in gratitude for bringing Sati into the world. In truth, the honor was a guilt payment from the city. Try as they might, her kin couldn't stand to live with her anymore. It had been easier to go, leaving her at least the shell of their presence to give her solace.

Softness was everywhere: the muted colors, the multitude

of pillows, the voluminous drapes. Even the floor was swathed in what must be three or four rugs atop each other. Unable to find comfort, Sati had surrounded herself with it.

There was a thump from a back room, and Lodesh sat down, cautiously feeling the chair to see if he would be able to get back up again. He hadn't been here for five years—not since her shaduf status had crashed down upon her. Lodesh grimaced.

As if drawn by the heat in his face, Sati appeared in the draped archway. She had dressed, donning her blue robe of office in a silent accusation. Lodesh winced at her choice of hair ribbon. It was faded and worn, still showing the blue of forget-me-nots embroidered on it. Sati's mother had once given it to him as a token of her motherly affections, an heirloom handed down through the generations. Lodesh had felt obligated to return it when it became obvious he and Sati weren't going to wed. Now, Sati wore it like a battle scar.

Striding across the room, she flung herself into a chair, almost disappearing among the cushions. She clutched a pillow to herself, looking like a lost child as she eyed him over it. "You didn't come tonight for my horse," she said stiffly.

"No." Lodesh shifted himself to the edge of his chair, remembering the soft feel of the ribbon's colors sliding through his fingers. Elbows on his knees, he placed his palms together, unable to meet her accusing eyes. "I have a question."

"You promised!" she cried, her grip tightening on her pillow until her fingers showed white. "You promised you wouldn't ask me anything!"

"No, I didn't." He hated himself for asking her, but it was clear by her distress she already knew both his question and answer. "I don't make promises—anymore."

Sati took a ragged breath. Lodesh knew she was considering if she was going to throw him out or not. "Fine!" she snapped, and he grew more anxious. "But it's going to cost you." Her jaw clenched. "I want a fertile seed from the mirth trees."

"Done."

"What!" Her grip on the pillow loosened, and it rolled to the floor.

"Done," he repeated, his face twisting. "I said, done!"

She sat up, confusion softening the lines in her face. Almost, it was his old Sati peering out through those haunted eyes. "I—I didn't think you would."

"I met your price, Sati."

"You really have one?"

Lodesh forced his hands apart. "It took me three weeks in the tops to find one, but yes. You are the sole owner of a seed that will germinate." Lodesh felt a touch of anger. He had made plans for that seed. It was likely going to be the only fertile seed he would ever find, and giving it to Sati was not one of them. "Now, do you know if Alissa and I have a future together?"

She abruptly stood and snatched her pillow from the floor. Lips pressed, she flung it to her chair and stomped, as much as her slippered feet could stomp, to the small nook that served as her kitchen. A kettle of water was set noisily over the low flames. Still silent, she stalked back and stood before Lodesh, her arms crossed. "Tell me about her," she snapped.

"Since when do you need to know—"

"Tell me!" It was a frustrated cry, thick with hurt and jealousy.

Lodesh sighed. "She's fair of hair and eyes," he said to the floor. "Her skin is dark. Her accent is Ese'Nawoer, but she claims to be from the foothills."

"I want to see her," Sati interrupted.

"Sati!" he cried, shocked.

"I don't want to meet her," she said in such a way that told him that was just what she had intended. "Just see her."

Thick unease settled over him. He looked up, then away from the hurt in her eyes. "I was going to invite her for a tour of the city," he offered slowly.

"Fine." Sati was dangerously calm. "I'll find you."

The silence soaked into Lodesh, disturbing him further. This used to be one of his favorite hiding places, full and warm with Sati and her family, everyone busy with their own lives but somehow keeping tighter than the closest weave. Now even the memory of the contentment was gone. "You— have my answer?" Lodesh prompted.

"Yes." It was barely audible. Sati turned to face the large hearth sheltering a small fire.

"Well?" he asked gently as he rose to stand behind her.

"Would you like some tea?" she said with a forced brightness. "You'll have a long walk without Frightful."

"Sati."

She turned, and Lodesh felt a stab of pain. Her face was frozen into a polite smile, but her eyes were desolate with loss. "Please, Sati?" he entreated, steeling himself before taking her cold hands into his. To his astonishment, there was no response from his tracings. She had indeed known he was coming and intentionally burnt her tracings to a temporary state of unresonating ash. "I know it must be hard."

"You know nothing!" she exploded. "I didn't ask for this!" Sati jerked free, and with a cry of frustration, she swung at him. Expecting it, Lodesh ducked and clutched her to him, trying to ground her, to give her something solid and real. She struggled, but he refused to let go. He felt he deserved far worse. Her muffled, shouted curses melted into shaking sobs, and she leaned against him, allowing him to hold her as she cried. It was the only release she had left. It was the only way he could show he still cared.

"I didn't ask for this," she wept as the tears slowed. "Knowing the tragedies of your neighbors before they do." She looked up, her eyes dark. "I met a boy today, Lodesh. His mother was so proud and happy. He . . . I . . . It isn't my fault!" she wailed, and the tears began anew, but they were for the boy and his mother this time, not her.

"Hush, Sati," Lodesh whispered. He tilted her head up, forcing himself to smile. "You will always be the sweet girl who threw dandelions at the night watchman with me."

"Maybe," she whispered. "But you're meant for another."

Lodesh's breath hissed out. He tried to keep the light from his eyes, knowing he failed when she gasped and turned away.

"But, Lodesh?" She hesitated, letting her breath out and

taking another. "I can't see if it's a good thing or bad. I only know your fates twine together."

"It's enough," he said, and he took a step back.

"Can you stay?" she asked, clearly knowing the answer.

His steps were soundless. The creaking of the door as he opened it pulled her gaze to his. "No," he said. "As you say, I have a long walk." And he shut the door behind him, leaving her standing alone and desolate as she had left him five years ago under the mirth trees with a blossom in his hands and the question of marriage standing shattered between them.

7

"Alissa, wake up." It was lovingly whispered, so she hid her smile and feigned sleep. If she were lucky, and Talon was absent, Lodesh's next words would be accompanied by a kiss upon her fingertips.

"Alissa?" His breath caressed her cheek. She mumbled, thrashing her arm to hit something. There was a muffled grunt, and she bit her tongue so as not to laugh.

"Please, Alissa. The Keepers are arriving for breakfast."

Keepers! she thought. Her eyes flew open as she recognized the stench of sausage, and her breath came quick in understanding. Smiling thinly up at Lodesh, she tried to disguise her dismay in finding the previous evening hadn't been a horrible nightmare.

A rough sound of disgust pulled her gaze to the door. Earan stood framed by the archway to the great hall. His disdainful gaze lingered on her jaw, and she swung her long hair to hide her healing scrape. Embarrassed, she stuffed her feet into the slippers Lodesh handed her.

"Lodesh tells me you're entitled to Keeper privileges," the bearded man said, "but I'll be ash before I share a table with you. You eat with the students."

"Earan!" Lodesh stepped between them. "You've no authority to banish her to the pit." Several new faces filed in, all in Keeper garb, all ignoring the ugly scene with a weary restraint.

"Until the formalities, she eats with the students," Earan said with a sneer.

"The mental noise they put out will drive her mad." Lodesh stood toe-to-toe with Earan.

"She already is insane!"

Alissa backed up nearly into the kitchen. Her head was throbbing. Mumbling an unheard excuse, she fled into her inner stronghold, only to halt in shock. "'Scuse me," someone said impatiently, and Alissa shifted so he could pass. His absence from the kitchen went all but unnoticed. There were only five people, but their dashing about made it seem as if there were twice that. Over it all was the nauseating stench of cooking sausage.

"Don't just stand there gawking, dearie. Do something!" came an exasperated shout.

Alissa spun to a generously endowed woman who looked as if she could be everyone's grandmother. Fixing upon Alissa's alarmed stance she laughed. "Oh! Beg your pardon. I thought you were one of my girls." Collapsing on a stool, the old woman peered at Alissa though well-earned wrinkles. "You must be that Alissa that Lodesh was going on about this morning. Aye," she murmured, "you'll do."

"Sorry?" Alissa stared blankly at the woman.

"He's a fine lad, that one." She patted Alissa's hand. "Just needs the right lass to settle his roving eyes apace."

"I'm sure I don't know," Alissa stammered, feeling her cheeks warm.

"Course you don't. If you did, it wouldn't be half the fun!"

A girl nearby cutting apples shook in silent laughter. Noticing Alissa watching her, the kitchen girl dramatically rolled her eyes. "Um," Alissa said, determined to change the subject. "Would you mind if I took some water? I haven't a room yet, and—"

"M-m-m," the woman interrupted. "You want a wash." She stood with a groan. "Kally!" she shouted, though it wasn't that loud in the room, and the girl at the apples set down her knife. "Pour Redal-Stan's tea water into a bowl for Alissa. No, not *there*. Over *here!*"

Alissa's eyes widened. "I can't take Redal-Stan's water," she stammered as a deep bowl was placed before her. It was quickly followed by a splash of water and a soft towel. Kally went back to her work but pointedly kept close enough to overhear.

"Nonsense!" the old woman huffed, seemingly unable to lower her voice. "It'll serve to remind him what it's like to be inconvenienced. He can wait for his breakfast. He deserves it, I say. Making you sleep in that smelly chair of his."

"I don't mind," Alissa said as she washed, shocked at the woman's accusing tone.

"In that drafty dining hall," she continued, waving at the heat.

"The fire was very warm," Alissa offered hesitantly.

"He needs a reminder who butters his bread," she finished as if Alissa had said nothing, but the woman's clear, green eyes stabbed into her, daring Alissa to contradict her again. There was a crash of pottery, and the woman rose along with the noise. "Oh, for the Navigator's Hounds!" she cried. "Must I do everything?" Then she shook her head. "My name is Mavoureen, but only Redal-Stan calls me that, the silly dear. Everyone else calls me Mav. And dearie?" She met Alissa's gaze knowingly. "After your wash, get back in there. Earan is a bully; he has been ever since he was knee-high."

A voice loud with anger slid into the kitchen clatter. "I'm not moving quarters for any half-witted Keeper. She can sleep with the students."

Alissa's chest tightened. She couldn't go in there. Not right now.

Mav pursed her lips and looked towards the archway. "M-m-m, yes," she said, snagging a plate from a stack headed into the room where the heated discussion was taking place. "Have you seen Talo-Toecan's garden yet?" she asked. "He keeps his students busy in there. I hear it's a sight to please the most discerning gardener. I haven't seen it in years." Her voice softened. "Not since a certain lad was courting me." She smiled a small, wistful smile. "I'm sure it's changed since then. But you will undoubtedly enjoy an early morning walk. Yes. You will."

Her hand hovered over a plate overflowing with sweet

rolls. Seeing Alissa's pleased smile, Mav chose one. A small teapot was next, and she guided Alissa through the commotion to the garden door. There was a welcome flush of cool morning air as the woman opened it and handed Alissa first the plate and then the pot. "Enjoy the morning," Mav said as Alissa's feet backed off the low step. "But, dearie? You'll have to confront Earan soon. A man like him won't forgive you for seeing him afraid."

Alissa felt a moment of worry, not sure what to think.

"Just bring it all back when you're done," the woman fussed. And she shut the door.

"Whew!" Alissa exclaimed as she stared at the blue of the door, distressed by the turmoil in what had been her quiet kitchen. Blowing her tension away in a soft huff, she started down the well-manicured path. Her gaze went to the clear sky to search for Talon, and a sigh escaped her.

It was blessedly quiet. Her footsteps kept time with her pulse, soothing her headache away. In the light of day, it was spectacularly obvious this wasn't the long-fallow garden she had started to tend but one bursting with care. She slowed as a flock of young exuberance came laughing and jostling around the corner. Spotting her, they attempted to settle to a smidgen of decorum, but as soon as they were past, they began whispering.

"That's the girl Ren said knocked Earan down," one said.

"Can't be!" another protested. "He said fire shot from her eyes. Hers are plain old blue."

Alissa smiled, imagining that by the end of the day, she would have not only knocked Earan down but broken his arm and eaten his horse.

The sight of the firepit sent a stab of heartache through her. "Strell," she said as her steps faltered. She was missing him terribly. She was missing Strell, missing Talon, missing Useless, and even missing Lodesh, for though he was here, he didn't know her. Miserable, she wandered until she found a small fish pond. It wasn't in her version of the garden, so she sat on the nearby stone bench to share her breakfast with the minnows, enjoying the novelty.

It was only when she reached for the teapot that she realized she had no cup. "Hounds," she swore, then jumped at a small scuffling on the path.

"Here, Alissa," came Lodesh's voice. "Mav sent me out with the cups."

"Your timing is impeccable," Alissa said as she patted the bench. Mav, she decided, must have forgotten her cup intentionally to give Lodesh an excuse to seek her out.

He sat with a happy sigh and poured out the tea, handing Alissa hers first. "After last night, I was afraid you might be able to craft a cup from your thoughts," he said.

"No." Alissa sipped at the tea, paying attention to the taste. "Only clothes."

"But not shoes, yet." He chuckled as he blew ripples across his tea. "I haven't even managed to fix a single form."

"Don't worry. You'll get your cup. Just watch the glazing."

He made a sound of agreement, then tilted his head. "You knew I was making a cup?"

Alissa's grip tightened, and she kept her gaze on the pond. "Everybody wants to learn how to make a cup," she said guardedly, and he relaxed. "I've just about given up, though." She picked up a pebble and tossed it in to make a soft splash. "I can't throw a pot to save my life."

"Perhaps you need a new teacher," Lodesh suggested.

"Strell is an excellent potter!" Alissa cried before realizing he wasn't serious. "Sorry."

"Strell?" Lodesh jumped to his feet, striking an overly dramatic, alarmed stance. "I have a competition before me. Tell me where he is, milady, so I may challenge him for the right to pursue your charms."

"Oh, Lodesh." She smiled up at him. "Don't be silly."

He abruptly dropped his playacting and sat down. "I'm not." Somehow he found her hand, but it was several heartbeats before she found the presence of mind to gently pull away. Lodesh was unperturbed; he almost seemed pleased. "I was wondering," he said lightly, "if you would like a tour of the city? Redal-Stan isn't likely to take you on as a student, and as all the other teaching Masters have succumbed to the fall wanderlust and are gone, you'll have the day free." He bent to find a smooth rock and skipped it across the pond to disappear into the bracken on the other side. "Redal-Stan is instructing Connen-Neute while his usual teacher is away, so I have the day to myself, as well. We can be to Ese'Nawoer and back before the Hold's doors are locked for the night."

Alissa's eyebrows rose. "Actually, I was supposed to meet Redal-Stan at the sixth hour. Do you know when that is?"

Lodesh looked at her in disbelief. "Come on." He stood and pulled Alissa to her feet. He tossed their tea out and gathered the cups. "You're late."

"Not again," she wailed. She snatched her plate and teapot, following Lodesh through the twists and turns until he gallantly opened the kitchen door for her. It was an absolute bedlam. She balked on the sill, reluctant to enter the swirling maelstrom of noise and heat.

"You should see the students' kitchen," Lodesh said, and he dived in, pulling her along.

There was a soft presence at her elbow, and Alissa looked to find Kally. "I'll take that for you," the girl whispered. Smiling her thanks, Alissa released the teapot and plate to her care.

Lodesh caught Kally as she turned away, whispering something. The girl's face lit up, and she glanced at Alissa.

"Lodesh?" Mav's shout made Alissa jump. "Be a dear and take up Redal-Stan's tray?"

"Yes, Mav, my most favorite of old ones," he said dramatically, performing a flamboyant bow as Kally vanished on an unknown errand. "Alissa and I will bring sustenance and charm to tame the beast that is Redal-Stan before his first cup of tea."

"Thank you, dearie," she said lightly. "So kind of you to go out of your way."

Lodesh's put-on air of self-sacrifice vanished as he leaned against a table to snitch a breaded sausage, devouring it in three bites. "We were headed there anyway," he said, wiping his fingers clean. "Redal-Stan bumped Connen-Neute's instruction to evaluate Alissa's skills."

"The old beast is taking another student?" Mav asked.

"Seems so." Levering himself up, he snagged a second sausage in one hand and the tray of cooked links Mav indicated in the other.

"Go on. Get. Before they get cold," Mav said brusquely as he gave her a peck on her paper-thin cheek, but she was beaming.

Alissa accepted the teapot Mav pressed into her hands. Taking a steadying breath, she followed Lodesh into the dining hall. It was twice as noisy as before, and she was glad to see Earan was absent. The barren spot above the hearth drew a frown from her, but perhaps the intriguing picture done in swirling blues had yet to be painted. Thoughts distant, she trailed after Lodesh into the great hall.

"Burn me to ash!" she whispered as she jerked to a stop. The great hall was gorgeous! The marble steps glistened in the sun. Elegant finials graced the banister. Waves of color hung from the high, open walkways. The rug showing the movements of the sun that she had found in storage was out, its subtleties not yet muted by centuries of use.

Alissa bit back a curse and ducked as something round and silver swooped over her head. "What," she exclaimed as she spun to follow it, "was that?"

Lodesh waited as she watched the head-sized sphere swing majestically back across to the far end of the hall like a giant pendulum. "I thought you said you were from the Hold," he said.

"I am," Alissa asserted, exasperated she had let her surprise show. "But—never mind," she finished sourly. She followed Lodesh up the stairs until they stood at the fourth floor landing. He was smiling expectantly, and she peered down to the floor of the great hall. Her mouth fell open in understanding. "It's a timepiece!" she whispered, leaning precariously over the railing. "The ball swings steady as the earth turns under it, marking off the hours as it goes."

Strong fingers grasped her shoulder to keep her from leaning farther. "See the hours sewn onto the rug?" Lodesh asked, sounding pleased. "It has to be reset every morning. Occasionally the students will alter the pendulum's swing in an attempt to explain their tardiness, and everyone runs about off their time until Redal-Stan resets it." He chuckled, and Alissa wondered how many times Lodesh had been responsible for such a prank. "Nearly broke my arm," he said, confirming her suspicions.

Alissa had seen the numbers on the rug when she and Strell had first rolled it out, but not knowing what the rug's purpose was, she had thrown it down any old way. Her eyes widened as she realized the pendulum was swinging halfway to the seven.

"Oh, Lodesh. I'm so late!" she wailed. Snatching the teapot and hiking up her skirt, she skittered up the remaining four flights until halting in confusion at the base of the tower. Lodesh took the lead until they reached the top. There he indicated the first of two doors. Alissa timidly tapped at it, jumping as Redal-Stan's thoughts came slipping expertly into hers.

"Alissa," he began pleasantly enough. *"Get in here."*

"Lodesh is with me," she thought hesitantly.

"Well, that explains your tardiness. Get in here."

Alissa fidgeted. *"As a Keeper, I shouldn't be able to hear you."*

There was a slight hesitation and the impression of a sigh, then, faint through the door came his shout, "You're late, student. Get in here!"

Alissa and Lodesh exchanged worried looks. With a dismal glance at her creased skirt, she pushed open the door and stepped inside.

The walls were stark white, absolutely bare of anything, reflecting the sun to make the room painfully bright. A sloppy desk took up one corner, covered with sheaves of paper, blunt quills, and pots of ink. Surrounding it were heaps of books—precious books—stacked knee-high along the wall as if they were annoyances. An archway led to an unseen second room. Alissa thought that was where Redal-Stan was, but then spotted him and Connen-Neute on the balcony.

The desk was a mess, but it was obvious Redal-Stan did his work in the wind. He sat in the morning sun, sprawled in a chair whose comfort astounded even her. Stones kept his papers from blowing away. It seemed they had interrupted a lesson, as Connen-Neute had a quill and paper in hand. As Alissa watched, he set his work carefully down and rose from an uncomfortable-looking stool, trying to fade into the sparse shade of the balcony supports.

Redal-Stan turned in his chair and frowned. "I don't recall inviting you for instruction this morning, Lodesh."

Unperturbed, Lodesh set the tray of sausages squarely on the small table atop the papers. He took the pot from Alissa and silently poured tea into a cup. Only after he ceremoniously gave it to Redal-Stan did Lodesh say, "I came to explain Lady Alissa's tardiness—and ask a favor."

"Lady Alissa, is it?" Redal-Stan grumbled, taking a huge quaff. He held out the plate of sausages to Alissa, his face going slack in surprise when she refused with a shudder. "You bring me breakfast," he said. "For that, I'll overlook your presumption, but your answer is still no."

Lodesh adopted a shocked expression. "You don't know what I want yet."

Connen-Neute disguised a laugh as a cough, steeling his face back to a somber meekness. Wanting to make amends for her mental slap last night, she offered him some tea, smiling as he warily accepted it. She remained beside him, squinting in the sun. It was glorious up here. They were so high she could see the roofs of Ese'Nawoer beyond the trees.

Redal-Stan took on a pious look. "Oh, Redal-Stan," he said, mocking Lodesh's speech perfectly. "The morning is too grand to sully it with study. Such a beguilingly beautiful woman should spend it in the woods or fields, or even the marketplace where her stunning presence will delight and inspire all those who partake of her vision. And who better than I to accompany her on such a noble and worthy undertaking?"

Snorting rudely, Redal-Stan gulped his tea. "Did I get it right?"

"Almost," Lodesh said in a hurt voice.

"The answer is no. I must ascertain where to begin her

studies. It appears," he said sourly, "that I will waste what's left of the morning in teaching her how to tell time."

Alissa flushed as Lodesh took one of her hands. "I can do no more, and I bid you a regretful farewell, milady," he said as Redal-Stan made an exasperated noise. "I leave you to bravely suffer the arrows of Redal-Stan's thoughts and demands." There was a light pressure on her fingers, and he bowed with a nobleman's grace. "Mav," he said as he moved to the door, "will be so disappointed."

Redal-Stan choked on his tea. "What? What's that?"

"Mav will be disappointed." Lodesh hesitated on the sill, his head bowed.

"Ah, Lodesh?" Redal-Stan shook the spilled tea from his hand and leaned forward to see him. "Why will Mavoureen be unhappy at Alissa studying with me this morning?"

Lodesh's toe edged back across the doorframe. "Kally has been granted a foal from the wild herd," he said hesitantly. "I promised Mav when I had a free day I would accompany her to choose a beast sound in body as well as sight." Lodesh looked over his shoulder and down the stairs as if unhappy with Redal-Stan forcing the issue.

"What has this to do with Alissa?" the Master asked.

"By week's end, all the good foals will have been chosen by the citadel brats who aren't troubled by such trivialities as work and responsibilities. It's a shame," he said softly, "that she will be punished for her endeavors while those who have none are rewarded. Mav will free Kally from her chores if only to see her get a good mount, however . . ."

"Yes," Redal-Stan prompted.

"It would be unseemly for me to accompany her alone. I was hoping Alissa could join us to serve as chaperone."

From beside Alissa came Connen-Neute's snicker.

"It would please Mav to no end," Lodesh finished hopefully.

Redal-Stan grimaced, his smooth forehead wrinkling halfway up his bare scalp. "And if I'm ever to see another candied apple, I will have to keep Mavoureen happy."

Alissa held her breath. She would dearly love to see Ese'-Nawoer with her people.

Noticing her eager hopefulness, Redal-Stan sighed. *"This is something you wish to do, Squirrel?"* he asked her soundlessly.

"Very much so. Please," was her prompt answer, wondering at the pet name.

"An entire morning wasted," Redal-Stan complained aloud.

Lodesh stepped back into the room. "I can teach her how to tell time."

"You think you can?" Redal-Stan chuckled, and not waiting for a reply, he said, "Fine. But if you fail, you'll light the students' dining hall for three consecutive nights."

"Two," Lodesh countered, and Alissa frowned at his lack of confidence in her.

"Done." Redal-Stan turned to Connen-Neute. "Do you wish to accompany them?"

"No, thank you," the young Master said silently. *"I've found it wise to not intrude upon Lodesh's schemes."*

"Verbally," Redal-Stan said with an impatient sigh. "We have Keepers present."

"No." It was a melodious voice, dark and rich.

"Wonderful!" Lodesh exclaimed. "Come on, Alissa, before he changes his mind," and he grabbed her arm, dragging her across the polished floor. "Kally is already in the stables," he added in a whisper.

"But my tea!" she protested as Lodesh yanked her into the hall.

"Enjoy yourself, Squirrel," was Redal-Stan's parting thought. Then they were gone, and halfway down the narrow tower stairs.

8

Alissa allowed herself to be pulled back down the narrow tower steps. The slippery stairs made of native stone shifted to polished marble at the landing where the Keepers lived, and it was there she managed to slow him down. "Ah, Lodesh?" she said, feeling a stab of worry. "What did you mean by Kally was already in the stables?"

He grinned, his breath fast as they brushed past the few students on the stairs. "I knew I could convince Redal-Stan to give you the day free. He'll do anything to keep Mav happy."

She bit her lip, her heart pounding from more than the pace. "No. I mean—stables?" Lodesh looked at her quizzically, and she added. "I don't know how to ride."

Lodesh slowed. "You really aren't from Ese'Nawoer, are you."

Embarrassed, she shook her head, recalling the one time she had tried to touch a horse at market. She had been six. The wild thing had broken its cart and run down an alley, dragging its harness and a trail of infuriated plainsmen.

Taking her elbow, Lodesh pulled Alissa down the stairs. "Don't worry. We'll get you a nice mount." His gaze went to the foot of the stairs, and a smile of recognition crossed him. Mav waited with three small sacks in her hand. The old woman looked uncomfortable outside of her kitchen.

"Young man," she said as she handed Lodesh the packages. "You make sure Kally picks out a nice foal."

Alissa's eyes widened. Was the entire Hold in on Lodesh's plans?

"Yes, Mav." He peered into a sack. The smell of bread and cheese tickled Alissa's nose.

"I mean it," the old woman warned, closing the bag about his fingers and causing Lodesh to look up. "She has been moaning all week about a certain pretty gray with a black hind foot. Thinks it's above her station, the silly girl."

Lodesh grew interested. "The one sired by the black that Reeve keeps chasing from the grove?"

The corners of Mav's eyes crinkled. "That's the one."

A faint smile hovered on Lodesh's face. "She'll get the one she wants."

"That's my boy," Mav said as Lodesh gave her another peck on her cheek.

Even before Mav had shuffled back to her fires and pots, Lodesh had pulled Alissa halfway across the great hall. Seeing the mouth of the tunnel leading to the stables, her fear rushed back. "Uh, Lodesh? Maybe we could just walk it?" she suggested hesitantly.

"Walk it!" Lodesh complained as they entered the cool shadow of the tunnel. "It will take all morning. And don't you dare suggest a cart. Even Mav would die before being dragged behind a horse like a sack of flour."

He was going to say more, but the terrifying scream of a horse shocked their feet to stillness. It was followed by another, then the crash of splintering wood. "Watch it! He's out!" Alissa heard Kally shout. "No! Get out of his way!" There was another scream.

Lodesh and Alissa broke into a run. Together they burst into the gloom of the stables and stood in the doorway. Kally was helping a pale-faced girl up off the hay-strewn floor. The young girl looked close to tears but seemed unhurt. The remains of a stall door hung from a single hinge. As Alissa watched, it fell, causing everyone to jump and the horses to call nervously. The girl backed to a rack of harnesses with her arms clutched about her. She was absolutely terrified.

"Easy, Coren," Lodesh murmured, pulling her to a bale of straw and sitting down before her with his hands about hers. "Everyone is all right. What happened?"

"I—I don't know," the girl whispered, pale and uncertain. "Tempest just went wild, broke down his door and ran away. No one was near him!" she protested. "We knew to stay away. Horse master Hilder will be so angry!" Tears dripped from her, and Alissa stood awkwardly, not knowing what to do.

"Hush." Lodesh gave the girl a quick, brotherly hug. "Perhaps a fly bit him."

Snuffling, she looked up. "I think he hurt his leg," she said around a hiccup. "I—"

"What under the Navigator's Wolves happened!" came a bellowing shout. The horses nickered a greeting, and Alissa spun. A large man filled an adjacent archway, reminding Alissa of an imbedded rock. It wasn't that his ragged hat nearly brushed the top of the doorframe, or that his shoulders were nearly as thick as the walls, or even that his legs were wider around than a good-sized tree. It was his presence. He was flanked by two skinny boys. All three were stained with the sweat of work.

Lodesh gave Coren a reassuring smile and stood. "Morning, Hilder," Lodesh said. "Tempest felt he was sound enough to be loosed."

"So I see." Frowning, Hilder turned from the wreckage. Seeing Coren afraid, he blinked, kneeling to put himself face-to-face with her. "This wasn't your fault, Coren," he said. His voice was kind, rumbling about the shadowy, dusty beams like grace itself. "I know you're too good with the flighty beasts to have done anything to cause this."

Relief flooded her face. Satisfied, the large man stood, the matter clearly in the past. As the horses continued to blow and stomp, he went to inspect the damage. One by one, Hilder peered at each piece. "Lodesh?" he muttered. "If you would please?" And there was a tug on her tracings as a soft glow blossomed, lighting the stables with an unaccustomed light. "Here it is," Hilder breathed, holding a piece up to Lodesh's light. "He's bleeding."

Lodesh ran a finger under the telltale mark of blood.

"We're headed for the field. I'll make sure he finds it all right and is moving well."

His light went out and Hilder grimaced, tossing the wood carelessly away. "I'd appreciate that. I'll have my hands full getting this lot calmed down again." He chuckled. "We haven't had an escapee for years. Wolves," he swore, watching the horses toss their heads and shift nervously. "It's almost as if a Master had come down."

Alissa froze. It was her. Tempest had broken down his door and fled because of her.

"Coren!" Hilder shouted, and Alissa jumped. The horses, however, seemed to calm.

"Yes, master Hilder?" The girl slid from her bale, her eyes downcast.

"If you have your scattered self together, get Kally a mount. One that isn't ready to bolt."

"Yes, master Hilder," was her relieved sigh. She and Kally disappeared through another archway. The two put their heads together, comparing the attributes of the horses they passed.

"You there!" This was directed to one of the boys, and he slowly pushed himself from the wall. "Get Frightful, and remember he takes the rope bit."

"Frightful is in the field, Hilder," said Lodesh. "May I borrow one of yours?"

"So he is." Hilder turned to an empty stall. "I should have recognized his magnificent absence." Grimy fingers ran through his hair under his hat. "There's Nightshade." He shrugged. "She's due for a spell in the field. You can leave her there or return with her as you like."

Lodesh nodded his agreement. "Cotton bit for her as well, please."

"She's not broke to it," Hilder warned.

"We'll get along fine," he said, stroking a long nose. Nightshade, apparently.

"As you will." Hilder turned to Alissa. She knew her smile must look rather sick as he chuckled and said, "You've never been astride anything larger than a goat, have you."

Alissa felt her face warm. "No."

"We'll put you on Sunbeam," Hilder said.

"Sunbeam!" Lodesh groaned in a soft disgust, and Hilder gave him a dark look. Turning to Alissa, Hilder put a heavy hand on her shoulder. "Sunbeam is a nice old lady. Gait as soft and mellow as her name. You'll be fine."

Alissa's smile was getting stilted, but she kept it in place. She had a bad feeling Sunbeam wouldn't like her.

Hilder's gaze dropped to her slippers, and he pulled a pair of boots from a high shelf. Lodesh's eyes widened. "Here," Hilder grumbled, extending them to her. "Wear these." They were light in her hand. Exquisitely detailed. Cream colored.

"Aren't those—" Lodesh began.

"Shut up, Keeper," Hilder growled. "It's not as if Keribdis ever got the chance to wear them. And do you see anything else that will fit those tiny feet of hers?"

Lodesh shook his head, clearly uneasy, and Alissa slipped them on before anyone could see the holes in her stockings. She put her slippers in a rack with the rest.

There was the unmistakable clatter of hooves, and Kally returned leading a brown horse. Kally had her own boots. Lodesh, too, had plucked a pair from a nearby rack. He sat between Kally and Coren upon a bale of straw to tug on his boots. The girls were teasing him, and he was thoroughly enjoying it. They were happy and content in their meaningless banter. Alissa turned miserable, missing Strell.

"Rest easy, miss," Hilder murmured, having misread her melancholy. "Lodesh has spent many hours with many fine ladies, but none has he cared to bring to my stables."

She looked up in surprise, and he grinned to show a missing tooth. Another clip-clop, this time slow and lazy, and a fat yellow horse, almost a pony, made her majestic way down the wide alley. It had to be Sunbeam. She was already saddled, and Hilder beckoned Alissa close.

"Here." An apple weighted her palm, small and yellow. "Give it to her on the flat of your hand, and she will be your friend forever."

Doubtful this would work, Alissa swallowed hard and did

as he suggested. Sure enough, the moment Alissa neared, the horse flattened her ears and backed up.

"Sunbeam!" Hilder bellowed, giving her a light slap on her rump. "What's under your blanket! Stupid beast," the large man muttered, gesturing Alissa should try again. This time, the "gentle old lady" bared her teeth. Alissa's knees went weak, and she backed up into Lodesh.

"Well, I'll be," Lodesh whispered as he gripped Alissa's shoulders to keep her from falling. Then he brightened. "It's the boots."

Hilder frowned. "Keribdis made 'em. I'd wager they reek of her. I won't send anyone out in slippers. Redal-Stan will have my liver if his newest student comes in with blisters."

Lodesh shrugged. "Try her on Tidbit. She has a nice temperament and has been conditioned to tolerate Masters better than any horse in your stable."

Tidbit, Alissa thought. *That sounds like a nice, small horse.*

Hilder made a grunt. "Worth a try. She needs to get out."

"And she's a lot faster than Sunbeam," Kally added, earning Hilder's dark look.

Alissa followed Hilder down the aisle, drawing back in alarm as he stopped before a tall gray. She was dainty and clear-eyed, elegance refined—and the most frightening thing Alissa had ever seen on four legs. "Ah. I don't think so," she mumbled, retreating to the center of the aisle.

"Nonsense." Hilder reached over the gate and Tidbit nuzzled him. "Give her the apple. If she likes you, she's yours for the day."

Not wanting Lodesh to think she was afraid, she offered the apple. Much to Alissa's amazement and dismay, Tidbit perked up her ears, and with lips both picky and soft, she took the yellow fruit. "That's nice," Hilder said with a chuckle. "Let's get her a saddle."

All too soon Tidbit was ready. Kally and Lodesh had already mounted—Lodesh upon a blanket instead of a saddle—and were smiling encouragingly down at her. "But she's so tall!" Alissa said as she balked at how high she had to reach for the saddle.

"We can double up if you like," Lodesh said.

"Ah, I'll be fine." Taking a breath, Alissa slipped her foot into Hilder's cupped hands and found herself quite a bit higher off the ground. Tidbit shifted uneasily, then settled. Proud and scared all at the same time, Alissa tried to smile.

"Now," the large man said as he fastened her pack behind Tidbit's saddle, "Tidbit is nice. She won't roll on you or brush you off. Lean forward to go, back to stop. Use the reins like this." And he showed Alissa how, slipping the thin strips between her fingers where they stayed to become hot and sticky.

"Keribdis made sure her horse was well taught, even though she never could get on the stupid beast," Hilder added. Seeing Alissa if not confident at least reasonably comfortable, he slapped Tidbit on her rump and shouted, "Off with you, before it gets hot!" and they were away, bursting out of the dark, cool stables into the sudden warmth and light of the day.

9

"*You let her go?*"

"Verbally, Connen-Neute," Redal-Stan corrected. "You need more practice."

Connen-Neute grimaced, straightened, and tugged at his wide sleeves. "Why?" he said, hardly enunciating the word.

For a long time Redal-Stan was silent, scanning a view virtually unchanged in the past five centuries. "It's more important she start making permanent ties than to begin her studies." Seeing Connen-Neute's questioning look, he rubbed his eyes. "She can't go back."

"*But you said last night . . .*"

"Verbally!" he barked, his frustration finding an easy outlet, then he shrugged in apology. "Please," he added.

". . . that she could," the young Master finished aloud.

Redal-Stan's brow furrowed. "At the time I thought she could. But I've been giving it some thought. She got here tripping the lines using a septhama point. It makes perfect, illogical sense, but it can't be done. The pathways used to shift and those used to trip the lines don't intersect. It can't happen."

"*It did,*" said Connen-Neute.

Redal-Stan sat back in unease, slumping in an unmasterly fashion, with his cup sitting precariously upon an elevated knee. "Yes, it did, and I plan to find out how. The shame is that even if I do, I still can't get her back."

"*Can't she do the same in reverse?*"

"Send herself back using one of her own memories?"

Redal-Stan's eyes tracked a flock of birds scared up by the students on their way to the fields. He absently rescued his cup as it began to slip. "No."

"Why?"

Redal-Stan turned, stiffening as he counted the sausages. One was missing, and he moved the plate closer as Connen-Neute brushed crumbs from his front. "She must send herself to a memory that doesn't include her, of a time when she's absent. She can't do that. No one can have a memory that doesn't include themselves. A shaduf can't see that far ahead. And though it would be possible to use a memory of another, no one here remembers a time Alissa has yet to live. That's assuming I can figure out how the patterns got crossed to begin with."

Connen-Neute was silent, then, *"She's here for good."*

His brow rose. "You don't sound pleased. Why not?"

"I'd rather not say," Connen-Neute hedged, standing up and turning his back to him.

"Verbally, please," Redal-Stan growled, his eyes narrowing at his student's refusal to explain himself. Then he slumped, deciding a different tack was in order. "I feel it would be best for Alissa to begin making ties to this time," he said. "It will help when she discovers her situation is permanent." Redal-Stan watched Connen-Neute's reaction to his next words. "Perhaps you could—take her under your wing? Keep her company?"

"No."

Surprised, Redal-Stan blinked. "True," he said in a deceptively uninterested voice, "she has markedly fewer years to her credit, but they've all been spent in her human shift making her physically, and for all accounts, mentally, the same age as you. Perhaps you should begin to consider the possibility that Alissa might—"

"No."

Intrigued, Redal-Stan hid his astonishment behind a sip of tea. Connen-Neute had been sheltered for most of his first hundred years, partly by design, partly by fate. His entire generation had been lost to accidents, leaving him to grow up more alone than was customary. It was unusual he would react this way to the chance to develop a real friendship, one that had the distinct possibility of growing into a more permanent relationship.

Redal-Stan warily set his cup on a stack of fluttering papers. He had found Connen-Neute to be overly sensitive to subtle patterns of thought even he couldn't sense. It was unfortunate that the young Master lacked the experience to interpret them. If Alissa made him uneasy, there was a cause for it.

Shrugging helplessly, Connen-Neute turned from the sun. "For some reason, she scares the wind from my wings," he offered hesitantly, sounding embarrassed. He returned to the view, his back stiff and his thoughts closed.

Redal-Stan shut his eyes as the wind rose to pull at his sleeves and thoughts. Worried, he wondered what might have fallen into his quiet, predictable life.

10

Strell slumped in Alissa's overstuffed chair before the fire in the dining hall. He had been there all night, the hours passing with him knowing them all. Only now, as the sun rose above the mountains, did he finally slip into a light doze despite the faint headache that had been plaguing him all night. The loss of her presence cut more clearly than if he were missing an arm. Sitting in her chair before the hearth had seemed to ease his heartache. So he had stayed, shunning his bed in the Keepers' hall, taking comfort in the curious scent of book paste and lace flowers that existed in her chair.

The distant sound of voices raised in anger shocked him from the edge of sleep, and his eyes flew open. The room was empty, the voices gone. *A dream,* he thought, as his head began to throb all the more. He stirred as the comforting feeling in Alissa's chair seemed to fade away.

Strell sat up to put his elbows on his knees and his head in his hands. The hiss of cooking bacon came faintly from the kitchen, and he rose to follow it in. Not acknowledging Lodesh busy at the hearth, he sat at one of the narrow tables. "That's not right," he whispered, and not knowing why, he shifted down two spots.

A plate of eggs and bacon slid in front of him. "Would you like some breakfast?" Lodesh asked cautiously.

Strell looked blankly at him. "No," he said, rubbing the top of his truncated pinkie with his thumb. "That's not why I'm here," he added, not knowing why he was.

Lodesh retreated to the hearth. He left the plate behind,

and it steamed. As the odors penetrated Strell's daze, he pushed it away. Alissa would be appalled at the meat. Strell wondered where Lodesh had found it.

The kitchen grew silent, and Strell vaguely realized that Lodesh had left. He didn't care. The kitchen now satisfied him, and he was as content as his sleep-deprived mind would allow. He rubbed his fingertips into his forehead, pushing back against the dull pain. His eyes closed, and he slumped. Again he drowsed, eyelids twitching as his body tried to find a deeper state of slumber.

Strell started awake at the crash of pottery and a high-pitched wail. Heart racing, he cast about the empty, sunlit kitchen. Only the water dripping from a rag broke the stillness. He watched another bead form and fall. "A dream," he whispered, gazing at the empty tables and silent pantry shelves. They looked wrong. "It must have been a dream."

But he rose and made his way into the garden. He shut the door behind him with a sharp click. The sound beat against his ears, and he picked at the last flakes of blue paint taking refuge between the wood and metal latch. His steps jolted up his spine in time with the throbbing of his head as he wandered the ragged path. Squinting from the sun, he stared numbly at the firepit's familiar lines. Then he continued, compelled by an unknown reason. The firepit wasn't right.

"But the bench is," he breathed as he came upon it and sat down. "I'm moonstruck," he said, his voice flat, not knowing what was happening but too grieved to care. Gazing blankly at the bright flowers, his vision blurred. The bench filled his aching emptiness. Lulled by the serenity, he dozed, half-asleep, half not, lulled by the sound of bees.

Quite distinctly, he heard the sound of a stone splashing into a small pool. He jerked awake. Heart pounding, he stared at the sunken flowerbed full of rushes and water iris. "I'm going insane," he breathed as the bench abruptly lost all its appeal.

Alarmed, he jumped to his feet. Now he inexplicably wanted to be somewhere else. Abandoning reason, he blindly followed the faint pull back up the path, through the kitchen, and up to the highest chamber in the Masters' tower. He stood in the echoing, empty white room, alert and aware, consciously willing himself to listen, searching with his heart instead of his senses. Pushing the heel of his hand against the pain in his head, he moved about, testing the air as if searching for a faint scent.

"Here," he breathed, his eyes closing as he found contentment on the balcony. He stood and soaked it in as if it were the sun, bathing his soul in the emotion. Strell's headache redoubled, and he gasped at the pain.

"But my tea!" he heard in his thoughts, and he reached and grasped blindly as she was ripped away. Stumbling, he opened his eyes, shocked at the emptiness of the room.

"No!" he cried. "Come back!" Down he ran. But he lost her on the stair. Frantic, he cast wildly about. She was gone. Half of him was gone. Someone was taking her away. He had to get her back!

Choking back a cry of frustration, he held his breath and slowed his emotions. He couldn't sense her when his thoughts were swirling. Standing at the center of the great hall, he forced himself to take breath after breath, each slower than the last, letting the tiny point of stillness within him grow. His head hurt, and he welcomed the pain, knowing it had something to do with feeling her presence. Gasping, he felt Alissa pass through him and continue.

"Wait!" he cried, slipping as he turned. He blindly followed, only to find himself hammering upon the locked and warded stable doors. "Back," he panted. Heart pounding, he ran to the great hall. He hit the inner set of the Hold's front doors, sending them crashing into the permanently open outer ones. He had to get out before the whisper of Alissa's presence faded.

He ran down the faint path to the woods, his thin shoes doing little to protect his feet from the jagged stones and sudden dips. He would do nothing but react, knowing if he tried to reason it out, logic would tell him sensing her across time was impossible, and he would lose her.

But he couldn't keep up.

Staggering to a halt, he bent low with his head between his knees. His breath came in ragged gasps that tore his lungs. His head pounded in time with his pulse. He felt as if he were going to be ill but didn't care. Alissa, his love, half of what made him alive, was slipping from him.

II

Hilder was right. Tidbit was sweet. The horse followed Lodesh and Kally in an easy gait that quickly relaxed Alissa. Her hands on the reins went from a death grip to one that was only mildly clutching. She began to look about, noticing what a beautiful day it was. "Strell?" she called breathlessly, then flushed. "Er, Lodesh?" she amended, hoping he hadn't heard.

Lodesh eased his mount's pace until he was even with her. Before she could remember what Hilder had said about how to stop, Tidbit slowed as well. Kally continued on until she was just out of earshot. Alissa wondered just who was actually chaperoning whom.

"Strell is someone you care for? Someone you left behind when you were drawn to the Hold?" Lodesh asked.

Embarrassed, Alissa hunched into herself. "Something like that."

"Then your slip is a compliment," he said. "What did you want to ask?"

"Who is Keribdis?" Alissa asked, thinking Lodesh wouldn't be interested in the odd shape of the oak tree she had thought to point out to Strell.

An honest smile came over him. "She is Talo-Toecan's often-absent spouse."

For a moment, Alissa pondered that. "Why does she have a horse if she can't ride it?"

"Ah, there's a story." Lodesh leaned to flick a fly from Nightshade's ears. "Someone once told her riding a fine horse at great speed must be very much like flying. She wanted to know if it were true. But as no horse will allow a predator on its back, she couldn't. When Tidbit was born out of season, Keribdis took the foal in. Fed her from a wineskin, slept with her in the stables all winter as Talo-Toecan wouldn't allow a horse into the Hold. Drove Hilder and the horses mad. Even so, Tidbit wouldn't let Keribdis on her back. Caresses and cuddling, yes. But any weight heavier than her hand produced only terror. So for the last five years, Keribdis has had to content herself with brushings and workouts at the end of a rope."

"Even when in her human form?" Alissa pressed.

"Rakus are carnivores, Alissa," he said. "Despite all the bread and apples they consume when passing as human, the smell of death lingers, betraying their—savage capabilities."

Alissa's brow furrowed. She was a Master, yet Tidbit let her ride. What was the difference? "Perhaps," Alissa suggested, "if Keribdis refrained from eating meat for a time?"

Lodesh made a small sound of agreement. "Perhaps. You should suggest it when she returns. She would be indebted to you if it worked. Keribdis dearly loves her little Tidbit."

"Maybe I will," Alissa whispered, hoping she would never have the opportunity. Flashing Lodesh a small smile, she turned the conversation to lighter topics until the way broadened and the smell and sounds of the city became apparent.

At the edge of the woods, Lodesh halted Nightshade with a subtle movement Alissa didn't catch. Tidbit drew even and stopped without direction. Kally too, halted, and together they stood at the edge of the damp shade of the trees to look over the sprawling conglomeration of homes and businesses. The noise of the city came faintly, and Alissa met Lodesh's delighted grin with her own. "There she is," he said, his voice soft with pride.

Kally put her heels to her mount and leapt forward. Before Tidbit could think to follow, Lodesh grabbed her bridle. There was a jingle of harness and a quick sidestep, and all was still. Alissa smiled with wide-eyed gratitude, but Lodesh had eyes only for his city. He didn't seem aware of the fall he had adverted. "Isn't she wonderful?" he asked as a dog barked.

"She's even more beautiful without her walls," Alissa

breathed, then realizing what she had said, she closed her mouth and leaned to rub a spot of dust from her borrowed boots.

"Walls, Alissa?"

She winced, then straightened. "Don't most cities have walls?"

Lodesh tossed a curl from his eyes. "Of some sort or another. Being so high in the mountains, we're afforded a measure of natural protection. And there's always the Hold."

"I guess you don't really *need* walls, then, do you," Alissa said, not sure if she should.

Lodesh broke his gaze with his city. His green eyes were full of a questioning innocence. "I can't imagine we do."

There was a thumping of hooves, and Kally slid to an exuberant halt. "Come on!" she moaned. "The citadel brats will finish their pastries and be out stirring up the field with their noise soon." She put a quick hand to her mouth. "I meant no offense, Lodesh."

His nose in the air, Lodesh adopted a haughty stance. "None taken," he drawled, every stitch the nobleman's son. "We privileged few born to the citadel *are* brats, of the highest caliber, myself included." A graceful bow, not easily accomplished on horseback, finished his act, and laughing, they rode into the city.

Alissa hated to admit it, but the farther they went, the more she gawked like the foothills girl she was. The streets weren't paved yet, and it was dusty. Her nose wrinkled at the smell of hot metal, reminiscent of the time Strell had let her favorite copper teapot run dry over the fire.

"Lodesh!" a strong voice called, and she turned to find the source of the stench. It was a smith, surrounded by his hammers and hooks. "Where's your magnificent steed?"

Lodesh raised his hand in acknowledgment. "The field, my most worthy man, the field. But not alone," he added slyly.

The blacksmith laughed and returned to work with a series of sharp clangs.

Across the way, a middle-aged woman with a basket waved frantically to catch Lodesh's eye. He drew Nightshade to a halt, a welcoming smile on him. "Lodesh, dear," the woman said as she drew close and placed a hand upon his knee. "I must thank you."

"Ah." Lodesh beamed. "My introduction of Pella and the baker's son was agreeable?"

Squinting from the sun, the woman pulled her scarf over her head to make a tent of sorts. "Yes. Pella is forever using the bread so as to have an excuse to get more." She looked down demurely. "I will admit, though, I'm sorry her attentions have turned from you."

Lodesh glanced nervously at Alissa. "Tell her I'll pine for her unattainable charms."

The woman eyed Alissa. "I will, but I don't think you will be lamenting for long." She patted Nightshade. "Frightful in the field?" she asked, and Lodesh nodded. "Good," she added, and they continued. Almost immediately a shout came from behind them, and Kally sighed.

"Lodesh!" it came again, and Alissa noticed a thin man with badly hemmed trousers struggling to overtake them. He was slumped under the weight of a young boy sitting astride his shoulders. "Lodesh!" he panted, giving Kally and Alissa a quick nod. "You must come to dinner. I've found the woman of my dreams. She works at the dye shop, the one you told me about this spring."

Lodesh touched his chin. "The one on the north side, third ring out?" he asked.

"That's the one." The man winced as the boy thumped his heels into the man's chest, shouting, "Go! Go!" as if he was a horse. "They had the most wonderful deep green as you promised," the man continued, "but an even more wonderful widow."

"Ah," was Lodesh's sigh. "Tarma is a jewel that shines when she's caring for someone."

Astonished, Alissa turned to Kally. Clearly Lodesh had intended they should meet. "Does he know everyone?" Alissa asked.

"Practically." Kally snorted. "He has introduced in one

way or another nearly half of the couples who have gotten joined in the last three years."

"You're jesting."

"No." She arranged the fringe of mane she could easily reach. "Anyone who needs anything and can't find it asks Lodesh. If he doesn't know, he knows someone who does."

Alissa glanced at Lodesh. The two men were deep in discussion: Lodesh's arms were flailing wildly, the boy's eyes were wide in awe, and the man's lips were curled in amusement. Seeing the direction of Alissa's gaze, Kally sighed heavily. "And it's a real bother when you want to do anything with him," the girl finished loudly.

The men looked up in a guilty surprise. "Yes, well," the thin man offered. "I don't mean to keep you from your afternoon, but if you're headed for the field, could you finish an errand for me?" His eyes pleaded as the child began bouncing mercilessly on his shoulders.

"Can I take the lad home for you?" Lodesh held out his hands, and the delighted boy was deposited behind Nightshade's neck.

"Could you?" was the man's relieved reply. "I found him wandering down here looking for a flower. He insists his mama sent him, but I think he slipped his nurse again."

Lodesh chuckled and tousled the boy's black curls. "Trook," he asked. "Does your mama know you went shopping?"

Alissa's smile froze. Trook? she wondered. Strell's grandfather had been named that.

"Uh-uh." Eyes blue and wondering gazed up at Lodesh in unconcern. "Mama wanted a white flower, and I couldn't find one in the garden."

"So you went off by yourself?" Kally cried in mock fright. "Weren't you scared?"

"Uh-uh." He shook his head solemnly. "Papa says I'm a brave boy and must do what Mama says. Mama wanted a white flower, and I couldn't find one." His face puckered in distress. "I can't find a white flower for Mama," he warbled, his eyes going dark and wide.

"Hey, now," Lodesh said. "You don't think I would allow you to go home with your quest unfinished, do you?"

"No?" His upturned face nearly melted with relief.

"Absolutely not," was Lodesh's firm reply. "Once a gentleman makes a promise, he must follow through to the best of his abilities. Right?"

"Right." The child enthusiastically thumped his heels into Nightshade's shoulders. The patient beast flicked an ear back, then forward. Lodesh whispered into the boy's ear. Immediately the youngster turned to the tall man. "Thank you for your hosp—hosp—" he stammered, deliciously charming.

"Hospitality," Lodesh prompted softly.

"Hospitality this morning, craftsman weaver," the boy said in relief. "And I ask you let me—ah—extend it to you full measure—um—someday," he finished, terribly pleased.

The man, who was apparently not the child's father, smiled. "It was my pleasure to entertain a member of the Hirdune household, young Trook."

"Hirdune?" Alissa whispered, her gut tightening. *It couldn't be. Not Strell's ancestor!*

"Did I say it right, Uncle Lodesh?" the boy asked, and her face went colder still.

"Worthy of any fine gentleman, Trook," Lodesh praised.

Alissa's eyes went unseeing. The child was Strell's ancestor. Not his grandfather, though he carried the same name. No, he was farther back than that. Lodesh once said his sister ran away with a man from the coast by the name of Hirdune. Swallowing hard, Alissa looked for any sign of Strell in Trook, finding none.

So disconcerted was she that she nearly fell from Tidbit when they leapt forward, Trook howling in delight. Mercifully, there were no more interruptions as Lodesh fended off all salutations with an overly dramatic, "We are on a most dire mission and cannot be detained!"

The proper flower was found, and in due course the brave lad was deposited into a tearful nanny's arms, which he immediately wiggled free from. Amid much noise, confusion, and many interruptions of smartly attired people, all was ex-

plained. Wilted flower clutched in a grubby hand, Trook
rested a sun-reddened cheek against his mother's shoulder
and struggled to stay awake as their final good-byes were
said.

Clattering from the tiled courtyard, they passed through a
maze of alleys, coming upon the field rather abruptly. By unspoken agreement, they halted. Alissa felt herself smile as she
tucked an annoying strand of her tangled hair out of the new
breeze.

Not yet surrounded by the city's most affluent houses was
a wide plain of ripening grass, fodder for the city's wild and
domesticated herds. Most towns had green fields, but Ese'-
Nawoer had designed theirs on a grander scale. Set to one
side, but still near the center, was the distant circle of mirth
trees.

There was a rumbling and the shrill bugle of challenge
from a small herd of horses. This, Alissa mused sadly, wasn't
in her memories of Ese'Nawoer. The field she knew was
silent of hoofbeats. "Bachelor herd," Lodesh offered. "And
there's Tempest, just where I'd expect him." Lodesh nodded
in satisfaction. "He looks fine."

The animals ran upon catching wind of them, their ears flat
against their heads. Lodesh stared, frowning. Nudging their
horses forward, they continued, unable to get more than
within hailing distance of anything on four hooves. Even
Alissa could recognize the fear in them, but it wasn't until
they came upon a spring that she found a way to distance herself and keep her secret.

"I think it's Keribdis's boots," Alissa said, wiggling one
out of the stirrup and holding it out. "They think a raku is on
the field."

Lodesh's brow smoothed. "I hadn't thought of that," he
said, then his frown returned. Alissa could almost see his
quandary. It wasn't as if she could take her boots off and go
barefoot.

"I'll wait here at the spring," she said, slipping from Tidbit in an ungraceful motion, stumbling as her knees refused to
work properly.

"Are you sure?"

Feeling like she was at the bottom of a well, Alissa squinted up at him, her breath catching at the green of his eyes. "Yes. Go on. I, uh, could use a moment to stretch my legs."

His smile turned knowing. As he reached for Tidbit's reins, Alissa pulled him closer. "You'll be sure she gets the gray?" she whispered.

"I wouldn't allow her to choose another," he whispered back. After darting a wary glance at Kally, he pointed to a dead-looking weed. "Can you hand me that?" he asked. "Watch the thorns. I only want the soft bits underneath."

Alissa angled her hand between the needles, surprised she had to nudge Tidbit away once the soft gathering of leaves was in her grip. Even Nightshade seemed interested, and Lodesh quickly tucked the greenery behind his lightweight coat.

Giving Alissa a final wave, Lodesh and Kally rode toward the nearby herd of mares and young. Tidbit trailed willingly behind them. Alissa settled herself on a large, flat rock half embedded into the spring's bank, watching as they ambled among the horses.

Lodesh's voice came faintly as he extolled the finer points of each foal they passed. To her surprise, he brushed past the gray Kally was interested in. Then Lodesh thumped her companionably upon her shoulders and directed her attention across the field. But he had, with that friendly pat, stuck that weed on her. The gray colt saw it, though. Ears pricked, he cautiously nibbled it from her. In an instant, it was gone, and he shoved Kally for more. Kally spun, delighted and charmed.

Still Lodesh pulled her reluctant attention to another horse, all the while placing another leaf of that weed on her shoulder. Then he turned away, pretending ignorance.

Lodesh purposely missed the look of rapture that befell Kally as the soft snuffling of the colt filled her ear, but Alissa saw it, and she felt the tears prickle as she knew Kally had a lifelong friend. The colt was hers and she was the colt's, more than they could possibly know yet.

"That one?" Lodesh called in mock distress, and Alissa smiled at Kally's hot reply.

Shaking her head, Alissa turned to the spring to watch the horses who had come to drink. The wind shifted her hair about her ears, and snorting in alarm, they dashed away in a rumble of hooves. "I'm not going to eat you," she muttered, then hesitated. One hadn't run. He looked like he might be diseased, and perhaps that was why he was risking the water. No self-respecting carnivore would touch him, looking like that.

"You must belong to someone at the Hold," she said, thinking the mangy beast was used to the scent of rakus. Pleased for the company, no matter how ugly, Alissa settled on her rock and soaked in the sun's warmth, eyes closed, listening to the insects.

The horse stirred her from her light doze with a soft nicker. Alissa sat up to find Lodesh striding toward her, leading Tidbit and Nightshade. Lodesh drop-tied them and sat down beside Alissa to watch Kally play with her new charge. The colt now sported a red ribbon plaited into his stubby mane, presumably a sign of ownership.

"What was that you stuck on Kally's back?" Alissa asked, her speech slow and lazy from the warmth of the sun.

"Ah—you saw that? Don't tell her."

Curious, she shook off her lethargy. "I won't," she promised. "But what was it?"

"Salt weed." Lodesh leaned back and gazed straight up. "The hardest part was putting it on her when only the little gray would see it. After that, it was a foregone conclusion."

"You knew this would happen?" With her chin, she gestured to Kally and her colt running circles around the patient mare.

His smile held the warmth of memory. "How do you think I got stuck with my horse."

"Nightshade?" Alissa said in disbelief.

"No." Lodesh sat up and gestured weakly toward the malnourished vision of long-legged awkwardness that still bided within earshot. "I mean Frightful there."

"That's your horse?" Alissa exploded thoughtlessly.

Lodesh winced. "Yes. He's something, isn't he."

"M-m-m," she said, but just what he was, she still wasn't sure.

Lost in what was apparently a fond memory, not a nightmare, Lodesh gazed at his ugly horse. "I was about Kally's age," he said softly. "Earan, my brother, took me out and stuck some salt weed on me, tricking me into choosing Frightful. He thought that by having an ugly horse, I would lose my bevy of girls."

"There were a lot, huh?" Alissa said with a laugh.

Lodesh wasn't embarrassed and only grinned. "There were quite a few—for a time."

"So what happened?"

"Girls," he said dryly, "like mothering the downtrodden." He laughed, and Frightful responded with a soft nicker. "They fell all over him. Brought him apples and grain. I didn't find out I'd been tricked until later when it came out during a—discussion." Gaze distant, Lodesh rubbed his chin. "But that," he finished, "is another story."

"Tell me?" Alissa asked.

"Later." Standing up on the rock, Lodesh looked into the east as the wind shifted his hair. Alissa felt a chill, realizing that Lodesh, her ever-familiar, always-predictable Lodesh, might already have a past he was trying to forget. "Come on," he said, extending a hand to help her rise. "I want to show you where I grew up."

"The citadel?" Alissa guessed.

His eyes sparkled eagerly. "No. The grove."

12

"**Y**ou there!" It was an angry shout, shattering the peace the circle of mirth trees had instilled in her, and Alissa spun. "Yes. You!" it came again. A squat, square man strode toward her under the trees, anger etched in every motion. "What are you doing here?" He started slightly as she felt Lodesh slide next to her, and the man's ire vanished in a single breath.

"Lodesh!" he called out, his pace never slacking, but now he gave off a sense of unconditional welcome. "Why didn't you tell us you would be back so soon?" he said as he halted beside them, his eyes full of pride. "Sorry, lass," he directed briefly at her. "I didn't know Lodesh had brought 'cha. I never would have shouted had I known. And why," this was aimed at the grinning Lodesh, "didn't you come to the house first? Your mother is going to be sore. I'll have to listen to her gripe all—"

"Father!" Lodesh broke in, giving him an expansive smile. "I'm at the Hold tonight as planned. I just brought someone to meet you while Kally picked out a horse."

Suddenly shy, Alissa dropped her gaze to the moss, damp under the shade of the trees.

Lodesh cleared his throat and took her hands. "Father," he said formally, "this is Alissa Meson, a Keeper of the Hold looking to Redal-Stan." Alissa's hands were transferred to the short man's, and she glanced up, startled at the heavily callused feel of them.

"The old beast took another student, did he?" the man mused, his sharp gaze seeming to go all the way to her core.

"Well," Alissa offered, "he was the only teaching Master there when I arrived."

"Ha!" he admonished. "Redal-Stan wouldn't bother unless he saw something in you." The unassuming man turned his attention to her fingertips, smiling at something he saw.

Lodesh shifted impatiently. "Can I finish?" he asked, then turned to her. "Alissa, I'd like you to meet the man I deem has the second most important job in the city, the caretaker of the mirth trees and the man I'm fortunate to say raised me from a small boy, Caretaker Reeve."

As Reeve bobbed his head in greeting, Alissa's fingers slipped from his in confusion. "But I thought your father was . . ."

Reeve chuckled and stepped back. "Ah, well, I didn't sire him, true enough, but Jenna and I raised him as our only child."

"You were abandoned!" Alissa blurted, then flushed.

Lodesh laughed, the sound lifting through the trees, seeming to belong as much as the moss under her feet. "No," he said. "They were forced to take me in."

"Don't listen to him," Reeve growled. "We wouldn't have had it any other way."

"I don't understand," Alissa said.

Reeve took one arm and Lodesh the other, leading her to a distant bench. "Well, you see," Reeve said, "one evening 'bout this time of year, Jenna and I were disturbed by the sound of a child's weeping. Being no one but us about, we went to investigate, finding Lodesh here nestled at the base of . . ." Reeve cast about. ". . . that tree there."

Lodesh caught her eye and discreetly pointed to another.

"He was only a wee bit of a thing then, not the great hulking giant he is now," Reeve continued. "No more than six, and sobbing as if a lifetime of woe was upon his soul. Jenna fed the tyke and rocked him to sleep as it was late. He never said a word, so, come morning, I took him to the Warden's holdings as that's where I would go if my child went missing. Imagine my surprise when I found the snot-nosed brat was the Warden's nephew."

Lodesh rubbed the back of his neck, looking terribly uncomfortable.

"The tears," Reeve said as he sat her at the bench, "were for his mother, recently overcome in childbirth." He paused as Lodesh sat down at the far end of the bench, his gaze ramrod straight.

"We never saw the tears again," Reeve said. "But *he* kept coming back. More often than not, we'd find him curled up at the base of a mirth tree, wet with dew and shivering. His mornings with us got longer and our partings at the Warden's gate harder, until it was decided he should stay with Jenna and me—providing I taught him something."

Reeve rested a foot on the bench between her and Lodesh. "By the way, son," he said. "What is, in your opinion, the city's most important job?"

Lodesh smiled. "The trashman, Father. The trashman."

"Course." It was dry and sour, and Alissa felt the last of the solemnity evaporate. Reeve then looked questioningly at Alissa. "But I thought everyone knew Lodesh's story."

"She isn't from Ese'Nawoer," Lodesh interceded before Alissa could open her mouth. "Alissa is straight from the foothills."

"Really?" Reeve squinted at her. "You're quite tall for the foothills, and dark. And your accent is decidedly Ese'-Nawoer."

"My father was from the foothills," she said, instinctively having no fear of recrimination for her mixed background from Reeve. "My mother is from the plains."

"Ah, well then." Reeve placed a meaty finger to his nose, and Alissa smiled, recognizing one of Lodesh's mannerisms. "You really are Ese'Nawoerian. Something of both, and not fully of either. How did you ever escape my son's notice through your Keeper studentship?"

"Alissa is rogue, Father," Lodesh said evenly.

Reeve pulled his foot from the bench and straightened. His

eyes were wide. "Rogue!" he exclaimed. "But you're of Keeper standing?"

"Yes." Lodesh glared at Alissa, daring her to deny it.

"Sort of . . ." she muttered, and looked to where the sun made it through the canopy. The dappled patterns shifted in the breeze that never reached the ground. Reeve let the silence sit, waiting. "Earan," she offered hesitantly, "seems to think I'm not."

"Earan is a fool!" Lodesh said with an unusual anger.

"To put a fine point on it, he's right," Alissa said. "I haven't been recognized."

Reeve nodded. "And likely won't until winter when a quorum of Masters is present."

Lodesh stood and began pacing, his outrage demanding action. "Earan makes a stink every time he sees her. He drove her to eat in the garden this morning!"

Thinking it must bother Lodesh more than her, Alissa drew her legs up and sat cross-legged on the bench. "I like the garden," she said. "And it's too noisy in the dining hall."

"Noisy?" Reeve eyed her with a sharp look.

Embarrassed at the fuss, Alissa shifted her shoulders. Reeve was silent, peering at her as if trying to solve a puzzle. Uncomfortable with his scrutiny, she uncrossed her legs and put her feet on the moss where they ought to be. Reeve grunted deep in his throat. "Well, if Earan won't let you eat in the Keepers' hall, you can walk in my grove." His brown eyes glinted in mischief. "Be it work or rest day, sun or moonlight. You're welcome."

Lodesh's mouth fell open. "Father!" he finally choked out.

"Be still, boy," he said, grinning at Alissa. "It's my grove. I'll invite who I want."

"But, Father!"

"I said be still!" He took Alissa's hands and drew her to her feet. "It's not as if I granted her citizenship to the city."

"You may as well have!"

Alissa gave the short man a smile as she took his arm. "Thank you," she said, delighting in his invitation to the grove for its own sake as much as for the bother it put Lodesh in.

"That boy of mine," Reeve said ruefully as Lodesh flung

his arms dramatically into the air and turned his back on them. "Always making more of a situation than what it is. And as for Earan? Things have a way of working out—if you watch them close and jump when you ought."

Alissa had no idea what he was talking about, but he smelled like dirt and growing things, so she went willingly with him as he escorted her among the trees. "It's a beautiful spot you tend, Reeve," she said, gazing up at the distant branches. "It must have been breathtaking this spring when they bloomed."

"Bloom?" Reeve said. "They have yet to bloom this year."

"Aye," came Lodesh's sigh from behind them as he gave up on his sulk and joined them. "It's been five long years."

Confused, Alissa turned from Lodesh to Reeve. "I thought they were a spring bloomer, even before the leaves opened."

Reeve glanced at the shifting boughs. "Spring or fall, sometimes in between—if they choose to do so at all." He hesitated, glancing at the shadows. "Alissa," he said, his tone going formal. "I have a question for Lodesh concerning a fungus that has become a problem recently. Would you mind if I stole him from you for a moment?" His eyebrows rose, saying more clearly than words that it wasn't fungus he wanted to talk to Lodesh about, and she nodded.

"You're most kind," Reeve said.

Lodesh opened his mouth to protest, and Reeve gave him a quick jab in the ribs. With a soft grunt, Lodesh's mouth snapped shut and he hunched. The square man led his tall, handsome, and sometimes dense son out of earshot, loudly explaining that the fungus was "over there, behind that far tree."

Chuckling at the spectacle of someone bullying Lodesh, Alissa turned to the grove. The trees seemed no smaller than she remembered. At the center of the grove was a wide circle of open ground surrounded by large hummocks of moss-covered earth, looking like ripples spreading out in ever-widening bands. It was, she decided as she got closer, a theater of sorts: the stage was the open circle and the seats were the rising mounds of earth. Apart from the theater, the grove looked the same as when she had left it.

"Except for . . ." Hiking up her skirt, Alissa moved to the largest tree. "You," she pointed accusingly and shifted her attention. "And you." She frowned at a second. "And you, I think," she muttered to a third. These three had fallen by the time she had found them.

"What do you mean by outgrowing your roots?" Alissa lectured as she ran a hand over the largest. "Reeve spends so much time with you, and you repay him by falling over. Shame!" She strode to the second. It was some distance. A bit breathless, she gave it a sharp thwack.

"Outgrowing everyone is fine," she said, looking up at the unlistening trees, "except when you forget it's your roots that keep you upright." It was the third tree's turn, and she walked about it, wondering how such a strong-seeming thing could fall. "What you don't show the world," she said gently, "is what allows you to reach the heights you do. Never neglect your foundation. Nurture it more than the handsome face of leaves and limbs you show. For even if they are destroyed, you can still rebirth from your untouched, unseen, never-realized roots."

Alissa let her hand drop from the smooth, gray bark, wondering if she should harken to her own words instead of heaping them upon helpless trees. "Grow," she sighed as she watched the toes of her boots. "And maybe bloom? Just a little? It would please Lodesh, so."

Not sure why she felt sad, she turned away. The western breeze gusted and dropped, and gusted again, sweeping under the trees to bring her a vague sense of unease.

13

Reeve pulled Lodesh nearly halfway across the grove before Lodesh dug in his heels and halted them. "You didn't take me from Alissa to ask my opinion of a fungus," he accused.

The man took his elbow again. "Don't be dense, boy," he muttered with a dour look.

Lodesh twisted his arm free. "What then?"

For a moment, Reeve looked him full in the face. There was a tinge of despair in his gaze, but he dropped his eyes even as Lodesh recognized it. Hunched and alone, Reeve continued on without him. "Your father came to see me this morning," he said over his shoulder.

"My father!" Lodesh glanced behind him to see if Alissa had heard, then jogged to catch up. "What—" he said as he drew him to a stop. "What did he want?"

Reeve hesitated. "He wanted to know if you're satisfied with the status I can give you."

"Yes! To tend the grove is all I want."

"Are you sure?" he asked with a soft persistence. "You could easily slip the skills I've taught you into a finer glove than that of a gardener."

Lodesh took a quick, almost frightened breath. "This is what I am," he said overly loud. "I have found what I'm good at, and I have found what gives me joy, and I'm lucky they're one and the same and that it didn't take me half my life to discover it."

Reeve smiled at him with a quiet pride. "When did you become so wise, Lodesh?" The man looked away, and Lodesh knew.

"They want me to return to the citadel," Lodesh said, tensing as Reeve nodded.

"It's believed your uncle's wife is barren." Only now did Reeve meet Lodesh's eyes, seeming to plead with him, as if to convince him it wasn't his fault. "Your uncle plans to shift the title to your father, the Masters and elder families willing. In due course, it will likely fall to one of his children."

Lodesh stepped back, cold from more than the shade of the trees. "I don't want it."

A thick hand took his shoulder in comfort. "Relax, boy. No one is going to make a twenty-two-year-old the Warden, but perhaps you should mull it about in your thoughts for the next decade and see how it fits."

"I know already it fits fine, but I won't do it," he said frantically. "They can pick someone else! There must be half a dozen of us."

"But as your sister declined her Keeper studies, only you and Earan have ties to the Hold."

"There have been Wardens who weren't Keepers," Lodesh asserted, reassured somewhat that they weren't going to descend in force and make him leave his home.

"True," Reeve admitted, his gaze on the branches high overhead. "But, Lodesh?" He hesitated. "Who would you rather see in the citadel?"

Lodesh took a deep breath and looked away. "Earan is the eldest. He's the logical choice," he said, his voice flat.

"The people don't know him," Reeve said.

"I'm sure that will change," Lodesh said miserably, knowing it wouldn't. But he couldn't leave his home, his trees, or his only memory of his first mother beneath them, singing softly while she rocked him to sleep as the mirth trees bloomed and the moon rose high.

There was a short silence. "Perhaps you're right." Reeve straightened, dropping the subject with an accustomed shortness. Turning, they spotted Alissa with her hands on her hips, regally assessing the ring of trees from her central position in the dancing court.

"What really brought you here today?" Reeve asked, a hint of amusement in his voice.

"I wanted you to meet Alissa."

The short man snorted, his tongue jammed in his cheek. Slowly he closed one eye. "I've managed to meet all your ladies, but you've never brought any to see me."

Lodesh felt himself color, and he tore his eyes from Alissa. "I can't seem to put my finger on it. It's almost as if she knows me already."

"Sometimes it's like that—at first," Reeve cautioned, and Lodesh laughed, the last of his unease melting away.

"Trust me. I have fallen in and out of infatuation so many times, I can spot it before the girl's overly protective brother does. No. It's *exactly* as if she knows me." He pursed his lips, struggling for words. "When I introduced her to you," he said, "she blushed. I can't make her do it. The Navigator knows I've tried. It's as if she's immune to me."

With a short guffaw, Reeve led them to where Alissa was walking disapprovingly around a wide trunk. "What *is* she is doing?" Reeve asked in wonder.

"I think she is scolding your trees."

Reeve clicked his tongue against his teeth in delight. "I knew I liked her."

Though he tried, Lodesh couldn't keep the excitement from his voice. "How come? You never liked any of my ladies since—you never like any of my ladies anymore."

Alissa slapped a smooth trunk, and Reeve started in surprise. "She's the only one who has dirt under her nails," he said.

"She does not!"

"You may not be able to see it yet, but wait until spring, my boy. It's there."

Lodesh accepted this warily. "I'm glad you like her. When the mirth trees . . . when they bloom again . . ." He swallowed hard. "I mean to give her one of their blossoms."

Reeve stopped so quickly it was several steps before

Lodesh realized he was alone. "Are you sure that's a good idea?" Reeve asked, his brow furrowed as Lodesh returned.

"I don't care if it's a good idea or not," he said crossly. "I spoke to Sati about her."

"Lodesh!" It was a hissed whisper of warning. "Do you really think that was wise?"

"No," he admitted. "But it's done. Sati said our fates intertwine, though she can't see how. That's enough for me."

"But remember what happened the last time?" the anxious man pleaded. "We nearly lost the both of you."

Lodesh gazed at Alissa. He knew his look wasn't far from hunger, and he didn't care if Reeve saw it. It was as if she was the only one who could save him from a life alone and afraid to care. "Alissa," he said evenly, "is already a Keeper. She can't also be a latent shaduf."

His head bowed, Reeve said nothing.

Lodesh closed his eyes as he gathered strength. That night had thrown him into a self-imposed seclusion, convinced anything he cared about would be ripped from him as was his mother and then Sati. It had been a small task to learn how charm could be used to keep an unhealthy distance between himself and any who would try to reach him. He was quite secure. Safe, untouched—and alone.

Reeve stirred. "I just worry, Lodesh," he said slowly.

"I have to ask," he whispered. "I don't care if she answers. But I have to ask."

Finally Reeve managed a smile, but disquiet still haunted his eyes. Lodesh blew in relief as Reeve put a hand on his shoulder, giving him his blessing even as the west wind slipped under the trees, bringing with it the sound of a horse ridden hard.

It was Earan, red-faced and sweating, who reined up before them. "Lodesh," Earan panted, sounding cross. "Your presence is required in the citadel."

"I'm busy—" Lodesh began, frowning at the lathered state of Earan's trembling mount.

"Now, little brother," Earan snapped. "There's been an accident. A wall under construction has fallen. Uncle and Father were under it. Uncle is dead. Father is alive but isn't expected to make it through the night."

"Father . . ." Lodesh whispered, his sight going vacant and his pulse quickening.

"You *do* remember Father, don't you?" Earan said with a sneer.

"Enough," Reeve said coldly, and he whistled sharply. Frightful thudded in under the trees, his neck arched and his bony head high. Dazed, Lodesh vaulted onto his back.

"Alissa." Lodesh turned to see her alone and small in the very center of the grove, her arms clasped tightly about herself. She had heard everything and looked frightened.

"I'll see her and Kally to the Hold," Reeve assured him, his eyes full of grief. Lodesh knew it wasn't for the Warden, nor even for his father, but for him. "Go!" Reeve shouted, and Earan yanked his horse about with a squeal of protest. Lodesh and Earan bolted from the shade of trees and into the blinding sun.

Slowly the man who had raised Lodesh moved to replace the moss torn up by the hooves, stomping each clump into the earth as if his life depended upon it.

14

Strell focused upon Talo-Toecan. "I'm not sure I understand," he said as he ran a shaky hand across his cheeks.
The thick stubble was harsh against his fingertips.

"I'm not sure I understand it myself," the Master said
somberly. Settling farther into his chair, Talo-Toecan sent his
gaze from his cup, to Lodesh, and finally to the pot of tea
upon the hearth in the Keepers' dining hall. Grimacing, he
topped off his cup. Lodesh had made the tea; Strell knew it
wasn't as good as Alissa's had been.

Is, he thought furiously, feeling himself tighten in panic.
As good as Alissa's is. She wasn't gone if Talo-Toecan was
right, just misplaced—Wolves, she was lost in the garden.

It had only been this morning that Talo-Toecan had
swooped down on his bat wings, nearly knocking Strell over
as he stopped him from running to Ese'Nawoer. In all fair-
ness, the only reason Strell agreed to return to the Hold was
Talo-Toecan's assurance that he knew what had happened.
Now that Strell knew, he wasn't quite sure he believed it. It
sounded too unreal.

Why not? he decided with a hopeless chortle. The idea that
Alissa had shifted herself to the past was only slightly more
insane than the idea that she could turn herself into a raku. He
forced his breathing even as his grief arose anew. She had
gone back using a septhama point. Sand and Wind, he hated
septhama points. They had something to do with ghosts,
and he hated ghosts. The plains were full of them. "You say

she finished her shift where the septhama point originated," he said. "Why didn't you warn her it could happen?"

The Master scoured his forehead in an unusual show of weariness. "I didn't know it could be done," he whispered.

"How could you not!" Strell cried in frustration. "You are her *teacher!*"

Lodesh turned from arranging the fire, shock in his eyes at Strell's accusation.

"Yes," the Master admitted, his eyes narrowing. "But I've done the same thing myself, as recently as just this morning, and never ended my shift anywhere but where I expected to. The patterns don't cross. It's impossible to run them simultaneously."

Strell slumped in on himself. "Where did she go?" It was a weary, heartfelt question. Exhausted and drained, he watched Lodesh turn his back on them and needlessly arrange the fire.

"There're numerous septhama points at the firepit," Talo-Toecan said. "It would be difficult to know for sure which one she fixed on. I wasn't paying that close attention."

Lodesh cleared his throat. "It can't be any more than five hundred sixty years, Strell. The Hold is only that old."

"The firepit was constructed long before the Hold," the Master said. "The garden was built around it much as the Hold was built over the holden. I don't know where she is."

"Did she get there safely?" Strell breathed, not caring how old the firepit was.

"I don't know."

Strell closed his eyes. "Can she get back?" he asked.

"I don't know," Talo-Toecan said again.

Struggling to keep himself intact, Strell breathed in her scent lingering in her chair. He had lost her. He would get her back. "I can feel her, sometimes. How is it I can do that?"

Talo-Toecan stirred. "I don't know."

15

"A re you sure, dearie?"

Alissa smiled as she pulled herself in from the window. "Yes, Mavoureen. I like this room." Turning her back upon the distant roofs of Ese'Nawoer, Alissa felt a wash of satisfaction as she sent her gaze over the familiar walls of her room.

The bed looked about the same, though the spread across it had clearly seen better days. Before the fireplace was what once was a chair. Now it was more suitable for firewood. Actually, all the furniture, sparse as it was, was mismatched and old. Only the shelves above the hearth had any shine to them, and they practically glistened under the varnish that Mav was energetically dusting. It seemed as if this was the forgotten backroom where the old furniture went when new was commissioned.

"The room next is empty too," Mav said, continuing her efforts though there was no dust and never would be. "No one thought to offer you these, seeing as their chimneys connect."

"I don't mind." Alissa shook out the moth-eaten curtains. Still no dust. The Hold's nightly sweep for dust was a blessing.

"You'd be the first Keeper who didn't," was Mav's tart reply. "Perfectly fine room going empty because you might hear your neighbor tending his fire."

"There's no one in there," Alissa added. "You would think at least one of these rooms would be used."

"Not them Keepers," Mav said caustically. "Darn fool sensitive if you ask me. Always harping on this or that." Then she blinked and smiled at Alissa with her clear, old eyes. "Present company excepted, of course."

Alissa grinned back. "Course."

"I'm surprised Lodesh, the dear boy, didn't want to show you these rooms himself. His room is only three down," she murmured as she pulled back the spread to find there were no sheets. "Good thing I brought up clean," she said, ripping the cover free with such gusto that Alissa didn't have the heart to tell her she usually slept in a chair before the fire.

Alissa took the spread as Mav extended it. "Lodesh stayed at the city," she said. "Didn't Kally tell you?"

"No." Mav snapped a sheet over the cot, and it settled with an enviable perfection. "The child hardly said two words to me when she got back. Mumbled something about potatoes and then ran to the storeroom annex. Didn't she get the gray?" She turned, her green eyes glinting in ire.

"Oh, yes," Alissa quickly reassured her. She went quiet, concerned for Lodesh. The loss of his father would be hard, even if they were estranged.

Mav grumped in relief, and together they shook out the blanket. The prickly sound of wool filled the air. "There, that's done," Mav said, patting the horrid, tiny pillow. "There's a necessity at the end of the hall," she said, laboriously bending to peek under the bed. "But you have a chamber pot if you'd rather. Can you ward your own windows when it rains?"

Wincing, she shook her head. Useless hadn't shown her how yet as it "wasn't needful." She could remove them, though, as he wouldn't risk her flying into a warded tower balcony.

Standing by the bed, Mav's brow furrowed in thought. "No reason to give Earan any more fuel for his fire. Have Lodesh ward them for you until Redal-Stan rectifies the situation." She gave a harrumph. "If he ever does. The inconsiderate beast seldom remembers anything that doesn't revolve around his comfort."

Alissa nodded, embarrassed to have admitted her ignorance.

"Just wait until I get a hold of Lodesh, the scamp," Mav grumbled. "Leaving you and Kally to make your way back alone. I thought I taught him better."

"Reeve brought us back," Alissa said as she began to lay a small fire for later. "It wasn't as if Earan gave Lodesh much choice."

"Earan? What about Earan?"

Alissa thought she would have to arrange for more wood soon, especially if she went without window wards. She wasn't going to admit to anyone she hadn't been taught how to work them yet. "Haven't you heard?" Alissa continued. "The entire Hold is buzzing with it."

"Heard what, dearie? No one tells me anything, except how the potatoes should have been cooked."

Still at the hearth, Alissa knelt and craned her neck, trying to spot where the flues joined. "A wall fell upon the Warden and his brother. It killed the Warden outright," she said into the chimney. "Lodesh stayed because his father isn't expected to make it through the night."

Satisfied the flues really did join, she backed out of the immaculately swept hearth. "Did you know the Warden was Lodesh's uncle?" she asked, but got no response.

"Mavoureen?" she said, turning to find her collapsed in a frighteningly small heap of flour-dusted cloth.

16

"You cold, cruel, inhumane piece of foothills—"

"Earan!" Lodesh shouted, looking up from Mav lying unconscious upon Alissa's bed.

"I'm sorry," Alissa whispered. She stood with her hands clutched about her arms. "I didn't know she was your grandmother."

Earan paced, the sound of his booted feet going through the thin rug to the floor. He halted aggressively before her. Alissa raised her eyes, running them up his rumpled clothes. They looked slept in. "Everyone else knows," he mocked.

"As you pointed out, Earan, she isn't from here." Rising from Mav, Lodesh removed his outer jacket. He glanced about, then tossed it to the rickety chair.

Earan's face grew ugly. "To callously tell an old woman her sons—her only children in the world—are dead. It's a wonder she's alive at all!"

Lodesh stiffened. "That's enough."

"I'm so sorry," Alissa whispered, slumping in guilt. "I didn't know."

Several voices whispered in the hall, but no one looked in, reluctant to get involved in a Keepers' argument. The hand Lodesh put on Alissa's shoulder was trembling. "Alissa has hardly left her side these two days," he said. "Tending her all this time."

"Probably waiting for the chance to stick a knife in her and steal her shoes." The huge Keeper began pacing, looking like a caged fox Alissa had once seen at market. "An addlebrained, rogue Keeper sends the last elder of my house into a death state so deep all I can do is watch her die. It's her fault. And you're defending her!"

Lodesh's fingers moved spasmodically and slipped from Alissa. "She may recover," he said, "and she is the last elder of *our* house, not yours."

Earan spun, his face flushed. "You never gave a breath of consideration to those that birthed you. Mucking about in the field with that worthless man, ignoring your responsibilities, and fostering your attentions on a no-account stand of trees!"

Alissa felt Lodesh's grip upon his emotions slip. "I have listened to you for two days as we settled Father's affairs," he said softly. "Shut up or leave."

"I'm not leaving." Earan's ringed finger went out and stabbed towards Alissa. "She is."

Knowing Mav's real kin should take over, Alissa obediently stepped to the door, halting as Lodesh took her arm. Her mournful gaze rose to his, and she read the anguish of what she had wrought with her careless, thoughtless words. Earan was right. It was her fault.

Her face must have shown her thoughts, because Earan adopted a confident stance. "See," he demanded. "She knows she killed Mav as surely as having given her poison."

"Get out, Earan." Lodesh's voice was so cold it was frightening. The tension in the room swelled. The whispering in the hall turned to an expectant hush.

"Don't tell me what to do—little brother." Earan stepped closer. His hands clenched.

"Get out," Lodesh demanded, "before you do something as foolish as your words are."

"And I expect you think you can make me?" Earan's face twisted as Lodesh stood toe-to-toe with his brother towering over him. Alissa held her breath, afraid. Lodesh didn't move, and finally Earan stepped back. "I'll leave," he said with a sneer, and her breath eased from her. Then she froze as she felt a ward go up. "After I dispense a Keeper's justice."

"Earan! No!" Nisi cried in horror from the hall.

"Don't be a fool!" Lodesh shouted.

"It's my right!" Earan bellowed. Face twisting with anger, he sent a burst of energy at them. There was a flash and boom of sound as Alissa defused the strike with a ward of light and Lodesh did the same with a ward of sound. Her heart pounded, and she fell back to the hearth, shocked Earan had attacked her.

"Stop it!" Nisi cried in the doorway, her hands over her ears. "Stop it, both of you!"

Earan's face was ugly. There was a tug of a second ward. Alissa gasped a warning.

Redal-Stan appeared beside Nisi. "What under my Master's Wolves is going on!"

Earan nearly fell in his haste to spin about. "It's my right!" he shouted wildly. Then he caught himself. The resonance of his ward across Alissa's tracings vanished.

No one said anything as Redal-Stan's unhappy gaze went from Earan's stained boots, to Nisi's wide eyes, to Alissa's frightened ones, to Lodesh's tense stance, and finally to Mav, unconscious on the bed. His jaw clenched, making him look old. "Would anyone," he said tightly, "care to explain why I was disturbed from my morning's studies with tales of feral men within the Keepers' halls?"

Earan stroked his beard and glared at nothing.

"I see." Redal-Stan entered and took an aggressive stance in the middle of the room. "Earan," he directed to the large man, "you're excused from your duties for no less than four days beginning now. You may use your newfound time to scrape the front steps."

"The front steps!" Earan took a protesting step back. "That's a student's punishment!"

Redal-Stan closed the gap between them. His face held a severe anger, and Alissa's eyes widened. "Which is exactly whom you were acting like." Earan opened his mouth. Redal-Stan took another, unnerving step forward. He arched his non-existent eyebrows. Only a finger width apart, he whispered into the startled man's face, "You wish to discuss it further—Keeper?"

Suddenly pale, Earan swallowed. His eyes bore into Alissa

for an instant, frightening her with his hatred, then he stormed out in staccato of boots.

Redal-Stan sighed. "Nisi?" he said gently, and she jumped. "Have Kally send my breakfast tray here, if you would. I'll be some time meting out punishment, and have no wish to let my breakfast go cold in the interim."

"Yes, Master Redal-Stan," she said, and she slipped away. The remaining Keepers trailed behind her in a rustle of hushed conversation.

Hunched, Redal-Stan moved to Mav. Alissa felt a stab of hope. He hadn't been able to help yesterday. Perhaps today he could.

The Master watched Mav's pupils shrink as he lifted her lids, and he counted her breaths and heartbeats. He felt her cheek for her warmth. Mav seemed to be asleep, sleeping so deeply and profoundly that nothing could rouse her.

Alissa had seen this before, lived it, and by the strength of Strell's compassion and her will, survived it. She felt cold, recalling last winter when she burned her tracings so badly she had no recourse but to retreat into her unconsciousness to escape the pain. Lost among Mistress Death's fog, she had abandoned any desire to return to a world where only heartache and suffering seemed to exist, until Strell's whispered words broke through to light the path back to the living.

Alissa knew she could find Mav and bring her back. She had spent the last two days trying to convince Redal-Stan to let her try. At first, the Master refused to believe Alissa had been hurt badly enough to have gained Mistress Death's attention and yet lucky enough to have slipped her snare. Showing him the memory of the burn she had endured finally convinced him, but he still refused to let her try. Today, though, perhaps.

Redal-Stan straightened from Mav, glanced at Lodesh, and cleared his throat. "Lodesh, join your brother on the front steps for this morning. Maybe you can come to an understanding." Pausing, he looked about Alissa's stark room with its ugly, castoff furniture. "Maybe not."

Somehow silent, though he, too, wore boots, Lodesh retrieved his coat. He bent low over Mav. There was a whisper and a kiss on her forehead. Eyes downcast, he stepped to the hall.

"And Lodesh?" Redal-Stan's soft words seemed to echo. "See that Earan doesn't use any of Mavoureen's tools. Find him something from the stables. It was months before I heard the end of it the time he used her best kitchen knife."

"Yes, Redal-Stan," he murmured. He left, looking empty and drained.

The tall, somewhat disheveled Master listened to Lodesh's steps fade before he turned to Alissa. "May I come in?" he asked, though he stood in the center of the room.

Grimacing, she gestured weakly. She went to the patch of morning sun and slumped to sit cross-legged within it. "I'd offer you a place to sit," she said, "but that's the only chair, and I wouldn't trust it to hold a kitten."

Redal-Stan gingerly bent to sit, regardless, jumping up as the chair creaked and began to give way. Silently he moved to the window and sat on the sill. He was blocking her sun, and peeved, she spun about, setting her back against the cold hearthstones.

"I would send you down to the front steps as well," he said. "But you would only make things worse between them."

Alissa slouched. "Earan is right," she said, gesturing to Mav. "It's my fault. Why won't you let me help her? Burn it to ash, Redal-Stan. I know where she is. I can bring her back!"

Redal-Stan held up a hand, stopping her. Rubbing his eyes, he drew his legs up and sat to take up the bottom half of the window. The hem of his long Master's vest edged the floor. He gazed over the barren walls and threadbare rug before settling upon her. "No."

She felt her mouth turn down. Against her will, memories of a gray, enfolding peace filled her thoughts as she exhaled. Mistress Death's gracious promise. Alissa clenched her arms tight about her drawn-up knees. The thought of the gray, muzzy nothing where Mav had hidden herself seemed to drive a spike of cold through her. She knew that to go back might allow Mistress Death to claim her due, but she wouldn't tell

Redal-Stan. Alissa gave herself a shake. "Then at least tell me why you won't let me try," she whispered, setting her chin on her knees.

"Don't you understand, Alissa?" he said in frustration. "I don't know how. The last Master who knew how to return from so deep within his consciousness died before the first stone for the Hold was set. I won't ask a student to go where I can't hope to follow. If you slip, I can't catch you." He took a steadying breath. "I am your teacher, Alissa. I'm responsible for you."

"And Mavoureen is my responsibility," she countered, frustration pulling her head up. "I can find her. I know it. And I won't slip. Please, Redal-Stan," she pleaded. "I can't sit here and watch her die. You know I've done this before. I don't need a teacher."

"No. You need a nursemaid," he said sharply. But he didn't leave as he had yesterday and the day before, so she silently waited. The wind fitfully shifted his sleeves, and with a slow exhalation, Redal-Stan turned from a Master of the Hold to a weary man from the desert, one too familiar with death. "I can't bear the thought of another morning without Mavoureen," he whispered. "Are you sure, Squirrel? You know the way back?"

A thrill of excitement went through her, quickly quashed by dread. "Yes."

"I want to try, too." Connen-Neute's quicksilver thought slipped unexpectedly into theirs, causing them both to start.

17

Alissa jerked her gaze to Redal-Stan. He looked as surprised as she, and she sent a trace of thought to find Connen-Neute in the room next door by the fireplace, eavesdropping. "Someone," Redal-Stan muttered, "needs to teach him some manners." Taking a huge breath, he shouted, "Verbally, Connen-Neute! And ward that ash-ridden door shut on your way out."

There was a flash of resonance on her tracings as the ward went up. Connen-Neute ghosted into existence beside her open door, his long face pinched with a worried defiance.

"Well?" Redal-Stan said wryly. "Are you going to invite him in? It's your room."

"C-come in," she stammered, flustered.

"This is exactly why no one wants these rooms, isn't it." Frowning, Redal-Stan stuck his head into the chimney and craned his neck. "I can't say that I blame them."

Glancing nervously between them, Connen-Neute sank down beside Alissa. He looked frightened at his spying having been discovered, and she gave him a thin smile, glad to know she wasn't the only one who got into trouble. "I want to try, too," he said, his voice low.

"No."

Connen-Neute opened his mouth to protest, then shut it. It suddenly struck Alissa that speaking aloud wasn't a natural task for rakus but a skill laboriously taught and diligently practiced. As if confirming her belief, Connen-Neute's thoughts slid into hers with a refinement his spoken words lacked. *"You're allowing Alissa. I-I claim the same right."*

"No. No. No!" Redal-Stan shouted, standing up. "It's too dangerous. She has gone before. You haven't. You'll get lost and die. And verbalize!"

"I can't get lost if I pickaback," he thought, looking anxious for his persistence.

Pickaback? Alissa wondered as Redal-Stan's eyes grew large.

"No!" he exclaimed, eyes widening in shock. "Neither of you can possess the finesse."

"We lose nearly three Keeper students a century to this wasting death," Connen-Neute said, his eyes darting. *"It's worth the risk to learn how to return them. And I like Mavoureen."*

"You don't need to," Redal-Stan said. "Alissa knows. One of you is enough."

"Alissa is leaving. You said it yourself."

Redal-Stan's eyes went furious. "You devious little—" he sputtered. "Go wait for me in my room!"

Connen-Neute went ashen. Remaining where he was, he tugged his red sash straight.

"Go to my room and wait, fledgling!" Redal-Stan shouted, red-faced.

Uncomfortable in witnessing their argument, Alissa cleared her throat. "Will someone please tell me what pickaback refers to?"

The silence was so profound, the singing of the Hold's gardeners below could be heard. Redal-Stan and Connen-Neute exchanged tense, almost embarrassed looks. The older Master was still angry, but it seemed their argument had been postponed by her question. Stiff and uneasy, Connen-Neute rose with an enviable smoothness and went to the window. He turned his back on them to gaze out into the hazy morning. "M-m-m," Redal-Stan murmured. "Talo-Toecan never explained . . ."

"I don't know," she admitted, wondering if she had broken an unwritten rule. "If you tell me what it is, I'll tell you."

Redal-Stan grimaced. "Well . . . ah . . . when Talo-Toecan instructs you on the trickier wards, his awareness is in your thoughts but most assuredly separate from yours. Correct?" She nodded, and he added, "Er, pickabacking is . . . ah . . . closer than that."

"How close?" she asked quickly.

"Your entire emotional state would be exposed." His attention flicked to Connen-Neute and back. "It's tantamount to standing naked in the center of the room."

"I see." Alissa frowned. "I don't think so. I'll find Mavoureen alone."

Connen-Neute spun, his long black vest furling elegantly. *"It's not that bad, Alissa."*

"Unfortunately he's correct," was Redal-Stan's unhappy agreement. "I won't lie to you. There's the potential for your thoughts to intermingle, but it's only a possibility. It's a matter of restraint, which either of you may or may not possess."

"So," Alissa mused aloud, "it's more like standing naked in a room where everyone promises not to open their eyes."

Redal-Stan's breath puffed out. "Exactly. But the penalty for peeking is far more than embarrassment. It invariably spawns a deep hatred. Put bluntly, one of you might eventually kill the other, not wanting to risk having your deepest fears known." Alissa knew her look had turned decidedly pale when he soberly nodded. "But first," he continued, "you have to keep from assaulting him outright. You," he turned to Connen-Neute, "you have never been tested that far, and you," he pointed a finger at her. "I don't know your limits at all."

"I won't peek," Connen-Neute offered meekly.

"That's the least of my worries." The old Master sighed.

Alissa took a deep breath. She didn't want to risk Connen-Neute spotting Beast. But if they could do it, the Hold would again have a Master capable of such a rescue, not to mention that Mavoureen would be saved. "You've pickabacked before?" she asked Connen-Neute.

"No."

Alissa found her fingers twirling her hair and forced her hands to her lap. "Then perhaps I should show Redal-Stan."

"Me!" It was an appalled shout. "Wolf's tears and sorrow. Absolutely not."

She turned to Connen-Neute. "But you will?"

Connen-Neute shrugged. *"I'm too young to have any secrets."*

Alissa furrowed her brow. *"Beast?"* she asked softly. *"Can you stay hidden from him?"*

"I don't know," she admitted. *"But if he should see me, won't he think I'm you?"*

Alissa thought about that, looking up at Connen-Neute's eager, expectant eyes. She slumped, knowing she had worn that same look on her face just moments ago. "Can we try it," she asked slowly, "and see what happens?"

"Yes," was Connen-Neute's intent whisper.

"No!" Redal-Stan shouted. He took in their obstinate frowns and closed his eyes in a long blink. "I'm losing control," he muttered. "I must loosen my hold further still." Slowly his expression grew still and, Alissa thought, devious. "Fine," he said, and her pulse leapt. "I'll allow it if Connen-Neute accepts responsibility for all mishaps."

"Done," Connen-Neute breathed. His glowing eyes met Alissa's suddenly wary ones. Redal-Stan had given in far too easily.

The old Master grimaced. "You may pull this ill-advised stunt off if you proceed as adults and not the giggling adolescents you are."

"Promise you won't look?" Alissa asked Connen-Neute.

"If you promise not to attack me . . . *again*," he finished wordlessly, pitching the word so only she could hear.

"Again?" she privately sent in confusion.

He fiddled with the toe of his slippers. *"The night you arrived,"* he mumbled.

"Oh!" Alissa laughed into his thoughts. *"That little slap! I'm truly sorry, but we hadn't been introduced, and you were being most impolite."*

"That was a slap?" he said in disbelief, and a chill ran

through her, shocking her. Though Connen-Neute had probably lived five times her years, he was still an innocent. He had never been hurt. He had no idea the risk he was taking, of the pain one Master could inflict upon another. He had learned of the ugly possibilities couched in stories, not the reality she had been forced to deal with to survive. She could hurt this young Master, and hurt him severely. Frightened, she looked up at Redal-Stan. *And he knew it.*

Redal-Stan's eyes became mocking when he saw that Alissa understood. Anger slipped into her. Redal-Stan expected her to burn him. He wanted to use her as his tool to curb Connen-Neute's newfound assertiveness! Her lips pressed together, and she frowned.

"Should I come in slow or fast?" Connen-Neute asked as he sat smoothly before her.

"Fast," she said, wondering if it was too late.

It was. Before Alissa could stiffen, he was there, or here, and it was Beast holding Alissa back from smashing Connen-Neute's presence with a blast of white-hot thought. *"Out! Get out!"* Alissa shrieked, then, *"Wait."* She wrenched her outrage back. Her breath caught as her fury crashed just shy of him, ripples of mental fire eddying up to the edge of his awareness as he seemed to shrink back, trying not to move. *"Stay,"* she gasped, shuddering. *"We can do this."*

His sudden, overwhelming presence in her mind had been like finding a spider on her neck and struggling not to strike at it while it skittered closer.

"You could h-have . . . You almost . . ." was his broken whisper of thought.

"I didn't," she stammered back, her stomach twisting. The urge to smash him held steady, and for a moment they did nothing but exist. Together they opened their eyes. Alissa struggled to focus, feeling ill and disoriented. She nearly panicked as she realized she was seeing through Connen-Neute's eyes as well as her own.

Tracks of sweat marked his face, and she felt warm from the sun he was sitting in. They stared blankly at each other. For an instant she was tempted to lift her awareness beyond her thoughts to see who Connen-Neute really was, but then she shuddered, afraid. Her pulse slowed to match his, and their breathing synchronized. As one, they raised a trembling hand to brush the hair from their eyes, though Connen-Neute's was too short to be a bother.

Redal-Stan's face was slack in alarm. "I didn't think you could. This will stop. Now!"

Together they shook their heads, their faces blank as they closed their eyes. It was easier without sight, and her nausea eased as they found a still point they could both tolerate. Slowly he went from a spider needing to be crushed to an annoying sliver. Connen-Neute's presence was as malleable as sand, pooling into areas of little-used thought. With a stab of anguish, she felt him settle into the gap that Strell had left.

"Strell . . ." she mourned, feeling the emptiness all the more, even as Connen-Neute squirmed, uncomfortable in it. And then she thought she could hear Strell's pipe, filled with his breath, playing a forgotten tune of promises, soothing her pain, making it bitter-sweet.

"What's that?" came Connen-Neute's intense question.

"A memory," she whispered, aching for Strell's smile. "We have to find Mavoureen."

"Wait," he persisted. "I want to hear more."

Too melancholy to answer, she turned from the music, trying to ignore its mournful, loving sound and focus upon Mav's consciousness instead. Immediately Alissa was overwhelmed by the cloying, gray presence of Mistress Death. The memory of Strell's music accompanied them; Alissa was loath to set it aside completely. Connen-Neute shrank into himself, soaking in the recollection of Strell's music like she soaked in the morning sun.

Together they drifted, going where the shroud was the thickest. Alissa slowed, feeling Mistress Death's hold tighten. Her thoughts became sluggish, distracted. The serenity slipped into her, pulled by the remnants of thought that remained from her first fall. The fog recognized Death's mark and followed it home. Rest, she thought, snuggling down, abandoning herself to oblivion. She had lost Strell. What did anything matter?

"Alissa! No!" came a piercing thought, stark with horror. The memory of Strell's music evaporated, replaced by an icy shock. The scent of death puckered her senses. She jolted back to awareness with a numbing fear.

"Ashes!" she exclaimed. *"Thanks, Connen-Neute."* But he didn't answer. Frightened, she cast about, finding him caught by the same promise of peace. *"Connen-Neute! Wake up!"* she cried as the gray thickened about him, making his thoughts hard to separate.

"Just a little longer, Mother," came a childlike lisp. *"The sun is so warm. The updrafts aren't blue enough to hold me yet."*

Panic drove the last of the cloud from her. She would lose him. Along with Mavoureen! *"Connen-Neute! Wake up. It's Death!"*

"Death?" he wondered with a child's innocence. *"Who is Death?"* Then he started. *"Wolves!"* he exclaimed, his thoughts regaining their familiar tone. With a shudder, he was free. She felt him gather his scattered emotions, shaking off his panic. Despite his efforts, a wisp of his fright spilled into her.

"Mavoureen will be difficult to free," Alissa said grimly. *"She's been here longer."*

"But where is she?" he asked.

Alissa hesitated. The gray still whispered its promise, but its summons fell upon minds warned and wise. The ancient memory of slow decay had become chokingly obvious. *"This way,"* Alissa puzzled, fancying she could smell the scent of baked bread. Focusing upon it, Connen-Neute and Alissa felt the gray shroud thin, and there she was. *"Mavoureen!"* Alissa exclaimed in relief. *"Thank the Navigator and all his hounds. Wake up. It's time to go back."*

Together, Connen-Neute and Alissa watched the silver blue of her awareness stir and gain definition. *"Who?"* she questioned.

Connen-Neute started as the woman's thought came softly

into theirs. It was the first time he had heard a human's thoughts, deciphered through Alissa's mind first. Mav, Alissa realized, had Keeper tracings, just not the training to use them.

"Alissa?" Mav questioned, as mild and soft as a moth. "Be a dear and shut the door on your way out? I'm taking a rest. . . ."

"What door?" Connen-Neute asked.

"She's fashioned a vision of familiar surroundings," Alissa explained. "It's as real to her as . . ." She paused. What was real anyway? Her entire life was a dream. Setting the uneasy thought aside, she tried again. "Mavoureen," she said. "You can't wake from this sleep alone."

"Oh?" the old woman questioned innocently. "I won't be long. Lodesh and Earan get along fine without me. Such fine men they've grown into. Just like their father." She sighed. "I'll just sleep for a space. I'm so tired."

A wisp of alarm stirred Alissa. She had never considered Mavoureen wouldn't want to return. "Kally!" Alissa pounced on the girl's name. "Kally misses you. She's in the kitchen, crying because you won't come down and bake the bread."

"Kally is fine," Mav said, her thoughts blurring to gray. "I've baked enough bread. Can't you see? Enough bread, enough dinners, enough apples . . . My hands are tired." Her thoughts mixed with the scent of toast and became faint. "I want to rest."

"But, Mavoureen!" Alissa insisted, starting to panic. "The day is so fine! The wind is from the hills, smelling of the first highland frosts. Please. Walk with me in the garden? You could tell me of the gentleman who once courted you there. Please?" Alissa begged, already knowing her answer. "Please tell me how he smiled at you?"

"No," she breathed. "Go enjoy yourselves. You'll find me later, and then we'll talk."

And with that, Alissa had lost. It was to have been for nothing. It was all her fault.

Beast made a rude harrumph. *"Yes, sleep, old woman. You're no longer an asset."*

Alissa stiffened. *"Beast,"* she hissed in warning, but went still when Mav's fading awareness pulled from the gray.

"The girl will take your place," Beast mocked.

"She will bake your bread, but she leaves the pans to soak. They will rust."

"Who . . ." came Mav's tremulous thought.

"She never sweeps the corners unless you tell her," Beast said slyly.

"Kally!" came Mav's indignant cry.

"Crusty pans, unswept corners. Vermin are gathering," Beast taunted.

"No!" Mav cried.

"Your best cheese knife is scraping moss from the front steps," Beast jeered.

"Earan!" It was a horrified shout, and Alissa waited, breath held tight.

Beast played her last card confidently. *"Lodesh,"* she said, *"wants to dance with you. The mirth trees are budding. You have only a day to find a hat to match the color of your eyes."*

"The mirth trees," Mav exclaimed in delight. *"Oh! If I don't hurry, the best will be taken. And there will be a festival. There always is when the mirth trees bloom. Kally will have to bring up an extra sheep or two from the fields, or perhaps a fine sow. And a second cart of produce."* She paused breathlessly. *"So much to do!"* she wailed, perfectly happy. *"Where—"* she balked in sudden confusion. *"How do I go?"*

Beast gave a satisfied snort. *"This way, Mavoureen,"* Alissa said, so happy she was almost in tears. *"Follow me."* Alissa gathered Mav's willing thoughts back into a natural sleep she could wake from, then led Connen-Neute to their uppermost thoughts. Opening her eyes, Alissa sighed contentedly. They had done it. Mav would live.

The look of fear Connen-Neute met Alissa with shocked her cold. With an agonizing jolt, he wrenched his presence from her. Gasping, she dug her fingernails into her palms so

she wouldn't reach out, clutching after his sudden absence.
Bone and Ash. He had seen Beast.

Alissa silently pleaded for understanding as she tried to
reach his thoughts, to explain, but he bolted out of the room,
terrified. "Connen-Neute," she whispered, and her outstretched hand dropped. Sick at heart, she looked to find
Kally and Lodesh standing beside Redal-Stan. A breakfast
tray sat forgotten on the floor beside him. The two were
poised expectantly, not caring that Connen-Neute had fled in
terror. Redal-Stan, though, eyed her warily. His gaze went
from her to the empty hall. His mouth opened with the obvious question, but then Mav sighed.

"And an extra tray or two of sweet rolls, I think," she said
clearly as she sat up.

"Mav . . ." Kally gasped, and she flung herself at her.
Alissa's eyes went suddenly damp.

"Oh!" came Mav's voice, muffled by Kally. "Did I fall
asleep?" The bewildered woman tried to disentangle herself
from Kally. "What are you crying for, Kally? Did Lodesh
choose you an ugly horse?" Her brow furrowed, and she shot
a poisonous look at Lodesh.

Lodesh beamed. In two enormous steps, he knelt to take
them both in an expansive hug.

"Oh, Mav!" Kally sobbed, wiping her eyes. "You scared
me."

"What?" Mav gazed at Redal-Stan as he were at fault.
"Can't a woman take a nap?"

Turning a tear streaked face up to Mav's wrinkled one,
Kally looked at her in wonder. "But Mav," she began, then
caught sight of Redal-Stan. He had his fingers to his lips, and
so Kally desisted, contenting herself with simply looking at
her.

Mav swung her feet to the floor. "Oh, so stiff. All my
years are showing today. Just look at where the sun is. It's
nearly noon, and no meal prepared. Odd," she mused. "I
thought we already ate." Then she laughed. "Silly old
woman." She stood, leaning heavily upon a willing Kally as
she adjusted her dress. It wasn't the same she had on two

days ago. Frowning, she hobbled to the door. Her movements were stiff and slow, but she was gaining strength every moment. Alissa guessed that by the time she reached the kitchen, she would be her old self.

"Come along, Kally," Mav said eagerly. "We have a lot to do today in my kitchen. The grove is budding!"

Lodesh jumped as if stung, his eyes alight.

"Did you hear the lovely music, dearie?" came her bird-light voice from the hall. "Such sorrow in that pipe. And Kally? You will get the corners when you sweep today, won't you?"

"Yes, Mav." The slow twosome made their unseen way down the empty hall.

"Lodesh," Redal-Stan said as Lodesh fidgeted, wavering between Mav and Alissa. "Run ahead and warn everyone to keep quiet about Mavoureen's nap. Take special care with the kitchen help. She has blocked it out. I'll explain tonight when I escort her home."

Lodesh nodded, darting to the threshold. Hesitating, he gave Alissa a heartfelt look. "Thank you," he said, and before she could respond, he jogged down the hall, calling after them.

In the new silence, Alissa sat on the floor and clutched her arms to herself, shivering with the cold memory of Mistress Death. She wished she could pretend to not remember. It would make things easier. "Mav does remember," Alissa whispered.

Redal-Stan returned to the windowsill. His shadow touched her, and she shivered. "Yes," he said. "But if everyone pretends ignorance, she won't lose her pride. I won't strip her self-imposed protection where others could witness it. This way, she will hate only me."

An uncomfortable silence grew as he tried to catch her eye. Finally he gave up and cleared his throat. "Why," he asked, "did Connen-Neute run away?"

Her eyes widened. Connen-Neute. She had to get to him before Redal-Stan did! He would tell Redal-Stan about

Beast! Rolling to her feet, she stumbled to the door, muscles stiff.

"Alissa," Redal-Stan said warily. "Where are you going?"

Shrugging apologetically, she bolted.

"Alissa!" came his irate thought. *"Get your winged-behind back in here and tell me what you did to Connen-Neute!"*

18

Alissa raced for the stairs, knowing she would have a precious few moments before Redal-Stan caught her. Chasing a mad Keeper through the Hold's halls was beneath his dignity unless it was at a properly sedate pace. Heart pounding, she sent a thought for Connen-Neute, finding him in one of the practice rooms two flights down. There was a distinct fuzziness about him, as if he had set up a field to hide his presence. She saw through it in a moment. Pickabacking had destroyed any chance of him being able to hide from her.

Setting up her own field to disguise her whereabouts from Redal-Stan, she jogged through the silent halls until she stood in the doorway of a practice room. She took a step in, blinking at the clutter as she waited for her breathing to slow. The tall, narrow room was filled with stacks of canvas, nasty-smelling, stagnant solutions of paint, brushes, screens, berries, bark, flowers, clay, and all sorts of things for making pigment. The sun poured in to make glorious puddles spilling from the disorderly tables and onto the jam-packed floor. There was hardly enough space to walk.

She entered quietly, not seeing him. Her eyes were drawn to a huge canvas, and her breath slipped from her in recognition. It was the intriguing picture she had found last winter in the annexes, the one done entirely in swirling shades of blue that she had set in the place of honor above the mantel in the Keepers' dining hall last year. Her attention went from the canvas to the window, and she went slack in understanding. It was the sky above Ese'Nawoer, swirling with the city's updrafts! She reached out a finger to find the exquisite thing was still damp.

"Oh, Connen-Neute," she whispered in awe, and he popped up from behind a stack of canvases so fast he nearly knocked them over. His narrow face was white with panic as he glanced furtively at the door behind her. She felt a wash of pity as she realized he must feel as if he were caged with an animal. Struggling to make eye contact, she edged from the door so he wouldn't be compelled to jump out a window to escape. "Wait. Give me the chance to explain," she said.

"Explain?" he said, his voice cracking. "There's nothing to explain."

Still he refused to meet her eyes. "I know you saw something that scared you," she said.

"I—I don't know what you're talking about." His spoken words took on the length and depth of his mental speech, as if he were afraid to touch her thoughts. She took a step closer, and he shouted, "Don't!" It was frantic, and she halted, frightened at the terror in his voice.

Keeping the length of the room between them, Alissa touched her chest. "She is here," she admitted softly. "Part of me. But she won't do anything I wouldn't do."

"It's feral!" he said. His long fingers gripped the chair between them until his knuckles went white.

Nodding a rueful acceptance, Alissa scooted up upon a cluttered table and swung her legs, trying to look harmless. "True," she said. "But I have civilized her somewhat." She smiled at a stray thought of Strell. "Charmed, perhaps," she added, "but definitely not tamed." Leaning across the narrow aisle, she arranged a line of chalk in order of size. "Let me tell you of how I found my wings," she said, "so you'll understand why I risk keeping her safe."

"Safe!"

Smiling, Alissa caught his gaze. He stiffened as she hopped off the table. "You know every raku generation, a human is born whose neural net is equal to that of a Master?" she asked.

He nodded. "I've studied the texts concerning the breeding necessary to achieve it."

Breeding necessary? Alissa thought darkly, then set it aside for later. "Put simply, something went wrong. I was drawn to the Hold thinking I was a Keeper, finding it empty but for Talo-Toecan imprisoned in the holden and an insane Keeper named Bailic trying to put the plains and foothills at war for his own use."

"A Keeper grounded Talo-Toecan?" Connen-Neute's eyes were large. "Where was everyone?"

"Somewhere else," she said, avoiding his question. "But Strell," she caught her breath in misery, "freed him, and my studies began in secret. Talo-Toecan never told me of my Master status. I assumed I was a Keeper."

"You didn't know you were a Master?" Connen-Neute whispered in disbelief.

"Not a hint." She snorted, judging he wouldn't notice if she took a step forward. "Eventually Bailic figured out I was the one doing the wards, not Strell, and he forced me to open the book of *First Truth* for him. "He," Alissa said scornfully, "thought that once opened, he could use the book's wisdom for himself. Instead, I absorbed its lessons."

"And shifted," Connen-Neute breathed, his eyes bright.

"Much to Talo-Toecan's dismay," she said cheerfully, edging closer yet. "There wasn't anything to keep me from flying. I was Beast," Alissa said dreamily, not caring that her eyes were glowing with an almost hungry look. "Thoroughly and utterly. I was joyfully feral. There was no reason to live but to fly. . . ."

Beside her, Connen-Neute shuddered. "Wolves' ashes," he whispered.

Alissa blinked, bringing herself back. "It was glorious. Talo-Toecan brought me down, and he along with Strell and Lod—uh—a Keeper tried to force me to destroy Beast."

He bobbed his head. "As every Master has. As is proper."

She stifled a surge of irritation at self-imposed fences. "I didn't want to. I refused."

Silently he digested that, frowning. "Why?" he finally

asked, and she scuffed to a halt before him. "You have to destroy the beast to survive."

She slowly shook her head. "I might have chosen to destroy her. Or I might have chosen to remain feral. But they took my choice away." Alissa took a breath, remembering how close she had come to dying. "So I did the only thing I still had control over. I chose to die." Her chin rose at her past defiance. "Strell realized what I was doing and freed me. He would have rather had me alive and feral then sentient and dead. Once I was free to decide what I wanted, I found it was possible to make a pact with her."

"With a beast?" He glanced at her and away in furtive, frightened jumps. "Don't you fear it—she will someday take over?"

Alissa smiled faintly. He still didn't understand. "Beast is more trustworthy than several Masters or Keepers I could name. She doesn't make promises with the intent to find a way around them. She can't lie. She doesn't understand how."

"But, Alissa," he protested, his fear clearly replaced by the desire to understand. "It can't be worth the risk."

Her gaze went unseeing, and she felt her breathing slow. The memory of the wind filled her with an aching longing. Freedom. Everything at her wing tips—hers. "I remember what it's like to be free," she whispered, closing her eyes until she was sure they wouldn't fill with tears. "So free it's a natural existence. Do you?"

Connen-Neute fidgeted. "I'm free," he said.

"Are you?" she asked, hearing his doubt, and he was silent.

"Redal-Stan will make you destroy her," he finally said.

"Then he had better not find out."

His head came up. "I won't tell," he said, his eyes holding an unexpected determination.

"Thanks." Relieved, she let out her breath in a heavy sigh. "Then you aren't afraid of me anymore?" She reached out and touched his hand.

Connen-Neute stiffened, then relaxed, and she knew she had won. "No," he said boldly, then grimaced. "Yes, well, sort of."

Now Alissa laughed. "Just as long as you don't quiver in fear at the sight of me."

"I never did," he protested loudly.

"You did!" she said cheerfully. "But we'll have to figure out what we're going to tell Redal-Stan." Connen-Neute squirmed uneasily, and a stab of angst went through her. It was obvious Redal-Stan had a tight rein on him. He still might tell. "Me?" she said slowly. "I'm going to ignore him. I'm not a child. My personal life is none of his affair."

From the corner of her eye, she saw Connen-Neute straighten with a new determination. A loud "Harrumph," from the open door made them both jump, and she spun to find Redal-Stan eyeing them severely with his hands on his hips. It was obvious he had just arrived, otherwise he would be more than irate. Incensed, probably.

"Have we reached an understanding, *children?*" he said dryly, then turned at the sound of rapid steps in the hall.

Ren slid to an excited halt behind him. "Redal-Stan!" he shouted, tugging his too-big shirt straight as he bobbed a greeting to Connen-Neute and Alissa. "The city. They say the mirth trees are budding!"

"I know," he muttered, spinning on a heel to quietly stomp down the hall. "Mavoureen told me." Ren hovered in indecision, then with an apologetic shrug, darted after him.

"How did you know?" Alissa asked Beast.

"You asked them to," Beast said, somehow giving Alissa the impression of a smirk as she settled herself back to slumber.

19

Strell sank into Alissa's battered chair before her hearth. Hot and sticky, he ran his thumb across the fabric so faded that the pattern of ivy could only be imagined. He had spent the last two days here in Alissa's room, learning the finer aspects of wraith detection until his head felt as if it was going to explode like a badly dried bowl in the kiln. But now he could tell when she left for her morning and evening walks in the garden.

He let his breath slip from him in a sigh, knowing it must look insane to Talo-Toecan and Lodesh as he haunted the Hold, following the whisper of Alissa's presence. Strell refused to believe her voice in the tower had been his imagination, and he would do anything if it meant he would hear it again. He lived for the hope she might hear him next time.

Strell pulled his shirt from his neck to cool himself, sending his gaze over her lavish room. It settled upon her shoes carefully set under her bed for her return, and he clenched in a flash of heartache. Left behind yet again.

The easternmost window's curtain was shut against the sun. It billowed fitfully in the breeze. The weather was from the coast. Unusual this time of year. The summers of his youth had been insufferably hot, but this sticky, heavy air drained one's spirit. And it was only morning.

The curtains blew outward again, and Strell took his pipe to sit next to Talon in the shaded, southern windowsill, hoping to catch the next gust. It was appreciably cooler in the annexes, but he wouldn't leave Alissa. The irritating buzz of a cicada rose to fill his world, dying in a harsh gurgle. In the distance, another answered. Strell's head thumped back against the sill, and he closed his eyes. Slowly he stilled his mind and reached for her thoughts. A sad, slow smile grew as he found her somewhere before the hearth. His head started a soft throb. Knowing the two were connected, he let his awareness of her fade.

The curtains shifted, and Strell raised his pipe and began to play "Taykell's Adventure" in a mournful, lackluster fashion. This was the only pipe he could play proficiently now, meticulously made with the last hole placed where his mutilated finger could reach it. He glanced to Alissa's mantel where his first mirth wood pipe lay. Though he had shattered it last year in a fit of frustration, Alissa refused to let him burn his family heirloom. And so it sat.

His tune drifted out over the roof of the great hall, seeming to wedge itself into the hazy, stifling sky without shifting the air at all. Talon drowsed, keeping him company. She shook herself awake in a rustle of feathers and oriented on a speck in the breathless heavens. Almost too quickly to be believed, the speck grew to a fearsome size and familiar silhouette. It was a raku, larger than Alissa would be but smaller than Talo-Toecan. Strell recognized it as the feral beast that had been haunting him lately.

Strell watched in cautious speculation as, with the smallest scrape of nail on stone, the raku lighted on the roof of the great hall. Carefully, Strell lowered his pipe and glanced at Talon. She was wary but unafraid. "Back again?" he whispered to the raku, and the beast shifted his wings as if threatening to leave.

"That's all right. I'd rather pipe than talk, anyway," Strell said as he began again, trying to entice the untamed fragment of mountain closer with one of Alissa's favorites. With ungainly, hesitant hops, the raku succumbed to his curiosity and flew through the oppressive air to land upon the roof of Alissa's room. Talon hunched, and Strell bobbled the easy, restful tune. The raku was right over them! He had never ventured this close before. Strell wasn't sure if he was pleased or frightened.

As sudden and unexpected as a soap bubble bursting, Alissa's presence became so tangible it hurt. Gasping, Strell stared slack-jawed into nothing. "Alissa," he whispered. Instinctively he reached out with his thoughts, hunching at the sudden ache in his head. This time, he agonized, this time she would hear him.

But something was wrong. She was drowsing and somnolent, reminding him of the time she had burned her tracings nigh to death. He stiffened as he realized she was with Mistress Death again.

"Alissa! No!" he exclaimed, startling Talon and undoubtedly the raku perched above them. He sagged in relief as he felt the gray shroud surrounding her thin and break away. She was safe. She had heard him.

"Ashes!" he distantly heard Alissa in his thoughts, and he clutched at the word as if it were a blessing from the Navigator. *"Thanks, Connen-Neute,"* Then, almost as frantic as he had been, he heard her shout, *"Connen-Neute! Wake up!"*

Strell started at the sudden clatter in the hall. Talo-Toecan and Lodesh burst through the doorway in a tumult of billowing sleeves and sliding slippers. Strell's fragile link with Alissa broke, and grief-stricken, he reached out to steady himself against the sill.

The two stumbled over each other to the curtained window. Flinging the heavy cloth aside, Talo-Toecan jumped onto the sill, his head nearly hitting the top of the frame. He leaned dangerously out, two long fingers and one foot the only thing keeping him there. His neck craned to the roof. Lodesh contented himself with leaning halfway out. "Look!" The Warden pointed, his eyes bright. "There he goes!"

With frantic downbeats, the raku took flight. Lodesh and Talo-Toecan silently watched as he flew a short distance to settle amid the trees, effectively hiding himself. "What under my Master's Wolves is he doing so close?" said Talo-Toecan.

Strell cleared his throat. "And good morning to you both, as well," he said dryly, rubbing his fingers into his forehead.

The two men spun. "Um, good afternoon, Piper." Talo-Toecan adjusted his vest—which needed no adjusting—and with as much dignity as he could find, stepped smoothly from the sill.

Strell remained where he was, reluctant to move, seething with disappointment. He had heard her, and now she was gone. But at least—at least she was safe. Wolves, he felt so helpless. "To answer your earlier question," he breathed slowly from the heat, "the raku came to listen to my music. He has for the last three days."

Showing an unusual lack of grace, Lodesh collapsed into Alissa's chair. "That would explain it," he murmured. "He was always one to appreciate a good tune."

"Connen-Neute liked even the bad ones," Talo-Toecan quipped, not seeming to mind the heat as he regally sat in the window.

Strell jerked forward at the name. "Connen-Neute!" he cried.

Lodesh and Talo-Toecan looked up. "Not that I was implying your piping wasn't up to its usual standards," the Master quickly amended.

"No," Strell said as he stood and looked out the window. "That was Connen-Neute?"

Talo-Toecan sighed. "Yes. He is."

"Alissa," Strell said, his words spilling over themselves. "I heard her. Just now."

"Oh, really, Strell," Lodesh scoffed.

"I know. I know," he admitted. "But when he was here, Connen-Neute, I mean, sitting on the roof, I felt Alissa's presence so much clearer."

Lodesh's face went blank. Then he made a small sound of disbelief.

"She was flirting with Mistress Death," Strell said hotly. "And she heard me!" Exhausted by his protest, he slumped back into the sill. "She did," he asserted, glaring at the mocking doubt in Lodesh's green eyes. "She thought I was Connen-Neute."

Strell froze in sudden thought. "Alissa is with Connen-

Neute," he said. "That means you can narrow the area of time she's in!" He turned eagerly to Talo-Toecan.

Lodesh cleared his throat with a tone of concern. "Perhaps you should come down to the cooler, lower levels for a while, Strell," he offered. "It's insufferably hot up here."

Angry, Strell rounded upon him. "I'm not sun-struck. I heard her. In my head. And though she thought I was Connen-Neute, she heard me!"

Lodesh's eyes narrowed, and his face took on an unusual anger.

"Excuse me, Lodesh?" Talo-Toecan stepped cleanly between them, breaking into their line of sight. "Go down and make a pot of tea."

"Tea!" Lodesh drew back. "It's too hot for tea."

"Nonetheless, I long for tea." Talo-Toecan went back to the window, his shadow lying between them. Strell and Lodesh eyed each other over it.

Lodesh's face fell into a knowing acceptance. "Of course. Tea," he said as he walked out. From the hall came his soft mutter, "If you want me to leave, why not just say so?"

"And let the pot boil by itself," Talo-Toecan called after him. Grimacing, he slowly lowered himself back onto the sill. "I want to enjoy my tea if I must drink it on such a day as this," he finished quietly.

Strell felt trapped by a truth no one held true. "You believe me, don't you?" he asked.

"What would you think . . ." The Master hesitated as if gathering himself. "What would you think if I told you I also could hear someone who is beyond my reach—occasionally."

Strell looked up, curious at the sound of shared vulnerability in Talo-Toecan's voice. "I would say to heed that call and follow it until you can go no farther."

"Aye." He sighed. "That's what I think as well."

"Then you don't believe I've had too much sun."

Talo-Toecan ran a hand over his shortly cropped hair as he glanced at Strell and away. "You have piped in a feral beast for, what did you say, three days running? I believe you."

Strell slumped, his relief was so great. With a short-lived

vigor, he crossed the room and sat on the edge of Alissa's chair. He hadn't liked Lodesh being in it. Elbows on his knees, he dropped his head into his hands. "She heard me, and now she's gone. How?" he asked.

The Master made a puff of defeat. "I have no idea. But that doesn't make it less real."

"Lodesh doesn't believe."

"Doesn't?" the Master asked, "or won't? Perhaps he's resentful that you can hear her and he can't." Shifting the curtains aside, he gazed toward Ese'Nawoer. "I'd like to know how you manage that, myself."

Strell closed his eyes, not sure if the pain of talking about it outweighed the pain of keeping it within him. "I think it was Connen-Neute's presence that made her clearer. But it never made a difference before." He rubbed the last of his headache away.

There was a scuff in the hall, and Lodesh entered, a steaming teapot and cups in hand.

"Thank you, Lodesh." Talo-Toecan held out an eager hand. Golden eyes expectant, he poured out the brew and offered it first to Strell, then Lodesh, who both predictably refused. "Strell has developed an interesting theory," Talo-Toecan said, "concerning why Alissa's presence is much more obvious at some times than at others."

Lodesh seemed to freeze, then reached for the pot, having apparently changed his mind. "Do tell?" he prompted. The two words sounded wary to Strell's trained ear, and he looked up.

"He believes Connen-Neute's presence heightens the clarity of Alissa's."

Lodesh hid behind his cup, and Strell's brow furrowed. The Keeper's actions were off. It was very subtle, but Strell's upbringing as a plains merchant picked it up. "Sometimes," Strell offered, watching Lodesh. He glanced at Talo-Toecan, seeing the Master had noticed the discrepancy as well. "There's something missing though. I haven't figured it out yet."

Talo-Toecan rubbed his temples and sipped at his tea.

Wincing, he set the cup down. "Making contact, real communication, such as you did today, is vital. If we can reproduce that, we may have a chance to get her back."

"How?" Strell asked as the old raku shook his head, his eyes unfocused.

Lodesh's grip on his cup seemed to relax, and Strell wondered if perhaps his own mistrust was from his worry. "Can you sense her now?" Lodesh asked.

Strell felt his gaze go distant. "Oh, yes," he whispered, hearing the haunted tone in his voice. "She's run out of the room and is in one of the practice rooms below us."

Talo-Toecan's cup hit the sill in surprise, and Strell stiffed. "When a piece of oneself is torn away," Strell said bitterly, "one becomes very adept at detecting the barest whisper of it."

"Unless one learns to ignore it," Talo-Toecan said somberly.

Lodesh made a rude noise. "You two can talk of maybes and somedays," he muttered, "but I need something tangible."

Talon squeaked, and Strell went to the window to look for Connen-Neute.

"This coming from a man who died over three hundred years ago?" said Talo-Toecan.

Strell turned to see Lodesh's eyes harden. "Excuse me," the Warden said, pulling a shield of formality about him. He set his cup on the mantel and strode to the door.

Talo-Toecan grimaced. "Lodesh, wait," he called.

"No," he said, and he left, his steps slow from the heat.

The Master seemed to gather himself in a long sigh. "This," he said in a soft disgust, "is the worst pot of tea Lodesh has ever made. I'm not going to drink it."

"So how can I establish a reliable contact with Alissa?" Strell said, not caring about the taste of Lodesh's tea.

Talo-Toecan's gaze roved across Alissa's room, his eyes brightening as he spied Strell's pipe. With a pleased sound, he reached for it, proffering it grandly to Strell. "I suggest you lure Connen-Neute back and see what happens."

Strell held the pipe loosely. "I told you. It's more than Connen-Neute."

"We must start somewhere," was his patient reply.

Taking a labored breath, Strell began a somber melody, sluggish from the heat. A sudden thought broke his playing midphrase. "Connen-Neute was in this room, or above it, in both now and then," he said.

"Yes. I think so, too." Talo-Toecan's agreement was lethargic. Strell knew it wasn't from the heat but his music. Alissa was the same.

"So perhaps if we mirror what exists in Alissa's time, we might make contact again," Strell said, hope making his breath quicken.

"Mayhap." Talo-Toecan shut his eyes. "As I have said, we must begin a dialog. How can we know what to mimic, if *she* won't tell us?" A slow, long finger gestured for Strell to continue, but Strell was too excited.

"She *is* in the past," he asserted, and Talo-Toecan nodded impatiently. "So why don't you remember her?"

He sighed as his eyes opened. "I was absent from the Hold occasionally," he admitted. "I may have just missed her, if she was ever really there at the time. Who knows?"

Having to accept this, Strell began to play with a renewed hope as the cicadas sang a harsh, irregular accompaniment.

20

"**G**ood morning, Mavoureen," Alissa called as she entered the kitchen. Beside the main hearth, Kally turned from her instruction to another of the kitchen's help and smiled.

"Ah, Alissa!" Mav said. "You're a spot of sunshine in a dreary day." Her strong, pale arms up to her elbows in flour, she continued to knead dough with a vigor one usually applies to an errant child's backside. "You'll eat your breakfast where you ought?" she said sharply.

Alissa gave her a sick smile. Her head was throbbing from the short walk through the Keepers' dining hall. It was crowded, and everyone had been talking at once, planning out their first day of the three-day festival. Everyone who could shirk their responsibilities was headed for Ese'Nawoer. The Warden's death hadn't been forgotten. His people had only grasped the opportunity to find solace. "Actually," she said, "I was hoping to eat in the garden."

Mav ceased her pounding and frowned disapprovingly. "You aren't avoiding Earan . . ."

Kally came to her rescue, a covered plate in hand. "Earan is already on the front steps. Alissa probably doesn't want to spend what time she has before her lesson in a crowded hall."

"That's it exactly," Alissa said in relief as she accepted the plate. "I haven't been under the sun in—so long," she finished lamely, not wanting to draw attention to Mav's two-day nap.

Mav lost her severe look. "Aye. But I don't think you'll see much sun this morning. It's a cloud we exist in."

"Even so," Alissa said with a wistful sigh, "it's too noisy in there."

Mav began to divide the dough into identical lumps. "Talk, talk, talk," she said. "That's all those Keepers seem to do—if you're lucky. No one tells them, Keepers I mean, to be still. They're worse than the students." She paused. "Present company excepted, of course."

Alissa grinned. "Of course," she said as Kally rolled her eyes.

The girl handed Alissa a teapot and cup, going before her to the garden door. "I want to thank you again," the girl whispered as she opened the brightly painted door.

Alissa glanced furtively at Mav, who was now bawling out a hopeless kitchen hand who had allowed tonight's pudding to scald. "Don't thank me," Alissa said. "I put her there."

Kally's eyes pleaded, and realizing that accepting Kally's thanks would free the kitchen girl's thoughts from blame, Alissa nodded. Content, Kally gave Alissa an awkward hug and turned away. "Mav," Kally called as she closed the door. "Let me help you with that."

Not sure what she should be feeling, Alissa balanced her unseen breakfast in one hand, gripped the teapot in the other, and made her way along the well-tended path. Damp gray brushed against her skin as the fog slipped about her, marking her passage in drops of dew upon her eyelashes. Its muffling gentleness soothed her as much as the sight of the familiar plants.

The mental noise the Hold put out was staggering. Only in the fleeting space before sunrise did it ever seem to slow. Alissa had found both the garden and the annexes to be unexpected oases, as the thick walls of the Hold blocked much of the mental backwash.

It had been yesterday while in the annexes under the excuse of looking for a new pillow that she found Breve searching for silver buttons for Earan. She thought she had been alone in the huge storeroom, and Breve's grin for having caught her softly singing what was obviously a tavern song broke the last of the somber man's mistrust. It had been

"Taykell's Adventure," and she had been mortified. When she had left, Breve was enthusiastically making up new verses concerning the misfortune-laden traveler, his well-schooled voice echoing against the ceiling with no regard to decorum. What surprised her was that Breve hadn't known the song already.

The buzz of a cicada broke the quiet, seeming to come from everywhere. Odd, she mused as she crunched down the pebbled path. Cicadas usually didn't sing unless it was hot. Rounding the final turn, she stopped and blinked. Lodesh was at the firepit, fidgeting. *Nervous?* she thought. *That is new.* "Lodesh?" she called, and he jumped, turning to beam at her.

"Good morning, Alissa." His voice was low and inviting. "Would you care to have breakfast with me?"

Alissa's gaze flicked to the blueberries, muffins, and the tea already poured and steaming. Awkwardly balancing her plate, she peeked under the lid of her plate to find . . . nothing. "Ah—all right," she said with a false sense of cheerfulness. Mentally cursing Kally and her misguided attempts at matchmaking, Alissa moved to join him. "How—how are you today?" she asked hesitantly, her thoughts returning to his father.

"I'm fine, thank you." Giving her a quick, stilted smile, he helped her down the shallow stairs. His simple act triggered a memory of Strell and her, dining here under the stars last winter. It had been foggy then, too. Her face froze, and she squinted up at the bright haze, trying to disguise her misery in analyzing the probability of the sun breaking through.

Lodesh hesitated and cleared his throat. "Here. Let me take your plate," he offered, and she looked to see a worried smile on him. The sound of flatware fell short in the muffling gray as he made good with the serving spoons. Thank the Navigator's Hounds Lodesh was here, she thought as she tucked her feet under her. Or she would go completely insane.

"Alissa?" Lodesh broke into her reverie, and she took the bowl of blueberries.

"Thanks," she said around a spoonful. "I haven't had blueberries since—never mind." Since she and Strell had found a patch behind the well, she finished silently, gazing at nothing.

Lodesh took a deep, determined breath. "It's Strell, isn't it?" he demanded.

Alissa nodded miserably. "I miss him, Lodesh. With you here, I can forget. But then I remember, and—" Blinking furiously, she looked away. She knew if she showed any tears, Lodesh would console her. And any show of sympathy would only make her cry all the more.

"You were planning on a future together?" he asked, but it really wasn't a question.

"T-trying to," she stammered, her eyes on her hands clenched about her bowl.

"Oh, Alissa," he murmured. "It only takes time."

"That's what I'm afraid of!" she wailed, only now admitting to what all the heartfelt looks and gestures of the Lodesh she first knew were all about. Curse him. He had known. He had known she would misplace herself, and he had never warned her. But she couldn't be angry at the Lodesh before her. He knew nothing of it.

Clearly confused, Lodesh drew back, turning to his breakfast to give her the opportunity to collect herself. There was the harsh whine of a cicada, and he set his bowl down. "Redal-Stan has kept your lessons in the morning?" he said, clearly trying to change the subject.

Alissa wiped her eyes and nodded. She knew they were red, and she wouldn't look at him.

"Then I would like to invite you to a gathering tonight."

Warning coursed through her as to where that might lead. "I don't know," she said.

"It's at the grove," he drawled confidently, and Alissa looked up at his dancing eyes.

"Really?" she breathed in anticipation, then grimaced. "All those people."

"It's after sunset," he continued. "Small gathering. Invited guests. The city has access during the day, but the citadel claimed that night as theirs. There won't be lots of people mucking it up. Just dancing and music."

But music reminded her of Strell, and she pushed her blueberries about with her spoon. She blinked in surprise when Lodesh tilted her chin up. "Music reminds you of Strell?" he asked, and Alissa gave him a sour smile. "Lots of storytelling, then," he asserted, and she winced. "That, too, eh?" he said softly. "Plenty of food," he began, then hung his head in mock sadness and held up a protesting hand. "No," he said with a forlorn sound. "I'm sure he eats."

Alissa couldn't help her smile at his playacting. "I'm afraid so."

His dramatic melancholy vanished as Lodesh took a sip of tea. "Well, there must be something I can do that doesn't remind you of him." His cup hit the bench in a soft clink. "Alissa," he said, serious. "I have made it my goal to see you happy."

"Don't say that!" she exclaimed, frightened.

"Why not?" His eyes flashed in defiance.

Alissa's gaze fell from his. "I'm going back to him."

"Oh." It was a short sound, carrying all his disbelief. "I see. When?"

"As soon as I learn how," Alissa mumbled over the rim of her cup, then hesitated. The tea was bitter. Had Lodesh made it?

"Learn how?" he asked.

Alissa put her cup down. "I meant, as soon as I convince Redal-Stan I have enough self-control to be off the Hold's grounds unchaperoned."

Lodesh leaned back, satisfied. "Ah. Rogue Keeper. All the responsibilities of a Keeper but the freedom of a student." He paused. It may take years," he cautioned.

Alissa's breath caught. "I'm well aware of that," she said, stiffening.

"It's how it is, Alissa," he said. "You've no choice."

"There's always a choice," she said tightly. "You just may not like it."

"Regardless," he countered. "If you leave without permission, you can't come back. And as you already have a source, your tracings will be burnt to ash so you can't use them."

She looked away, her lips pursed. Still, he persisted. "The harsh reality is he likely won't wait the possible twenty years necessary for you to return. And even if he did, he won't be the same man or you the same woman."

Alissa glared, angry he was forcing her to come to grips with this. Twenty years? She was looking at over three hundred if she couldn't get back.

"Don't look at me like that," he protested with a hint of anger. "I've seen it happen. Just because I've only walked the earth for twenty-two years doesn't mean I haven't seen pain."

Her anger abruptly softened. "I don't think that at all, Lodesh."

Appearing lost in a memory, Lodesh went still. "I don't want you to suffer that," he said. "I want to see you happy." His eyes cleared, focusing on her with a familiar longing that made her go cold. "I want to see you happy with me. I can see in your eyes that you could be happy with me. Why squander your time on a maybe?"

"I love him, Lodesh," she whispered.

Lodesh took her bowl and put her hands in his. His face was frighteningly neutral. "Love springs from many sources. It need not be channeled into a single path."

Unable to meet his gaze, her eyes dropped to her hands cradled in his. A scuff of gravel jerked their attention up and she pulled away. It was Nisi in the fog with a plate in her hand. "Nisi!" Alissa exclaimed, relieved. "I looked for you in the dining hall."

"Yes, what a surprise," Lodesh echoed distantly as he shifted away.

Nisi hesitated. "If I'm intruding—"

"No," Alissa interrupted. "Not at all. Come sit down."

"Yes. Stay," Lodesh said faintly.

Smiling, Nisi edged down the stairs and sat beside Alissa. She silently eyed the blueberries. "A group of us girls are going to the city this morning, Alissa. Want to come with us? There's a little candle shop, fourth arc out, where if you ask them, they will—"

"Alissa has lessons this morning," Lodesh interrupted.

Peeved he hadn't let her answer, Alissa glanced at him.

"Oh. I forgot." Nisi's brow furrowed and she sipped her tea. "Perhaps tonight?"

"Alissa is going to the grove with me tonight," Lodesh asserted.

Nisi drew back, the tips of her hair swinging to brush her shoulder. "All right." Looking put out, she rubbed a spot on her cup.

Not liking how he had made Nisi feel, Alissa frowned. "I haven't said yes, yet," she said.

Lodesh opened his mouth, and as she gazed at him with wide, mocking eyes, he looked alarmed. "Yes!" He exploded into motion, jumping dramatically up onto the bench across from them and striking an elegant pose. "Alissa does as she chooses! And I hope," he stepped down and took her hand, "she chooses to accompany me to the grove tonight." His gaze probed her expectantly.

Nisi gave a short bark of honest laughter. Alissa's grin couldn't be deterred either, and she nodded, forgiving him. The sound of running feet turned their heads as Ren jogged around the last turn. "Hey! Hi!" he exclaimed breathlessly as he came to an unsteady halt. "Am I late?"

Lodesh shook his head with a cheerful resignation. "No. Have a seat. Use my cup. I've already had my tea."

Ren flopped to the bench, taking a huge quaff. "Ow!" he cried, leaning forward and dabbing at his lip. "Hounds, that hurt. Now I won't be able to taste anything all day."

"Have you had breakfast?" Alissa asked, willing to share.

"No, thanks. I'm not hungry."

Nisi gasped. "Get the surgeon. Ren's not hungry!"

"What's going on, Ren?" Lodesh's eyes ran over the restless student's attire. "Isn't that your good shirt? And a new pair of boots?"

Ears red, Ren glanced at the brightly colored leather. "Yes. Mav gave them to me. Today is my anniversary."

Lodesh and Nisi exchanged knowing looks. Nisi patted Ren's knee. "Good luck. I'm sure you will be recognized this year."

Ren smiled weakly. "Ashes. I hope so. The students' hall is getting obnoxious. It would be grand having a room with a door, four walls, and a window." He sighed dreamily.

Nisi chuckled. "And a floor *you* sweep, and a hearth *you* supply with wood, and—"

"No!" Ren wailed, waving a protesting hand. "Let me dream."

Alissa turned to Lodesh. "Anniversary?"

Lodesh paused midchew, then nodded. Swallowing, he said, "That's right. You've been here less than a week. It seems longer," he added, and Alissa silently agreed. "Every year, a student is evaluated for possible Keeper status."

Nisi raised the pot of tea. Seeing Alissa's smile, Nisi topped off all the cups. "Ren has been a student for twelve years," Nisi said. "And though seventeen is young for a Keeper, there's precedence."

Ren fidgeted. "The younger you start, the easier it is," he explained.

"So," Alissa exclaimed, "today you might become a Keeper?"

"I wish it was that easy." Ren slumped, then straightened. "But I'll find out if I will be considered for such. The decision must be sanctioned by a caucus of Masters. There won't be enough of *them* here until the first lowland frost and they start flocking back to the Hold."

From Alissa's side came Nisi's sigh. "Then it's back to lessons and practice. I do so enjoy it when the wanderlust hits them this hard. Everyone gets a well-deserved break." Nisi looked at Alissa apologetically. "Well, almost everyone."

Reminded, Alissa rose and brushed the crumbs from her skirt. "Speaking of which, I ought to go."

Lodesh rose with her. "I'll come with you."

Alissa smiled wickedly. "Redal-Stan will remember you owe him two days in the students' dining hall. He might insist you start tonight."

"Just as far as the kitchen," he said, taking her empty plate and cup and helping her up the steps and onto the path.

"Yes, go," came Ren's quick agreement. "Don't get him in a mood, whatever you do."

"I'll do all I can to further Redal-Stan's good humor," she said, warm with the feeling that she might be starting to fit in.

Ren shifted awkwardly and mumbled, "Thanks."

Together, she and Lodesh walked to the kitchen. The path was designed for one, but they managed it side by side. She kept her eyes lowered, feeling awkward not for his closeness, but for the silence he kept. He was clearly thinking, and that worried Alissa. The bright blue of the kitchen door showed through the fog when he pulled her to a stop.

"Alissa," he said. "You'll think on what I said?" he asked.

Her gaze went to the path. She knew he wasn't speaking of going to the grove but of his words concerning love. Her eyes rose to his against her will. His hope and vulnerability shone like honesty in a child. "Yes," she said softly, not knowing why. Gathering her scattered self, she snatched the dishes from him and ran to the door.

She would get home. She would get back to Strell.

21

Distracted by her worried thoughts, Alissa slowly ascended the stairs. The pendulum hung unmoving below her in the middle of the great hall. It had been so ever since the Warden's death. In her grip was a bowl of cooked ham chunks. Kally had pressed it into her hands with the assurance it would help put Redal-Stan in an accommodating mood.

She slowed as the passage narrowed at the base of the tower, more from melancholy than from being out of breath from the climb. Alissa glanced at Useless's shut door in passing. Part of her would be relieved to see his familiar face, but she knew it would be a false security. Seven more flights, and Alissa wearily found herself before Redal-Stan's door. She took a deep breath before she tugged her skirt straight and knocked.

"Alissa. You're late. Get in here," came his sour thought.

Stifling a sigh, she pushed open the door to find him writing at his paper-strewn desk. His head came up at the disgusting scent of ham, and he set his quill down with meticulous care. "Morning, Redal-Stan," she said, then turned to the balcony. "Connen-Neute."

Redal-Stan's hand met his desk in a sharp slap. "Bone and Ash!" he cursed in disgust.

"Told you," Connen-Neute crowed as he moved from the shadows of the balcony's pillars. *"I told you she has keen eyes."*

"What," Alissa asked in confusion, "are you talking about?"

His expression sullen and cranky, Redal-Stan sank back in his chair and stared into space. "Connen-Neute and I were discussing who was going to mind the Hold tonight and who was going to the citadel's gathering." He briefly met her eyes. "I don't like to leave the Hold entirely empty of Masters. No telling what might happen."

Alissa silently agreed. "So what does that have to do with my eyes?"

Clearly pleased, Connen-Neute sat on the long couch before Redal-Stan's desk. *"He didn't think you would notice me under a ward of obscurity. I knew you would."*

"Burn it to ash. I lost," Redal-Stan moaned, his eyes on the ceiling.

"There will be other gatherings under the mirth trees," Connen-Neute said, and Alissa felt the ward drop from him.

Redal-Stan stiffened, glaring irately. "Verbalize, infant," he growled, then pointed at her. "I see Lodesh failed to impart even the beginnings of telling time to you."

Shrugging, Alissa set the bowl of ham on his desk, just out of his reach. "He tried, all the way to Ese'Nawoer. I can't seem to get it. I can read the pendulum. But relating it to the sun?"

Gaze fixed intently on the bowl, Redal-Stan leaned forward. "I'm not surprised. Lodesh owes me three days in the students' dining hall."

"It was two days," she said, more than a little peeved. With a single digit she pulled the bowl away as he reached for it. From beside her came Connen-Neute's horrified intake of breath. "And why are you not surprised? Do you think me that stupid?" she added.

Redal-Stan pursed his lips, standing up to take firm possession of the bowl. "Nothing of the sort," he said as he fell back into his chair. "No Master can. And would you care for some?" He proffered her the bowl.

Shuddering, she refused, then sat beside Connen-Neute on the couch. "I was raised foothills. I don't eat anything that has feet."

The Master blinked, the long-handled fork halfway to his

mouth. Eyes wide, his jaw snapped shut and the fork dropped. He glanced at Connen-Neute and back. "You don't eat meat?" he asked in a hushed voice. "A raku who doesn't eat meat? Don't you get hungry?" Not waiting for her reply, he leaned and offered her a forkful. "Here. Maybe if you tried some."

"No, thank you." Alissa struggled not to gag as he waved it under her nose. Undeterred, he extended it farther, brow high in encouragement. "I don't eat meat, Redal-Stan!" she cried.

"Perhaps if you tried it," he persisted, then drew back at her fierce expression. "Maybe you just don't like ham?" After a moment to be sure she was serious, he abandoned himself to the bowl's contents. Alissa looked at Connen-Neute, surprised at his wistful dismay.

"It seems," Redal-Stan said between bites as he returned to their original topic, "that we're too much in tune with the sun to be shackled with the self-imposed rules humanity indulges in to give predictability to their lives."

"But I wasn't born a raku," she protested.

"But your mind is arranged as are theirs."

Alissa sighed, wondering if she was forever doomed to be behind her time.

Redal-Stan sat back in thought. Wiping his mouth, he reached for a small box hidden under a sheaf of papers. He rummaged in it with several intriguing clatters. "There it is," he said, snapping the box closed and handing her a single object.

She weighed its heavy presence in her palm. "A ring?"

He slumped into his chair with a very unmasterly sprawl. "It's a clock."

"It's a ring," she said, holding it up and squinting. "With a hole where the stone fell out." Connen-Neute shifted uneasily at her challenge, and she looked at him. "Well, it is."

"It is—a clock." Lips pressed, Redal-Stan dared her to contradict him again. "If the sun were brighter, I'd show you how it works. It's yours."

"Mine!" Blinking, Alissa extended it back. "I can't. It's too precious."

"On loan, then, until whenever," he replied lightly.

"Thank you." Alissa slipped it into a pocket. It was too big to fit her finger. Later she would find a length of twine and wear it about her neck.

"Hm-m-m." Redal-Stan frowned. "I've asked Connen-Neute to sit in on the cataloging of your abilities so he may see that lack of knowledge is a natural state that must be rectified slowly, not all at once like a dog consuming a haunch of venison."

Losing his usual dignity, Connen-Neute slouched into the cushions. *"He means to prove I'm not the only one who lacks the basics that a Master should know."*

Redal-Stan placed a piece of ham in his mouth and chewed. "Hush."

"Half the Keepers know more than me!" Connen-Neute cried.

"Enough! And verbalize!"

Alissa watched in amusement, thinking the exchange was very familiar.

"Well?" Redal-Stan said loudly, and she couldn't help but jump. "What can you do?"

Put on the spot, her mind went predictably blank. "Uh," she stammered, "internal and external fields." She hesitated. "Both permeable and impervious."

Redal-Stan blinked. "Wolves!" he cursed. "I forgot that."

"What's an impervious field?" Connen-Neute asked.

Redal-Stan waved absently. "Later. What else, Alissa?"

"Um, wards of ignition, illumination, warming, stillness, sleep, silence, obscurity, and from you, calming. I can also maintain the appearance of scar tissue from that burn I showed you over my tracings with no conscious effort, and block my whereabouts from a mental search. Took me three months to learn how to do that." She sighed with remembered frustration. Connen-Neute slumped, and thinking to bolster his spirits she added, "I've seen but have been asked to not practice several wards of offense that I can demonstrate."

Redal-Stan's eyes were closed. He said nothing, and she began to wonder if she had done something wrong. "Wards of stillness, silence, tracing disguise, and wards of offense," he finally said. "By my Master's Wolves, Alissa. Where were you schooled? A war field?"

She fussed with her sleeve and said, "Yes. I can also hide one ward within another to—"

"Stop!" Redal-Stan raised a quick hand. "Perhaps you should leave, Connen-Neute."

It wasn't a request, but the young Master didn't move. His eyes turned determined.

"That's about it," she hurriedly added as Redal-Stan's brow furrowed at Connen-Neute's blatant defiance. "The only other skills I have are wards of creation and—ah—line tripping."

"That's it, eh?" Redal-Stan was decidedly sarcastic.

Alissa nodded uncertainly. "The former I have free rein in. The second I know the theory and a small bit of practice. Talo-Toecan had sent me several times among the lines." She turned to a disgusted Connen-Neute. "That's why he was teaching me so soon. He was afraid if he didn't, I would guess enough," she bit her lip, "to get myself in trouble."

Redal-Stan looked rather put out as well. "Your instructor—and I use the term loosely now—he sent you among the lines in the first place for what reason?"

Alissa took a slow, deliberate breath. "To frighten me away from the Hold."

Redal-Stan ran a hand over his nonexistent hair. "You didn't mention several wards that are generally taught to beginners, such as, oh, window wards?"

"That's right," she said, feeling herself warm. Connen-Neute brightened and ceased his irritating knuckle cracking.

Almost in disbelief, Redal-Stan leaned forward. "No?"

Face flaming, she stammered, "It wasn't needful."

"Can you unlock doors?" Connen-Neute asked.

"Those keyed for general entry," she admitted, and he smiled with a smug satisfaction.

"How about a ward of deflection?" Redal-Stan shot at her, and she shook her head. "Misdirection? Ward of truth?" he added.

"No."

"Can you preserve food?" Connen-Neute was thoroughly pleased now.

"No! That's it!" she exclaimed, embarrassed.

Redal-Stan had the audacity to laugh. "You see?" he said to Connen-Neute. "Everyone is skilled in different areas."

"But she possesses all the exciting things," he complained.

"Maybe." Alissa couldn't keep the disgust from her voice. "But how often does one need a ward of silence? I would much rather know how to close my own window."

"And your book studies?" Redal-Stan asked. "I don't suppose you can read yet?"

Positively affronted, Alissa reached to a nearby stack of books and opened one. "The undesirable premature mixing of the populations," she read, "can be accomplished by a physical barrier such as in mountains or seas, or mentally by using a bias or prejudice. The former is more reliable, but once breached is nearly impossible to contain. The secondary method has the potential to be less secure, but aberrations are generally few and can be dealt with on an individual basis rather than resorting to—"

The book was snatched from her grasp and closed with a snap. Redal-Stan put it out of her reach and settled himself. "Ah, yes," he said, refusing to meet her glare. "You can read."

Alissa made a mental note of which book it was, planning to find it later. She had a suspicion she was the aberration that must be dealt with on an individual basis.

"Connen-Neute appears impressed with your—ah—considerable accomplishments," Redal-Stan muttered. "Let's move on."

"She's been at it for almost *a year,"* Connen-Neute thought, moaning.

Ignoring this, Redal-Stan steepled his fingers. "I suggest we spend the morning exploring the mechanics behind what you did to get here. Alissa, show me the tracings you use to shift."

"Now?" she questioned, glancing at the balcony with wide eyes. The whine of a cicada split the fog. In the distance, another answered. "In daylight? What if someone sees me?"

"We're sixteen stories up, Squirrel. One raku is much as another at that height. Besides, you aren't going to shift. I only want a resonance." He leaned across his desk, squinting. "You can show a resonance without invoking a ward, can't you?"

"Of course," she huffed, affronted. She took a breath to settle herself, then set up the proper pattern. She blinked slowly at Redal-Stan, fighting to keep her mental vision and her sight of him at the same time.

"It's perfect," Redal-Stan grumbled as his gaze went distant, checking the resonance against his own tracings. "You're using the expected pattern exactly." He frowned to himself, his scalp wrinkling. "Show me the pattern you use when tripping the lines with a septhama point," he demanded suddenly. "Try to hold them simultaneously."

Alissa froze. What if she did it again? Who knew where she would end up!

"Sand and Wind. Just set it up!" he exclaimed, exasperated. "You are not—I repeat, *not*—to engage the ward. Understand?"

She glanced nervously at Connen-Neute, then closed her eyes so as to concentrate better. The pattern used to shift still glowed in her thoughts. Swallowing hard, she set up a ward to trip the lines. In an eye blink she was done. As expected, the first ward was gone. They didn't use any of the same paths and so couldn't be run together.

Slightly depressed they hadn't found the answer, she opened her eyes to find Redal-Stan waiting. His gaze went distant and unseeing as he studied the resonance. A heavy sigh shifted him as his sight cleared. "Yes. Exactly what I would expect," he said, and she winced. "It's perfect. Talo-Toecan managed that right, at least. No extra paths, and you couldn't hold them concurrently. There's not the slimmest way the patterns for shifting and tripping the lines can cross, triggering them both into play. By my Master's Wolves, Alissa. What did you do?"

"I don't know." Unhappy, she lowered her gaze and dropped the ward.

No one said anything, and Redal-Stan cleared his throat in the uncomfortable silence. "Connen-Neute, I was going to send you on an errand, but why don't you stay? I want to see Alissa trip the lines, to make sure she isn't doing something odd, and there's no harm in pushing your studies up. You know the theory; you know the patterns. It's high time you actually went."

Connen-Neute jerked upright. A gleam of anticipation curved the corners of his mouth. Ignoring Redal-Stan's snort for his enthusiasm, he hid his hands in his sleeves and tucked his feet under him as he sat on the couch. Just to be contrary, Alissa put her feet firmly on the floor.

Noticing what she had done, Redal-Stan arched his nonexistent eyebrows. "Well, set the ash-ridden ward up!" he exclaimed, making her and Connen-Neute jump. "But I want to check the pattern again before you invoke it, and—ah—don't use a septhama point." He closed his eyes and pretended to shudder. "Use one of your memories."

Alissa's heart gave a thump. She was going to do it. He was actually going to let her trip the lines by herself! Redal-Stan was watching her expectantly. His fingers were steepled in a startling mimicry of her papa, who probably got it from Talo-Toecan, who assuredly got it from Redal-Stan. Well that, she thought, was something she was never going to do, and she uncrossed her legs and set her feet firmly on the floor, not remembering having put them back under her. Eyes open, she set up the pattern needed.

Redal-Stan's eyes went distant, and then he nodded. "Perfect," he muttered. "Connen-Neute, look sharp. You'll be asked to duplicate this later. Take special note in the amount of energy used. Alissa seems to have a knack for knowing how much is needed for a good resonance without engaging the ward." He turned to her. "Where will you take us?"

Her breath came in a quick, excited surge, and she forced her shoulders to the back of the couch. Her legs curled up under her and, resigned to their presence, she ignored Redal-Stan's soft chuckle. For a moment, she considered. *Strell?* she wondered. Her thoughts of him were the strongest, but she couldn't bear the idea. "Talon," she said firmly.

"Who?" Redal-Stan asked, his eyes wide in wonder.

"Talon," she reaffirmed. "My pet kestrel. She has been with me since I was twelve."

"A bird!" said Connen-Neute in dismay. *"Out of all the excitement you have lived, you want to tell us of a pet bird? Why not that insane Keeper, Bailic?"*

Using anger to cover her fright of Bailic's memory, Alissa rounded upon him. "I don't like Bailic. I want to show you Talon," she snapped. "And if you don't think it's exciting, you can just—just— Pursing her lips, she gestured to the balcony railing. "Take a flying leap!"

"Temper, Squirrel," came Redal-Stan's calming laugh. "I'm sure your recollections of Talon will be most enlightening."

Mollified, Alissa adjusted her skirt to cover the tips of her shoes with a quick, abrupt motion. She gave Connen-Neute a final glare—seeing he wasn't sorry at all—then turned back to Redal-Stan. "What do I do?" she asked nervously.

"Set up the ward, place your thoughts upon your memory, and allow the ward to direct your awareness to the proper paths. I would suggest you concentrate on the more earthy sensations until the memory is in full motion. Scent, and to a lesser degree, touch, are powerful triggers of memory. Just give Connen-Neute and me a moment to get our own tracings alight in preparation to follow," he murmured, slipping into a light trance with an enviable quickness.

Connen-Neute and Alissa exchanged a look of shared excitement, then he, too, leaned back into the cushions and appeared to go to sleep. His long, somber face was quiet and still. Putting her thoughts on Talon, she set her network aglow and slipped easily into the memory she had chosen as the clearest: The day they had made their acquaintance.

22

It was hot. Too hot for early summer, and Alissa loved it. On her knees in the freshly turned dirt, she breathed in the comforting fragrance of warm, moist earth, even now beginning to fade as the day grew warmer. Sitting back on her heels, she ran a hand under her hat and gazed down the long row.

"Beets," she muttered. "I hate beets." But they stored well and were good for trading with the flatlanders if nothing else. Plainsmen loved them. Still, sixteen rows took forever to weed out. It had rained two days ago, and the grass had sprung as high as her knees. Squinting from the sun, Alissa stood. She glanced at the house and wondered if it was worth the trouble to get the hoe from the barn as her mother had shouted out the window not long ago. Sighing, she brushed the pressed soil from her knees and moved to the low building beside the sheep pen.

The barn door creaked and groaned under her tugging, finally yielding enough so she could slip inside. It was cooler, and she shivered. A soft rustle telling of mice whispered. Mother couldn't seem to keep a cat. She would try every spring, and every spring they would be back on their home doorstep before the sun went down. Traps were set for the mice, but who knew how much grain they lost every season. The rust-blemished hoe lay where Alissa had left it, and promising to oil the dratted thing this time, she snatched it up and went to the field.

Swinging it in short arcs, she tugged the weeds from the

blood red beet tops, leaving a flattened trail of dying vegetation behind her. The afternoon sun spilled over her, doing as much as her exertions to rid her of the barn's chill. A soft flutter over her head drew her attention, and Alissa paused to watch a small kestrel hover, waiting for the insects she was scaring up. Seeing her watching, he darted away. Alissa smiled and returned to her work. He'd be back. They had resident kestrels for as long as she could remember.

Lulled by her work, she almost missed the small falcon's return. A large grasshopper took to the air with a startling buzz. Its flight was astonishingly short as the kestrel dove, snatching it midjump. Pleased she had provided the hunter with an easy meal, Alissa continued, putting off resting in the hopes he would come back.

For the longest time there was only her and the sound of her work. Then, so quietly as to be only imagined, came the fluttering of wings. Grinning, Alissa ignored him. As she watched for any darting shapes, there was a startled whistle and gust of wind. A shadow fell cold across her. She looked up, blinding herself with the sun.

Gasping, she dropped the hoe and covered her eyes. The heavy ash handle hit her shin. Clutching her leg, Alissa heard, rather than saw, a crashing among the brush at the edge of the clearing.

"By the Hounds?" she whispered as she stared at the still shifting branches. How could a bird make that much noise? She glanced at the house before hobbling to the edge of the meadow and peering into the scrub. Green silence greeted her. There was a sharp crack, and she jumped at the whoosh of air and muffled thump as a branch fell.

Alissa cautiously stepped under the cooling shade, clasping her arms about herself in the chill. A kestrel tumbled on the ground. "Oh, you poor thing," Alissa whispered, watching it flop its wings and swish its tail side to side in an odd way. Upon seeing her, the small bird hissed, daring Alissa to come any closer.

"Let me see?" she coaxed, taking a step despite the obvious warning. Immediately it took flight, or tried to, smashing

*its way back through the underbrush to the meadow in a fren-
zied attempt to put distance between them.*

Alissa's predatory instincts took hold, and she was after it.
It was hurt, she reasoned. She was going to help it whether it
wanted her to or not. She quickly regained the open meadow
and stopped, watching the tops of the grass. It wasn't hard to
tell where the bird was, and Alissa confidently made her way
to where it sat panting.

"Careful, now," she whispered as she eased into a crouch
two arm's lengths away. "I won't hurt you. I just want to see
if you're all right. You don't fly very well."

The robin-sized falcon hissed and opened its wings, trying
to cow her. Alissa watched with a mix of pity and amusement as
it stood in place and stridently beat its wings, trying to become
airborne. Finally it admitted defeat and sat in a miserable-look-
ing lump.

"Are you done fanning the grass?" she said with a
chuckle, and it seemed to stiffen. Clearly she would have to
charm it, and as her mother always said, the best way to
charm a beast was with food.

Alissa turned and began looking for anything edible. "La-
dybug . . . no," she mused. "Spider . . . definitely no." Shuddering, she moved a step away. "Flies." Lots of flies, but she
couldn't catch them. Sitting on her heels, she looked at the
bird. It was a she, Alissa guessed by the larger size, though the
coloration was more in line with that of a male.

"How," she said to the bird, "do you ever find enough to
get by?" Much to her delight, the bird bobbed her head as if
in agreement.

"Skinny green caterpillar!" Alissa exclaimed, then grimaced. She wouldn't give that to a plainsman, though he
would probably eat it. Then Alissa saw it. A cricket. That she
could catch. She wouldn't get pinched or stung. Licking her
lips, she edged closer, her eyes wide in anticipation as she
lunged.

The smooth, spiny shape of the cricket filled the pocket of
her closed hand. Fortunately, the kestrel hadn't moved, and
holding the violently struggling insect between her thumb and

*forefinger, Alissa slowly proffered it. "Come on," she coaxed.
"Your mother used to do the same thing. Just pretend I'm her."*

*The kestrel hesitated. Clearly nervous, she looked from
Alissa to the cricket. Then, much to Alissa's delight, she cautiously stretched out her neck and took the horrid thing.*

*"There." Alissa sighed, letting out the breath she hadn't
known she had been holding. Then she frowned. The bird
wasn't eating. The cricket was in her beak, kicking violently,
but the bird was doing nothing with it. In fact, she looked most
peculiar. "Go on," Alissa prompted. "That's what you're supposed to eat."*

*As if responding to her voice, the bird shifted its feathers
and pinned the cricket to the ground. Tearing it to pieces, she
delicately chose what she would and wouldn't eat. By the time
the kestrel was done, Alissa had another cricket. Scooting
closer, she offered it as well. Three crickets, one grasshopper,
and a slight sunburn later, Alissa had the bird pinching her
stocking-wrapped hand as she walked cautiously back to the
house.*

*"Mother?" she called softly, her eyes upon her new pet. "I
think I found a way to rid the barn of mice!"*

Taking a slow, deliberate breath, Alissa snapped out of the
mild trance. She opened her eyes with a blissful smile of
remembrance, finding Redal-Stan waiting for her. "Well
done, Squirrel," he whispered from under half-lidded, somnolent eyes. "Very well done."

From her other side came a desperate moan, and they
turned to find Connen-Neute curled up in a black and gray
clothed ball on the couch.

"What's your problem, student?" Redal-Stan said irately,
then broke into a knowing grin. "Got a headache!" he
shouted.

Connen-Neute whimpered, shuddering in pain.

"Oh, please," Alissa said, pleading for sympathy. "It's
agony the first time."

"I remember," Redal-Stan admitted with a rueful chuckle.

"It's not anything one can easily forget." Relenting, he leaned over his desk, and she heard a whispered thought. *"Watch. You need to put in a shunt to relieve the excess energy. Like this."*

Connen-Neute sagged in relief. Taking a hesitant breath, he slowly uncurled and stared at them with haggard eyes. *"Wolves' Ashes,"* he cursed. *"Why didn't you warn me?"*

"Sorry, I forgot," Redal-Stan and Alissa said together.

"So!" the old Master boomed. "What did we learn besides kestrels like crickets?"

"It hurts if you don't have a shunt already in place," offered Connen-Neute sourly. He rose and shakily went to the long-cold pot of tea, warming it with a quick thought.

"Besides that." Redal-Stan stood and went to claim a cup. Alissa rose as well, hoping that if she stood by the teapot and looked wistful, Redal-Stan would make her a cup.

"Tripping the lines is only a mental journey—usually," she drawled.

"Usually," Redal-Stan agreed. "And it will stay that way until I'm convinced we have a foolproof way to send you back."

Connen-Neute went still. Taking his cup, he glanced at her and turned away. Immediately Alissa went wary. "I want to go now," she said, staring at Connen-Neute's stiff shoulders. It had been five days. Only the thought that she would see Strell soon was keeping her calm. And that comfort was wearing thin.

"Hush, Squirrel. We must make sure the clouds are empty before you fly through them."

"But I just tripped the lines," she asserted. "I can do it. I want to go back *now!*"

"You must be patient."

Connen-Neute moved to the narrow band of afternoon sun on the balcony. He completely turned his back on her. Alissa stared. Something was wrong, and Connen-Neute knew it. "I went back to one of my memories," she said, her brow furrowed in thought.

"Yes, you did." Redal-Stan's voice was cautiously congenial. He sat on the edge of his desk and crossed his arms before him. He frowned at Connen-Neute over Alissa's shoulder.

"When I came here, I used a septhama point," Alissa said. Her breath quickened.

"Correct." Redal-Stan stood in a rustle of brown fabric, all pretense of disinterest gone.

"Septhama points only work backward," she whispered, going cold.

"Alissa," the old Master warned as he took a step forward.

"No! Listen to me," she exclaimed, and Connen-Neute turned. His face was creased in pity, and she panicked. "I used a septhama point to get here," she said, her voice cracking. "There's no one here who has a memory farther forward than mine, which I can borrow. I can't send my thoughts to a time I haven't experienced, and I can't experience it until I have gone—back." Her last words were a haunted whisper.

Only now understanding, she reached out a blind hand and felt Redal-Stan steady her. "I can't go back," she said.

"Easy, Alissa," Redal-Stan said gently. "Come sit down."

"I can't." Dazed, she could do nothing but blink. "I—I have to go," she mumbled, and pulled away. "I have to find Strell."

"Alissa. It'll be all right. Come sit down."

She felt a ward of calming resonate in her thoughts. "No!" she cried, smashing the passive ward with a blistering thought. She had to get out. To get back to Strell! Her heart pounded, and she stiffened, taking in the shut door and Redal-Stan's tight grip on her elbow. She tore from him, spinning to the balcony.

"Connen-Neute!" Redal-Stan shouted. "Get away from the window! She doesn't know a window ward. Get out of the way!"

The window! Alissa made a slight moan of despair as she felt his ward go up.

"Alissa."

She turned to see Redal-Stan with his hands raised, confident he had her trapped. "You're fine," he said. "You're going to be fine. Strell is gone, but you will be fine."

"No!" Breath fast, she turned to the sky. "I have to find Strell!" she cried. Before her heart finished its beat, she set her tracings to break the window ward. Panicked, she cast her ward from her without giving it a field to contain it. Made strong by her anguish, it spread from her in a silent wave, visible as a faint shimmer.

Her will to flee tore through everything it encountered. A thunderous boom shook the Hold as hundreds of doors flung open. The ward to clear the window had transcended itself, acting upon anything closed.

"Wolves!" Redal-Stan cursed and flung himself to the floor. A protection ward was tight about him. He didn't know what her ward contained.

Connen-Neute stood by the window, rocking slightly from the mental force. He hadn't put even the barest protection over himself. Alissa caught a sad look as she jumped from the balcony, shifting even as her feet left the railing. Then the Hold was gone and she was free, streaking to the east.

23

The stones Redal-Stan had pressed himself against shivered as Alissa's will hit the roots of the mountain and reverberated back. "Wolves," he whispered as he looked up. "She said she didn't know window wards. I think she opened every ash-ridden door in the Hold!"

"She said she couldn't make them, but would you chance your student smashing into a ward as she tried to land on a balcony?"

"No." Feeling old and foolish, Redal-Stan used a chair to get to his feet in stages. Upright, he glanced at his open door and back to Connen-Neute. Seeing him unafraid, Redal-Stan grunted in surprise. Eight quick steps, and he was next to him, eyeing the empty skies. "I'll be back," Redal-Stan said tersely. He put a foot up on the thick railing, finding himself held back by a long hand. "I have to catch her," Redal-Stan snapped, tugging his sleeve free. "She is likely to go feral over this, if she hasn't already."

"She won't," came a quiet thought into his.

Redal-Stan paused, his drive to follow postponed by Connen-Neute's strong conviction. "Even so, I will be hard-pressed to find her."

"I know where she is," was the young Master's soft reply.

"How!" he barked, then shot a glance at the hall. The sounds of excited Keepers and students were coming closer.

"I could find Alissa were the great plain between us," Connen-Neute breathed, his gaze on the horizon. "You didn't know that, did you, about pickabacking?" He turned, his eyes filled with an almost wild look, and Redal-Stan stifled a shudder. *"I can recognize her thought signature now as if it was my own. But I know already where she went."* Connen-Neute jumped to the railing, halting his momentum with a practiced ease.

"Tell me where she is. I'll get her," Redal-Stan demanded.

"She doesn't trust you. She would fly away, and I don't think you could catch her." And with that, Connen-Neute leapt from the balcony and shifted.

There was a snap of wind against wing canvas, and he was gone. Redal-Stan stood alone, wondering at the confidence Connen-Neute had found in the mere days that Alissa had influenced him. The raku's golden form was lost in the hazy sunshine as he headed east over the mountains. "Perhaps," he worried aloud, "the wind has been kept from his wings too long."

Redal-Stan turned at the growing tumult in the hall. A large group of students came to an uneasy halt outside his door. Kally pushed her way to the front, ignoring her lower rank. She stared at him with wide, wondering eyes. "The lids popped off the flour tins," she said, "and I can't close the door to the garden. Would you please come down and help me?" Behind her, more of the Hold's inhabitants came to a silent, questioning halt.

No one asked what happened, and he refused to volunteer anything as he made his brooding, methodical way through the passages and halls. He stopped at every chamber, removing the ward that had fixed the doors so that the Keepers couldn't shift them by muscle or ward. By the time he reached the floor of the great hall to find the outer doors of the Hold immovable slabs of wood, he was more than a little concerned. Just whom, or what, had Connen-Neute gone after?

24

Knees drawn to her chin, Alissa sat on a large flat rock amongst the damp scents of gathering dusk on the other side of the mountains. The wind spilling from the nearby peak was chilly, and she shivered in the last remnants of the sun. A pile of stream-smooth pebbles was beside her. One by one, she flicked them into the meadow. She was aiming for the crickets.

Another stone hissed through the yellowing grass to find the earth, and the field went silent. Her breath caught. As she wondered if she had hit one, a familiar touch brushed her thoughts. She relaxed, realizing why the crickets had silenced themselves. The graceful shape of a raku executed a sharp turn and landed a wing length from her. "Hello," she muttered, her gaze returning to her pile of stones.

Settling himself in a comfortable crouch between her and the setting sun, Connen-Neute propped his head upon his forearms and curled his tail about himself. *"May I join you?"* he asked, his eyes closing in a sleepy blink.

"You're bigger than me," she said as she sniffed. "It's not as if I could stop you."

His golden eyes opened. *"I'll leave if you ask."*

"Sorry." Feeling as pleasant as pond scum, she managed a sour smile. His eyes closed, and she added in warning, "I'm not going back to the Hold. You can't make me."

Connen-Neute rippled his hide, giving the impression of a shrug. He disappeared in a swirl of pearly white, solidifying in his human form to sit in an elongated oval of flattened grass.

"You know something?" she said. "Talking to you is worse than talking to Talon."

He grinned.

The crickets began to reassert themselves, and so Alissa resumed her game. "I'm surprised," she said as a rock went swishing among the dry stems. "I would have thought Redal-Stan would have been the one to follow me and try to drag me back."

"I didn't follow you," he said aloud in his gray voice. "I knew where you were going."

Alissa squinted into the setting sun, holding a hand above her eyes to see him better.

"You're lost," he said in explanation. "You went home."

"Isn't it wonderful?" Alissa gazed over the open field. "Over there by that rockslide is where the sheep's winter shelter will be. The house," she looked upwind, "will be where those hemlocks are now. The well will be behind it, right about where that stream is." Alissa paused. The stream wasn't in her memories of home, but her papa had dug the well exactly where it was flowing. Frowning, Alissa turned to Connen-Neute. "We're in the kitchen garden, and this rock," she patted it, "is where the snakes will sunbathe."

Thoroughly depressed, Alissa slumped. The Navigator's Wolves should hunt her. It was more dismal than the time Useless had accompanied her back to her parents' farm to tell her mother she was all right. The farm had been abandoned: the sheep were gone, the fields sat fallow, and the house was empty. The chickens, though, were still there. The note Alissa found said her mother had returned to the plains, then went on with other motherly sentiments that sent Alissa into tears. Useless had placated her with promises to help her find her mother, once she was skilled enough to pluck her mother's thought signature out of the untold thousands of plainsmen. To Alissa, that meant never. Now, she didn't even have that.

In a rustle of gray and black silk, Connen-Neute joined her on the rock. "I was raised in the high reaches," he said as he sat down beside her, his eyes on the nearby peaks. "It seemed I was always cold, but it was a great deal safer. A raku child must be sheltered from most neural-net resonances lest a ward be picked up prematurely." She looked at him blankly, and he added, "Would you give a toddler a ward of ignition?"

She shook her head, finally understanding why her papa had never let on he had been a Keeper. "All but parental contact is minimized," Connen-Neute continued, "until the level of self-control is adequate to handle temptation."

"Sounds lonely," she said, thinking of her own childhood spent with imaginary friends.

Connen-Neute shrugged. "It was, especially later, but it was my adolescence, and I wouldn't change anything. Once it was determined I had developed mastery of my impulses, I was introduced into society. I was about thirty then."

"That's awful," she sympathized, wondering how old he was. He didn't look thirty.

Turning his unreadable gaze to hers, he said, "It was safer, though. I was the only child of my kith to make it past my first thirty years." Alissa stared, trying not to look appalled, and he added, "All my siblings were lost. Some to flight accidents. A young raku isn't very coordinated, and is small, about the size of a pony, until about fifteen. When growth starts, it's explosive, making it difficult to keep up with the changing shifts in mass and momentum. But a few," he sighed, "were lost when they found their neural nets and began to play. Those were the worst," he finished somberly.

Alissa could say nothing. The trials of her childhood were nothing compared to that.

Connen-Neute stirred, adjusting his collar with his long fingers. "That's where I found my self-control. Watching their fatal mistakes. Where did you learn yours? It's considerable, seeing as you were raised by a commoner."

Alissa shook herself. "Uh—my mother at first," she said, and he smiled knowingly. "But it took a burn across my tracings I should have died from before I began to see the benefits of holding one's temper," she admitted, shielding her eyes from the sun and squinting at him.

There was a tug on her awareness, and a bright orange paper hat winked into existence. Connen-Neute silently placed it upon her head to shade her eyes. "Hounds, thanks," she said as she took it off to look at it. "That's right. You mastered crafting paper from your thoughts. Very nice." She turned it over, examining it thoroughly. "I'd wager you're great fun at parties," she finished dryly as she placed the wide-brimmed, eye-hurting monstrosity back on her head.

Connen-Neute straightened in pleasure. *"You know I mastered crafting paper?"* he said, slipping back into his more familiar thought-speech.

She gave him a friendly shove on his shoulder. "Everyone knows Connen-Neute crafts the highest-grade paper. You can tell by the smell."

"Almonds," he breathed. "You have free rein in crafting matter. What do you excel in?"

Alissa aimlessly threw a stone. "I excel in making trouble." Then, seeing his disappointment, she relented. "Clothes. That's it. Nothing interesting like cups or paper hats."

"Clothes are invariably the first," he said. "But what do you plan on specializing in?"

The eagerness in his voice pulled Alissa's attention from the darkening field. Suddenly she realized he saw her as a contemporary, something he probably never had before. Her next flippant answer died, and she smiled, pleased. "I don't know," she said as she took a handful of pebbles. "I had hoped pottery, but I seem to be lacking something."

Thoughts of Strell surged through her. Eyes closing in heartache, she slumped. "Ashes," she whispered. "I have to get back home, Connen-Neute. There must be a way."

He took a pebble from the remainder of her stack. "Redal-Stan thinks it's not possible," he said hesitantly, and he threw it.

Frustrated, she reached out a thought and caught his tossed stone in a field. The pebble hit the edge of her field and rolled to the bottom, hanging in an unreal display of control. "Redal-Stan would have said I couldn't get here, either," she said hotly, allowing the rock to fall.

Nodding, he whipped a second stone almost straight up. It arched up into the black, barely visible against the purpling skies. "Still," he said mildly, "I've known him to be correct in most situations." He paused as the stone reached its highest point. "Now," he whispered, and he and Alissa fought for control of it.

"That's a very safe answer," she scorned as she mastered the rock, then let it fall.

"But it's true." Connen-Neute sent another rock after the first. This one, he caught.

"Well, he's wrong this time," she said defensively. "I'll get back. I—" Her breath caught at the thought she might not. "I will," she said, as her pulse pounded in her temple, seducing a headache into existence as she refused to cry.

"No." His voice was as gentle and persistent as rain. "You need a memory of your time that doesn't include you. And even if you had that, you don't know how the patterns crossed."

"I'm going to get back," she said flatly. She couldn't feel herself swallow or breathe, but her arms clasped about her shins were trembling, so she knew she still lived.

"You can't." His words were so soft, she wasn't sure if he had said them aloud. "Strell is gone," he said mercilessly, despite the tears spilling hotly down her cheeks. "He's gone!" he said, giving her a shake as she tried to hide her face. "And what are you going to do about it?"

His question remained unanswered as she watched the peaks blur and dissolve from her tears. Her misery, the aching emptiness, seemed worse here than surrounded by people. Taking a breath, she held it until she had to breathe again. For a long time, only the crickets and her intermittent, tattered gulps for air shifted the night. The sun had set, replacing the glare with a soothing gray. There was a tweak on her thoughts, and a soft sheet of paper was pushed into her hands. "Thanks," she said raggedly.

"It's mostly cloth," he offered, seemingly eager to have something to say. "I wanted to see how soft I could make paper. Don't show Redal-Stan. He'll make me craft a cart-load of it."

Alissa bobbed her head and used it to blow her nose. "I can see other uses for this," she mumbled, glad for the distraction.

Then he sighed, and Alissa knew he wasn't finished with her yet. "Accept it, Alissa," he said regretfully. "Strell is out of your reach. You could fly away and hide for four hundred years to rejoin him when you catch up, but even then, he's gone. You'll be a stranger to him." He threw a pebble at the field. "Four centuries leaves an indelible mark."

"Yes, I can see that," she said, too raw and sick at heart to be angry.

"Love, like the wind, can come from many sources. If you accept he is lost to you, perhaps you might consider—"

"Connen-Neute!" she protested, embarrassed.

"—someone else," he finished innocently. He flicked a stone into the field, and there was a startled squeak as it found a mouse. Then he turned red and coughed, carefully placing his last pebble back on the stack. "Just don't start making eyes at me," he added, realizing where her thoughts had gone. "I don't like Beast. She's too—Ashes, she scares me." He shivered, and then, trying to make it look as if it were from the chill in the air rather than the chill in his soul, he turned a concerned eye to her. "Would you like a fire?"

"No," she said, her thoughts returning to what he had said concerning his upbringing. It was more than Useless ever explained to her. "Connen-Neute?" she asked, wondering how much she could pry from him. "Why don't you speak more? You have a wonderfully dark voice."

His teeth gleamed in the faint light as he smiled. "I spent my first fifty years almost entirely in the shape I was born in. Talking is a hard habit to form."

"Fifty years?" Alissa's mouth fell open. He looked her age. "How old are you?"

"One hundred sixteen seasons this winter, but Redal-Stan seems to think I'm sixty."

"But your schooling is so far behind mine!" she stammered.

Connen-Neute gave her a slow, sideways grin before casually tearing off a handful of grass and beginning to work it into a chain. "Not exactly."

"What do you mean, not exactly?" she asked, not liking his smug attitude.

Daisies, looking ghostlike in the pale light, joined the ribbon of grass he was fashioning. "What I mean is, I would be willing to wager I'm a better flyer than you."

"Are not."

"A better hunter than you."

Alissa snorted in disgust, not caring.

"My wards, though simpler, are probably faster."

"I doubt that!" she exclaimed, momentarily silencing the crickets.

"Are, too." He bit off the stray stems of his garland and placed it about her neck.

Alissa winced, imagining what she must look like. "I guess I'm ready for Lodesh's gathering," she said. "The poor little foothills girl has a new hat and stunning jewels." She dropped her gaze and sighed. "Let's go. I feel more alone here than at the Hold somehow. But at least the cicadas will be quiet now that it's dark."

Connen-Neute slid from the rock and extended his hand to help her down. "Cicadas?"

"Yes. They drove me to distraction this morning."

"I hadn't noticed," he said. His hand was different from Strell's, thinner, smoother, a great deal longer. Alissa paused, never having held a Master's hand in hers before. Her toes went damp as she found the ground and his hand slipped from hers.

"It will be dark by the time we get there," he continued, pulling his gaze from her hand. "No one will see you arrive and shift back." He winced as he looked at her feet. "I don't know what to do about your shoes, though. I could make you a pair, but they would be too big."

Embarrassed, Alissa scrunched down. "I've a pair of boots in the stables," she said. "We can pick them up first. I should probably tell Redal-Stan where I am, too." A flush of guilt took her and she quashed it. She would never have fled if he hadn't tried to pen her in.

Connen-Neute nodded. "Everyone else will be in boots. And on the way, I'll show you what several thousand years of study and a hundred sixteen years of flight practice can do."

"Oh, really?" Alissa said in friendly challenge. "I'd wager Beast can beat your thousand years of sentience any day—or night."

Connen-Neute eyed her suspiciously. "We'll see." He stepped away and shifted.

Setting her hat and garland on the rock, Alissa minced a few steps away. She wanted to keep her daisy chain and didn't want to risk breaking it down to nothing when she shifted. Beast stirred as she took true Master form, and together they looked Connen-Neute over.

Alissa's suspicions were borne out. She *was* smaller, annoyingly so. He was as muscular as Useless but markedly smoother of hide. He might, she decided, be able to outfly Beast.

Connen-Neute's gaze lingered on the healed scar on her wing. *"I ran into a tree,"* she said, her embarrassment easing as he closed his eyes in a sympathetic-looking blink and held up a long foot, one of the knuckles bent at an odd angle.

"Tripped over a cliff edge," he said by way of explanation. *"By my Master's Hounds, Alissa,"* he asked, *"Where did you get such a length of tail?"*

"Talo-Toecan says it's from him," she said, demurely wrapping it around herself twice.

The young raku blinked. *"Talo-Toecan gave you his cellular pattern to proof your own?"*

She nodded. *"But I don't see what difference it makes. All he has is that stumpy thing."*

"His tail wasn't always that short." Connen-Neute's eyes were bright with amusement. *"We never found out how he lost a third of it, and Keribdis isn't talking, either."*

Suddenly uneasy, she snatched her garland and leapt into the dark, careful to not disturb her abandoned hat, a silent testimony to her and Connen-Neute's conversation.

25

Alissa leaned one hand against Connen-Neute's hulking thigh as she tugged Keribdis's boots on. The dry smell of Ese'Nawoer's field rose up with the stored warmth of the day, comforting in the light of a newly risen moon. It mixed with the clean smell of the flowering mirth trees. The scent of pine and apples invigorated her.

"I don't see why you had to get your boots." Connen-Neute sighed, causing her to nearly lose her balance. *"I frightened that stable hand out of three years' growth, not to mention the horses!"* A shiver traveled across his hide. *"You can't even see your feet under your skirt."*

Lips pursed, she sat on his foot to finish lacing up the boots.

"It's not as if you're from the foothills, anymore. You're a Master of the Hold, and as such, no one could care less if your feet are covered or not."

His words struck a sore spot, and she sent her heel into the ground with a hard thump, just missing his clawed toes. "I'll always be from the foothills, Connen-Neute."

The raku swiveled his head, his eyes glowing. *"As you will. Are you* finally *ready?"*

Though dwarfed by Connen-Neute's massive form, she felt tall in her borrowed boots. At her hesitant nod, he shifted, reappearing in an outfit she had never seen before. It was cut to a similar style and was still black and gray, but the fabric was finer. The red sash around his waist was vibrant, and his shirt had the shadows of ivy woven into the pattern.

Alissa ran a hesitant hand over her skirt. She could only make the one outfit. It was clean and crafted from what she had once considered the finest of materials, but next to Connen-Neute's, it seemed common. "Maybe this isn't a good idea," she mumbled as the faint sound of a woman's laughter came softly across the damp field.

True to form, Connen-Neute said nothing as he replaced her daisy chain about her neck. Lifting her skirt free from the dew-wet grass, Alissa picked her way behind him, pulling him to a stop at the edge of the trees. She took a steadying breath.

People, lots of people, greeted her eyes. A small fire and pot were surrounded by elegantly dressed guests with hats and long coats. Their laughter burst forth occasionally, lending credence to Alissa's belief that they were keeping the mulled wine from running away. The center of the grove was full of peeps, thumps, and whistles as a group of professional and what were obviously amateur musicians found their places. Much to Alissa's surprise, they were concentrating on a small arc of the rising mounds of moss and not the flat center. Someone had put down a series of planks there. With sudden understanding, she realized it was a dancing platform.

Connen-Neute's eyes were fixed hungrily upon the musicians, but it wasn't until Beast quivered at the sudden outpouring of a pipe that Alissa realized why. Connen-Neute was enthralled by music, as any proper young raku should be.

The grove was lighted by head-sized kettles of fragrant, flaming oil suspended on long ropes from the trees. The dancing boards were lit by wards of illumination; there were at least six Keepers present. And over it all was the clean scent of the blooming mirth trees.

Alissa's breath caught as she spotted Lodesh. His hands were on his hips, and he watched all with a pleasing mix of authority and congeniality. He looked splendid, every part the nobleman's son in a dark green outfit, the shade that looked so well on him and Strell. Her shoulders slumped.

She would find a way back to Strell. Redal-Stan was wrong, but even as she thought it, a sliver of doubt dug itself deeper.

As if feeling her gaze, Lodesh fixed firmly upon her. He grabbed the arm of a passing man and gave him a set of preoccupied instructions, never dropping Alissa's eyes. Done, he tugged his jacket straight and made a beeline for them. "Connen-Neute, Alissa," he called, extending a welcoming hand as he drew close. "I'm glad," he said softly, "that you *chose* to join me tonight, Alissa. Redal-Stan said he saw you headed this way but was unsure of your plans."

Alissa couldn't help her grimace. "I just spoke with him. He knows where I am."

Lodesh blinked. "Spoke to him?" Then he brightened. "Oh. Through Connen-Neute."

"Yes," she said faintly, tucking that little slip away. "We spent most of our day together."

Looking askance from her to Connen-Neute, Lodesh paused. "With Connen-Neute?"

Alissa's lips pursed. "He has a lot to say if you take the time to listen."

"Connen-Neute?" he persisted in disbelief. "This one right here?"

"Yes. I've been helping him with his verbalization skills."

Pulling his attention from the musicians, Connen-Neute shrugged. His golden eyes focused on something behind Alissa, and he paled. "Excuse me," the Master muttered, and he edged away, losing himself in the throng of people.

"By the Navigator's Hounds, Alissa," Lodesh gasped. "What did you do to him?" That's the most I've heard out of Connen-Neute my entire life."

Alissa looked behind her to see Reeve stomping toward them. "If Redal-Stan wouldn't hound him, his speech would come easier," she said, making room for Lodesh's adopted father.

Reeve smiled a distraught greeting at Alissa as he came even with them. "Lodesh," the man admonished. "You said only a few people. They've set up a dance board!"

Lodesh winced. "I asked them to, Father. So they wouldn't damage the moss."

"Aye," he agreed ruefully. "But you said only a few."

"I only asked a few. The rest just showed up. I couldn't very well tell them to go."

"They'll leave things," Reeve warned. "Just watch. And whose door will they knock on all day tomorrow? Mine. That's who."

"I'll put up a sign." Giving her a wink, Lodesh put an arm over Reeve's shoulder and began leading him into the shadow. Alissa followed.

"No one had better climb my trees," Reeve warned, and Alissa chuckled, imagining the well-dressed adults capering about the branches.

"Please, Father. You're scaring the guests," Lodesh said. "Everyone will behave."

"They had better." The squat man put his hands squarely on his hips and planted his feet firmly at the edge of the shadow. "If there's one nick in my trees, one branch bent—"

"I know," Lodesh interrupted. "I'll never be able to have another gathering again."

Reeve scowled at Lodesh's exasperated tone. "Just so," he muttered, then turned to Alissa. "Keep him in my good graces, will you, Alissa?" he said. Before she could answer or even say good-bye, he turned and stomped away.

"That was close," Lodesh breathed. "If he knew Connen-Neute was here, he might have asked everyone to leave."

Alissa's thoughts returned to Connen-Neute's frightened look and the speed at which he left. "Why? Aren't Masters welcome?" she asked, feeling a tinge of worry.

"Not Connen-Neute." Taking her arm, he strolled Alissa back to the light. "Father caught him climbing the mirth trees three years ago, searching for a fertile seed on a wager he made with Talo-Toecan. Then he bodily dragged him down and chased him out."

Alissa's eyebrows rose in astonishment. "Connen-Neute *is* afraid of him!"

Lodesh beamed. "Absolutely one hundred percent terrified."

"But he's a Master of the Hold." Alissa gestured helplessly. "He's so much more—"

"Powerful?" Lodesh finished. "True. But do you crush the bee that buzzes at you when you're weeding out the vegetables?"

She shook her head. "It won't sting me if I leave it alone."

"But you're so much bigger," Lodesh drawled. "What could a little sting do to you? Why not just get rid of the bee, and the risk, completely?"

Alissa nodded in understanding. He smiled, clearly going to continue, but hesitated as a single piper and drum began a steady cadence. Breve's deep, resonant voice cut through the noise, and her eyes went wide as she recognized "Taykell's Adventure."

"Listen to that," Lodesh said, angling toward the crowd. "Breve found a new tune."

Alissa felt an odd anticipation as Breve sang the first stanza. That and the refrain were the only parts that could be counted on as being familiar, for as she explained to Breve, the fun was making up new, and sometimes embarrassing, exploits for the woeful farmer to deal with.

"Taykell was a good lad, he had a hat and horse.
He also had six brothers; he was the youngest one of course.
His father said, forgive me lad, I've nothing more to give ye.
His name forsook, the path he took, to go to find the blue
*   sea."*

The crowd lit into the refrain, leading Alissa to believe Breve had been singing it nonstop since having learned it. They bellowed it out more enthusiastically than her village ever had, and she warmed. Ashes, who knew what they would have Taykell doing by the end of the evening?

Lodesh looked at her, his jaw dropping as he made the proper jump of thought. "You taught it to him?"

She nodded, growing more embarrassed. It was a tavern song. She ought not to know it.

"Then, come on," he said, pulling her closer. "I want to hear it."

Ignoring her protests, Lodesh pushed them through the crowd until her toes edged the circle about the musicians. As a heavyset man wearing a silk jacket and an orange paper hat sang a second verse, she hesitantly raised her gaze to the happy faces. She couldn't say who was from the plains or foothills. Their features were as mixed as hers. It was obvious the animosity between the two cultures hadn't begun. No one stared. No one whispered "half-breed." There was no spitting at her feet, no thinly veiled disgust. She slowly realized that for the first time in her life, she could get lost in a crowd. Her shoulders eased, and she clapped softly as Breve snatched what looked suspiciously like Connen-Neute's paper hat from the large man and placed it on his own head. The Keeper grinned at Alissa and sang to her a verse she had taught him.

"Taykell met a maiden, fair as a summer's day.
He told her he was homeless; she asked if he would stay.
Pleased to find a wife and roof, he quickly then said, yes.
And far too late, he learned his fate. How could he have
*   but guessed?"*

The company roared into the refrain, pounding it out. She watched in amusement as Lodesh held out his hand for the hat, his eyes showing a delighted anticipation. Setting the paper hat on his soft curls, he waited until the surrounding people finished. All eyes were on him, and playing up to the crowd, he waited for the piper to play a few bars of music alone before he sang,

"But the maiden had a suitor, of elegance refined.
He gave her much attention, and with her was most kind.
Stunned by the deep devotion, and the love her suitor
*   shown,*
Taykell beat a quick retreat, and soon set off alone."

Alissa's jaw dropped, as the surrounding people laughingly sang the refrain. She was shocked he would use "Taykell's Adventure" to convince her to forget Strell, but his good humor was infectious. And it was an acceptable way to publicly test the waters. Heart pounding, she snatched the hat from him and placed it on her head. She had never sung before people, but she couldn't let Lodesh have the last word. Her hands began to sweat as the refrain came to an end. Focusing on Lodesh instead of what she was doing, she spontaneously sang,

"Taykell's maiden, all alone, she did some thinking long.
Keeping house and drudgery, for her seemed all too wrong.
Doing what she wanted, instead of what she should,
She stole a horse, ugly of course, and ran away for good."

The knowing cheers that followed brought a quick heat to her cheeks. She pulled the hat from her head and willingly gave it to a brown-eyed woman already wearing a hat bedecked with feathers. Perching Connen-Neute's hat atop the impossible arrangement, the woman waited for her turn. Alissa tried to back away, but Lodesh wouldn't let her, and the woman sang, her eyes riveted purposefully to Lodesh's,

"She found Taykell a'pining, by a tree within a wood.
And snuck up slow behind him, to surprise him if she could.
But he felt his love approaching, and he spun with great
    delight.
Into his arms, and simple charms, they kissed with all their
    might."

Face flaming, Alissa wiggled her way backward. Lodesh followed, and she kept her eyes lowered as the crowd cheered. The tune continued on without them, and she held the back of her hand to her cheek to try to cool it. She had always thought Taykell ought to have a companion on his journeys. Perhaps if her invented verse stuck, he would.

"I quite like your new song," Lodesh said slyly as soon as

they were far enough away to be heard over the music. She snuck a glance at him, her knot of anxiety easing as she saw only a relaxed good humor on him. His gaze was fixed across the field, and his smile suddenly widened. "There's Marga," he said. "Let's sit with her before she gets a ring about her."

Alissa's new carefree state vanished. She stopped short, letting Lodesh go three steps alone. Drawing up sharply, he eyed her in question. She ran her gaze over her plain attire and bit her lip. Everyone was so nicely dressed. Her Keeper attire looked rather bland.

Lodesh waved a hand in dismissal. "It's only Marga," he cajoled, escorting her across the grove. Alissa's unease tightened. Marga was young Trook's mother. She had been nice but rather imposing when Alissa had met her: so many attendants, such a fine house. Alissa had felt positively primitive, though Marga was as free and honest with her smiles as Lodesh. And what if the woman had heard her singing?

Tonight, though, Marga's attendants were gone. She sat alone on a blanket embroidered with mirth flowers. Her hair was piled upon her head with pins and ribbons, lending her a calm grace that denied she had a child. Dressed in three shades of cream, she looked as perfect as an uncut cake. As was proper, her hem had been pinned up to show her boots, blackened with soot in mourning for her father and uncle. Marga's eyes widened in delight at Alissa's daisy chain, and Alissa dropped her gaze. Marga had a length of polished silver.

"Marga!" Lodesh exclaimed. "You remember Alissa."

"Don't be silly. Of course I do." Leaning eagerly forward, Marga offered Alissa her hand, palm up, and Alissa briefly covered it with her own. "You never did allow us to properly thank you for finding Trook."

Alissa sat at Marga's invitation, and Lodesh settled between them. "No need," Alissa said. "I was just tagging along." She hesitated, her gaze flicking to Marga's darkened boots. "I'd like to extend my condolences," she said. "It's hard when Mistress Death comes suddenly."

Marga turned to rummaging in a basket, avoiding everyone's eyes. "Father always said the mirth trees are a better judge of character than most men. That they chose to flower for his wake is a great comfort." She set a bowl holding cheese molded into the shape of flowers onto the blanket, and Alissa's eyes widened. The bowl was made of glass! And Marga had it outside holding food as if it was common.

"I'll never understand why Father, may he be feasting at the Navigator's table, objected to you tending the grove, Lodesh," Marga added as she gestured for Alissa to help herself. Alissa was half-starved, not having eaten since morning, and she politely nibbled a cheese flower, reaching for a tiny roll in the shape of a fish to go with it.

Lodesh chuckled. "Father was well-known for his leniency with his children, and you should count yourself lucky for it."

"What is that supposed to mean?" Marga halted her motion to pour out a wineskin into a glass cup. Only a drop fell, looking like a red jewel.

Lodesh glanced at the musicians and sighed dramatically.

"Sarken is a fine husband!" she said, shoving Lodesh willingly over onto the moss.

"I wouldn't know," he said, flat on his back and staring up at the unfallen mirth flowers. "But I do know he's young, ragged looking . . ."

"He's not ragged." Marga glared at her brother. "He's just—fashion deprived."

"Fashion deprived!" Lodesh sat up. "The man couldn't pick a matching shirt and pants from the same vat of dye."

"Stop it!" Marga cried, not really upset. "He makes nice things for me and fills my head with his aspirations."

Alissa hid a smile behind a second roll as Lodesh frowned. "Huh," he grunted. "Aspirations my horse's—"

"Lodesh!" Marga cried.

"—hoof," he finished, grinning. "He just wants to take you away from the rest of us."

Marga's gaze went to the dance boards as she handed Alissa a cup. "Sarken is a wonderful artisan, Alissa," she said, ignoring Lodesh's repeated jabs at her foot.

Alissa sipped her drink, marveling more at the container than this year's unfermented wine in it. "Is he here?" she asked, hoping he would look like Strell, then praying he wouldn't.

Marga's eyes glowed. "He's on the music risers." Shifting eagerly onto her knees, Marga searched the scattered rows of heads. "He crafts pottery for our keep, but his first love is his music. There he is," she said, waving. "He's the one with the pipe."

Heart in her throat, Alissa followed Marga's gaze, expecting to see Strell. Much to her relief, Sarken was a tall man with a narrow, bearded face and extremely straight, jet-black hair cut longer than hers. There was no Strell about him.

Under Marga's gaze, Sarken sent a trill of sound through his pipe, a phrase of music to act as his distant greeting. It cut over the boisterous noise of "Taykell's Adventure," and Alissa caught her breath with a stab of anguish. Strell had inherited his talent.

"He has two professions," Marga said smugly. "Lodesh is jealous."

Lodesh choked on his drink. "Of him?" he sputtered. "I just don't want you to follow him back to the coast."

"I'm not."

"You're not?" Radiating relief, Lodesh set his drink aside and took her hands.

"No." Marga smiled. "He wants to go to the plains now."

"The what!"

"Hush," she admonished. "I think they're ready to play."

Marga didn't see the look of despair that flooded Lodesh, but Alissa did. He hid it behind his efforts to arrange his cushion, but the shadow of it remained, even as he smiled at Alissa.

The crowd cheered as the song ended. In twos and threes the people cleared the dancing circle. After a series of false starts that set the professional musicians' eyes rolling, they finally settled upon a fast-paced dance tune. Several couples returned to the boards, their feet stomping. Alissa's pulse quickened, and she felt Beast grow restless. The music had a similar effect on Marga. The young woman's hands began to softly clap, and her feet began to shift.

Lodesh winked at Alissa. "Watch," he mouthed silently as he tightened his laces. Done, he leaned back against the moss and closed his eyes. Only his fingers kept time, thumping against his lower chest.

"Lodesh?" Marga murmured. "Let's dance."

"Hum?" His fingers stilled.

"Come on," she cajoled, pulling him into a sitting position. "Just one tune's worth."

"Now?" Lodesh complained. "You know I don't dance until the moon rises over the trees. And besides, I want to dance with Alissa. If she chooses to," he added quickly. Blinking in sudden consternation, he searched her face. "You do know how to dance, don't you?"

"Course I do," Alissa offered hesitantly, still embarrassed for having sung before a crowd.

"Come on. . . ." Marga pleaded. "As hosts, we have to put in an appearance. Alissa won't mind." She turned to Alissa, and Alissa waved them away. "See!" Marga cried, and she pulled him unresisting to his feet.

As they moved to the platform, Marga's dress shifted to show the dark green underskirt hidden behind the panels of her overskirt. The color peeping behind the slits matched Lodesh's outfit perfectly. Lodesh turned, and over his shoulder he sent a silent, *"Thank you, Alissa."*

They hesitated at the edge, waiting for a spot, then plunged in. Lodesh, Alissa wasn't surprised to find, was a good dancer. Very, very good. Marga was no beginner herself, and could almost keep up with him. Flinging skirts, kicking ankles, and quick whirls caused explosions of color as underskirts were suddenly revealed and hidden. It was eye-riveting.

Surrounded by his friends among the music of drums and pipes, Lodesh smiled, clearly enjoying the challenge of the dance. He looked at peace with himself. Alissa had never seen that before, and it pulled a pang from her. Knowing his miserable future of guilt and shame made his happiness now all the more precious. She would fix him and Ese'Nawoer into her memory as they were tonight: vibrant, beautiful, and innocent.

26

There was a rustle of fabric, and Alissa turned with a welcoming smile, expecting to see Connen-Neute. A gaunt woman in a simple blue dress had sat upon the moss beside Marga's blanket. Alissa's smile shifted to a noncommittal greeting, which the woman answered with her own. Alissa turned back to the dancers, but Lodesh and Marga were lost in that single instant.

"They dance well together, don't you think?"

It was low and tired, and Alissa looked at the thin woman beside her. "Yes. They must practice a lot." She fidgeted, feeling her stomach give a twinge. That juice, she decided, must have been somewhat fermented after all.

The woman made a small, sour shrug. "They used to. Lately their attentions have been diverted to more *mundane* paths."

She sounded bitter, and Alissa glanced up uneasily.

"Look at me!" The woman laughed a shade too gaily. "I've forgotten my manners. I'm Sati," and she extended her hand, leaning across the small distance between them.

"Alissa." As her hand brushed the woman's, nausea swept through her. Alissa snatched her hand back and buried it under her arm. She gulped wildly. Beast jerked her attention from the music, and Alissa had to struggle to keep her feral consciousness from running them away.

Sati watched Alissa's reaction with raised eyebrows. "You aren't a Keeper," the woman accused. "You're a Master." She paused, her fingers going to her mouth. "Hounds," she cursed quietly. "No wonder I couldn't see to answer his question clearly." Her eyes went wide. "Lodesh doesn't know, does he. I've got to warn him!"

Eyes wild, Alissa reached out, drawing back as if stung at her feeling of illness. *Warn him? About what?* But Sati was on her feet to find Lodesh. Steeling herself, Alissa stood and grasped Sati's sleeve, pulling her beyond the torchlight, and into the fragrant shadows. Nausea rose high, and Alissa paced a tight, frantic circle before the woman, trying not to retch. Something was wrong with Sati. With her tracings. "You," Alissa stammered, only now realizing the significance of her blue dress. "You're a shaduf."

"Shaduf Sati, as you will it," she said, making a short, sarcastic bob of her head. "And now that we've been properly introduced, I'll be warning Lodesh before he goes and proposes." She turned, anger clear in her sharp, quick strides.

Alissa took a deep breath and stepped into her path. "Sati, wait," she demanded. The sense of wrongness crashed over her anew. Clamping down upon both Beast and her upwelling nausea, Alissa stared at her. "Please," she gasped, an acidic taste in her throat. "Let me explain. No one is supposed to know I'm a Master." Then she hesitated. Her discomfort almost seemed to vanish as Sati's last words penetrated. "Propose?" Alissa said.

Taking a haughty stance, Sati all but sneered at Alissa's confusion. "You're astonishingly good. Your shift to human is almost perfect." She wiggled her fingers. "You're still off on the eyes, but gray is closer than gold. Redal-Stan teach you that?"

"Propose?" Alissa stammered.

"Yes, propose," she snapped. "Are you stupid or just deaf?"

"I-I," Alissa stammered, and then her eyes narrowed at the insult. "How do you know he's going to propose?" she demanded. "Shadufs can't see into a Master's future."

"See it?" she all but barked. "I don't need to see it. I've lived it! First," she gestured roughly, tossing her head so her hair began to spill from its white ribbon, "he will wait until the moon is all but crested, then pull you to the shadows on some excuse or other."

"Sati, I . . ."

"Then he will whisper how his life will mean nothing if you aren't there with him."

"Sati, please," Alissa pleaded, but then stopped. Sati's face had softened, and her shoulders had drooped. She stood, not tight and angry but lost in memory.

"And," Sati whispered, "when the moon rises beyond the trees, pooling about your feet, the mirth flowers will begin to slip from the trees in a gentle shadow of scent."

Sati was crying, the tears slipping unnoticed down her face, its weary lines gentled with a tragic sorrow. She was beautiful in her misery, and Alissa's throat tightened with shared loss.

"Then he will take your trembling hands, forming a bowl to catch the sweet rain of flowers to accept the one he gives as his token of his love, a symbol of his offer of marriage."

The torchlight outlined Sati in a shimmer. Alissa stood, unable to move. Something had ruined this woman, taking her life, her hope, leaving an empty shell animated by nothing. There was no grace but in memories for her. "Sati," Alissa whispered. "What happened?"

Awareness flooded back. Dropping her head, she tucked her hair back under its tie and hunched into herself. The harsh angles reappeared. "I thought everyone knew," she said. Sati moved farther into the shadow to stare out into the moonlit field. "I'm a shaduf," she said. "That's all. My abilities broke into existence all at once on an evening much like this one."

She turned to Alissa with her haunted eyes. "A shaduf's abilities generally trickle into being, first as night terrors, then daymares. Plenty of time to realize a curse has been set upon you. Time to prepare for the monstrosity your existence will become. But no," she drawled sarcastically. "Not me. My abilities crashed full upon me in a heartbeat."

"But what happened?" Alissa persisted.

"Remember?" Beast interrupted. *"The first future a shaduf lives is his or her own death. Lodesh's proclamation of*

*love triggered her abilities, tainting her love for him with the
stench of her death."*

"By the will of the Navigator," Alissa whispered in horror,
feeling herself go cold.

Sati spun, her frown bitter. "The Navigator had nothing to
do with it. I found myself dying in childbirth. Lodesh's child.
It took two days for us to manage, my daughter and I. It ended
with my daughter beside me, preceding me into death just
barely. My daughter lived long enough for me to grow to love
her." Sati turned away. "Then I died as well."

Alissa could do nothing, say nothing, staring at her in
shock.

"Lodesh was very brave," Sati said lightly, "but to see his
eyes lying to me when he said I would be all right was worse
than the physical pain. I don't recall the pain anymore." She
sat down at the base of a tree as if unable to stand. "But his
eyes," she said distantly. "Those I see. Those I remember."

The tears ran unchecked from Alissa. Sati's eyes were
frighteningly dry. "I think I went mad when the Seeing was
over and I found myself in Lodesh's arms, under the moon
with the scent of the mirth trees thick in the air. Lodesh didn't
know what had happened. He only knew I was suddenly terrified of him. I've never told him of his part in my death."

"I'm—I'm sorry," Alissa said, knowing it was wholly inadequate.

Sati's gaze was empty. "Could you live with someone
knowing their death?"

Alissa sat down beside her, unable to simply walk away.
"So you won't die in childbirth," she offered, then immediately regretted it, but Sati smiled harshly.

"No. Now I die of a bloody cough, or a sharp pain in my
chest, or once even a bad case of the stomach pains. It depends," she lectured, "upon what I habitually do, periodically
shifting as I shun certain foods or tasks, or even places.
Everyone else's death stays the same, but once you know, you
can't help but shift it, even when you try not to."

Alissa was silent, imagining the horror of knowing.

"I wish I had more courage," Sati whispered.

Feeling eyes upon her, Alissa turned to see that Connen-Neute had pulled himself from the musicians and was watching her. Not knowing what he wanted, she shook her head. He turned away as a whistle's solo attracted his attention.

Sati shook herself. "Look at me," she said ruefully. "I only came to spill a glass of wine on you. If I had known I was going to like you, I would have burned myself first."

"Beg your pardon?" Alissa blurted.

Shrugging her too-thin shoulders, Sati looked at her feet. "I have a small box. I made Lodesh buy it for me. It's warded shut. When I try to open it, I suffer a mild burn." Misunderstanding Alissa's horrified look, she quickly added, "It's warded for me alone. It's perfectly safe for anyone else. It hurts like, well, I'm sure you know, but it's worth it."

"But why?" Alissa stammered, feeling her naïveté was serving her badly.

Sati seemed to understand. "Burned tracings don't resonate. You wouldn't have to fight to keep from vomiting. A Keeper wouldn't notice me at all, and," she added, sounding almost guilty, "until they heal, I'm unable to See. "Once," she said dreamily, "I burned myself so badly I had nearly three days." She sighed. "It was spring. I could almost forget. Lodesh had promised to visit, and I couldn't bear to see him cringe. He tries to hide it, but, well . . ."

Alissa closed her eyes. Something was terribly wrong when the only way to feel joy required an equal payment of pain. *"Burn her,"* Beast said.

"Burn her?" Alissa whispered.

Sati's head jerked up. "You can? Alone? They said it was too late. Did they lie to me?"

"I—Sati. Wait." Alissa took a step back. "I never meant—"

"Burn her tracings to permanent ash," Beast demanded. *"Give her something back. A crumb to her is worth more than a feast to any other."*

"But the pain," Alissa pleaded as Sati stepped forward, her pinched features tightening in hope. "I don't know if I can channel that."

"*It's not so much the amount of energy as the force behind it,*" Beast said, shaming Alissa with her courage. "*We can spare her some of the pain. Take it upon ourselves. This woman-shadow will survive.*"

"Alissa! Look at me!" Sati pleaded, forcing her hands to her side as she started to reach out. "I don't care about the pain."

"I don't know if I can," Alissa whispered, her excuse sounding shallow even to her.

Spots of color showed on Sati's cheeks. "That is a lie!" she snapped. "Your kind has burned lesser shadufs before they mature. They refuse to grant me peace because I'm the best they have. Look at me!" she cried. "I can't allow myself to care about anyone or anything! My love for Lodesh has mixed with my death so freely that I can't separate the two anymore. I know I could remember how if I could only stop Seeing!" She took a ragged breath. "Please, Alissa. How can I smile at a child, when I know someday he will beat his wife to death?"

Terribly frightened, Alissa searched Sati's face. She took a deep breath. "Not here. I'll come to you tomorrow."

Sati went from hopeful to frantic. "No! Now! We can go into the field. Wherever you want, but it must be now!" Seeing Alissa's alarm, Sati lowered her voice. "They watch you so close, the Masters, I mean," she whispered urgently. "Connen-Neute would stop us now but for the music distracting him. Tomorrow Redal-Stan will forbid you."

"No one," Alissa said hotly, "forbids me from anything."

Sati laughed sourly. "He will threaten you, and the result would be the same."

Alissa tensed, knowing Sati was right. "Hounds. Do you realize what you're asking?"

Sati stared at her with her hollow, empty eyes. "Yes."

Alissa was silent. She looked from Sati to the content, happy people that Sati could watch but never join. "Come on." Alissa extended her hand, snatching it back as their fingers touched, then firmly grabbed it and pulled Sati deeper into the shadow of a mirth tree. Its huge girth was between them and the light, but she still could hear the song and laughter.

They settled themselves facing each other, the clean smell of the mirth trees mingling with the powdery scent of the goldenrod and asters. The dew had risen, and the moss was damp. Alissa was worried they would be caught and scared silly they wouldn't.

"You'll make it quick?" Sati said, her voice trembling.

Alissa nodded, recalling her own, accidental burn. "But it will seem to last an eternity. And, Sati?" Alissa hesitated until she looked up. "Promise me you won't hide from the pain. The only refuge is death. You must endure it. It will be so bad you'll pass out."

"Then I'll lie down." Looking small and vulnerable, Sati settled herself upon the moss and clenched her wrap about her. She couldn't be much older than Alissa but had died more times than Alissa dared guess. "Please hurry," Sati whispered. "Please. They'll stop you."

"May I see your tracings?" Alissa asked, and at Sati's uneasy nod, Alissa slipped a thin, unnoticed thought into Sati's consciousness. The feeling of nausea rose full force. Beast took most of it, leaving Alissa to try to decipher the tangle of tracings Sati's neural net was. It was hopeless. She'd have to burn them all. The pain would be hideous.

"I can't burn everything," Alissa whispered to Beast. *"She would die from it!"*

"Ask to see a resonance," Beast said.

"Beast! You're smarter than three Masters combined."

"Faster, too," Beast said smugly.

"Sati?" Alissa called, and the woman jumped, her eyes flashing open. "Show me what tracings you use by doing whatever it is you do to see the future," Alissa said. "If I can burn only the parts that are wrong, the pain won't be as bad."

"You decide," Sati said softly. "Decide who and the question. I won't be responsible for knowing any more futures."

Alissa drew back. She didn't want to know anyone's misery before it happened. Knowing Lodesh's was bad enough. The sound of a pipe mimicking the song of a wren cut clearly through the night, almost as if it were a sign. "Ren," she said firmly. Nothing bad could happen to him. "Do you know him?"

She nodded, her gaze beginning to go distant.

"Will he gain his Keeper status?" Alissa said, seeing no harm in that.

With a slow exhalation, Sati's eyes unfocused and closed. The nausea rose high. Alissa's tracings seemed to give a hiccup as fragmented pieces of a broken pattern tried to resonate in a harsh discord. Sati's tracings were faintly glowing from the unsupplemented force the woman held. It was clear what needed to be burned and what could remain untouched. Sati was almost tripping the lines of time but using linkages Alissa didn't have.

Alissa felt a stab of panic as Sati's pattern began to overwhelm hers. Her thoughts became light and disconnected. She was going to trip the lines. She couldn't stop! *"Beast! Help!"* she cried, but it was too late, and together they slipped into Sati's dream of the future.

"*W*arden!" *It was a hateful cry, filling the cold, dawn air with frustration.*

"Warden!" This time it was a scream of defiance, pouring from Ren as he exhaled, the tightness in his chest giving it the force to pound against the walls surrounding the city he had once called his. A flock of birds upon a slate rooftop took flight and flew away in a smattering of feathers. He was alone. His army had abandoned him. He hadn't cared. He hadn't asked them to come; he had simply given direction for their separate pain.

"I know you're in there, Lodesh. Talk to me!" Dust turned him the color of the walls. He slumped against the gates until he slid to the ground. "You owe me that," he all but moaned.

There was a scuffling from the walk atop the wall, and a fair head peeked over. "By the Wolves, Ren? It's been you?"

Ren gave a bark of sarcastic laughter. "You remember me," he whispered. "I'm flattered." He took a breath. Finding the strength to stand, he backed to face the city, its walls shining yellow under the new sun. He removed his hat and performed a low, graceful bow. "Are they feeding you well in there?" he called softly. "The plains and foothills are empty of all but death and famine." His mocking words came clearly through the air, finally stilled of the sound of drums and marching feet. Even the insects had been crushed out of existence. Nothing broke the stark quiet but his harsh breaths.

"Ren," Lodesh said warily. "Why did you do this?"

"Me?" It was an unreal bark, and he replaced his hat to cover his eyes lest Lodesh see the pain. "I'm not the one hiding behind walls thicker than Mav's pestle pudding."

There was a guilty hesitation. "I didn't cause the plague of madness," Lodesh said, "but I must protect my people. I'm their servant. I have no choice."

"There's always a choice!" Ren all but screamed, feeling his head begin to pound. "Unless your reason has been stripped from you and you're a beast." He looked defiantly up at the top of the wall. "Are you a beast, Lodesh?" he taunted.

"If we had let them in," Lodesh called down, "the plague would have ravaged the city as well. Everyone would have been lost."

His strength left him, and Ren sank to his knees. "They weren't all sick. She only wanted you to save her children, our children." Ren caught a sob. "Those she kept from my murderous hands." A low, eerie moan stirred from him, and he let it grow, frightened at its sound but more afraid of what it would do to him if he didn't let it go. It rose to an unbearable feeling of despair until it broke in a sharp sound of anguish. He took a gasping breath, wondering if he was still sane.

"I couldn't stop," he whispered. "The dreams burned in my head. Horrible dreams, Lodesh. Urging me, goading me, promising release if I only made them true. I thought I was alone, and I hid my dreams from Kally, but she had them, too—and the children. Oh, the children! We went mad, along with the rest of the world. All mad," he moaned, "with the soft thought of killing keeping us from sleep. It promised if we *could only kill enough, that it would go and leave us in peace."*

Finding strength in the telling, Ren raised his voice, unable to stop. "The children succumbed to the promise first," he said dispassionately. "Murdering the livestock. You could tell it must have been difficult, especially for the younger ones. They weren't very strong. They used whatever they could. What they left was painted over their killing field." He took a breath. "The trees turned early that year, Lodesh, painted rust in the summer's heat."

The walls were silent.

"I tried to stop," Ren said, feeling ill and lightheaded. "The promise never grew, never lessened, and never ceased. I know what I did. I watched from behind myself. I could hear myself screaming, but those hands around my daughter's neck weren't mine!" Ren raised his head. "They weren't mine!" he raged, his voice echoing against the walls. His eyes were dry. "The sound of her fear, I might forget, but the silence afterwards—I never will."

"Ren," Lodesh said, his voice hushed in horror.

"Shut up, Warden," Ren snarled. "I won't call you by your name any longer. You aren't a man. You've traded your humanity for your cowardly walls."

A small stone slid from the top of the wall, making a puff as it landed with a muffled thump. "I didn't start the plague," Lodesh said. "I'm only protecting what I can. The rest of your army has left, come to their senses. Go home with them."

"I have no home," Ren breathed, but he rose, brushing at the dirt out of habit, not making a difference in the dust-caked cloak. "Are you that blind?" His voice was a thin, weary ribbon. "You may not have started the plague, but your Masters did."

"That's enough!" Lodesh shouted, anger coloring his voice.

"What are you going to do?" he said with a bitter laugh. "Come down and thrash me?" His arms hanging at his sides, Ren stared at the gates and Lodesh standing atop them. "We're nothing but stallions and mares to them," he said, *"designed to bring Keepers into existence. But not too fast!"* he admonished, becoming agitated. *"Oh no!"* he taunted. *"They might lose control, and that,"* he finished gaily, *"wouldn't do."*

"Ren," Lodesh protested, *"what you say—"*

"Makes perfect sense!" he shouted, pointing with a trembling finger. Slowly his arm dropped. *"It takes a very specific background to make a Keeper. And they had lost control."*

Lodesh sank to his knees atop the wall, horror etched in his face in the bright sun.

"First they reduce the population," Ren said. *"Then they divide it. This time they decided to use hatred to keep the foothills and plains apart. Much more certain,"* he mocked, *"than a physical barrier. And just as hard to surmount."*

Ren paced before the locked gates, his anger growing as the sun warmed. *"The foothills blame the plains. The plains blame the foothills. And the coastal folk!"* he raged, spittle coming from him, *"conditioned to believe in magic, won't cross the mountains for fear of the winged demons that inhabit them!"* Ren stopped. *"Perfect, isn't it,"* he said with a false calm.

"Ren. You're wrong," Lodesh whispered. They wouldn't go to those extremes."

"Ask Redal-Stan," Ren interrupted coldly. *"Or better yet, Talo-Toecan. I would be willing to wager he was the one who suggested your cursed walls to begin with. Didn't want to lose,"* he taunted, *"his precious city, no doubt."*

"Talo-Toecan has been gone these last three years," Lodesh whispered.

"Coward!" Ren cried.

"Ren," Lodesh persisted. *"I can't believe it."*

"Can't—or won't? Did your precious Masters lift even one wing tip to help or offer a suggestion to combat the sickness?"

"No." It was a hushed whisper.

Ren looked down at his hands. *"I didn't think so."* He looked up. *"And I'm left with the blood of those who looked to me for protection staining my hands. Well, I won't take the blame for this!"* Ren raised his hands stiffly to the sky. *"I will not accept the responsibility for the deaths of Kally and our children. Do you hear me, Warden!" he screamed. "I give my guilt to you and all who hide behind your walls of shame and fear!"*

The air began to tremble, stirred by a force so low it could only be felt.

"You!" Ren scorned, an ebony glow enveloping his upraised fists. "You will be cursed, though you should live for a thousand years, Lodesh. My anguish, my pain, my shame shall be my gift to you, and you will never rest until you prove yourself worthy of the name! Do you hear me, Warden!" he sobbed, as his upraised hands became lost in a darkness even the new sun couldn't penetrate. "The death of the world is on you!"

A cry of rage escaped him, and as it reached its peak, the blackness silently exploded from his hands. For an instant, it was as if the sun winked from existence.

Then the blackness was gone.

A cock crowed from behind the walls and was silent.

Ren slumped where he stood, shattered and drained. He was done. As he turned to go, a gentle rumbling began. Feeding upon itself, it grew to a great unrest as the very earth protested the curse. From the east, the noise echoed along the walls in twin paths to the west. They met at the gate, and with a mighty shudder and groan, the gates fell, outraged at the strength of the ward set upon those it once sheltered.

Ren never looked back. "Believing you had no choice has made it so," he whispered.

With a frightening snap, Alissa's awareness returned. She gasped in panic of what she had seen. *"Burn it!"* Beast screamed. *"Burn it now!"*

So she did. The icy wash of hot thought filled Sati's resonating pattern. The horror of what Alissa had learned was cauterized in the sharp, clean flow of destruction. Alissa took her share of the pain, then reached for more, multiplying her agony, trying to take it all, to find release, to make amends for what she had witnessed.

It was too much, and as Alissa silently screamed into her phantom agony, she fell unconscious to see no more.

27

"**B**urn it to ash, Alissa!" Lodesh shouted over the noise of drums and stomping feet. "Why didn't you tell me you could dance?"

"Huh?" Alissa blinked twice and stopped dead in her tracks.

"Hey! Watch out!" someone shouted, and she was knocked from behind. Her ankle gave a twinge, and she stumbled. She would have fallen if Lodesh hadn't hauled her off the dance boards. Alissa stared in bewilderment at the spinning figures. The music and pounding feet were overwhelming. It was all she could do to not cover her ears. What was she doing on the dance boards, and how had she gotten there? The last she knew, she had been with Sati.

"Sati," Alissa whispered, turning to the edge of the torchlight.

Lodesh leaned close, his breath fast and his eyes bright. "You want to sit down?" he asked, misreading her motion, and she nodded. They picked their way through the watchers, the noise becoming almost bearable. Alissa pointed to Marga's empty blanket, and he angled them to it. It was as far from the dancing boards as they could get without retreating into the darkness.

They sat down beside each other, and Alissa took her sore ankle in hand. Worried, she checked her tracings. They were clean. The pain had been only a phantom. *"Beast?"* she called.

"What?"

She sounded guilty, worrying Alissa further. She wanted to talk to Beast but was afraid Lodesh might hear; he was terribly perceptive. "Lodesh?" she said, fanning herself dramatically. "Would you fetch me a drink, please? The dancing has made me thirsty."

His eyes went wide in mock dismay. Jumping to his feet, he performed one of his extravagant bows. "How beastly of me!" he cried. "I have neglected you sorely, milady. Would you perhaps desire another mulled wine?"

Mulled wine? Alissa thought. Was that the odd taste upon her tongue? "Tea, I think."

"But, of course." Lodesh bent to retrieve her hand, and she laughed as he continued his pretend bowing and scraping over it. A final flourish, and his fingers slipped reluctantly from hers. He strode away, giving those he passed a friendly nod.

Alissa watched until he was gone, then centered herself. *"Beast,"* she called warily. *"Why were you dancing with Lodesh?"*

"I wasn't dancing with Lodesh," she protested. *"You were."*

Alissa took a breath. *"No. I was unconscious."* Though her tone was casual, she was concerned. Beast had relinquished control when Alissa woke, so it wasn't a breach of their arrangement—from a certain point of view—but such slips had been happening a lot lately.

"It's not my fault," Beast whined. *"You took more than your share of the pain, almost all of it."*

Alissa shifted on the blanket, remembering. *"I had to. I needed it, deserved it maybe. How can I look at Ren and Kally, knowing all that? Sati was right. Her life is misery."* Alissa shuddered, wishing she had a shawl. She had met Lodesh knowing his past, or future rather, but Ren and Kally . . . They, perhaps, she could spare without shifting what had to be.

"Where is Sati?" Alissa asked. *"What happened?"*

Beast seemed to sigh. *"You fell unconscious,"* she accused, *"but you weren't lying down at the time. Your arm was pinned. It hurt."*

"You feel my pain?" Alissa asked in surprise.

"It's my pain as much as yours," she said jealously.

"Oh." Alissa frowned at this newest revelation. *"Sorry."*

"So I sat you up. Sati woke before you. She smiled at me," Beast said, a wondering tone in her thought. *"She said thank you and gave you something. I put it in your boot so you wouldn't forget and accidentally break it down when you next shift."*

"What is it?" Alissa asked, realizing the bump under her toes wasn't the stone she assumed it was. She began to unlace her boot, but Lodesh was coming, and she desisted.

"I don't know. A white pebble?"

Lodesh had an expectant look in his eyes as he approached. "Here you go. Fresh brew."

Alissa gingerly accepted the thick-walled mug, took a sip, and set it beside her. Lodesh sank down with a contented sigh, sprawling himself out every which way until, with an embarrassed grunt, he straightened, glancing at Alissa as if to see if she had noticed.

"But why were you dancing?" Alissa whispered into her thoughts. She watched Lodesh closely, but he didn't seem to hear.

"I was good. I stayed where you left me. But Lodesh found you and asked if you wanted to dance. I didn't want to speak. We don't sound alike."

Lodesh turned to her. "I'm sorry, Alissa. Did you say something?"

"No." She gazed up into the fragrant cloud of unfallen mirth blossoms.

"I had to say yes," Beast whispered. *"I could do nothing but nod my head."*

"You could have shaken it no."

"But I didn't want *to."*

Alissa sighed. Beast was very much like a child.

Lodesh heard her sigh and bent close in concern. "Tired?"

"No, not really."

His eyes went to her hands, wrapped securely about her ankle. "Is your foot all right?"

Alissa smiled ruefully and wiggled it. "Yes. It's fine. It's given me problems ever since I twisted it falling into a ravine." Reminded of Strell, her face went slack.

"You're jesting," Lodesh said, disbelief arching his eyebrows. "I've been watching you all night. Everything reminds you of Strell." He reclined upon an elbow. His eyes were twinkling, but she could tell there was a sliver of truth to his contrived sadness. "The music, Sarken, the mirth trees, the fire, and now your ankle." He fell back against the moss. "How can I compete with that?" he said to the sky.

Alissa laughed. This was the Lodesh she recalled, and she clung to the memory as if it were the only thing real left to her. Perhaps it was.

He sat up, his green eyes glinting. "I'm determined you will enjoy yourself tonight!" he said as his hand found hers. "There must be something here that doesn't remind you of him."

"Dancing," Beast said wistfully, loud enough to reach Lodesh's thoughts.

"Dancing?" Lodesh caught his breath.

Alissa's face went cold. *"Shut up!"* she hissed into her mind, but it was too late.

"Strell doesn't dance?" he asked, but it was more of an exuberant statement, and he jumped to his feet, looking down at Alissa. "I dance! Are you rested? Let's go!"

Her heart thumped at the thought of his arms around her through the steps of a dance, closer than he really ought to be. "I, uh . . . My foot still hurts," she blurted.

"You just said it didn't. Ashes, Alissa. I think they would have cleared the dance boards for us to finish that last one alone if I hadn't misstepped and thrown you off your beat." His enthusiasm dimmed. "You don't want to dance *with me* anymore," he said, sounding hurt.

"Of course I do," Alissa protested, knowing Lodesh had nothing to do with her falling out of beat. "It's simply—there are so many people."

"It didn't bother you before." He sank down to a crouch.

"I think you're afraid. I think you're afraid they will clear the boards for us, and everyone will be watching us dance alone."

"I'm not afraid!" Alissa said, and Lodesh grinned in challenge. "Well, maybe I am afraid," she admitted, but not for what he thought. Lodesh slumped. He looked so unhappy, she couldn't leave him like that. "Maybe," she offered hesitantly, "if we danced here, instead?"

Immediately he brightened, giving credence to her growing suspicion that dancing in the shadows might not be a good idea; he looked far too eager. "Next round," he said, settling back.

Alissa looked slyly at him. The music was low and coaxing. She knew this tune. It was the introduction to a complicated number that required careful forethought of partners. Even as Alissa watched, the buzz of participants were finding each other, arranging themselves, shifting as more threesomes decided they would attempt it. Many would start. Very few would last to the end, exhaustion and a lack of finesse bringing them down. It was harder on the musicians. Her pride was still stinging from her admission of fear, so it was with no surprise she heard herself say, "Why not this one?" A rumble of drums rose and faded, and she shivered.

Lodesh froze. Slowly he turned. "You know the Triene?"

Alissa smiled at his surprise. "My mother taught me."

He was clearly doubtful, shaking a blond curl from his eyes. "We've only two people."

"So you play two parts." Alissa stood and pulled him to his feet. The pace of the music was increasing. It had almost begun. "I'll be the fair maid," Alissa said, "and you will be—"

"The dashing hero!"

"Actually," she said. "I thought the dastardly villain. He shows up first."

Lodesh frowned. "That's the hero in my version. Perhaps we should compare stories."

Alissa softly clapped in time, waiting for the dance to begin. Her pulse quickened, and she felt Beast stir. Beast ought to enjoy this. It was very much like flying.

"Here it comes," he warned as a stringed instrument took precedence. "Three, two, one!"

They began, stepping carefully so as not to mar Reeve's moss. From the dancing boards, the sound of synchronized boots hitting wood came strong, and the watchers cheered. "Well, the fair maid is in the hills," Alissa said, the soft thumps of her feet in time with the noisy ones from the dancing boards. She twirled, picking nonexistent flowers in a circle about a stationary Lodesh. He started to clap, the music to pick up speed.

"Yes," he agreed. "So far it's the same." He watched her, making a sharp nod as the complexity of Alissa's footwork increased with the volume of music. His pleased expression said she would be a suitable partner, as skilled as he. His smile shifted from evaluation to appreciation, and Alissa felt a thrill of something dart through her. It was more satisfying with real musicians and not her mother's breathless humming mixed with helpless laughter.

Alissa's steps grew subdued, mirroring the music. "And she gets lost," Lodesh said.

"Ha!" Alissa said. "In my story, she wanders too far to get home before dark and simply has to make camp." Her circle became wider. On the dance floor, there were laughs and shouts. People were getting in each other's way. It was a tricky dance, and there had to be eight pairs on the dance floor. But that, apparently, was half the fun.

Lodesh began to mimic her as she circled. Strike for strike, his feet met the sound of the drums' pulse. The pace was already faster than what she was used to, and it was only going to get worse. On the dance boards, one couple bowed out, accompanied by friendly jeers and calls. The gap was closed, and seven continued on.

Weaving an elaborate pattern of twists and stomps, Lodesh moved from her left to her right, but always behind her. "Then she's found," he said breathlessly, drawing close. "And is swept off her feet," and he did just that.

Alissa gasped, then laughed in delight to cover her surprise. There were shouts from the dancing boards, and two more couples retreated. "My mother never taught me that version," Alissa said with a giggle as her feet lightly touched the moss, and they proceeded with the daring challenge and answer of footwork.

Lodesh's eyes were fixed upon hers. "Ah," he said, his breath coming fast. "Perhaps it's unique to Ese'Nawoer."

"I think it's unique to you," she shot back. She wasn't thinking any longer. She had only time to react.

"What happens next?" Lodesh whispered.

Alissa moved closer so he could hear her breathless words, never slowing. "The villain—a fallen nobleman—escorts her to his humble holdings and tries to convince her to stay."

It was Lodesh's turn for a solo dance, and as Alissa's footwork eased so as to catch her breath, her mouth fell open in awe. He had been holding back. "By the Hounds," Alissa breathed, astounded.

It was a free-for-all on the dance boards as the remaining couples tried to outdo each other. The sound of slamming feet and clapping hands was a physical force, but she couldn't look from Lodesh to see. Lodesh, ever mindful of the moss, was less extravagant in his footfalls, but he more than made up for it with his fervent looks. His eyes had locked upon hers almost hungrily as he circled. Alissa felt Beast respond as their pulse beat in time with the drums. By the sounds of it, three more couples had left the circle, exhaustion pulling them down.

Lodesh glided in stealthy, ever-tightening loops, his motions becoming more seductive. Alissa spun to keep him in her sight, her breath fast. "Then what?" he whispered, his words warm and quick upon her cheek as he drew close and then away.

"They dance together as she thinks it over," she said, suddenly uneasy.

"That's what they do in my story, too," he said as he took her hands, and her feet instinctively did what was expected of them.

On the circle, the music and the crowd grew subdued and

darkly expectant. The pipes dropped to a low thrum, and the drums fell to a low cadence that steadily grew.

Alissa's fingers never left Lodesh's. The drums beat. Her pulse pounded. Her breath came fast as she strove to keep up with him. Her feet moved in time with his, feeling herself begin to slip. Just as she felt she could bear it no longer, he spun her into a wild turn that ended with her in his arms, crushed against him.

Lungs heaving, Alissa stared wide-eyed at him, her hands clamped firmly upon his shoulders, his around her waist. They stood unmoving as the music broke in a communal shout from the boards, and the dance continued without them, pounding, and pounding.

"And then?" he breathed, his eyes wild and his breath fast.

Her mind went blank, lost in his arms and his gaze and his presence. "Um . . ." she stammered, trying to drop her eyes, but Lodesh refused to let go. "The hero, her love, who has been searching for her, finds them. She must choose."

Lodesh never loosened his grip, and she wasn't sure if she wanted him to. "In my version," he said huskily, "that would be the villain." His eyes were deep with an unspoken question. "There are no villains here."

Behind them, the remaining couples were joined by their last participants. The music crashed to nothing. Silence broke upon the circle, aching in her ears after the thunderous fall of drums. But the dance wasn't over. A single, mournful pipe rose as the maiden made her decision. The outcome was different every time. It was up to the dancers, and the watchers waited in breathless anticipation.

The moon had risen above the trees. As if drawn from its presence, the mirth flowers began to fall, spilling down like light itself. A sigh of emotion rose from the people as they realized it. The intoxicating scent of the mirth trees crashed over them.

Alissa's eyes widened. Lodesh was going to propose, and at that instant, she didn't know if she could say no!

"Student!" Redal-Stan's thought came shocking into hers. *"Come home. Now!"*

"I—I have to go," Alissa heard herself mumble, not moving from Lodesh's arms.

Lodesh's eyes went wide. "Wait," he said urgently. "It's not what you think."

"Now," Connen-Neute whispered into her thoughts. *"If we're late, they won't let us into the quorum."*

"Lodesh," Alissa protested mildly. "I have to go."

"Alissa, if you're not airborne by the count of twelve, you lose your vote. One. Two. Three."

"I have to go," she repeated, but she couldn't pull away. She felt Connen-Neute slide behind her. Lodesh's grip tightened, and his eyes flicked briefly over her shoulder.

"I know," he said, clearly distressed by the Master's presence but determined to continue, "that your heart has been lost to another. I can't battle with a phantom and hope to win. You must banish him yourself. I won't ask anything of you tonight, but Alissa?" His eyes went deep into her, pulling into existence a surprising response. "I will—someday."

A flower drifted onto her shoulder and he reached for it, placing it into her palm and curling her numb fingers about its silky fragrance.

"Seven. Eight."

"I have to go, Lodesh," she said, but he didn't hear the significance of her words.

Connen-Neute stepped closer, and Lodesh released her. His eyes did not. She stumbled after the Master as he pulled her into the field. Her gaze was on Lodesh, alone in the shadows.

"Nine."

Nearly tripping, Alissa broke eye contact. She ran into the grass, searching for the dark in which to shift. Connen-Neute assumed his natural form, and his eyes glowed impatiently.

"Ten."

"Wait!" she called, struggling with Keribdis's boots, frantically tugging them off.

"Eleven."

"I'm coming!" She shifted with a quickness she had never attempted before, snatched up the boots, and leapt into the air.

"Twelve. Did she make it, Connen-Neute?"

"Just."

"Harrumph."

One of Keribdis's boots slipped from her grasp. It fell to the damp grass with a thump. Winging about, she went to find it, cursing her ineptness.

"Leave it, Alissa," Connen-Neute said. *"I'll come back tomorrow and find it."*

"Promise?"

"Promise."

Alissa obediently swung herself to the west. Silently they sped to the Hold through the moonlight, her breathless thoughts remaining in the grove with Lodesh. *"Beast?"* she whispered. *"You really feel everything I do?"*

"Everything," she said, sounding so dazed, Alissa grew more worried still.

≥8

Connen-Neute and Alissa sped toward the Hold. It sat like a heavy shadow at the base of the peak. Damp and comforting, the night air slipped about them like silk, the updrafts looking pearly and unreal in the almost-full moon. Beast was humming in delight to be in the air, but Alissa was worried. Her feral consciousness had never taken so much interest in what was going on. And Beast's emotions concerning Lodesh were most disturbing. Sighing, Alissa dismissed her concerns. Perhaps it had been from the music.

Redal-Stan's balcony blazed with a welcoming light. Alissa angled towards it, circling the tower behind Connen-Neute to lose her momentum. *"Um, Connen-Neute?"* she thought. *"What did Redal-Stan mean when he said I might lose my vote?"*

"We decide tonight who will be the next Warden."

"We decide?" she blurted. *"I thought the city decided."*

"Yes and no," was his slow response. *"Because the Warden holds sensitive wisdom, we have a say in the matter. The citadel families meet tonight to pick a candidate. So do we."*

Alissa stalled, backwinging in alarm. *"Talo-Toecan is here?"*

"Hounds, no. We meet by thought."

Reassured, Alissa followed him to alight upon Redal-Stan's balcony railing. Keribdis's boot hit the floor with a dull thump. Alissa shifted, tugging her skirt down to cover the holes in her stockings. There was a tweak on her thoughts, and a gray pair of slippers appeared. Smiling gratefully at

Connen-Neute, she jumped from the railing and slipped the oversized monstrosities on. They were lined with a gray fur, and her face warmed as she imagined what they would feel like on her bare feet.

Redal-Stan poked his head from his bedchamber. "Finally," he muttered, running a hand over his bald head. Striding forward, he motioned for them to sit. "Come on. Come on. They've already begun."

Connen-Neute stayed on the balcony. He wouldn't fit into the room unless he shifted, but he looked content enough as he closed his golden eyes and slipped into a light trance.

Wrapped in a velvety brown throw, Redal-Stan sprawled in his chair and eyed her expectantly. "Well?" he snapped.

Alissa perched on the edge of a chair. "I have no idea what's going on," she admitted.

He blinked. "You've never joined a conference? Why not?"

"There's only Talo-Toecan," she reminded him, angry for having to say it aloud.

"Oh. Yes." He dropped his eyes and plumped up the pillow in his chair. "Um, tell you what. You can't vote, seeing as you aren't supposed to be here. Put your thoughts lightly into mine so you can listen in. That is, unless you can hold sixty-three fields simultaneously?"

She shook her head. "Only five."

"Five!" exclaimed Connen-Neute, his eyes flashing open in surprise. They abruptly closed at his teacher's disapproving frown.

"It's a start," Redal-Stan reassured her. "Anytime you're ready."

Alissa settled herself and sent her thoughts to his. Immediately she felt as if she were in a large room surrounded by hundreds. She wasn't, of course. There were only sixty-three of them, sixty-four if you counted her. It was more than slightly oppressive, as if she was being jostled and bumped by unseen shadows. Whispers and snippets of conversations slipped about the edges of her awareness, making her slightly queasy.

"There's no help for it," Redal-Stan whispered. "The crowding must be endured. To be heard, one must shout.

"Where," he thundered unexpectedly, "does the vote stand?"

"It's about time!" came a chorus of irate thoughts, and Alissa struggled to maintain Beast's calm. She didn't like this at all.

A firm, feminine thought cut through the babble. "Welcome, Redal-Stan. Connen-Neute has given us his vote, and so we stand at an informal count of one absence, two for Marga Stryska, eight for the abolishment of the Wardens completely, four for choosing a new Warden line, six for grooming Trook Hirdune, and forty-one for Keeper Earan Stryska."

"Earan!" Beast cried, and Alissa shushed her, terrified Redal-Stan would hear.

"Thank you, Keribdis," Redal-Stan said loudly, and Alissa's fear multiplied. That strong-minded thought was Keribdis? She would spot Beast in an instant. She was trained for it!

"Soon as we know your preference," Keribdis said, "we may commence the bargaining."

"What about Lodesh?" Beast said clearly into the mental hush.

Alissa cringed as pandemonium erupted. "Lodesh? Lodesh Stryska?" were the cries. "You're jesting!"

"Be still," Redal-Stan hissed, thinking it had been her, and Alissa felt a wave of irritation from Beast, surprising and worrisome.

"Qui-i-i-iet!" Keribdis thundered, and silence fell. "Redal-Stan," she drawled into the new hush. "Am I to understand you have brought Keeper Lodesh Stryska under consideration?"

There was a long pause. "Apparently," he muttered, and the resulting upwelling of protests made Alissa cower.

"Very well." Keribdis sounded peeved. "The vote is one absence, two for Marga—"

"You may as well drop your bluff," interrupted an anonymous voice. *"Marga won't have the presence of mind to administer to a city when her children go shaduf."*

An angry thought snapped, *"It's wrong. Sati is all the shaduf we need. The union between the Stryska line and the coast should have been postponed."*

Postponed? Alissa thought. *Marga's children shaduf? What is going on?*

". . . eight to abolish the Warden post completely," Keribdis continued.

"There's a good idea," came a sarcastic thought.

". . . four for choosing a new Warden line . . ."

"Even better!" someone shouted.

". . . six for young Trook, forty-one for Earan, and one—for—Lodesh." Keribdis seemed to take a deep breath. *"Any voluntary changes in the order? No? Then—"*

"Wait." Connen-Neute's familiar thought came clearly, sounding subdued but determined. *"I change my vote from Marga to Lodesh."*

The gathered rakus stirred, and Alissa felt the beginnings of unease in her. Earan could have the title. Lodesh's life would be changed for the better. She had been a coward for keeping silent before. What was her life compared to the untold misery of Ese'Nawoer?

"I change mine to Lodesh as well," another piped up.

"Me, too."

Hot protests and sharp accusations rose loud, and Alissa wished she could cover her ears.

"Fine!" Keribdis shouted. *"Wyden? Make a new count, please?"*

There was a soft sigh. *"Yes, Keribdis,"* and the noise subsided to a slow mutter.

"See what you've started," Alissa thought at Beast, and Beast sniffed in annoyance.

"May I have a word with you, Redal-Stan?" came Keribdis's thought, soft into Alissa's.

"Of course. But don't expect we won't be overheard," he said, and Alissa winced at her unhelped-for eavesdropping.

"What the Hounds are you doing?" Keribdis said. *"I've*

*had this issue grounded since yesterday. Lodesh is fluff and
flotsam. Are you trying to make my life difficult on a whim, or
is this a political ploy?"*

"Neither." Redal-Stan sighed. *"Lodesh isn't as scatterbrained as you've been led to believe. He's very popular in
the city."*

Keribdis paused. *"Well-liked? A pawn then?"*

"Wolves no," he cried. *"He's far too clever for that. Actually,"* he said reluctantly, *"he moves easily between the common and Keeper fractions."*

Alissa's heart sank.

"Really," Keribdis mused. *"So you're serious about this?"*

"Apparently." It was a very dry comment.

"Very well. We will do it the hard way." Alissa felt Keribdis gather herself. *"Wyden?"*

Wyden's presence grew strong, giving Alissa the impression of clearing her throat. *"We have a movement to three absence, fifteen Lodesh, and forty-four Earan. And yours, which
is?"*

"Earan," Keribdis said. *"I assume everyone knows who
has sided with whom and why?"*

Silence.

"Then," she said, *"who wants to go first?"*

Again the silence. Not even a whisper.

"Come now," Keribdis cajoled. *"Someone must have
something somebody else wants."*

"My tour of Hold duty is upon me in three seasons," came
a masculine thought. *"I'll come in early and free someone if
they switch their vote back to Earan."*

"I'll do it," chimed someone. *"I have four seasons left in
the Hold with two students who lack the restraint to make
Keeper. I'm sure they could be encouraged to leave soon."*

"Fine," the first voice agreed, *"but I want no new students
for five years, minimum."*

"You want a tower room but no obligations?" cried a third
voice. *"That won't happen."*

*"I'll take anybody's responsibilities for the next eighty
years,"* bellowed a new voice, *"but I want a vote for Lodesh!"*

"Eighty years! They'll all be dead by then."

Confused, Alissa whispered to Redal-Stan, *"What's going on?"*

"Vote buying at its most honest, Squirrel, vote buying."

"You mean," Alissa said quietly, her outrage growing, *"the decision of the next Warden isn't based upon merit but on who wants the summer free and who will do whom's chores!"*

"I'm 'fraid so."

"That's wrong!" exploded Beast, shocking Alissa to a stunned silence. *"The city wants someone they trust, depend on, someone they like! Not a self-serving, egotistical bully who will willingly bow to whatever you want out of fear or loyalty."*

"Quiet," Redal-Stan hissed privately at her. But it had been Beast. She had shut Alissa out, leaving Alissa struggling frantically for control.

"I will not be silent!" Beast shouted, and the buzz of dealings hesitated. *"Lodesh has studied those he lives among. He knows what will make the baker agree to the blacksmith's ideas so both are pleased. He appears simple because it's easier to get things done that way!"*

"I said shut up, Squirrel!"

"You're Masters of what?" Beast raged. *"Everyone? Try mastering yourself. Look at you, bargaining with the helpless to shirk your responsibilities. Loosen your grip,"* she warned. *"You're strangling your children, the very ones who freed you."*

"Who," came Talo-Toecan's startled thought, *"is that?"*

Redal-Stan formed a field about himself and Alissa. The stunned silence was replaced by Redal-Stan's angry presence. *"Get out,"* he snapped, and he booted her from his thoughts.

Her eyes flashed open to find Redal-Stan glaring at her. Connen-Neute's eyes were wide with shock. She stared at Redal-Stan, frightened that Beast had taken control so easily. Alissa hadn't been able to stop her. Beast had called her bluff and won. Panicking, Alissa opened her mouth to explain and ask for help, but Beast took control again. Alissa felt her face harden. "Fine," Beast said aloud through Alissa, and Alissa found herself standing up.

Redal-Stan pointed a trembling finger at the door, and she walked out. "I didn't want to stay anyway, old one," Beast snarled, and slammed the door.

Beast stormed Alissa down the stairs, earning several stares and raised eyebrows. Beast wasn't paying attention, so Alissa managed to divert them to the garden and the firepit. They sat in the dark on the cold stone: Beast fuming, Alissa panicking. Alissa didn't think Beast knew she was in control, or they would have shifted and flown away. Alissa struggled to move a finger, blink, anything, becoming more frightened until, like a soap bubble bursting, she was back in control.

Alissa gasped at the sensation. A wave of cold assailed her. Beast's thoughts turned panicked. Alissa had been right. Beast hadn't known she was in control. She did now, though, and Beast's wail of dismay flooded Alissa's mind.

"I broke my word!" Beast cried. *"I stole your wind as I said I wouldn't."* She hesitated. *"You're going to destroy me. You must! I can't be trusted!"*

Alissa's wildly thudding heart eased at Beast's obvious dismay. And as Redal-Stan hadn't known what happened, they could work this out by themselves. *"Beast,"* Alissa said firmly, trying to disguise her fear. *"You made a mistake. Why? What was different?"*

"You're not angry?" Beast asked tremulously.

"I'm furious," Alissa said softly, *"but clearly you weren't aware you had taken control."*

"No," she whispered.

"It's been happening a lot lately." Cold from more than the night, Alissa lit the wood already laid out and leaned close to the flames. The Hold loomed dark above her. The same walls, the same stones, full of life but empty of the one she sought.

"I know," Beast said meekly. *"I'm sorry."*

Alissa sighed, wondering why she was having so much trouble with Beast lately. *"And now Lodesh has gone from a fool to a candidate for Wardenship."*

Beast said nothing, all but disappearing in a wash of misery.

Alone in her thoughts, Alissa allowed her worry at Beast's slip to come flowing back. Accident or not, it had happened. She sat and stewed, reluctant to move. She felt more herself at the firepit than she had all day.

The moon was set and the sun nearly risen when Connen-Neute spiraled silently down and woke her from an uncomfortable doze. He gazed at her, his golden eyes full of worry. He knew it had been Beast speaking, not her. "Well?" she prompted with a feeling of futility.

"Lodesh is the Hold's choice. It was realized his foolishness is indeed a ploy to avoid responsibility. His apparent gullibility is more of an asset than Earan's loyalty. And Earan's recent attempt to burn another's tracings in anger raised questions as to his control."

Alissa felt a tear form and her shoulders slump. She never meant for this to happen.

"If it helps," he offered awkwardly, *"Beast's words had nothing to do with the decision."*

"Please go away," she said. Not wanting him to see her cry twice in one night, she put her head in her hands, and he silently left. She didn't know if it bothered her more that Lodesh was going to be the Warden or that Beast's words of shame had been heard and ignored.

29

Strell sat at the firepit, shaking inside. Warm rain slipped down his collar as he clutched the stone bench with a white-knuckled fervor and stared at the damp night. Steam rose from the warm earth, adding to his feeling of unreality. "Thanks," he whispered raggedly to Talon, and the small kestrel chittered from her sheltered position in a bush. His heart slowed, and he forced his grip to loosen. Putting his elbows on his knees, he dropped his head into his hands. Alissa's presence filled the firepit, and he basked in it.

"That wasn't a good idea," he whispered. He squinted into the dark as a gust of rain and wind, accompanied by Talo-Toecan, descended. The old raku said nothing, preferring to remain in a form that didn't mind the wet. "I'm not going to do that again," Strell said defensively.

The raku rumbled a question.

Strell wiped the rain from his eyes. "I purposely stopped following Alissa as you suggested. Your idea that she would sense my lack of presence as I had sensed hers was a good one, Talo-Toecan," he stammered. "But she wasn't paying attention. Something was distracting her. And then," Strell breathed, remembering his fright, "I lost her completely."

With a savage, clawlike finger, the Master gestured for him to explain.

Strell struggled to find the words. "I followed her thoughts to Ese'Nawoer's grove—"

Talo-Toecan expressed his wonder with a rumble.

"I know that's where she went," Strell said. "I can sense

her even at that distance now, and that's just it," he pleaded.
"I followed her flight back and felt her settle in the tower, one
of the upper rooms, and then, nothing." He looked up, his
pulse quickening in the memory of his fear. "She was gone. I
ran upstairs, thinking if I could juxtapose ourselves again, she
might reappear, but even the memory of her was gone."

Talo-Toecan raised his head in alarm, and Strell held up a
reassuring hand. "Talon led me to her. As soon as I reached
the firepit, she was there to be found."

The raku's eyes narrowed with puzzlement. He shifted in
a swirl of gray almost indistinguishable from the rain and
dark, appearing with an ugly, wide-brimmed hat atop his
head. "A moment," he said, stepping down into the pit. "The
involvement of Talon aside, you want me to believe your lack
of proximity to Alissa triggered a disillusionment of her?"

Strell frowned, uncaring if the Master believed him or not.

"Perhaps," Talo-Toecan offered, "you simply lost your
sensitivity of her."

He shook his head, feeling his hair stick to him. "She was
gone, then she was back."

His expression deep in thought, Talo-Toecan adjusted his
hat and bent to sit.

"Not there!" Strell shouted, and the Master halted halfway
down. Giving a small grunt, he edged three steps to the left
and sat. Strell rubbed his forehead, pinching it to try to drive
the soft headache away. His fingers were slick with rain.

"Strell?" came Talo-Toecan's slow, wary voice. "What are
you doing?"

"Nothing," he said around a sigh. "Nothing. I can't seem
to do anything."

"No," the Master said. "My tracings are resonating. Por-
tions of it, anyway. And Lodesh is skulking in the kitchen, too
far away to account for it."

Strell looked up, his astonishment mirrored by Talo-
Toecan's in the soft dark. "May I look at your tracings?" the
Master asked softly.

Strell blinked. "My—" His breath caught at the implica-
tions. "Yes."

Talo-Toecan's gaze went distant. Strell held himself still, his pulse hammering, knowing Talo-Toecan was peering into his mind, able to see his tangled tracings but none of his thoughts if what Alissa said was true. Even so, he kept his emotions carefully blank. Talo-Toecan's head tilted, and his jaw snapped shut. "Wolves," the Master said, his face ashen as he stared at Strell.

Hope lit through him. "A pattern?" Strell asked. "Did you see a pattern? What am I doing? Am I a Keeper?"

Talo-Toecan shook his head vehemently. "No. No Keeper, Strell. Keeper tracings are very precise, as are Master's, and you're neither. I can promise you that." His eyes went distant. "Wolves," he whispered again.

"But I'm doing something?"

"Yes." He dropped his head into a hand, and Strell's eyes widened at the unusual show of unease. "Tell me, did anyone in your ancestry have, by chance, a foothills background?"

Strell stiffened on the wet bench. The suggestion was an insult to someone born in the plains. Then he swallowed his pride, knowing it had no place in his new, hard-won view of the plains and foothills. "My grandfather had blue eyes," he said shortly, still affronted.

Talo-Toecan took a deep breath. "The Hirdunes are a chartered name, yes? Can you follow your line back to the coast?"

Taking a stick, Strell began to sketch in the soggy earth, the marks washing away as quickly as he wrote them. "Yes," he said uneasily as he finished. "Lodesh is right. My far-back grandmother is his sister. I don't know her background—I imagine Lodesh could tell you—but my far-back grandfather came from the coast." He looked up, reading surprise in the old Master's expression. Strell swallowed a smirk. What did Talo-Toecan expect? Strell had a chartered name. His lineage had been part of his sister's dowries. Of course he would know it.

But the Master had returned his gaze to the fire. "Why were there never any Keepers?" he was muttering intently. "Someone scarred the entire family line and is trying to destroy the evidence." His head rose. "Keribdis?" he breathed.

Strell's jaw clenched. His family had a disturbing history of narrowly escaping annihilation from plague, fire, and more recently, flood. "Why is she trying to wipe my family out?" he demanded. "What the Wolves is wrong with me? With us?"

Talo-Toecan started. "Um," he stammered. "Nothing. I think your misaligned tracings are what's allowing you to find Alissa through time where Lodesh and I can't. The few fragments I can see resonating in my thoughts would be used to find septhama points, among other things. I think you're somehow tapping into that."

"Septhama points are where ghosts come from," Strell said, feeling a stab of alarm.

"Not really, but that's pretty much what Alissa is right now, isn't she?" Looking across the wet night at Strell, his golden eyes seemed to glow, sending a shiver through him. "I have a few mental exercises to help smooth the scar tissue across your tracings," the Master said softly. "I'd have mentioned it earlier, but it seemed pointless. It will help get rid of your headaches."

Strell's eyes went wide. "How do you know I'm having headaches?"

Talo-Toecan stirred as if Strell had confirmed a suspicion. Adjusting his hat so the rain fell at his feet he said, "They stem from a lack of clean flow of energy through your tracings."

"But you said they were a tangled mess."

"They are. But it might help." He hesitated. "Perhaps . . . perhaps you shouldn't say anything to Lodesh about this," Talo-Toecan said. "Until we know for sure."

Strell's breath left him shakily. It sounded like a good idea to him.

30

"Lodesh!"

Lodesh's elbows slid off the narrow table. His breakfast dishes rattled, and he looked sheepishly at the woman who had raised him, standing above him with her hands on her hips.

"For the third time, dear. Will you please take the ward off the window? The morning has grown warm."

"Yes, Mother. Sorry." The ward vanished. The scent of mirth flowers drifted in to mix with the rhythmic, soothing sound of Reeve sharpening his shears.

"Collecting daydreams so early?" his mother said as she settled across from him so the light fell across her sewing.

Reeve gave a small harrumph. "I expect our son still has his thoughts on his gathering last night. From the amount of noise they put out, I would say it was a success."

"Aye," she answered dryly. "A huge success."

Lost in finding the bottom of his cup, Lodesh smiled. It had been a resounding success.

"M-m-m," Reeve grunted. "That reminds me. Someone tore the moss under the westernmost tree. See that it gets replaced. And use the moss still damp with dew so it settles in properly," he admonished, his eyes firmly on his shears.

"Yes, Father." Lodesh flushed. He hadn't known his and Alissa's dance had done any damage until he had gone out to inspect the grove this morning. He had anticipated a severe chastisement. This calm acceptance was unexpected.

His mother squinted as she threaded her needle. "I'm surprised you managed to drag yourself out of bed this early."

"Haven't seen my bed, yet," Lodesh admitted. "I've been helping the stragglers home."

"With Alissa!" his mother cried, setting her work down.

· "No. She left at moonrise. She was called back to the Hold."

"You let her return unescorted?" she said, even more shocked.

"No. Connen-Neute took her." Lodesh's eyes flicked worriedly to Reeve, but he seemed unusually complacent this morning, contenting himself with only a slight grimace.

"Connen-Neute, you say?" his mother mused aloud. "Reeve, dear. What do you suppose Redal-Stan wanted from a Keeper that couldn't wait until morning?" She bit her thread free, and a freshly mended apron fell back into the pile of never-ending mending.

Reeve gave a noncommittal grunt.

Lodesh stacked his dishes to make room for his tea. *What had Redal-Stan wanted?* he wondered. True, Alissa had left early, but he said everything he had intended. And his words had been well-received. Alissa hadn't wanted to leave; Connen-Neute had dragged her away.

Reeve tested his shears' edge before resuming his work. "Too bad such a closed-mouth lout had to take her home."

"Posh," his mother admonished. "It's only a short trip by horse."

Reeve snorted. "It'd be a long walk with Connen-Neute."

"He wouldn't make her walk!" his mother protested. "It would take half the night."

Lodesh smiled, his eyes unseeing out the window. "She walked it. Horses don't like her. It's the oddest thing. She can't get on any but Keribdis's, and Tidbit is in the Hold's stables."

"Oh, the poor dear," his mother sighed. "Just imagine that long, silent walk home."

Lodesh speared a bit of egg he had missed. "Alissa likes his company," he said. "Spent all day with him, helping his speech." Lodesh smiled. "He said two words to me last night."

"Fancy that," his mother said with a gasp. "A *Keeper* teaching a *Master.*"

Lodesh looked up at her tone, but her head was down, busy with the decision to mend the knee of Reeve's favorite work pants or her old bonnet. The pants won.

Lodesh helped himself to the last piece of toast. He spread the strawberry jam thick, wondering how Alissa had earned the trust of the shy Master so easily. He paused, licking a drop of jam before it fell.

Reeve's rhythmic strokes faltered. "I see you've collected their leavings?" he said slowly.

"Huh?" Lodesh blurted, then nodded, his eyes going to a large basket by the door.

Reeve spat on his sharpening stone. "That's an odd assortment. Look. There's even a boot. A *lady's* boot." His eyebrows arched. "Too much mulled wine."

Grinning, Lodesh stretched out and snagged it with a fingertip. It looked suspiciously like Alissa's, or Keribdis's rather. He had found it in the field. There was a soft rattle in the toe, and he tipped it. His heart seemed to stop as a mirth seed rolled into his palm. White-faced, he stared at it. Sati had a mirth seed, but the boot was too small for her. Had Sati and Alissa met?

"How do you lose one boot?" was Reeve's question. "Two I can understand." He smiled and blew a kiss from his oily hands to his wife. "Going barefoot in the meadow is for the young."

"Reeve!" his mother cried, looking ten years younger in her pleased embarrassment.

"But one boot," he continued. "I don't know. . . ."

Lodesh put the seed deep into his pocket. It couldn't be Alissa's boot. He placed the boot on the sill as there was no room on the table. Picking up his toast, he chewed methodically.

Reeve cleared his throat. "I wish you would have let me take you down, dear. At least to laugh at the tipsy ones."

"You know me. I can't stand the noise."

"Aye," he said. "Just like a Master, you are. Too many people, and you hide in the shadows."

A smile passed over Lodesh. Alissa was like that. He cupped his chin in his hands and gazed dreamily out the window. How delightful, wanting to dance in the shadows.

"I would have liked to introduce you to Alissa," Reeve said loudly. "She reminds me of you when we were younger. She even had a daisy chain about her neck. Remember me making you those?"

"Yes, love." She tittered. "But now I know you're jesting. The daisies have been gone for weeks. You'd have to go to the lower elevations for them, nearly the foothills."

The rhythmic sound of metal on stone halted for a moment. "M-m-m. Nonetheless, Alissa had one, fresh as—well—a daisy."

Lodesh hesitated as he lifted his cup. His mouth shut, and he set his tea down. Connen-Neute could have gone to the foothills for them, but Alissa had said she had been with him all day. He wouldn't have left her alone for the time it would have taken to get them and return. Connen-Neute, therefore, must have found them in the city.

Lodesh smiled in anticipation, sipping his tea. He'd ask around, find out who had learned to grow such a late bloomer. He could arrange for a bouquet, now that he knew she liked them.

His mother stirred uneasily. "Lodesh," she scolded gently, "do take that boot off the sill."

Lodesh took it in hand just as a tremulous knock intruded. "I'll get it," he offered. "It's probably someone looking for their hanky."

Reeve bent over his work, never looking up as Lodesh opened the door and his welcoming smile turned to astonishment. "Connen-Neute!"

Dreadfully frightened, Connen-Neute's eyes flicked to Reeve, then the boot. "Thanks," he muttered as he grabbed it and bolted away with a hurried, dignified gait. Clear of the house, he dropped the boot and shifted. Sharp talons grasped the boot, and he took flight, scrabbling to regain the boot as it slipped from him. Then he was gone.

Lodesh stared at the empty field. "It's Alissa's," he whispered. "How did she get home with one boot? Connen-Neute can't carry her. A horse won't carry her. She'd have to . . ."

"No," he said to no one. He closed the door. In a daze, he sat by the fire, suddenly chilled. *She's a Keeper,* he told himself. *Her fingers aren't long, and her eyes aren't those of a Master.* "But neither are Redal-Stan's," he whispered.

And Alissa can ride a horse, he rationalized. *But only Keribdis's,* he thought, his eyes closing in the realization, *and only because she doesn't eat meat.*

Wolves! he thought. *She can craft clothes from her thoughts. But not shoes—not yet, she had said.* Lodesh paled. "Clothes," he mouthed silently. No Keeper spends the effort to learn to craft clothes from their thoughts. The only reason would be if she could—*shift.*

His stomach clenched. How could he have been so blind! He found her in the garden, in the dark, with no shoes. She had spent her afternoon in the foothills making daisy chains with Connen-Neute. That's why she got along with the young Master so well. She was one!

No! he asserted more strongly, refusing to believe it. Alissa wasn't a Master. He couldn't marry a Master. She had to be a Keeper!

Reeve took a breath as if to say something. Then his head dropped, and the rhythmic scraping resumed.

31

"Five . . ." Alissa breathed, eyeing the spheres of flame glowing above the fire in her room. Contained by her fields, her fire had a decidedly odd look. It was quiet, almost the middle of the night, and not a sound disturbed her. Slowly a new sphere formed. Her delight faded as she realized one of her originals was gone. "Hounds," she cursed. After seeing Connen-Neute's smug expression last night, she was determined to master holding six fields before quitting.

She had been trying to practice all day, finding herself continually distracted by Redal-Stan's various, spontaneous, and nonsensical demands. Connen-Neute had been suspiciously scarce, and she wondered if Redal-Stan made a habit of barging into the young Master's thoughts from the top of the tower to send Connen-Neute to fetch something.

Alissa jumped at a soft tap on her door. Her fields collapsed, and she sent her thoughts to find Ren. Sati's forecasting rushed back, twisting her stomach. Steeling herself, she wedged her feet into Connen-Neute's slippers, threw a blanket over the nightdress Nisi had lent her, made a sphere of light, and opened the door.

"Ren!" she said in surprise, for he was dressed for travel, a full pack by his feet.

"Um, hi, Alissa," he stammered, tugging his shirt back into place. "Did I wake you? I saw the light under your door, and I thought maybe . . ."

"I was practicing my fields," she said as she stepped into

the hall, her hands cupped about her globe of light. "What are you doing?" she asked, though it was obvious.

"Um, would you see if you could open the front door for me?" he asked, and Alissa's eyebrows rose. "Downstairs," he rushed. "The front door. Someone warded the outer doors open. Redal-Stan can't close them, so now the inner doors are warded shut for the night." His eyes pleaded. "I don't know how to open those."

"Ren. You can't leave," Alissa said, immediately knowing it was the wrong thing to say.

"Sorry I bothered you." He snatched his pack up. "I'll find a window to climb out of."

"No, wait." Light in hand, Alissa ran after him, the shadows bobbing wildly. She caught him on the landing and put herself in his path. "I never said I wouldn't help," she said breathlessly. "Just tell me what's going on."

Hands clenched, Ren looked at the ceiling, searching for words. Alissa's shoulders drooped. "You were denied Keeper status," she whispered.

"For at least another year," he finished bitterly.

"Ren, you have time. . . ."

"Stop!" he demanded. "That's what Redal-Stan said. I'm tired of waiting. Tired of somedays. He all but promised. Then up and changed his mind. No explanation. Nothing."

Alissa's ire rose. Redal-Stan had sold his vote, and Ren was the one paying for it. "Come on," she said, taking his arm and pulling him to the tower stairs.

"Alissa, wait," Ren said. "It's too late for that."

"But it's not fair!" she insisted.

"No." Ren pulled away. "I'm done. I just want out. I would have left years ago if not for—" Dropping his gaze, he turned away.

Sati's shaduf-dream weighed in Alissa's thoughts like cold clay. *If not for Kally?* she thought. "You have the potential for great abilities, Ren. Don't leave now."

He laughed, not sounding at all like himself. "Potential is useless without a source, and the Masters won't give one to someone they don't trust. They know once I'm done with

my training, I'm leaving." His brow pinched, and his words
grew hushed. "Last year, Yar-Taw caught me listening to an
argument between Talo-Toecan and Keribdis. The Masters
are up to something, Alissa. They're using people somehow.
That's why they won't give me a source. They're afraid if I
have any strength, I might interfere with their plans. I think
the only reason they keep teaching me is so they know
where I am. Or they aren't sure how much I heard."

Alissa clutched her arms around herself, suddenly cold.
"What plans?" she asked, her thoughts returning to Strell's
claim that his family's accidental demise had been ordained.

Ren's eyes dropped, and he shuffled, glancing down the
hall. "Never mind. Forget I said anything. I just want to
leave. Can you open the door?"

Alissa met his eyes, not liking the uneasy feeling he had
instilled in her. He wasn't going to tell her any more, but she
could guess enough. "All right," she said. "I'll try."

"Thank you."

The trip downstairs was silent—both of them not knowing what to say—but the locked inner doors wouldn't open
for her either. "Wolves!" Ren swore, bobbing his head
apologetically. "I have to be away before Kally comes to
start breakfast. I'll lose my nerve if I see her."

Frowning, Alissa thought it over. Ren was going. If Kally
knew, she might go with him. If Alissa could keep them
apart, perhaps the shaduf-dream would remain only a dream.
"I know another way out," Alissa said softly. "Come on."

Ren followed her without question through the dark
kitchen and out into the moonlit garden. The damp smell of
vegetation hung heavy as they wove their way down the
well-manicured paths. Alissa paused, pulling her blanket
tight against the autumn chill, looking at the tower to get her
bearings. "Here, I think," she said, and she squished through
a freshly weeded bed of bergamot, grimacing at the dirt on
her borrowed slippers.

Ren watched as she stared at the wall. "What are you
doing?" he finally asked.

Her arm was cold, stretching out past her blanket as she

held her light high. "Looking for the door," she said, then paused. It was exactly what Useless had said to her last year. Shaking the odd feeling off, she placed her hand upon the chill wall and felt the lock release. Pleased, she opened the door and stepped aside. Her smile faded. "Ren? Be careful."

"I will." He gave her a mirthless smile and stepped past the wall. Taking his knife, he carefully scratched a word on the outside stones. Alissa didn't look; she knew what it said. She hunched into herself, miserable for her apparent inability to change anything. "In case I come back," he said, looking grim in her light. "Be careful, Alissa," he added. "They want something. Nothing is given for free, especially power."

She ignored her wash of emotion. "Ren?" she asked softly. "Where are you going?"

"The plains," he said. "As far away as I can get."

Alissa glanced back at the tower and followed him past the garden's wall. "Go to the coast," she said, trying to change his life for the better.

He squinted in her light. "The coast?"

"It—it's almost too late to make the foothills before the snow," she lied, glad she had stepped beyond the Hold's truth ward.

He shrugged. "All right. I guess it doesn't matter." His gaze dropped. "Here." Ren handed her a thin ribbon, intricately braided with five shades of blue. Alissa blinked, holding the length of fabric in a loose grip. Giving a ribbon was a sign of deep devotion in both the plains and foothills: from man to woman in the foothills, but woman to man in the plains as they refused to do anything the same way those in the foothills did. According to her mother, unmarried plainsmen kept them as a public sign of a young woman, or young woman's mother's, favor.

"It's not for you," Ren blurted, red-faced as he understood her confusion. "It's Kally's. Give it to her for me?" he said, unable to look up. "And tell her good-bye, and that I'll miss our breakfasts together." Hunched, the young man turned away. There was the faint sounds of his footsteps, then nothing.

Alissa listened to the night, unusually silent as the insects had been stilled by the cold. Shivering, she returned to the garden. The door grated shut, and she leaned against it, depressed.

"Sati said you can change the future once you know of it," Beast said, unusually alert.

"So why do I feel like I've sent him to his death?" Alissa whispered. Levering herself up, she made her slow way through the dark, blessedly silent halls to her room. Sleep, though, was elusive, and she found herself turning in her chair. Kally's ribbon lay on her mantel like a silent accusation. The moon was too bright, and the room stuffy. The fire was too smoky and the mice loud. Then, to cap it off, someone decided it was the perfect time to practice their piping.

It was a dance tune, and the rhythm of it drove into her skull like new nails into soft wood. Alissa stared up at the ceiling, growing more and more angry, until, mercifully, it ceased. "Finally," she muttered, and snuggled under her covers. But it started up again. Groaning, Alissa buried her head under her pillow. No wonder the Masters lived in the tower. Much to her exasperation, Beast actually began to hum along.

Alissa stiffened as she recognized the tune as "Taykell's Adventure," cursing herself for having taught Breve the tune. Not only did someone have the audacity to be playing in the middle of the night, but from the sound of it, they were right next door.

"Fine!" she snapped. Her nightdress tangled as she lurched to her feet and stormed into the hall. A soft, polite knock was ignored, and a fierce thought found the room empty. They must know how to block her search. "You in there," she whispered loudly. "Stop it!" But the music continued. Alissa knocked again and tried the handle. It was locked.

"Connen-Neute!" Alissa wailed into the young Master's

thoughts, and his frightened presence jumped to wakefulness.

"*Alissa! What? Are you hurt?*"

"*No-o-o-o,*" she moaned. "*Someone is playing a pipe in the room next to mine. They've locked the door and they don't hear me.*"

"*There's no one there,*" he mumbled. "*Go to sleep.*" And he sighed sleepily.

"*Windmate!*" Beast snapped. "*Come open this door.*"

"*Huh!*" Connen-Neute was suddenly very much awake. "*Coming.*"

Alissa paced the hall, going more angry when she realized her steps were in time with the music. After what seemed an exorbitantly long time, Connen-Neute's light appeared at the end of the hall. "Finally," she whispered as he stumbled even with her and touched the door.

"Alissa," he mumbled, just this side of sleep. "No one's in there. That's my lock."

"Ashes!" she cried. "It's driving me moonstruck. Can't you hear it?"

He shook his head, confused. There was a flash of resonance across her tracings too quick to catch as he unlocked the door. She triumphantly shoved the door open to find . . . nothing. The room was empty. But the music remained.

The piper began an achingly familiar tune, and Alissa gasped, recognizing it. "That's my song!" she cried, staring at Connen-Neute. "The one Strell wrote for me!" And then the empty spot that Strell had left in her was empty no longer. "Where?" she cried, frantically spinning about. "Strell! Where are you?"

"*Alissa. Thank the stars that guide us!*"

It was Strell. She heard him, and she panicked. The faint whisper of his presence faded. "*No!*" she shouted into her mind. "*Strell! Come back!*"

"*Listen,*" Strell soothed, his thoughts so faint as to be almost imagined. "*Talo-Toecan says you must put yourself entirely at a still point, or we will lose everything.*"

She took a shuddering breath, focusing on the thinning threads of Strell's thoughts, gathering a line here, one there, struggling to bind his presence into something she could hold. "Still point," she whispered. Sinking to her knees, she appeared to go comatose.

3²

Connen-Neute watched with little surprise as Alissa turned white and sank to her knees. Her wild, frantic eyes closed, and she collapsed. It might have been alarming, but he had come to accept the unusual when it came to Alissa. He wasn't worried yet, just concerned.

With a last, wistful thought of his interrupted sleep upon the Hold's roof, he placed his and Alissa's lights atop the mantel and gathered her up to set her in the room's only chair. He draped her blanket over her, tucking it under her chin. Alissa's light abruptly dimmed, and he frowned. That shouldn't have happened. Gone out? Yes. But not dim. She hadn't consciously shut it down. It had been left to run at an involuntarily reduced rate. Only now did he think to call Redal-Stan, and his gentle, tentative query was met with the expected grumbles and groans.

"Unless someone is on fire, go away," came the Master's barely recognizable thought.

"Ah, it's Alissa," he offered, feeling Redal-Stan snap awake. *"I'm with her in the Keepers' hall. She's collapsed into a deep trance. At least, I think it's a trance."*

Unease filled him. Perhaps he should have told Redal-Stan immediately. *"Redal-Stan?"* he called, then turned as the old Master slid to a halt in the hall. He appeared more harried and disheveled than usual in a plain robe. Not acknowledging Connen-Neute, he strode into the room and set his light beside the other two. He crouched by her, frowning.

"Start from the beginning," Redal-Stan said tersely.

"She was complaining of music being played in this room."

"But you locked it," he interrupted.

"Yes. I told her no one was in here, but Bea—er—she insisted I come and open it." Connen-Neute shook his head. *"She really can't open any door but those keyed for Keepers."*

The old Master gestured impatiently for him to continue.

"So I opened it. There was no one in here. But I might have heard music."

"Really." Redal-Stan stood, his sun-darkened face creased in worry.

Connen-Neute nodded. *"She then became agitated, called for Strell, and collapsed."* He fidgeted with his sleeve, glad Redal-Stan was here to shoulder the responsibility.

"Aye," the Master said as he bent low over Alissa. "It's a meditative state. It's a good thing you woke me. This is exactly what I wanted you to watch for." He reached to touch her, but just before contact, Alissa's eyes jumped to a wide-eyed alertness.

"Alissa!" Redal-Stan said, taking a startled step back. "You're all right!"

Connen-Neute's feeling of unease solidified into a sour lump as her frightened eyes flicked from Redal-Stan's to his. Burn him to ash. It wasn't Alissa. It was that beast! His heart pounded and he almost bolted, but he froze at her panic. She looked scared, like a child discovering the adult she'd been following belonged to someone else. With any luck, Redal-Stan would think it was Alissa. But even as he thought it, Redal-Stan peered sharply at her.

"Alissa?" he whispered, then straightened, his breath slipping from him in a hiss. "Slow now," he said to Connen-Neute. "Move to the window." Never taking his eyes from Beast, he backed up and fumbled with the door until it latched.

Ramrod straight, Connen-Neute held his uncertain ground.

"Move," the old Master said. "She's gone feral, though I've never heard of it happening while one is still in a human form."

Connen-Neute shifted from foot to foot but didn't move.

"I said sit in the window, fledgling!" Redal-Stan whispered. "We might still be able to salvage this. She hasn't flown yet. Perhaps because it's night, she can't."

Beast stiffened, looking affronted. "I can fly at night just as well as you can, old one." Her eyes widened, and she clasped her hand over her mouth. Her accent was odd and precise, every syllable spoken with care.

"You speak!" Redal-Stan stood stock-still.

Beast's mouth twisted. The look she gave Connen-Neute spoke of a sophisticated humor he hadn't expected. She knew her words had destroyed any chance of passing as Alissa. With a resigned sigh, she settled herself. Her blanket pooled about her knees, and Connen-Neute blinked. Her smallest movement had a sultry slyness, and her slow voice carried the same.

"Of course I speak," she said. "I know everything Alissa does, and a few things she's forgotten. And as for keeping me grounded? You couldn't catch me." She turned an appraising eye to Connen-Neute, and he took an alarmed breath. "Neither could you, windmate." She paused. "Not yet. Alissa's teacher is the only one who can bring me down, and he cheated. He didn't want to play at all." Beast pouted.

Redal-Stan's mouth gaped. "Wolves," he finally managed.

"Wolves, indeed," she said with a sniff.

"Redal-Stan," Connen-Neute interrupted. "I'd like you to meet Beast."

Beast extended her hand, and Redal-Stan backed away. "What the Bone and Ash is going on!" he cried, his voice echoing painfully. "Alissa is feral, and you act as if it's nothing!"

"It is," Connen-Neute said dryly, deciding he could sit in the windowsill if he wasn't being told to do so. He winced as his teacher's befuddlement predictably turned to anger.

"You said you would tell me of any atypical behavior!" Redal-Stan shouted, pointing at Alissa. "What the Wolves do you call this?"

Connen-Neute allowed a whisper of anger to color his

words. "This is typical behavior for Alissa. Talo-Toecan allowed her to keep her feral consciousness."

"What!" It was an appalled shout.

Beast curled her legs under her. "Allowed isn't the word I would choose. He hasn't figured it out yet, is all."

Redal-Stan looked at her in horror.

There was a soft knock. "Alissa?" came an urgent whisper from behind the closed door. "Are you in there? I heard shouting."

"Come in, Lodesh!" Beast called, her eyes glowing with a sudden desire.

"Go away, Lodesh!" Redal-Stan thundered as the door was flung open and Lodesh all but fell into the room, catching himself as he saw Connen-Neute and Redal-Stan. "I said, go away," Redal-Stan growled. "This doesn't concern you."

"Really, Redal-Stan," Connen-Neute said apologetically. *"I didn't break my word. You told me to watch for atypical behavior, not to necessarily tell you about it."*

Redal-Stan froze. Slowly he turned to Connen-Neute.

"And this is normal," Beast added. Then she bit her lower lip. "For the most part."

There was an audible snap as Redal-Stan closed his mouth. He turned to Lodesh standing uncertainly by the door. "Out," the Master demanded, his expression turning choleric when Lodesh shut the door and leaned back against it to become nearly immobile.

Lodesh swallowed hard. "With respect, I'm not leaving until Alissa asks me to."

Turning a bright red, Redal-Stan pointed to the hall.

A low sigh drew Connen-Neute's attention, and he froze. Beast had curled up with her knees to her chin, her arms clasped about her legs to make her look both defenseless and artlessly alluring. "I'm glad you're here, Lodesh," she said, her gray eyes almost black.

Lodesh grew pale. "That's not Alissa," he whispered.

Redal-Stan gave him a mirthless, disgusted look. "Do you think? Sure you want to stay?"

The Keeper took a step back. "What . . . what's wrong with her?"

Running a hand over his bald head, Redal-Stan closed his eyes in a long blink. "Alissa has an alter consciousness. She is insane, remember?" He turned and paced before the hearth. "Beast, meet Lodesh. Lodesh, Beast."

"We've already met," she said.

Connen-Neute could almost see the Keeper's thoughts fall into place. "Hounds," Lodesh whispered. "That was you on the dance boards. That wasn't Alissa, that was you," he said, and Beast beamed.

Redal-Stan fumbled for the edge of the unmade cot and sat down. "You mean to tell me you've been flopping back-and-forth like a card? How many times has this happened?"

Beast's face fell, turning her from a sensual goddess to a child. "Three—I think."

"That was you dancing the Triene?" Lodesh said, sounding disappointed.

Beast smiled a wise, ancient smile. "No. That was Alissa. Mostly. I think."

"You think?" bellowed Redal-Stan, and Connen-Neute watched his teacher struggle to maintain his composure and regain control of the conversation all at once. "Can't you tell?"

"Mostly." Beast winced. "But it's getting hard." She looked up, her eyes growing frightened. "It's never been so before. I try to be good," she said. "I promised. But she keeps leaving. And I don't like it!" she finished with an unhappy cry.

Silence fell in the small room lit by three globes of warded light. Lodesh moved to a corner, clearly trying to stay out of Redal-Stan's sight and therefore keep himself in the room. Seeing Beast begin to tremble, Connen-Neute made a robe and draped the soft gray over her shoulders as she didn't seem to know to pull her blanket back up. Whether her shaking was from the cold or her fright, he couldn't tell.

"It's her disconnection from Strell," Connen-Neute said quietly, and Lodesh turned at the unfamiliar voice. Connen-

Neute's brow furrowed. He had more to say, and because of Lodesh, he should say it aloud. Glancing at Beast, he gathered his courage. If she could speak in entire paragraphs, he could, too.

"From what I have guessed," he said slowly. "Strell was instrumental in restoring her sentience less than a year ago. She hasn't had time to find other reference points, and without him, there's nothing left to hold her to the now." He turned to Beast. "Am I right?" he asked, and she nodded, looking scared. "And if you don't find a way to return, Alissa will eventually go feral?" he finished.

"I think so." It was a frightened whisper, and Connen-Neute hated having to force her to admit it aloud. For all her feral wisdom, Beast had a child's ability to cope.

Redal-Stan put his elbows on his knees, his anger replaced by curiosity. "You're frightened," he said. "I would have thought you'd be pleased."

Beast looked mournfully at him thorough Alissa's gray eyes. "Alissa has gifted me with something far beyond the small wisdoms I have shared with her. I don't want her to lose her sentience," she whispered. "A beast doesn't remember love."

At that, Redal-Stan sat back in undisguised astonishment.

Beast blinked, her gaze going distant for a heartbeat. Then she grew dismayed. "Oh, the string is going loose. She can barely hear him now."

"Him?" Redal-Stan questioned, and Connen-Neute strained, hearing a distant something on the edges of his awareness.

"Her piper." Beast glanced about the room as if looking for something.

"No," Redal-Stan said. "I won't accept that Alissa can hear a commoner across time."

"Time," Beast lectured, turning irate at his disbelief, "is no barrier for thought, old one, or distance, if the string is taut and strong."

"Not true," he argued. "If you go beyond the curve of the earth, you lose contact."

Beast looked at him smugly, a sliver of her original sultry air returning. "You're very learned, old one. But in this instance, you're less correct than usual."

From the corner came a small sound. "Time?" Lodesh whispered.

"Do you know what you're implying?" Redal-Stan sputtered.

Connen-Neute would have laughed in other circumstances. "She said you were wrong."

"Not that," the Master snapped. "What she suggests is impossible."

"She can hear commoners?" This time, Lodesh sounded bewildered.

"Impossible for you, maybe," Beast said. "But I taught Alissa how to listen, and she taught a beast how to love. Which do you think is more impossible?"

Redal-Stan's mouth snapped shut.

Beast rose in a supple movement so seductive and graceful that Connen-Neute caught his breath with a thrilled alarm. Slipping to Lodesh, she took his hand. His eyes widened, and she pulled his head against hers and whispered, "Alissa is frightened to admit it, but I think you ought to know that she does love you, not like her piper, but loves you nevertheless." She gave him a faint smile. "I'm here, Lodesh. Dance with me again?" Her gaze grew frighteningly aroused, filled with a desire and want so guileless that it shocked Connen-Neute.

Then, with a sigh and a slow blink, Beast slipped away. Awareness filled Alissa's gray eyes. She stepped back as if to catch her balance and dropped Lodesh's hand. Drawing her robe tighter about her shoulders, she took them in. "I guess," she offered slowly in her own voice, "I have some explaining to do?"

33

Alissa breathed deeply, looking for the smell of the missing rain. It had been warmer, too, in Strell's time. There was a fire in her room next door, but Strell's presence was here, even if she couldn't hear him anymore, and she wouldn't leave. Exhaling, she turned to Redal-Stan and Connen-Neute. "But I simply can't go feral. I explained that."

Redal-Stan shook his head, offering her the honey-soaked veal Lodesh had brought up. The Master had been keeping Lodesh out of the room with a variety of tasks. Currently he was in search of tea. Shuddering, Alissa refused the meat, and Redal-Stan set the plate down with a disbelieving slowness. Connen-Neute slid closer, and the nasty bits began to disappear.

Unaware of his pilfering, Redal-Stan settled himself on the ugly cot with his elbows on his knees. "It's inevitable," he said. "You lack a connection to this time, and it's going to do everything it can to minimize your impact." He hesitated as he realized the plate held less than it had a moment before. Frowning, he moved the plate to the cot. "Just by being here you're making changes. Small ones, but they're building on each other."

Connen-Neute rose. Pretending to stretch, he resettled himself closer to the plate.

"Time, I believe, isn't so inflexible that it can't accommodate small shifts," Redal-Stan said. "One does have free will." He smoothly took up the plate as Connen-Neute reached for it, setting it down on his other side. He deliberately chose a bite and slowly chewed. "But time, like water, takes the shape of the vessel it's in."

Alissa sighed. "Meaning . . ."

"You don't belong." He shifted his shoulders. "Events will occur that will minimize your impact. If you didn't help Connen-Neute with his verbalization, someone else would."

She nodded. "You mean I'll go feral or die."

"Hounds, Alissa," Connen-Neute thought as he gasped. *"Don't be so morbid."*

Redal-Stan blinked, surprised as well at her matter-of-fact facade. "Probably," he said. "Considering our conversation with Beast, I would say the former. The changes you have made will either be buried beneath an accumulated history of events, or your actions would have been performed by some-one else to begin with."

"Or," Beast said dryly to Alissa alone, *"we are here to do these things."*

"But how does that make me feral?" Alissa protested.

"Ah." Redal-Stan nodded. "That is the second half. Connen-Neute is correct. Your reference points are wrong. Last spring, you completely redefined yourself. You went from a foothills girl to a student of a supposed legendary fortress, to a Master of the same, all in six months. Sand and Wind, Alissa. You had to reconcile a lifetime of beliefs with a new set of seemingly conflicting ones. It's no wonder we go insane when we first shift. We lose our first, most real iden-tity: our physical self." He glanced at the door, clearly want-ing the tea. "It takes time to create a new self-image," he continued. "Time and stability. A single summer isn't enough. A decade of summers, maybe."

"But I shift fine," she said, grimacing as Redal-Stan of-fered her the last piece of meat.

"Reconciling a new physical form is relatively easy," he said. "It's the mental image that is harder. You've lost a life-time of references, and your self-image has become fuzzy about the edges."

Connen-Neute slumped on the sill. *"And once a certain threshold is reached?"*

"She will go feral and stay that way," Redal-Stan finished. For a moment there was silence. "When Strell returned your sentience, I believe you unwittingly made him your lodestone. You undoubtedly were building on that, forming additional reference points as you found what was fixed and what was subject to change, but your core was centered about him."

"And he's not here," Alissa whispered, feeling cold.

"You're relying upon imperfect reference points," Redal-Stan said.

"The Hold," Connen-Neute interrupted. *"The grove, her room, the garden."*

"Which would work," Redal-Stan said, "except they aren't exactly the same points that you've been building upon the last six months. The subtleties aren't there. The slant of the sun, the scent of the air; they're betraying you even as you struggle to make them fit what you already know. I believe the only reason you didn't go feral the moment you got here is because of your familiarity with your—er—alter consciousness. Anyone else would have gone feral within the span of six heartbeats." His eyes went distant in some private thought.

There was a whisper of fabric as Connen-Neute turned to the door. Faintly she heard Lodesh returning with the tea, and nothing more was said until he appeared in the open doorway.

"Ah, Lodesh!" Redal-Stan held out an eager hand. "Thank you. There's a long night ahead." Redal-Stan poured out the tea into three cups, leaving the fourth empty. "But there's no need for you to endure a sleepless night. You should return to your bed. You will have a busy day tomorrow."

"But I want to stay!" he said. "I don't care that Alissa has two selves." He dropped his eyes, furtively glancing at Alissa. "I—don't mind Beast."

Alissa felt a rush of gratitude, but Redal-Stan ran a hand over his head. "Go to bed. We have to get rid of Beast, not promote her. Blessed randy Stryska boys."

Lodesh drew himself up stiffly. "That's not what I meant." It was at that unfortunate moment Alissa set her mug of tea down with a grimace. It *was* bitter. She could taste it clearly.

Lodesh saw, and her frown shattered what little pride he had left.

"Ashes. I can't even make a decent pot of tea, can I," Lodesh said tightly.

"It's fine!" Alissa said, taking a gulp and forcing a smile.

Lodesh looked from her anxious expression, to Redal-Stan's untasted cup, to Connen-Neute's drink set carefully out of arm's reach. "Yes, I can see that," he muttered. "I'll leave. There's no need to send me on any more useless errands."

"Lodesh, wait," she pleaded, but he was gone.

Alissa rose in an awkward lurch to follow him, only to be held back by Redal-Stan's dark hand. "We have more pressing issues," he murmured.

"More important than Lodesh's feelings?" she snapped. "He's the only one besides me who thinks Beast is not a problem to be weeded out."

"Lodesh's future," Redal-Stan said. Reminded of last night's decision to offer him as Warden, Alissa sat back down in dismay. There was the distant sound of a closing door.

"The chartered families have predictably chosen an alternative Warden," Redal-Stan said, and Alissa held her breath. Perhaps Lodesh would be spared. "They have chosen Earan," he finished. "The city will decide between them tomorrow."

Her hopes died to less than ash. The masses would choose Lodesh. She knew it.

Redal-Stan sipped his tea, swallowing as if in pain. "It falls to me to accompany him to Ese'Nawoer tomorrow." He paused. "I don't want to. You will take him."

Alissa looked up in annoyance. "I don't want to, either."

"I don't care," he said mildly. Connen-Neute stirred uneasily at her defiance, but Redal-Stan was unruffled. "I wasn't the one who suggested he be considered," Redal-Stan said dryly, shifting Alissa's anger to guilt.

"I'll go," she whispered.

"That's what I said," he drawled. "Besides, no one but you will be able to keep him from running once he realizes we want to make him Warden. Connen-Neute will go as well, as the official representative of the Hold."

Redal-Stan stood and stretched for the ceiling, looking like a tired plainsman, not a Master, in his nondescript robe. Collapsing in on himself, he motioned Connen-Neute to fetch the two remaining lights from the mantel. "I suggest you get what sleep you can," Redal-Stan said. "You leave shortly after sunrise."

Alissa didn't move from the uncomfortable chair that somehow existed in both versions of Strell's room. "You said we had a long night," she said. "Aren't we going to find out how to get me home?"

With a series of hand waves, Redal-Stan ushered Connen-Neute out. He hesitated before grabbing Lodesh's pot of tea. "Go to sleep, Squirrel," he said in the new shadows. "I never said I was going to bed."

The door shut with a creak. *"Strell?"* Alissa called, getting no response. Not surprised, she burrowed farther under Connen-Neute's robe, unwilling to leave for even the moment it would take to get her pillow. Strell was here. She wasn't going to move, even to shift the empty, rank-smelling tray of veal to the hall.

Alissa closed her eyes before the cold hearth in a room that wasn't hers, clothed in a nightdress that belonged to someone else, covered by a robe given to her by yet another, falling asleep to the sound of Beast humming a lullaby into their thoughts.

34

"Curse you, Lodesh," Strell shouted, trembling in his anger and frustration. "I talked to her! I still would be if you hadn't scared Connen-Neute away!"

"I said I was sorry about that." Lodesh stood just inside the piper's door. His words were sincere, but Talo-Toecan could see a shadow of insolence, or perhaps relief, in his stance. It took all his restraint not to respond to the Warden's growing lack of tact. Almost, it seemed as if Lodesh was glad he had broken the link between Strell and Alissa.

"Lodesh," Talo-Toecan said, edging forward in the hard chair before the piper's unlit hearth. "I feel the dampness in the air tonight." He hesitated. "Go make tea."

The Keeper took a breath to protest, then, realizing he was being asked to leave, spun and strode away. The sharp sounds of his booted feet faded. Talo-Toecan listened to the night's rain as he gathered his thoughts. In direct opposition, Strell began to pace. Seeing his long, jerky steps, Talo-Toecan wondered if the piper might be just this side of insanity.

Little air made it through Strell's one small window, and it was stuffy. Talo-Toecan's tired gaze ran over the bare walls and ugly furniture. It seemed cold, though the night was balmy. His globe of light made sharp shadows and hard corners. Strell's room looked like a cell. "You're free to search the annexes for anything to make your stay more comfortable," he said.

Strell halted, startling him with the wild look in his eyes.

"Why? Alissa is the only one who ever thought your offer of shelter was made out of any genuine attempt at hospitality."

Talo-Toecan blinked, peeved at the wash of guilt Strell's words evoked. Giving up trying to find a comfortable position on the hard chair, he moved himself to the floor and put his back to the cold hearth. The rain gusted in to mist the piper staring in frustration out the window. Talo-Toecan began to fashion a ward to keep it out, then halted. Strell hadn't asked him to.

He was, Talo-Toecan realized, serving the piper badly. Strell was doing all he could to get Alissa back, while the Warden did nothing. Less than nothing. Talo-Toecan's eyes drifted to the crack in the wall. He would fix that, he decided.

Strell came to rest on the sill, slumping with an exhaustion that told of little food and even less sleep. "She finally heard me," he said with a sigh, the harsh lines of worry relaxing. "Hounds. She felt so good as her thoughts melted into mine." He stiffened as he looked at Talo-Toecan. "She says she's all right," he said nervously. "But worried about the lapses of control she has been having."

Talo-Toecan smiled. "She isn't used to having anyone tell her what to do. With any luck, she will return to us better than she left."

"No." Strell shook his head. "I don't think that's what she meant." Driven from the sill by the rain, Strell hovered uncertainly before sitting on the edge of his bed. "She's sometime before the walls go up at Ese'Nawoer," he continued. "Most of the Masters are gone for the fall season. There are only two about, Connen-Neute and a Redal-Sen or Stone."

"Redal-Stan," Talo-Toecan offered, and Strell nodded. Talo-Toecan's brow rose. Lodesh had been about during that time. His eyes narrowed as he considered the possibility that Lodesh was keeping something from them. "I think," he said slowly, "I have an idea of when she is, but more important is her ideas as to why your contact is unreproducible upon command."

Strell leaned forward. "She doesn't know. But if we can talk, won't the rest follow?"

Turning from his hopeful expression, Talo-Toecan felt a stab of worry. "I don't know," he said. "Next time you reach her, ask what Redal-Stan believes. He was the foremost authority on tripping the lines. Taught it to most of the Masters in his day. After discovering the ward of healing, he was granted a leave of absence from his duties to study tripping the lines in more detail. We never found his remains."

Breathing deeply of the night, Talo-Toecan looked for the missing scent of book paste. Redal-Stan had been like a grouchy uncle, a proud father, and a demanding teacher all in one. Strell was silent; even the nervous shifting of his foot had stilled. "I'm sorry," he offered.

Talo-Toecan briefly met his eyes. "I was the last to see him. We expect either he did something that blew himself to ash, or a bloodthirsty zealot out to revenge his sheep surprised him while he was tripping the lines. We lose most of our feral kin that way," he said with a sigh. "They let humans get far too close, underestimating their deadly capabilities." A gust of mist blew in, darkening the floor. "Redal-Stan would know if she can return."

Strell's head rose, his eyes dark with an inner pain. Talo-Toecan watched him take a deep breath, shifting his entire body as he exhaled. "There has to be a way to get her back," Strell said. "She's proved the impossible can be done. We have to find out how."

Unable to bring himself to agree, Talo-Toecan looked away. It was a fool's hope. The sound of Lodesh coming with the tea prompted him to pull the battered footstool closer.

"There's got to be a way," Strell agonized as the Warden walked in.

Not looking at anyone, Lodesh set the pot and three cups on the footstool. Talo-Toecan served the tea, the sound of liquid pouring into the cups mixing with the rain. He suspiciously watched Lodesh take his first, hot sip. There was only one autumn the Hold had been so empty of Masters. And Lodesh had been there. Was this guilt he was seeing?

"If only," Strell whispered, seeming consumed by his misery, "you hadn't frightened Connen-Neute away. We might have talked longer, perhaps figured this out."

"How many times do I have to say I'm sorry," Lodesh muttered, then froze as he noticed Talo-Toecan's eyes mistrustingly upon him.

Talo-Toecan's long fingers interlaced about the cup. "So, Strell. Are you still convinced the more parallel we make our separate situations, the better our chances to make contact again?"

"Yes." Strell straightened. Fear, anticipation, doubt, and hope showed in him.

"Then perhaps I should leave," Talo-Toecan said slowly.

"Leave?" It was a horrified shout.

"I was in the plains that particular fall with—with Keribdis." Talo-Toecan gulped the bitter tea to distance himself from the memory. Almost he had understood her. Almost she had understood him.

"You don't think it's that sensitive, do you?" Strell asked. "Wouldn't a raku length be enough? I've always had to coax Connen-Neute that close before I noticed any difference."

Talo-Toecan eyed Lodesh. "What do you think, Warden?" he said, and his pulse quickened as the man flushed. It was so subtle, any eyes but a Master's would have missed it.

"I would think," Lodesh said slowly, "that a raku length of distance would be sufficient."

"Then you *do* believe I talked to her!" Strell cried.

Lodesh frowned. "I guess I do," he admitted.

Talo-Toecan watched the exchange with interest. The question now was whether he should believe the Warden. He took a sip of tea and set the cup down in disgust. "By the Hounds, Lodesh," he complained. "Didn't you even boil the water?"

"There is nothing wrong with my tea," he said, standing up and storming from the room.

Strell watched him go, his eyes wide. "What's bothering him?" he asked.

Talo-Toecan's brow furrowed in mistrust. "I'm not sure—yet."

35

There were three of them in the predawn darkness of his room in the Keepers' hall. Lodesh mumbled, shifting his covers to look through his cracked lids. He sent a whisper of thought to see who they were. Before he could get an idea, one said, "He's awake. Get him."

Lodesh bolted upright. A blanket tangled him. An arm went about his neck, a hand over his mouth. Something pinned his ankles. A muzzy field settled over him, keeping him from sensing anything with his tracings. Frightened, he set his thoughts to a ward of destruction.

"Wait!" he heard Alissa call. "Lodesh. Wait!"

Immediately he stopped, and the hand fell away from his mouth. "Alissa?" he whispered. A blindfold quickly replaced the blanket, too fast and skilled for him to glimpse anything. He gratefully breathed the cooler air.

"Lodesh. I'm sorry," Alissa pleaded. There was a tentative touch on his arm. "You're going to be all right. I promise." Someone swung his feet to the floor. "I promise," she repeated, sounding as if she were trying to convince herself.

"Foot?" a gray voice said, and Lodesh started. Connen-Neute? What did the young Master want with him? There were repeated taps on the floor, and Lodesh obligingly lifted his foot. The familiar fit of his riding boots slid onto first his right then his left foot.

"You need the necessity?" came Breve's recognizable grumble, and Lodesh shook his head. He'd only been asleep a few hours, and he felt ill from the lack of sleep.

A firm grip on his shoulder pulled him up. "Put this on," Breve muttered, and Lodesh slipped his arms into a long coat whose hem bumped about his calves. It smelled of mirth trees.

Fumbling fingers tried to fasten the buttons. "I'll get them," Lodesh said, annoyed. The heavy buttons were metal, and the pattern graven on them teased a memory. He left the lower half of the coat open. He had on boots; they were going by horse. But where?

"All right," Breve said, sounding tired. "Let's go."

His door opened, and he balked. "Alissa? What's going on?"

Her touch drew him into the hall where a more aggressive attempt would have turned him violent. "I'm sorry, Lodesh," she said unhappily. "No one will hurt you. I promise."

Lodesh counted the stairs all the way to the floor of the great hall. It was quiet, before the students woke. Then someone coughed, and he realized the students were assembled, and he was walking through them to the door. His warded thoughts could sense nothing. Only his trust in Alissa kept him from digging in his heels and demanding to know what was going on.

It was in relief that he heard the Hold's doors open and the comforting, jangling sounds of saddled horses. A familiar nicker and a nudge in his chest brought a nervous smile, and his hands fluttered over Frightful's bony head. The horse's ears flicked back at Connen-Neute's presence. "Can't I just walk?" he heard Alissa complain, and Breve's gruff, sympathetic answer. There was a soft jingling followed by a short gasp, and Lodesh knew Alissa was mounted.

"Your turn," Breve directed at him. Still blindfolded, Lodesh swung onto Frightful. As soon as he was settled, the Keeper yanked his arm, pulling Lodesh's ear close to his mouth. "And if you're thinking of taking off that blindfold and bolting, I warn you that sorry excuse of an animal you're on is tied to Tidbit. Alissa will fall." He hesitated. "Understand?"

Lodesh nodded, and he felt the weight of a hat hit his head. Slowly he straightened, raising a hand to its unfamiliar shape.

He was kidnapped and forced to wear clothes he couldn't see. But he was too worried to be outraged.

"Shall we wait?" Alissa said.

Breve made a small sound. "I can bring him out myself. Lodesh is the more difficult of the two. Connen-Neute?" His tone shifted to respect. "Would you care to accompany Alissa? These two horses show less fear." And with Alissa's nervous laugh, they moved forward.

The morning sun was upon his face. Its autumn strength gave little warmth, and he was glad for the hat and coat. They rode slowly east to Ese'Nawoer. It would have been wonderful riding with Alissa, even with Connen-Neute along, but he barely heard the birds or felt the wonderful snap in the air, so consumed by his worry was he.

What had he done? Was he being publicly punished? He felt his hat again, searching for the ropes of ridicule, but it seemed ordinary Keeper garb. The coat, too, was of a fine fabric, not the coarse cloth of the damned. He strained his ears as they went into shadow and the acidic smell of rotting leaves and hemlock came to him. Soft thumps told him there were four horses, the last two some ways behind. "Wolves take you, Breve," he heard his brother Earan curse faintly. "Tell me what's going on, or I swear I'll shove you from your horse."

"What do you think is going on?" Breve snapped back.

With a quick breath, Lodesh knew. Earan was up for Wardenship now that both their uncle and father were gone. That meant he . . . was . . . too! "No." A shift of balance, and Frightful halted. "I won't do it," he said, reaching for his blindfold.

"Please," Alissa pleaded, sounding scared as she stopped him. "Don't make this harder."

"I won't be the Warden. They can't make me," he said, hearing panic in his voice.

Small and alone, Alissa whispered, "Yes, they can."

"You said everyone had a choice!" he exclaimed.

"They do," she said unhappily. "But sometimes, someone else makes them for you."

Frightful sidestepped, nickering nervously. "A problem?"

Connen-Neute's voice ghosted out of Lodesh's enforced blindness.

Terrified of what was happening and unable to stop it, Lodesh weighed his options. He could refuse, he rationalized frantically. Yes. He would refuse. They couldn't make him do anything. "There's no problem," he said stiffly.

"Thank you," Alissa whispered, and he jumped at her touch on his arm as they resumed.

They entered the city in an unreal envelope of silence. He never would have known it but for the clop of hooves echoing against the houses and hard-packed streets. In the distance he heard the rhythmic clanging of a blacksmith's forge, then nothing. The scent of spice cakes came to him, and he placed himself: third arc out on a small street headed for the field.

Behind him he heard, "Where are we, Breve?" and Breve's hushed reply, "West quarter."

Everyone was gone, Lodesh decided. Gone or silent, he couldn't tell with that cursed ward over him. He had never felt so alone. The clop of hooves became thuds, and the smell of damp earth rose high. Frightful grew frisky as a bachelor herd swung close and shied away at the scent of Connen-Neute. Their rumble vanished, leaving only the sound of the grass against the horses' chests. Slowly the rich, intoxicating scent of the mirth trees came to him. A faint rumble drifted on the air, unrecognized. Frightful halted of his own accord with a nervous head toss.

"You'll be walkin' from here," Reeve muttered from right before him. "I'll not have those horses on my moss."

"Good morning, Reeve," Alissa said, hardly recognizable for the guilt in her voice.

"Alissa," he replied stiffly. "I'm telling you I don't like this."

"Neither do I," she said with a sigh.

"Here," Reeve said to Alissa. "I'll help you from that flaky beast before she spills you."

Lodesh hastily dismounted to stand helplessly by Frightful. "Father?" Lodesh pleaded. "Don't let them do this to me."

"Hush, boy," he said gruffly as the sound of Breve and

Earan grew close. "We don't have to like all the choices we make."

"But, Father," Lodesh whispered, and he turned at Alissa's touch. She was trembling, and he grasped her arm as she stumbled and nearly fell.

"Sorry," came her breathless murmur. "I don't feel well all of a sudden." She leaned heavily upon him. "Ashes, my head hurts. Give me a moment."

Alarmed, Lodesh cast sightlessly about. "Father?" he called.

"By the Hounds, Alissa!" Reeve exclaimed, and Alissa's weight vanished. "There you go. Hold my arm. You can sit in the tent. Did that fool of a Master let you come out here when you weren't feeling well?"

"I was fine this morning," she protested weakly. "I didn't sleep much last night."

Lodesh reached for his blindfold. "Enough," he said, finding his arms pinned to his sides.

"Not yet, Keeper," came Connen-Neute's voice, low and silky.

"But Alissa . . ."

There was a hesitation. "She's fine." Worry colored Connen-Neute's voice, and the Master's grip vanished. "Just pale."

Connen-Neute escorted him under the chill shade of the mirth trees until he felt the walls of a tent about him and his blindfold was removed. He blinked in the amber light filtering through the yellow folds of fabric. Alissa sat cross-legged upon a cushion in a corner. Her head was in her hands, and she looked as exhausted as if she had run to Ese'Nawoer instead of riding. She smiled weakly up at him and mouthed the words, "Feeling better," but he knew she wasn't.

Earan and Breve were in a corner. His brother was dressed in a short, gold-colored tunic with matching trousers. It was elegant, with braided coils and silver buttons. He looked every finger-width the Warden, and he gave Lodesh a forced smile. Lodesh dropped his eyes to his own attire, and his eyebrows rose. The coat was his usual deep green, and though simpler of decoration than Earan's, it was exquisitely cut.

"Where did this come from?" he said in awe, looking over his hat. It was as tasteful as the rest, something he would commission if he dared dip into his birth father's coffers.

Reeve gave a pleased grunt. "Your mother and Nisi picked it out with Marga's help."

Lodesh's face went slack. It would take weeks to commission a suit this fine. "You knew this would happen?" he asked.

"Not till last night," he said with a sad smile. "They used to be your father's."

"Oh." Lodesh grew thoughtful, fingering the silver buttons engraved with the likeness of a mirth flower. He thought he remembered them.

There was a chorus of frightened horses, and Redal-Stan stormed into the tent in a billow of yellow fabric. "Everyone here?" he said brusquely. "Fine. Let's begin." He took position in the center of the tent. "Guardians, bring forth your charges and petition your case. Breve?"

Taking Earan's elbow, Breve stepped forward.

Redal-Stan nodded respectfully. "What has this man been taught?" he asked.

"I have taught him the strategies of war and peace, skill with the sword and pen, eloquence with words and deeds, and the balance between the want and the have," Breve said.

"What are his skills?"

Breve shifted, looking discomfited. "That of the hunt and deed."

"His strengths?" Redal-Stan asked.

"They rest within the loyalty of his convictions."

"His failings?"

Breve's eyes flicked away briefly. "His pride."

There was a heartbeat of silence. "Well answered," Redal-Stan praised. "Who speaks for Keeper Lodesh?"

Alissa struggled to rise. Connen-Neute motioned for her to stay as he moved forward. But it was Reeve who boldly stated, "I do," and Redal-Stan's eyes widened.

"He's a gardener," Earan whispered too loudly. Connen-Neute gave him a poisonous look, and Earan's ears reddened.

"What have you taught this man?" Redal-Stan asked.

Reeve removed his hat. There was dirt under his nails and he smelled of outside. Lodesh knew the squat man looked coarse next to him, and Lodesh was proud to be his son. "The joy of living things and the nurturing of them," Reeve said clearly, and Earan's grin turned patronizing.

"To strive for an end result his grandchildren's children might see," Reeve continued. "The ability to listen to the words of people and hear the truth behind them . . ."

Earan's smile faltered.

". . . and the difference between desire and need."

Redal-Stan held his face still. "What are his skills?"

"To recognize a large problem when it's small and how best to prune it to a proper path."

"His strengths?"

"His love for his city," Reeve said solemnly.

"His failings?"

Reeve hesitated. "His love for his city."

For an instant, surprise showed in Redal-Stan's eyes, then he nodded. The Master waved for everyone to step back. "I deem both petitioners are equally worthy, and I give the decision to the people, who must abide with it. Connen-Neute? Would you help me, please?"

Lodesh turned as the Masters untied the back panel of the tent, letting it fall away to reveal the field. It wasn't empty, and Lodesh's mouth fell open. The entire city must be assembled. As the crowd caught sight of them, the low rumble grew to an exuberant cheer. From the corner of his sight, Lodesh saw Alissa slump with a hand over her eyes.

Redal-Stan took three steps out of the tent, his feet edging into the sun. He raised a hand above his head. "Ese'Nawoer!" he cried. "Greetings!"

A thunderous noise swelled and grew, and Lodesh blanched. The sound dimmed to nothing as Redal-Stan lowered his hand. "I am, as you know, Redal-Stan, ranking Master at the Hold. I called you before me so I may ask your opinion on a matter of great importance."

The crowd answered eagerly. They knew why they were here.

"The city stands without a Warden," Redal-Stan said as the noise subsided. "It cannot remain so. The citadel has given you a candidate, and as choice is necessary for self-worth and satisfaction, the Hold has offered you another."

Redal-Stan waited until the crowd's small noise ceased. Clear and soft, his voice floated out over the multitudes, carried to the edges of the field by a ward. "The decision, Ese'-Nawoer, belongs to you." Turning, he whispered, "Step forward, both of you. One on either side."

Lodesh moved in a daze, overwhelmed by the throng and what was happening.

"Do you know the supplicants?" Redal-Stan said, and the people roared their approval. "Is there a third consideration?" he asked, and field went silent. "Then we will waste no more of the morning." Redal-Stan turned to his right. "Earan Stryska, Keeper of the Hold, eldest son of Marl and Lucian Stryska, step forward."

A thunderous noise rose, stunning everyone before the yellow tent. Earan raised a firm hand, acknowledging them. He was flushed, holding himself confidently. Lodesh drew a careful breath. Perhaps it would be all right.

"Thank you, Earan," Redal-Stan said over the noise, looking as relieved as Lodesh felt. "If you would step back." The Master drew a large breath. "Lodesh Stryska," he said loudly. Keeper of the Hold, youngest son of—"

The crowd surged forward, drowning out his last words in a sound so loud it was a physical force, rocking everyone but Lodesh into taking a step back. His mouth hanging open, Lodesh took a hesitant step forward. The people redoubled their efforts. Terrified, Lodesh turned to Redal-Stan. "You can't make me do this," he said, ashen faced. "Then he turned the other way. "Father," he pleaded. "Don't let them do this to me."

"Buck up, boy," the short man said. "I didn't raise you to turn from those that need you."

"But I don't know anything about governing a city."

Reeve's frown melted into a smile. "Listen to them," he said. "They don't want someone to run their lives. They want someone to stay out of their way. Someone who will listen when things go wrong. Someone who will put their needs before his or her own wants."

"But your trees," Lodesh said. "Who will care for them?"

Reeve hugged him fiercely, giving him a rough kiss on his cheek. "You will," he whispered. "You will, my boy, in due time. Now go greet those who look to you."

Lodesh turned to his brother. "Earan, I didn't want . . . I wasn't trained . . ."

Earan made a sour-looking shrug, trying to hide his disappointment but not doing very well. "Neither was I, little brother. We were never meant to administer, but I don't think they care." Earan nodded to the crowd, now beginning to stir uneasily.

"Decide quickly, Lodesh." Redal-Stan was suddenly at his side. "Either accept their will or not. A city scorned is more vicious than a proud woman wronged."

Lodesh's eyes widened as he realized the trap was secure. "I can't refuse them," he whispered. "Anything I say will sound like an insult." He turned to find Alissa. She smiled proudly from her cushion, looking as if she were trying not to cry.

Redal-Stan gestured flamboyantly for him to step forward, and the field went silent. As if in a dream, Lodesh moved. There was a tingle of a ward. His words, however soft, would be heard by all. The wind brought the hot smell of the field to shift his hair, and the mirth flowers drifted down peacefully behind him. One settled on his shoulder, and he reached for it, taking strength in its familiar scent. He would be all right. He wouldn't have to leave his grove forever.

"Ese'Nawoer," he said into the hush, then hesitated. "I'm overwhelmed, honored," he raised his flower, the traditional token of affection between two lovers, "and completely at a loss for words." He grinned, and the crowd burst into a thunderous cheer. They had their Warden.

"Wolves," Earan whispered. "He was the Warden even before we lost Uncle," and Redal-Stan gave a short grunt of agreement.

Behind him, Lodesh felt Alissa collapse. He and Redal-Stan turned as one, but it was the Master who moved first. "Quick, Connen-Neute," Redal-Stan snapped. "Help me get her out of here. Why the Wolves didn't that sorry excuse of a raku teach her a ward of shielding!"

Lodesh was half a step to her when a strong arm caught him. "Hold, little brother," Earan admonished. "If you leave without giving them the satisfaction of a speech, they'll know something is wrong and go home uneasy, thinking your service has begun with a bad omen."

Shaking his arm free, Lodesh watched in frustration as Connen-Neute rolled Alissa into the back flap of the tent. The two Masters shifted, grasped opposite ends of the sling, and struggled into the air. Redal-Stan was almost gray from his worry and age, dark about the muzzle and tail. By contrast, Connen-Neute was young and inexperienced in carrying heavy loads in tandem. Lodesh watched them dwindle into the distance. They would make it back to the Hold safely. They had to, he thought, forcing himself to believe it.

He took a rough breath and turned back. The crowd had noticed the departing Masters, and an uneasy buzz had begun. Lodesh resolutely set his worried thoughts of Alissa aside. He had to. The people of Ese'Nawoer were sharp and canny. They would recognize any worry, any hesitation, and like a jealous lover, know if his thoughts weren't with them and them alone. But he loved them, too, this stubborn, bullheaded, benevolent people, and to them he belonged. He looked at them proudly and took a breath. "People of Ese'Nawoer . . ."

36

Her shoulder was agony. At first, that was the only thought Alissa's muzzy head could comprehend. That and the nasty taste in her mouth. Her tongue felt thick and her throat raw, as if she had been shouting. *"Beast?"* she called into her thoughts, and a blinding wave of pain thundered through her head.

Whimpering, she curled up into herself on her side, knees to her chest. It was back. Her infamous headache. Hurt washed over Alissa in time with her pulse. Shoulders hunched, she kept her breaths shallow as the agony diminished. It even hurt to breathe.

Waking up in pain had once been a habit with her, one she didn't enjoy, but at least she had learned to deal with it. And so, before making her traditional moan, she examined her tracings. They were clear and pristine. Satisfied she hadn't burned them into a temporary state of ash, Alissa counted the days and decided she could do a ward of healing.

The first influx of warmth infused her and dissolved the pain. Blessedly quick, the spikes of pain in her shoulder became dull throbs. Her head felt light, and her headache disappeared. Sighing, she burrowed farther between the blankets, wanting to go to sleep with that intoxicating sense of well-being. But the sheets smelled like book glue, and the surprise brought Alissa alert. Not only was she in someone else's bed, but she had no idea how she had gotten there.

"Ashes," she whispered, opening her eyes and sitting up. The room was very tall, very large, and very full of books carefully shelved against three walls. One high window tried to light it. From the shadows, she would say it was late afternoon. A white screen was set up in the center of the room. Alissa guessed she was in Redal-Stan's bedroom.

She closed her eyes and tried to remember how she got here. Maybe Beast would know. *"Beast?"* she whispered carefully, feeling the throbbing echo of her headache return. It wasn't debilitating this time, and she closed her eyes and endured it.

"What?"

It was very subdued, frightened almost, and Alissa grew concerned. *"What happened?"*

"I did it again."

The four words sent a wash of alarm through Alissa. It was mirrored by Beast's separate emotions, but hers were tinged with guilt. *"You, ah, took over?"* Alissa said hesitantly.

"Yes." Beast's thoughts grew untamed. *"And it was so easy,"* she breathed, sending a chill through Alissa. *"It was as if you never existed until I heard his music."*

"Music?" Alissa strove to hide her fear, not wanting Beast to know how scared she was at her admission. *"Strell's music? You heard him?"*

"Yes," Beast admitted. *"They dropped you on the balcony. That's why your shoulder hurts. I almost shifted and flew away, but then I heard his music and remembered. . . ."*

Alissa gulped at her near escape. *"And?"*

Beast turned frightened, like a small child. *"I got scared. I forgot you again! Then I got angry because I hurt. Then everything got worse. The old one knew I almost forgot you. He said I would again. He said he wanted to help me to go to sleep until you woke up. I told him I would stay awake to protect you, and that if no one hurt or scared me, I wouldn't forget my promise, but he wouldn't listen."*

Alissa gripped the bedclothes, frightened of things she didn't remember.

"I told him no," Beast continued. *"And he said yes. Then I said a few things I shouldn't have. And he said a few things he ought not. Then,"* Beast grew indignant, *"they sat on me and*

tied your hands! They held your nose and made me drink that—dirt-water! *And then I fell asleep.*" Beast's thoughts turned fearful. "*It was so fast. I didn't want to go to sleep.*"

Alissa took a deep breath. Her fingers were trembling, and she gripped them into fists. "*Well,*" she thought shakily, "*it's done, and I'm all right, and you're all right.*"

"*But it's going to happen again,*" Beast said miserably, hiding herself.

Seeming to be alone in her thoughts, Alissa tried to settle herself. Slowly her headache eased. She was beginning to believe Redal-Stan was right in that she was going to end up feral. That Beast didn't want it either somehow made it worse. Restless, she swung her feet to the floor. There had to be a way to get home before Beast forgot her completely.

A note on the bedside table caught her attention, and she picked it up. It was addressed to Squirrel, and Alissa frowned, pulling it closer to make out the swirling characters in the dim light. "Squirrel," she read. "No Keeper visitors. No nonverbal talking with anyone. You bruised your tracings, and until they heal you will have a headache. My room is warded to block most of the Hold's background noise, so stay put. I'll be back by sundown tomorrow to talk to you. And stay out of my books." It was signed Redal-Stan.

Alissa let the paper drop back to the table. It came to rest beside a thin book. Glancing at the title, she frowned. Her papa had once read to her from this before he left. It was a child's book concerning a scatterbrained squirrel and his never-ending predicaments caused by his temper. Now realizing why Redal-Stan called her Squirrel, her frown deepened.

Irate at the pet name, Alissa rose to investigate Redal-Stan's room. She found all his books, with the exception of the one on the bedside table, were warded shut. The screen in the center of the room sheltered a bathing tub of all things, and after regretfully deciding she had no way to fill it, she wandered out into his main room. All the books there were warded, too. Deep among the clutter she found her book, *First Truth.* This one couldn't be warded against her, but the wash of baffled emotion coming from the book when she bypassed its protective wards with a claim of ownership dissuaded her from opening it.

Trapped, she thought darkly as she sat atop Redal-Stan's desk. *Told to stay put and not talk to anyone.* She felt like she had the plague. Would they remember to feed her? After that ward of healing, she was starving!

The wind gusted in from the balcony, tugging at Redal-Stan's papers, safe under their paperweights. A cup of forgotten tea sat atop the largest stack, and she toyed with the idea of lifting it in spite to let them all blow away. A smooth rock pinned the stack beside it. This she took in hand, placing the papers under the teacup. The rock's river-washed smoothness filled her grip pleasantly.

Alissa tossed the rock from hand to hand. It was just the right size to make a cup. It would take some time, but time was exactly what she had. Her tools were three hundred odd years away, but she could improvise.

Feeling a faint stir of anticipation, Alissa snatched Redal-Stan's wooden writing board. A cloak made of thick leather went over her good shoulder. Several paperweights were next. She could use them as hammers. Her cup would be crude, not the polished perfection she could manage given time and the right materials. But if she used the fine-grained sand Redal-Stan had to rub out mistakes in his writing, she could polish out at least the inside, especially if she used the pestle from the mortar kicked under the desk.

Smiling, Alissa took her tools and moved to the bed. Yes, she thought. A cup would be nice. And if she worked it right, she might even fix the memory of its making into her thoughts.

37

Lodesh paced stealthily to his door. After dimming his ward of light, he cautiously levered open the thick slab of ornate ash. Breath held, he peeked around the frame. His gut tightened as the man sent to watch the hall straightened.

"Would you like a plate of sup before retiring, Warden?" the man in citadel livery asked.

"No." Lodesh sighed. "Could you . . . tell me what time it is?"

The man beamed. "I would rightly guess it's a good two hours after sunset, Warden."

Lodesh thought for a moment. "You're Krag, right?" and the man puffed out his substantial chest in obvious pride. "Go to bed," Lodesh said. "And not in front of my door." He turned and muttered, "If I want something to eat, I'll get it myself."

Krag grinned, settling himself more firmly at his spot as Lodesh shut the door. Escape past Krag would be impossible. Tugging his short vest straight, Lodesh strode across the room to the window. He shook his head in disgust. His upper-floor apartments took up more space than Reeve's entire home and kitchen garden put together. The window, too, was oversized, though not big enough for a raku to land at.

The night breeze tugged at his hair, bringing him the distant scent of mirth flowers as he stood at the window with his hands on his hips and brooded. Large as it was, the four walls of his room were confining. He wanted out, if only for a breath of air. And while he could stroll among the garden's roses and moonlight with impunity, the idea lost much of its appeal knowing his walk would be with Krag. "At least I can smell the roses," he said sourly, reaching past his window to worry a flower free from the thorny vine that snaked up the trellis to the roof.

Lodesh froze at a sudden thought, a grin stealing over him. He looked down at the ground, and with a sharp nod, strode to his closet for the outrageous stockings he was supposed to wear tomorrow. They were purple, and they looked terrible, but he hadn't the heart to tell the woman who chose his clothes. They would be more productive in protecting his hands.

Again at the window, Lodesh wrapped the hose about his palms and fingers and pulled tentatively upon the trellis. It held firm. Slowly, carefully, using all his balance and finesse, Lodesh climbed out onto the wall. His breath slid easily from him in a relieved sigh. There was an ominous creak, and his smile faltered.

It was followed by the sound of a small crack, and he tensed. The eye-opening sound of metal pulling from stone split the night, and he knew he was going down.

He scrambled frantically up. Thorns bit at him. A rung snapped. There was a frightening moment of drop. He gasped at the sudden pain in his shoulder as he jerked to a halt.

A long-fingered hand was wrapped securely about his wrist.

Feet scrabbling against the insecure trellis, Lodesh grasped the lip of the flat roof with his remaining hand and tried to pull himself up. A sharp heave flung him to sprawl on the roof. Rubbing his shoulder, he squinted up at the shadow before him. Immediately he made a light.

"Connen-Neute!" he exclaimed. "Thank you. I was just—" He halted, his relief turning to embarrassment. "Just checking the top buds for aphids."

The young Master arched his eyebrows and sank to sit cross-legged across from him on the flat roof. Lodesh put his knees and elbows in order. He unwound the stockings from his hands and brushed the broken thorns and leaves from him.

"Is there something I can do for you?" he asked. Then his face grew cold. "Alissa!" he cried. "Is she all right? How could I have forgotten about her!"

Connen-Neute raised a placating hand. "Not Alissa," he said quietly, his dark voice seeming to belong to the night as much as the owl and the wolf. "Marga."

"What about her?" he said, suddenly afraid for his sister.

Connen-Neute looked to the west, to the Hold, his golden eyes seeming to glow eerily in the warded light. To Lodesh, he looked anxious, ready to take flight at the least provocation. Realizing the young Master was frightened, Lodesh forced himself to relax. Whatever it was must be important, or Connen-Neute wouldn't be here. "Please," he said softly. "Tell me."

Connen-Neute nodded, his long face serious. "It's my belief the chances have increased tenfold that Marga's unborn children will be allowed to turn shaduf."

Lodesh's breath hissed out as if he had been kicked. "By the Navigator, no," he whispered, stunned. Not Marga. Not his sister. It would tear her apart, watching her children turn cold and bitter as the knowledge of a thousand deaths fell upon them.

Feeling as if he might be sick, Lodesh turned his cold face to Connen-Neute. "How do you know?" he said brokenly, then felt his face harden. "What do you mean, *allowed* to turn shaduf? You can stop it?" He stood up, angry. "Could Sati have been stopped from turning?"

Connen-Neute rose as well, standing very still. "I shouldn't have come."

"No!" Lodesh said with a whispered urgency. "Wait." He forced his arms to his side. "I'm sorry. I'm not in a position to condemn anyone. But you're here. You wouldn't be if you could do something to change it."

"Change?" the young Master said, mouthing the word slowly as if it was made of wool. "No. Prevent." He looked uneasily towards the Hold again, then sat down. "I need help."

Lodesh forced himself to sit, knowing the effort he was making to get the words out.

The Master's eyes seemed to glow. "I must know when Marga is with child."

Lodesh shivered from the multitude of questions that simple statement gave rise to.

"The earlier the better," Connen-Neute added. "I have reason to believe a mild burn—"

"You would burn a child's tracings before it's born!" Lodesh exclaimed in outrage.

Connen-Neute's eyes hardened. "Shall I leave?" he said, and Lodesh eased back. "It need only be a gentle burn if the timing is good. You wouldn't feel it, and neither will the unborn."

Slowly Lodesh nodded, still unsure. "But an infant?"

"A neural net is very . . ." Connen-Neute took time with his next word, ". . . susceptible as it's forming. To wait until birth would necessitate a stronger, painful burn."

Lodesh shifted uneasily. "Marga's children won't be shaduf."

"Or Keeper," Connen-Neute added softly.

He frowned. "What of Trook?"

The white evenness of Connen-Neute's teeth gleamed in the faint light. "Keeper," he said.

"You know already?" Lodesh beamed with pride as if he was his own son.

The Master nodded. "I looked as soon as I could without Redal-Stan becoming suspicious."

Suddenly the furtive glances to the west became clear. Connen-Neute was acting on his own, against a course of action that the Masters had agreed upon. It put him in a precarious position if his actions to prevent Marga's children from going shaduf were discovered. "Why are you doing this?" Lodesh asked, wondering what had changed in Connen-Neute for him to risk it.

Connen-Neute stood, his lips pursed. "I'm not brave enough to voice my beliefs and fight for them," he said. "My hidden actions will have to suffice until I find the strength."

"Redal-Stan says actions speak louder than words."

Lodesh rose as well. "You're braver than you give yourself credit for."

Clearly unused to such praise, Connen-Neute shifted his shoulders awkwardly. "Be subtle when telling me when I'm needed. Brave or not, I've no wish to be tried for sedition." He shuddered. "You tell Marga."

Lodesh nodded. Their meeting was obviously over, and he glanced at the edge of the roof, wondering how he was going to get back down. He had no doubt Marga would want Connen-Neute's help and tell him as soon as she thought she might be with child. Lodesh paused, frowning. That is, if she *could* tell him.

"Connen-Neute, wait," he called as the young Master distanced himself in preparation to shift. "Marga is leaving for the plains this coming spring. Can you look in on her yourself? Perhaps every few months?"

The Master tightened the red sash around his waist in agitation. "They'd become suspicious, especially when her children appear as commoners." He frowned. "A few years and they will guess."

A wash of hopelessness rushed through Lodesh, leaving him feeling ill. Sarken was determined to go. "Perhaps a box, such as the one you warded for me to give Sati." Lodesh flushed in guilt. "She can take it with her, a going-away present," he added. There was something wrong when one felt compelled to give one's sister a gift to burn her children.

Connen-Neute's eyes went thoughtful. "That's better. It would be hard to link it to me."

Lodesh watched Connen-Neute straighten. His speech, too, had improved dramatically, even over this short conversation. No wonder Alissa liked him.

"Not a box," the young Master said softly, seeming unaware he was talking aloud. "They know I've done that. Something else. Something valuable so it isn't lost. Something that performs a task in order to invoke and then check the ward. A continuous burn, no matter how gentle, will be noticed."

"I have a metal brooch," Lodesh suggested. "It opens—"

"I'm not skilled enough to ward metal. Wood perhaps?"

"Mirth wood," Lodesh said. "No one would lose worked mirth wood. I have something left over from when my father thought I was going to be too shy to win a wife." His eyes went distant in remembrance. "Poetry, music, swordplay, he tried everything until realizing that the only thing I was good at was dancing. I have a pipe downstairs made of mirth wood. They moved all my things." Lodesh peered over the edge to find the ground lost in shadow. "Marga's husband is a musician, so no one would ever suspect it. You could ward it tonight, and I could give it to her in the morning. That is, if I can get down from here without breaking my neck."

Connen-Neute's mouth curved in a sly smile. Beckoning Lodesh to follow, he took Lodesh's light and brought it close to his feet, running it across the roof until he made a satisfied noise. Lodesh wasn't surprised when the Master levered a part of the roof aside to reveal the top of one of his closets.

"Your grandfather," Connen-Neute said, somehow managing to keep a straight face. "He liked to play cards. Talo-Toecan would come out here when Keribdis was—gone."

Lodesh looked down at his two pairs of shoes, stacked neatly upon what could obviously pass as a ladder. "Why am I not surprised?"

38

Alissa broke from her trance with three deliberate breaths, startled by the sound of a soft knock. The room was dusky with shadows. Her back was achy and stiff, and she was filthy with stone chips and sand. Cramped and abraded, her fingers sported several small gashes. With a flush of guilt, she realized she had gouged Redal-Stan's writing board. His cloak was ruined. And in her hands was a shallow cup. A smile eased over her.

There was a scuff at the dark archway, and Alissa looked to see Mav, a candle in her grip and a bundle of cloth under her arm. She set it all on the bedside table and extended her hand. "May I see?" she asked. Alissa grinned and handed it over. Blowing the dust from it, Mav examined the cup thoroughly. It was more of a palm-sized bowl than a cup, being small and shallow and having no handle. Strell would call it a thimble. She sighed at the reminder of him.

"This is very nice," Mav said.

"Thank you." Alissa straightened her legs and winced, rubbing at her knees.

Mav handed it back. "Well. Let's see you try it." Caught off guard, Alissa stared. "Weren't you trying to fix a new form into your thoughts?" the old woman added as she sat on the edge of the bed. "I've climbed the tower five times since yesterday afternoon, and each time you said nothing to me, buried in concentration. I missed eavesdropping on the dinner crowd for this. I want to know if you've done it."

Alissa vaguely recalled gulping cold tea and gritty toast.

Her eyebrows rose, and with anticipation stirring in her, she set her cup on the scarred board and shut her eyes. Wards of creation were tricky things. There was a basic pattern they all followed, but deviations were rampant due to the nature of their task. The ward drew upon memories, and depending upon where those memories were stored, different pathways were used. It was because of these irregularities that it took so long to learn a new ward of creation. Specializing in one media helped, but still, fixing a new form was tedious and time-consuming.

Taking three breaths, Alissa set the basic pattern alight as she concentrated on her cup. A thrill went through her as new tracings were added, making the pattern larger. She relived the entire night and day in less than a heartbeat, gave the memory substance, and with a curious twinge on her thoughts, turned her source's energy to mass. Alissa's eyes flew open. There in the candlelight were two cups where one once stood. "I did it!" she exclaimed, beaming at Mav's satisfied nod.

"That you did, dearie. That you did." She beat Alissa's reach for the new cup and blew the dust from it. "And now I would ask a favor?" She smiled mischievously. "Promise me I can be there when Redal-Stan sees you craft one for the first time."

"Redal-Stan!" Alissa's hand went to her hair. Back protesting, she rose. "He said he'd be back at sundown. It looks like it's nearly that now. I'm filthy!"

"That you are." Mav stood as well. "He's been gone all of yesterday and today, off on a Master's business important enough to be done in person. Connen-Neute's been minding the stairs. Won't let Keeper or student higher than the eighth floor. Love a duck, that child is so serious and solemn. I told him you would be all right, but he wouldn't risk anyone damaging your tracings further until they've had a day or two of rest. Now, do you promise?"

Alissa blinked. *Oh, yes. Make a cup when Mav was present.* "All right," she said, deciding she couldn't chance Mav seeing her shift to a raku and back so as to clean up.

"I drew you a bath last time I was here," Mav said as she pulled the gritty sheets from Redal-Stan's bed and threw them in a pile by the door. "The water is probably cold, but it won't be chill. Redal-Stan, the old goat, is the only one in the Hold with a private bath. He fills it from a catch basin on the roof. Empties it with a pipe through the wall, all the way to the ground."

Alissa stiffly moved to the white partition. Grimacing at the temperature, she warmed it with a ward, then another until it steamed. With a last look over the panels, she wiggled from her clothes and slipped into the tub. A sigh slipped from her. It was as good as a healing ward. She attacked her hair with a thick cut of brown soap smelling of mint. Grit slid beneath her fingertips. The soap found every scratch and abrasion, setting her teeth on edge.

"Nothing like a bath to loosen stiff muscles," Mav was saying. There was the sound of sheets being snapped over the bed. "I'll stay and chat," she said. "Keep the riffraff out until you're decent. I've brought a set of clothes for you, something other than that Keeper garb. A girl needs more than one set of clothes."

Alissa held her breath and went under, scrubbing the soap from her scalp. She felt, more than heard, a soft thumping through the water. Alissa sat up in a wash of water, listening. Faint through the walls was the sound of stomping feet. Redal-Stan.

Alarmed, she stood up. Water went everywhere. Frantically wrapping a towel about herself, she scrambled out of his tub. Mav met her gaze questioningly, spinning with hands raised when Redal-Stan burst into his outer room.

"Alissa!" he bellowed, and bright light lit the archway.

Mav jumped in a whirlwind of feminine outrage to the outer room. "Out!" her frail voice commanded shrilly. "Get out, you old beast. She's bathing!"

"Alissa!" he thundered. "I want to talk to you."

"I said, get out!" Mav's trumpet hurt Alissa's ears. "Give the girl a chance to breath!"

"She's had two days to breathe. I want to talk to her!" He

appeared at the archway with a light in hand. Mav was boiling mad at his elbow. Seeing Alissa by the tub with a towel
wrapped about her, too scared to move, he stopped short. His
mouth opened, then shut, and he turned away, a hand running
over his bald head. "Why didn't you tell me she was
bathing?" he groused.

"What do you think I've been doing!" Mav swatted him
with her apron strings.

He frowned at Alissa's puddle on the floor. "Get dressed. I
want you in my reception room." He held up a finger. "Now."
He spun on a heel and left. The room went dark.

"Well!" Mav huffed, coming to sop up the water with another towel.

Not liking his tone, Alissa resolved to take her time.

"Now, Squirrel!" came his distant bark, and she jumped,
dropping the stockings Mav had laid out. They had no holes
in them. How novel. Flustered, Alissa's fingers fumbled with
the laces of the new yellow dress Mav had brought up. It was
embroidered with gray-blue flowers across the neckline to
match her eyes, and Alissa made a light to see it better, liking
how it fit.

"Don't mind him." Mav tried to arrange Alissa's hair, and
she squirmed under the attention. "I don't think he's angry at
you. He probably found out about his Shaduf Sati burning
herself to uselessness."

Alissa's breath caught, and Mav went still. "Oh, Alissa,"
she breathed. "You are in a pudding." Her eyebrows bunched.
"Perhaps I'll make some tea." Looking tired, she blew out her
candle, took up the sheets, and went to the archway. "Maybe
a plate of ham." She paused uncertainly. "You know how he
loves his ham."

"Mavoureen?" Alissa said, not wanting to go out there just
yet.

"I wouldn't keep him waiting," she said as she slipped
away.

From the outer room came Redal-Stan's respectful, "Good
evening, Mavoureen," and her thin, piping reply. Alissa heard
the door open, then shut to leave an ominous silence.

She found her shoes and slipped them on. With a worried gulp, she allowed her sphere of light to go out and peeked past the archway.

Sitting behind his ward-lit desk, Redal-Stan gave Alissa the impression of an angry cat. Seeing her, he pointed at the couch placed dead center before his desk. Alissa meekly sat on the very edge of it. The sound of night crickets filled the silence.

"Why!" he barked, making her jump, "didn't you tell me you were having headaches?"

Alissa's eyes widened in surprise. She took a breath, and he raised an irate finger.

"Ah!" he admonished. "Don't interrupt. Why didn't that ash-ridden excuse for an instructor teach you a simple protection ward?" Redal-Stan stood, his stance stiff.

Alissa opened her mouth.

"Yes, I know," he interrupted, and her mouth snapped shut. "We cataloged your accomplishments and you didn't mention them, but I thought it was an oversight." He paced in jerky steps to the dark balcony, and she turned to keep him in view. "It's not really a lesson," he said. "It's a necessity, like, like . . ." He gesticulated wildly. "Like breathing!" he finished.

Tired of being cut off, Alissa's lips pursed. "Well?" he exclaimed, and she took a breath.

"You could have severely damaged your neural net," he began again, not noticing her glare though he was staring at her. "You're lucky, you know, that Connen-Neute and I were able to manage your weight and carry you free of the city. Channeling the emotional backwash of an entire city synchronized in thought, whipped up to that kind of frenzy, could have resulted in irreparable impairment of your ability to communicate—or worse."

"Then I'm all right now?" she asked, pleased to have gotten the words past him.

"Quiet!" he snapped from the shadowed balcony. "I'm not done." Finding Connen-Neute's tall stool with his toe, he sat down on it as if he had meant to. He stared at her, and she at him. "What have you to say for yourself?"

"Thanks?" she said uncertainly, and he stiffened in disbelief. "Thanks a lot?" she tried again, and he stood, turning to clench the railing. Alissa felt a stirring of anger. "Don't get mad at me!" she exclaimed, and he spun about. "I was brought up in the foothills, alone with my mother. Market gave me headaches, but I blamed it on the heat or the dust or that everyone was staring hatefully at me. And as for Ese'Nawoer," she said, rising to join him on the balcony, "it's empty! He saw no need to teach me to block out the mental backwash of three people!"

"Three?" The anger in Redal-Stan's face vanished.

"Three!" she said, flinging herself into his balcony chair, suddenly depressed.

"Then maybe I should show you!" he said, loud enough to make her ears hurt.

"Maybe you should!"

"All right then!" Redal-Stan leaned back against the railing. "Look," he said sarcastically as she felt a twinge upon her thoughts. "See?"

Beginning to calm, Alissa unfocused her attention to find her tracings. The pattern resonating was absurdly simple, and she nodded as she memorized it. The resonance faded.

"Set it up within an internal containment field," he said, sounding disgusted, "and let it settle over your network as you do for disguising your tracings."

Pleased with having learned something, her anger vanished. "Like this?" she chirped, and he sighed at her mood shift. His eyes went distant and his posture slumped as he checked it.

"Yes." He sounded tired. "For day-to-day existence in the Hold that's fine. Strengthen it when confronting fourteen thousand prideful people. I would suggest you not use it until you heal so you don't develop a dependency upon it." He frowned. "Stay out of Ese'Nawoer."

Alissa's fingers tapped the arm of the chair.

"Fine!" he snapped. "Do what you want!"

Mollified, she stilled her fingers and dropped the ward. "So I can resume my usual activities?" she asked meekly.

"Ignoring my instructions?" he grumbled. "Taking leaves of absence without permission, interfering with the peace of my other students, and generally making yourself a pain in my side? Of course," he half sang in exasperation. "Go ahead."

Alissa's frown returned. "I meant practice my wards, talk silently to Connen-Neute."

"Yes," he grumped. "A pain in my ash-ridden side." Alissa exhaled heavily, and he relented. "Yes and no." He glanced at the black outlines of Connen-Neute's stool, clearly wanting to sit down but refusing to sit on a student's chair when she was in his. "You're not entirely better. Test the air carefully, Squirrel. I wouldn't talk soundlessly to any Keepers for a few days. Most lack a certain finesse."

She shifted her shoulders. The only Keeper she had ever cared to speak silently to was Lodesh, and he was a subtle as Connen-Neute.

Redal-Stan seemed reluctant to say anything more. Their previous conversation was too much like an argument to lead gracefully into talk. She thought he was waiting for her to go, but she had come to appreciate his oasis of quiet at the top of the tower and was reluctant to leave, despite the awkward silence. Besides, she had nothing to go downstairs for. Lodesh was probably imprisoned in the citadel.

"Redal-Stan?" she questioned, arms wrapped about herself. "How is Lodesh?"

Redal-Stan drooped. He turned his back to her, placing his hands upon the railing to look over the cricket-laden fields to the city. The lights from Ese'Nawoer's homes were unseen, but the stars were eclipsed by the smoke from its fires. "Like a hand into a glove," he said. "Like a hand into a finely crafted glove. One he really doesn't want to wear, though it suits him well."

Alissa's gaze dropped. Redal-Stan continued to gaze into infinity. The light behind them made the shadows uncertain, but she thought she saw a grievous sadness reflected in the old

Master who had grown up in the plains as a boy. Seeing him sorrowing after Lodesh's plight, she realized she and Redal-Stan were destined to be apart, even among their adopted kin.

They might wear a Master's clothes, perform a Master's tasks, fly in the mist on a moonless night, but they would always be who they were before: a farm girl growing up alone in the hills and a half-starved adolescent struggling to survive the plains. Their background marked them as much as their normal eyes and fingers, and their propensity to delight in even the smallest task their structured neural nets allowed them. They alone understood the quickness of the human existence, the tragedy of choice, and the strength that lay behind both.

Alissa stood and reached for his sleeve, allowing her unshed tears for Lodesh to make their appearance. He turned, knowing why her eyes were full. "They don't understand, do they," she whispered around her tight throat, and he shook his head.

"No. For all their wisdom, rakus don't understand the sacrifices men and women make."

His arm went about her shoulder in a quick, fatherly embrace. Giving her a stern look, he took a step back. "No tears for Warden Lodesh," he admonished, and she gulped. "He wouldn't understand. It would leave him uneasy and do him no good."

Alissa smiled sickly up at him, and he turned back to the city. "The Stryska line is strong," he said. "Even with the sorrow, he will endure. He will do wondrous things."

Feeling the cold of the night on her cheeks, Alissa wiped the tears from them. She gave him a mirthless smile. A decisive knock startled them both, and Redal-Stan turned, blinking. "Mav?" he questioned. "Come in."

Mav shuffled in, followed by an anxious-looking Connen-Neute with a tray in his long hands. "Thank you, dearie," she said. Her sharp eyes swept the room, lingering on Alissa as she sniffed loudly. "Kind of you to help an old lady," she added. "I'll take it from here."

Connen-Neute willingly surrendered the tray with its

teapot and three covered dishes. Hovering just inside the door, the young Master worriedly touched his shoulder. *"It's fine,"* Alissa said wordlessly, and he visibly relaxed, stepping farther into the room.

Mav's eyes narrowed at Alissa's red eyes, and the woman set the tray down beside Redal-Stan's moth-circled light with an attention-getting clatter.

"So glad you came back up, Mavoureen." Redal-Stan ghosted past Alissa, intent on the sight of the covered dishes. "But I'm afraid you've missed the locking of the Hold's doors."

"Then I'll be resting my achy bones in the stables tonight. It won't be the first time," she said dryly. She stepped in front of the plates, causing Redal-Stan to stop short with a comical haste. Feigning unawareness of his abrupt halt, Mav raised a questioning brow to Alissa, seemingly for approval. With a jolt, Alissa realized the kitchen's matriarch thought her tears had been caused by Redal-Stan. Alissa smiled and mouthed the words, *Not his fault.*

Mav frowned in disbelief, and Redal-Stan's eyes narrowed. But as soon as she moved out of the way, he forgot his annoyance and started lifting lids. Mav slapped his hand with a preoccupied motion and arranged a small supper on his desk. Drawn by the promise of food, Alissa and Connen-Neute drifted closer.

"Redal-Stan?" Mav said. "Connen-Neute and I were discussing on the stairs the possibility of a Keeper or Master learning how to craft an object of metal or stone from their thoughts." The final cover was removed, and Alissa took an eager breath. Sweet drops!

"Now." Mav gingerly eased her body into a chair with a surprising show of familiarity. "Connen-Neute assures me that because they are so, m-m-m, *dense* did you say, dearie?"

Connen-Neute nodded. Alissa edged closer to the plate of sweets only to have Redal-Stan intercept her reach, pulling the plate away. Her lips pursed, and she frowned.

"Dense, yes," Mav continued. "He tells me it would be impossible to craft, say, buttons or—a laundry kettle."

Alissa blinked, her ire vanishing in surprise. No one had
told her that. And it hadn't been that difficult. She looked at
Mav in astonishment, and the old woman slowly winked, not
looking at her at all.

"He's right," Redal-Stan said, and while he was distracted
by Mav, Alissa slipped the sweets from him, retreating to the
couch with her prize. "Metal," he continued, "stone, and even
mirth wood to some degree, are too dense to be dissolutioned
easily, so it's impossible to craft them with your thoughts."
Plate in hand, Redal-Stan turned to offer Alissa first choice
from one of the two plates of meat. Surprise brought him up
short as he realized she had absconded with the sweets.

"I see," Mav mused aloud. "But you can craft clay."

"True," he agreed, turning back to Mav. "But clay is malleable in its natural state."

"Metal is malleable when it's hot," she challenged.

Nodding, Redal-Stan carefully chose his first morsel of
ham. "But in its natural state, it isn't. And if it's too dense to
break down, it's too dense to craft from your thoughts."

"M-m-m." Mav closed her eyes as if in thought. "I still
think it could be done." Stifling a grin, Alissa licked the honey
from her fingers, knowing where this was headed.

Redal-Stan smiled indulgently as he seated himself upon
his desktop. He dangled a long leg down to the floor, effectively dominating the two plates of ham. "If it were possible,
wouldn't someone have done it already? Metal, perhaps, with
much study and concentration, terrible concentration. But
why bother? And you can't dissolution stone, so you can't
form it from your thoughts." Secure in his convictions, Redal-
Stan deftly speared a ham slice with a long-handled fork, unaware that Connen-Neute was quietly screwing up his
courage.

Mav sighed. "I would think it worth the effort to try," she
said slowly. "A Master who could craft, say . . . needles or
candleholders would be very popular."

Connen-Neute took a resolute breath. Alissa watched in
wonder as he straightened his vest, strode to Redal-Stan, eyed
him, then reached for the second plate of ham. The scrape of

the dish on the desktop seemed painfully loud. Slowly the young Master returned, sitting smoothly at the opposite end of the couch from Alissa.

Redal-Stan said nothing, but his look was of astounded dismay. His student could no longer be bullied and would have to be treated with more respect.

"Redal-Stan?" Mav's eyes glinted at Connen-Neute's revolt. "I would wager with you."

There was a clatter as Connen-Neute's fork hit his plate. His face was fixed in alarm.

"A wager, you say?" Redal-Stan's tone was far too casual.

"Yes." The chipper woman sat straighter, daring him with her bird-bright eyes. "You know that small pantry behind the largest hearth?"

"Yes," he drawled, arranging his three remaining ham rolls in order of size.

"If I can find someone willing to try crafting an object in stone or metal, I want it."

Redal-Stan chose the smallest piece. "What for?"

"To sleep in, of course!" she exclaimed, and Redal-Stan ceased his chewing. "I'm tired of dragging my bones from Ese'Nawoer and back every blessed day."

Redal-Stan swallowed. "You know I can't sanction that. You aren't a Keeper, or even a past student. Talo-Toecan has forbidden it for a very good reason."

"Strell isn't a Keeper," Alissa offered. "Talo-Toecan allowed him to stay."

If Redal-Stan could be any more surprised, he would have fallen off his desk. He waved his fork wildly. "It doesn't matter," he growled, stabbing another ham roll. "You can't dissolution metal, mirth wood, or stone. Therefore you can't craft them from your thoughts."

Mav leaned forward, delicately snitching the last, largest morsel of meat from his tray. As he watched helplessly, she ate it. "I don't see your logic, old goat."

Connen-Neute gasped and began shoveling his remaining slices of meat into his mouth. Redal-Stan looked as if he were ready to strangle someone. Cool and confident, Mav sedately chewed, knowing she had goaded him into the response she wanted.

"Fine," he snapped. "If you can get someone to craft metal, not try but actually do it, you can have your closet, cheeky old woman. I'll fix it with Talo-Toecan somehow, but you," he stabbed a finger at her, "will be dead by the time you convince someone to even try."

"Ha!" It was a carefully contrived bark of sound. "I haven't baked my last candied apple yet. But I want Kally to be allowed to stay as well. She's too great a help to me."

"Burn you to ash, woman," Redal-Stan exclaimed. "No."

"Yes," she countered. "And I'll find someone to craft stone. That's got to be harder."

Beside Alissa, Connen-Neute whispered, "No, Mavoureen. He'll have your firstborn." Alissa squirmed, wanting to show them it was possible.

"Stone, eh?" Redal-Stan calmed, looking more like a shifty plains trader than usual. Fine," he said. "Since we are entertaining the ridiculous, I agree. If I get a candied apple on my breakfast tray every morning whether you win or lose."

Mav gasped. "Do you know how hard those are to make?"

"You should have plenty of time," he taunted, "if you're staying in the Hold."

A shaky hand went to cover her eyes, supposedly in dismay, but Alissa knew it was to hide her eyes, gleaming in victory. "Kally can stay," she said softly. "I can stay. You get a candied apple once a week."

Redal-Stan leaned confidently back. "Every day."

"A full tray once a month," she countered as she looked up.

"Done and done," he agreed. "I should like a tray of yellow apples first," he drawled.

Alissa waited for Mav to announce Alissa's new skill, but the old woman merely gave her a knowing smirk and levered herself up with a heavy sigh. Mav reached for the teapot, now fully brewed. There was a tweak on Alissa's awareness as someone warmed it up.

"Perhaps red, though," Redal-Stan pondered aloud. "Red apples are generally sweeter."

Pouring tea into two cups, Mav handed them to Redal-Stan and Connen-Neute.

"Until, of course, the red and green mix apples are ripe," Redal-Stan continued. "They're by far the sweetest." He reached for a cup, pausing at the two empty ones on the tray. "Aren't you having any tea?" he questioned Mav. "The doors are locked. You'll need something to keep you warm in the stables. That closet is still mine."

Mav swirled the pot, estimating how much was left. "Yes. I would enjoy a cup of tea before I retire, but I would rather have it in one of Alissa's cups. They don't slip out of my old hands as easy as yours."

Alissa grinned as the two Masters turned to her. "Alissa's cups?" Redal-Stan said.

At Mav's encouraging nod, Alissa made two cups in quick succession. Mav triumphantly blew the dust from them and filled them with tea. More pleased than anyone had a right to be, the woman sank into her chair, the steam glowing in the illumination from Redal-Stan's light.

"But . . ." Redal-Stan stammered as Connen-Neute shook off his surprise and began to laugh. The wonderful sound was contagious, and Alissa grinned all the more. "Bone and Ash!" the old Master of the Hold shouted. "Let me see that!" He grabbed Alissa's cup from the tray, yelping in pain as tea slopped over to burn his hand. "You said you couldn't craft anything but clothes."

"I was bored," Alissa said, grinning. "And you wouldn't let me read any of your books."

The towel Redal-Stan had conjured to dab up the spilled tea hit his desk. "No," he said. "You expect me to believe you made this," he pointed to her cup, "in less than a day?"

"Of course not," Mav said. "It took her all of last night and today."

Redal-Stan froze, his hand halfway across his head. Alissa couldn't stop smiling, pleased and embarrassed at the same time.

"Would anyone care for a hand or two of Slats and Shanties?" Mav dipped into her apron pocket. "Now that I'm in no hurry," she added slyly. Connen-Neute eagerly pulled a small table close between the couch and Mav's chair. The soft sound of sliding cards joined the crickets.

"What happened?" Redal-Stan breathed vacantly as he set her stone cup down.

"Here, Alissa," Mav called merrily. "Sit on my right. Make Redal-Stan go last."

"I don't know how to play," she admitted as she slid down the couch, and Mav waved an impatient hand.

From his desk Redal-Stan whispered, "You have a bed made up in that closet already, don't you."

Mav beamed, her wrinkles falling into themselves. "Are you going to play or not?" she asked, and he turned his back on them, sucking on the soft part of his hand he had burnt.

Three cards slid to a stop before Alissa. "Not yet!" Connen-Neute cried as she reached for them, and Alissa snatched her hand back.

"So, tell me, dearie." Mav touched Alissa's arm. "What did you do to calm the old beast down so quickly? I thought he would be raving all night." She turned over six cards in the center of the table, and Connen-Neute chuckled for some reason.

"He wasn't mad about Sati," Alissa admitted, "but about me bruising my tracings."

From behind his desk, Redal-Stan gave a grunt. Slowly he turned, the inspection of his hand apparently forgotten. "Sati?" he said. "What about Shaduf Sati?"

39

Alissa's eyes went wide, Connen-Neute lost his grin, and Mav sucked in her breath. "Um," Alissa stammered.

"Can't you ever keep your mouth shut?" Beast said dryly in Alissa's thoughts.

"Alissa?" Redal-Stan said warily.

Quick, old fingers gathered the cards up in a tidy pile. "I think I'll be going now," Mav said as she slipped her cards into her pocket and stood.

Connen-Neute rose, gulping his tea in a single, hurried swallow. Redal-Stan loomed behind his desk. "Alissa?"

"Good night, dearie," whispered Mav. She gave Alissa a pitying glance and left, not even taking the time to gather the plates and cups.

"Good luck, rather." Connen-Neute edged out after her.

Alissa stood, feeling rather sick. "I should go, too. Good night, Redal-Stan."

"What about Shaduf Sati?" Redal-Stan came out from around his desk, standing so close she fell back onto the couch.

"Um, she's a nice lady," Alissa offered.

"Nice lady! You met her? How could you stand it?" He paused, his eyes going wide in a sudden thought. "You didn't . . ." he whispered, and Alissa shrank into herself. "Alissa," he said. "Please tell me you didn't."

She bit her lip, miserably looking at her shoes.

There was a sigh as Redal-Stan fell heavily into Mav's chair. "Wolves," he breathed. Alissa looked up, afraid of what she might see. But he had no expression, staring at the moths hammering at his globe of light. "How did you keep her intact through the pain?" he asked.

"I—we took most of its echo," Alissa said in a small voice.

"We? You mean Beast?" he asked, and Alissa nodded. "Wolves take you, Beast."

"It was—uh—a selective burn," Alissa offered. "That lessened the pain dramatically."

Redal-Stan's eyes looked flat and unreal, and she shivered. "You asked to see a resonance?" he said in a monotone, and she nodded. His reaction was frightening her.

"You tripped the lines?" he asked, and she nodded again. "Whose death did you see?"

"Ese'Nawoer's," she whispered.

"Wolves." He sat quietly, not moving at all. Moth shadows fluttered over his face. "I should have gone to watch you myself. I thought Connen-Neute was mature enough to not allow music to distract him so thoroughly." He turned his tired eyes to hers. "Can't I let you out of my sight for even one evening without you destroying something?"

Alissa felt a flush of shame, then squelched it, replacing it with a more familiar defiance. "She asked for a burn. Demanded it. She was going to lose her mind." Alissa steeled herself, preparing for a loud, aggressive lecture, but Redal-Stan seemed to grow more despondent.

"I'm not going to argue the morality of capitalizing upon her misaligned neural net," he said heavily. "It's an old argument, one never resolved."

Alissa stiffened. Sati was right! They had bred the woman into existence, like a better sheep with thicker wool.

"All that work," he breathed, his eyes fixed into infinity. "Six generations of study and observation—useless." Unaware of Alissa's anger, he rose and went behind his desk. Taking a large book from a stack, he set it before him with a spiritless thump and waved the moths from his light. Still standing, he leafed through the book. "Burn it to ash. There's no question now as to allowing the Stryska line to produce a replacement. This is worse and worse."

"Ren was right," she said sharply. "We're nothing but broodmares and stallions to you!"

"Broodmares?" Redal-Stan's head came up, his brow furrowed. "Do you have any idea the time and effort it takes to build a profile on just one family line? You have to go back generations to catch sight of those cursed recessive traits, and then not even know for sure if they're there in their descendants. Then," he slammed his book shut, "there's always the joy of trying to work around what some stubborn Keeper wants to do, and you warn them, but do they listen? No-o-o-o. So you end up with shadufs popping up all over the place!"

Beast came to the forefront, her outrage temporally overshadowing Alissa. "You tell them who they may join with and if they may engender offspring?" she exclaimed through Alissa. Then Beast stopped short, apologized to Alissa, and hid herself.

He strode to a stack of books and snatched one. "If only it were that easy, Beast." His attention on the yellow pages, he returned to his desk. "Ash-laden moths," he muttered. Gathering them up in a field, he bodily threw them over the balcony railing. "We do have some scruples. Keepers have children with whom they want, but you try keeping an accurate profile of even half the population at risk."

"Risk?" Alissa whispered, her outrage hesitating.

"I'll admit we discourage or occasionally prevent certain joinings." Redal-Stan sat down and looked up from his book. "You've got it wrong, Alissa, for the most part, anyway. We aren't trying to engender shadufs. We're trying to minimize them. Mostly."

"Then you do admit to manipulating the population!" she accused hotly.

Redal-Stan gave her a dry look from under his brow. "Let me explain. Obviously Talo-Toecan hasn't, and I can't allow you to run about with dangerous information unless you understand the whole of it. A little wisdom in your hands is a threat to civilization." He ran a peeved glance over his desk. "Where's my writing board?" he grumbled, then swept an arm to shove everything but his light to one end. Glancing up, he noticed she hadn't moved. "I'm not angry about Shaduf Sati. No one told you not to. We'll leave it at that."

Still Alissa sat, fuming. Redal-Stan had plucked a quill and ink pot from the mess and was scribbling on a sheet of paper. His brown eyes rose to hers. "You do want to know the difference between a Keeper and Master, don't you?"

Despite her ire, she dragged Mav's chair closer.

"Now." He looked up. "You grew up on a farm. Do you know the practical side of animal husbandry?" Alissa nodded, and he steepled his fingers. "White hen, red rooster give you red and white chicks, not pink, right?"

"Yes." Alissa sat straighter. "But it varies with the two chickens. Sometimes the chicks are all red, and when any white do show up, it's usually about half."

"Half, eh? Very astute. What about two red chickens? What does that give you?"

Alissa shrugged. "All red, usually. Sometimes a quarter of them are white."

"A quarter." He gave a satisfied grunt and leaned forward. "Want to know why?"

Shoulders shifting in surrender, she put her elbows on his desk. Chuckling, he took his quill and scribbled some more. "This," he said, shoving the paper at her, "is our key."

She picked it up and read, "RR is red; rr is white; Rr is red carrying the masked—" She hesitated at the unfamiliar word, never having seen it before.

"Allele," Redal-Stan prompted.

"Carrying the masked allele for white," she continued, hoping he would explain. She let the paper fall. "I don't get it."

He paused in thought. "Every living thing has instructions for mass. Uh, for the way it looks. For reasons I don't want to go into, these countless instructions just happen to come in pairs. Now, when I say pairs, I don't mean the separate parts of the pair are identical. That chicken, for example, can either be red or white."

"All right," she said, wondering what he was talking

about. He pushed her cup at her, and she took it, warming her fingers.

"A white chicken is white because both parts of that pair tell it to be." He circled the rr.

"Why not write it as W?" she asked.

"It just isn't. Don't interrupt. A red chicken is written as RR, or Rr." He circled them. "Now let's say we have a white hen and a red rooster."

Alissa leaned forward watching him scribble rr x RR.

"Their chicks need only one pair of instructions, so they get a half from each parent."

Alissa squinted at the paper. "Wouldn't having both pairs be better?"

"No. Trust me on this." She made a face and he added, "So all our chicks get an R from their sire, and an r from their dam."

Alissa looked to where he had enthusiastically scribbled Rr. "They would be red, right?" she said, glancing at the key. "Even though half the—uh—pair tells them to be white?"

"Yes!" He smiled as if she had said something clever. "The white instruction is weaker than the red. It's recessive, over-powered by the other. Even though the chick looks red, half its instructions tell it to be white. The white won't show up in the chicken, but if it passes its white instruction to its off-spring, they might be white."

Her brow pinched. "What does this have to do with Masters and Keepers?"

He blew out a slow breath and waved at a moth. "It's more complex than that," he admitted. "Though the Masters would like to deny it, the difference between a Master and a Keeper is small. Only three pairs of those untold number of instructions are critical to transcending a human background and becoming a raku. Get those in the proper configuration, and the rest can be smoothed out in the first shift."

"Oh!" she exclaimed. "That's why I had to bind Talo-Toecan's nail the first time. His instructions were in it, weren't they?"

Redal-Stan nodded. "Yes. The three pairs of instructions,

or alleles, rather, concern the complexity of your neural net. They're called P, C, and F."

"Plains, coastal, and foothills," she guessed.

"Ah, yes." He shifted uneasily and reached for his cup. "The plains are unusually numerous with the recessive p instruction, the foothills in the f, and so on. A raku is recessive in all three and is written thus." He scribbled, ppccff. "That's what is known as a signature. If you have even one dominant instruction, you aren't a raku, or Master, rather."

"So my signature is ppccff," Alissa said hesitantly.

He grinned, showing his teeth. "Since before you were born. Keepers have two dominant instructions fouling up their neural nets. Any two. It doesn't matter which. Three or more creates so much chaos in their tracings that they're a commoner."

Deep in thought, Alissa sipped her tea. "What do you get when there is only one strong instruction messing up their tracings? A very powerful Keeper?"

Redal-Stan shook his head. "It's called dominant, Alissa, not strong. If it's C or P, you get a shaduf. A single dominant F gives you a septhama." He shuddered in mock horror. "Very rare, almost as rare as you, and just as much trouble."

"So," Alissa said softly, ignoring the small jibe. "Sati was almost a Master."

Stretching for more tea, Redal-Stan cleared his throat nervously. "No. Sati was an unhappy accident. Highly unlikely, but it happens when Keepers are stubborn."

"An accident you capitalized upon," Alissa accused.

He sighed in exasperation. "Should I have gone to her parents and forbid them to wed?"

"Yes!" she cried, then dropped her gaze. "No, I guess not."

"See? It's difficult." Redal-Stan settled back to prop his feet upon his desk in an unmasterly fashion. "Her mother was a Keeper. She had been told of the risks, though not the reasoning behind them. It was far more likely she would have commoner or Keeper children. The calculations are hard, even when having followed the family lines as far back as I have. Except in the obvious case of a shaduf, you can't tell if someone is carrying recessive alleles unless they pair up. You can't see it hiding behind a dominant allele. That is, except in the coastal allele. Those function together as codominant. The phenotypic expression of the alleles show a blend of the phenotype rather than the dominant masking the recessive."

Wishing he would stop talking, Alissa put a hand to her head and sighed. Codominant. Phenotypic alleles? Expressions? Did he really expect her to remember all this? she thought.

"Uh," he amended. "Neither of the two kinds of instruction is dominant over the other. It would be like getting pink chicks from red and white parents."

"Then why didn't you just say that?" she muttered under her breath, then louder, "What about septhamas? Can you spot them?"

Redal-Stan shook his head. "No, unfortunately. That single dominant F throws their tracings so far from ours that their neural net looks like a commoner's. That's why they don't make us ill with half-resonances as shadufs do. Several appear every century, throwing off everyone's expected ratios. We usually find them by an upsurge of Keepers in a family line that was expected to produce commoners." Redal-Stan grimaced. "They're nothing but trouble. The only reliable way to spot a recessive instruction is when they pair up. That *can* be seen."

"Like white chickens," Alissa said, thinking she might be starting to understand. She stretched for the teapot and refilled her tiny cup. "What do people with a double weak pair look like?" she asked, warming the cup with a quick ward.

"It's called a double recessive, Alissa," he said irately, "not a double weak pair. But to answer your question, what a person looks like depends on which pair you're referring to." His eyes narrowed. "I'm not going to tell you."

Alissa frowned, and Redal-Stan arched his nonexistent eyebrows, daring her to push the issue. "I," he boasted, "remember Ese'Nawoer's population when it was a small cluster of huts about a central community fire. Except for the newer families, I can tell you who has the potential for carrying a hidden recessive trait. It helps tremendously in calculating the expected probabilities for the next generation of Keepers. You, for instance, were probably a one in sixty-four, possibly one in thirty-two." He took his feet from his desk and put them on the floor. "Highly unlikely. But I'm surprised they allowed your parents to have any children."

"Allowed!" Alissa said, her anger flooding back. "You're all self-serving hypocrites."

He shook his head in exasperation. "Let me tell you a story before you judge," he said quietly, his eyes falling from hers. "When the first of my line of teachers was young, younger than you, she existed on the coast before being recognized for her potential and rescued."

Rescued? Alissa thought. "She was born human?" she asked, not needing to see his nod.

"Her name was Mirim, and she was the first human to manage the shift to Master. All the human folk were on the coast at that time," he said. "The mountains and plains belonged to the Masters. It was their playground—theirs and the feral beasts. There were lots of them, as it had recently been discovered how to shift to a human form. Losses were high until they got it right."

He paused, and his voice was somber when he next spoke. "The genetic heritage of the coastal people at that time was diverse, much as Ese'Nawoer is today. But there were untold thousands more. I've made a study concerning Mirim's memories, and it was a horrendous existence. No one bothered to instruct the latent Keepers. Some knew how to use their tracings. Taught one another stolen resonances. More often then not, a power-hungry Keeper slaughtered the one who taught him to prevent a future betrayal." His eyes went sorrowful. "Without the teachings of control and restraint, they made a shambles of their society."

"Wars?" she asked hesitantly.

He shook his head. "Wars are at least organized. It was more of a continuous multifront battle that ebbed and flowed with the seasons. The common folk suffered the most." Redal-Stan watched the moths battling his light. "The Masters had a practice of making forays into the safer areas—smaller towns, a fishing district on market day—and finding as many rogue Keepers as they could. Then they'd burn their tracings to ash to try to break the cycle. That's how they found Mirim."

He looked up. "Her townsfolk had beaten her and left her for the crabs and tide. They beat an eight-year-old nigh to death when someone caught her playing with fields. They would rather see her dead then grow up to join the ranks of the tyrants that stole their food, burned their homes, and assaulted their wives and daughters."

Alissa swallowed, imagining being beaten for playing with fields.

"When they discovered her tracings were perfect, the Masters didn't burn her network. Instead they took her in, tended her broken body, and eventually gave her a source. When she got older, she managed the jump to Master, then went on to write the book of *First Truth*."

She shivered, never knowing where the wisdom had come from before. Her hands trembled as she reached for her cup.

Redal-Stan eyed her from under his nonexistent brows. "Mirim shifting into a raku threw their beliefs of superiority into chaos," he said. "Their 'pet' had to be taken seriously, and it caused a savage rift in the conclave, the echoes of which we're still battling today." Again Redal-Stan gathered the moths in a field, watching them through his fingers. "Somehow the Keepers discovered the origins of source and that it made them stronger," he said as he rose and went to the balcony. "They began to lure feral beasts. Rope it. Kill it. Burn it. Bind the ash."

Alissa sat in a horrified silence, her fingers gripped tightly about her cup.

"They only knew it gave them more strength. They didn't know why. Thankfully they were able to retain only a small amount of source for all their efforts. Most would have been lost to the wind. It takes a special field to capture the source from a death pyre without snuffing out the flames that free it." He released the moths, turning to give Alissa a thin smile.

"Only a few Masters every generation bother to cultivate the concentration necessary for such a skill."

Feeling ill, she said, "I'm sorry."

He returned to sit on the edge of the couch, his elbows on his knees, his eyes downcast. "Something had to be done. Mirim was an adult by that time, and not well-respected because of her human origins. Alone, she gathered as many humans as she could who had two dominant coastal alleles. The people trusted her; her eyes were green, her fingers were normal, and she knew the culture.

"For nearly two hundred years she led them through the passes to the east, family by the family, soul by soul, enticed by promise of peace and freedom from the current tyrant. They tamed the sheep and goats, learned to respect our feral kin, and had children who utterly lacked recessive coastal alleles."

Alissa shifted uneasily. "How did that make anything better?"

He dropped his gaze. "It didn't. It's still unclear what her thoughts were at that time. Whatever they were, everything fell apart when a young Master was enticed to his death with music and burned alive for his source."

Her stomach clenched, imagining Connen-Neute writhing in flames, unable to escape.

Redal-Stan spoke to the floor. "The Masters went all but insane, striking out against the coast, purging from it the recessive trait that became known as the plains."

Alissa caught her breath, unwilling to believe what he was saying.

"Yes." His eyes flicked up and away. "Anyone with the possibility of a recessive plains allele in their signature was killed. Entire families. They knew Mirim had a population in the foothills with an abundance of that recessive trait. Removing it from the coast would reduce the chance of the coast engendering Keepers. Problem solved and revenge satisfied in one—neat—package."

Alissa stared at him. "That's—that's . . ."

"Yes, it was," he admitted, his gaze haunted, "which is

why Mirim's memories are still passed down. The atrocity can't be allowed to be forgotten."

Alissa's knees came up to her chin, and she clutched her arms about them. No wonder Talo-Toecan was so reluctant to tell her about the past. It was horrific. The silence began to grow, but she didn't think this was the end of the story.

"That was the way it was for four centuries while everyone caught their breath and buried their dead." Redal-Stan looked at her horrorstruck face with a sad acceptance. "Just as they thought they had gotten control of the situation, the population east of the mountains began to spontaneously separate. Mirim had settled the area with people with no recessive coastal alleles, and it was found every time a dominant F and P linked up without at least one recessive coastal allele to moderate, the result was lethal."

Alissa's eyes widened.

"They didn't expect that." He stared into his long-emptied cup. "It explained why their calculations of probability had always been slightly off. Needless to say, they promoted the separation."

"The foothills," Alissa whispered, "were mostly the stronger F, and the plains were mostly the stronger P. If they married, there would be no weak coastal instruction in their children. They would—" She couldn't say it.

"It's extremely rare that a child from a mixed marriage survives to term," Redal-Stan finished for her. Alissa looked at him, aghast, seeing the reason for the hatred that stretched back thousands of years. "It isn't foolproof," Redal-Stan said. "There was, and still is, a continual, unhelped migration over the mountains. Bring in one recessive coastal allele, and the plains and foothills can have children between themselves. Before long, you're right back where you started."

Alissa straightened, wondering about her own birth. "Keepers, Shadufs."

"Yes." Redal-Stan glanced at her. "All too soon Keepers began to appear."

"And you?" she whispered.

He smiled bitterly. "Eventually me. They planned their sixth child very carefully."

"Sixth child?"

With a rude snort, Redal-Stan set his empty cup on his desk. "I speak metaphorically, of course. Masters, unlike our feral kin, have children. Lots, if fortune smiles upon them. But everyone works to bring about the culmination of a transeunt. In a way they are a child." He pointed a finger at her. "You're the seventh. I'm the sixth. Mirim was the first."

"Oh." So she was a transeunt, Alissa thought, not sure she liked the title.

"Keepers are again painfully numerous," he murmured uneasily. "And though they're being taught restraint now, there has been hidden mutterings of purging the eastern populations of the recessive coastal allele once more. They're ignoring Mirim's memories of the horror and devastation they wrought upon the coast. Ese'Nawoer, they say, is where their next child will come from." He eyed Alissa. "Clearly this didn't happen."

Alissa shook her head solemnly, realizing she was playing with the ends of her hair. A soft, hesitant knock at the door pulled her hands down. Giving Redal-Stan a stilted smile, she hid her discomfort behind her cup, surprised to find it empty.

"What is the point of being at the top of the tower if everyone knows where you are?" Redal-Stan grumbled. He took a deep breath, and Alissa wished she could block her ears. "Go away!" he bellowed.

"Don't punish Alissa," came Connen-Neute's faint thought. It was the equivalent of a whisper, as if he were afraid to hurt her tracings further. *"I was sent to watch her. Sati's loss is my fault."*

Redal-Stan's nonexistent eyebrows rose. He tilted his head to the door, a crafty look in his eye. "Come in."

The door opened enough for Connen-Neute's tall shadow to slip in. His gaze flicked between hers and Redal-Stan's as he cautiously took the chair farthest from the desk. "I'll take her punishment," Connen-Neute said, his eyes level and undaunted. "Whatever it is."

"Uh, Connen-Neute?" Alissa said, only to find her shin kicked. She glared at Redal-Stan.

"How noble of you," Redal-Stan drawled, and Alissa grew angry. No one but Strell had tried to take her punishment before, and she would be lying if she said she didn't appreciate it. "But she has no punishment," the older Master finished.

"She hasn't?"

"No. But your offer to help me search the texts to find the appropriate family line to watch for a replacement shaduf is appreciated," he finished.

"I didn't—" Connen-Neute hesitated and, appearing to have swallowed something sour, whispered. "Of course."

Alissa frowned. "You won't let me read your books. Why are you letting him?"

"He's not letting me," came Connen-Neute's whispered thought. *"He's forcing me."*

Redal-Stan rose with a stretch. Moving to a shelf, he tugged the largest tome free. It hit his desk with a thump, and he opened it, scanning the names listed. "Only because you don't want to," he said. "Take this one with you when you go."

Alissa gritted her teeth in frustration.

"You can't win, Alissa," Connen-Neute advised. His long face grew solemn. "How is your shoulder?"

"It's fine," she grumbled, angry that Connen-Neute could read Redal-Stan's books and she couldn't. It wasn't fair.

"No, really. How is it?" he persisted. "I'm sorry I dropped you on the balcony. I thought I might have . . ." he lowered his eyes, ". . . have broken it."

"You very nearly did," she said, flexing it experimentally. "I ran a healing ward as soon as I woke up." She eyed him darkly. "It was the only reason you managed to pin Beast down, you know."

Bent over his books, Redal-Stan slowly looked up. "What was that?"

"Uh," Alissa stammered, wishing she hadn't brought up Beast's impropriety. "I'm sorry," she said, her fingers twining her hair into knots. "I talked with Beast. She promises not to do it again, fight you, I mean."

"I did not!" Beast cried, but only Alissa heard her.

"No. Not that." Redal-Stan stood still as stone. "The other thing."

"I fixed my shoulder?" she offered, wondering at their gaping looks. Then she rolled her eyes. "Yes," she grumped. "I know. Learning a ward of healing before a window ward isn't proper, but Hounds. I had to take my lessons when I could."

Leaving his book open, Redal-Stan ghosted from behind his desk. He sat down onto the couch beside her. "M-m-m, ward of healing?" he said mildly.

"Yes." She eyed her empty cup, wishing she had started with a bigger rock. "Do you call it something else? Sometimes my terminology is off."

Redal-Stan waved Connen-Neute to silence. "Describe it to me," he suggested. He saw her gaze on her cup. "Here. Let me fill that for you," he murmured, doing just that.

Hot cup in hand, Alissa settled back uneasily. Redal-Stan was being most attentive, and Connen-Neute looked positively intense. "Well," she said, "it's the ward that speeds up healing. Three days' worth in a moment—you know—and allows you to do the same for anyone else. That's why my tracings don't hurt. Much," she added in afterthought.

"You mean other Masters, of course," Redal-Stan said.

"No." Surprised, Alissa set her cup down. "Anyone."

"Show me?"

It was a plaintive whisper, and she looked up, not believing it had been Redal-Stan's. That wistful tone usually came out of her. Her mouth fell open in understanding. "You don't know a healing ward!" she cried, afraid.

Redal-Stan took a sharp breath, shattering his obvious longing. Again the self-assured, slightly egotistical plainsman-cum-Master was before her. Giving a gruff "Harrumph," he settled back into the couch, then slipped to the edge again. "No," he said. "Will you teach me?"

Alissa felt a grin creep over her. "All right. Under one condition."

Immediately he grew defensive. "What?" he said flatly.

"I want to show Connen-Neute, too."

Connen-Neute's breath came in a quick sound of gratitude.

"Yes," Redal-Stan agreed, settling back. "That would be fine."

40

Redal-Stan glanced up as Connen-Neute's empty cup touched his desk with a small click. *"If I might retire?"* his student questioned. *"It's late."*

"Verbalize, please." Redal-Stan rubbed a hand over his tired eyes. "You speak to Alissa. Why won't you speak to me?"

"Because," was all the young Master would say, and Redal-Stan grimaced.

"Go," he grumbled. "Go to bed, or the roof, or wherever it is you're sleeping these days. But don't leave my book where it can go damp."

"The roof," Connen-Neute mumbled. He straightened his vest as he stood. *"Would you like me to watch her tomorrow?"*

Stretching, Redal-Stan reached for the ceiling. His back cracked several times, and he groaned softly. "Yes. If you would."

"What about tonight?" he persisted. *"She refused to take the sleeping aid."*

Redal-Stan chuckled. "You saw her palm it off into my cup, too, eh? No. She won't go feral tonight as long as no one gets Beast upset or frightened." He paused. "I'll check on her."

Connen-Neute nodded. *"But tomorrow she might go feral?"*

"Yes." He felt his forehead crease with worry. "Tomorrow, the day after, next week. It depends on things I don't understand yet. I'm hoping the longer we can stave off Beast flying away, the better the chance Alissa has for finding new reference points."

"She might find a lifetime of points in two weeks?" Connen-Neute asked hopefully, slumping when Redal-Stan shook his head. "Then tomorrow I will accompany her," he said aloud. "To remind Beast if she becomes—dominant."

Redal-Stan closed his eyes in a long blink. "If she gives you any trouble, tell her I've charged her with getting you to speak aloud more. I'll take the day after on the excuse of lessons. The daylight hours I'm not too concerned about. It's at night Beast seems to grow strong."

Giving him a nod, Connen-Neute took the book and left, closing the door behind him.

Redal-Stan went to his balcony, drawn by the newly risen moon. As Connen-Neute had said, it was late, but his thoughts were spinning. It was unlikely they would lend themselves to sleep. There was a tug on his thoughts as Connen-Neute shifted on the roof, and he smiled. Redal-Stan had spent many nights himself watching the air currents stream about the stars. But now, in his long-lived agedness, he contented himself with his balcony. The open sky was for the young.

Falling carelessly into his balcony chair, he flexed his hand. The slight burn from the tea was gone. It was an odd feeling, being at the receiving end of the student/instructor relationship again. Alissa had the bearings of a born teacher, answering all his questions with a patient understanding very unlike her usual temper. And his hand—he looked at it in wonder—was healed.

Redal-Stan leaned his head back and closed his eyes as he recalled her intent instruction. "No," she had said. "You don't need to know anatomy and such. *You* aren't healing anything, just focusing the surrounding energy to a fevered pitch. The body uses it as it sees best, and the body knows how to heal itself."

And it felt so good! he thought, unable to stop his sigh. Like being in a sunbeam, or having a sunbeam inside you. Just the memory of the ward seemed to warm him. Connen-

Neute had nearly fallen asleep when Alissa demonstrated the ward upon him. After seeing the young Master's bemused expression turn into a languorous stretch and nodding head, Redal-Stan had decided he would heal himself, thank you all the same. He had memorized the resonance, and after getting his "teacher's" permission, he tried it only to all but fall asleep anyway.

A breath of wind carrying the promise of morning frost slipped over him. He retreated back inside at its sudden chill, longing for the bone-soaking heat of his plains for the first time in centuries. Restless, he went to his desk for a paper and quill. A quick thought and the globe of light he had left upon his desk doubled its intensity. Alissa, he mused, couldn't be allowed to go feral. The idea of her irksome, exasperating, nimble-minded presence joining the ranks of the lost was intolerable. But he gave her less than a week, even with Beast's cooperation.

It wouldn't be an easy loss, either, but long and drawn out, painful to both. Already Beast was beginning to assert herself. Alissa still maintained control, but it was slipping. Soon, he imagined there would be a nightmarish period of confusion where you might ask a question of Alissa and Beast would answer. He was sure Beast would be unhappy and apologetic, but it would continue to happen with an increasing regularity. A day or two of that, and Alissa would fade further, leaving a distressed Beast to cope with a world she barely understood. Eventually Beast would wake one morning with no memory of Alissa and fly away.

It was inevitable. It was unthinkable. It was not going to happen. Not if there was a way he could stop it. But he knew there wasn't. He had to stop thinking there was and focus upon the even more impossible task of getting her back to her own time. Back to her lodestone, Strell.

"Strell," he whispered, dipping his quill. What if she did get back? She said there was no one left but Talo-Toecan. And Talo-Toecan wouldn't willingly sanction a Master/commoner union. Master/Keeper, perhaps, considering the apparent lack of suitable matches.

He hesitated, reaching for his tea. It was to his lips before he remembered the sleeping draught. Smiling, he rose and threw the liquid out over his balcony.

"Strell is a commoner," he whispered as he returned and began to write the possible signatures for a man from the plains. He eliminated any with four or more recessive alleles that would make Strell a Keeper. Those with any dominant plains, two recessive coastal, or two recessive foothills alleles were also ignored as being highly improbable. The lethal combinations were, of course, omitted. When done, he pondered the remaining signatures. Any of them were possible. None would instill Talo-Toecan with any desire to allow Alissa to have children with Strell. He scribbled more, sighing as the truth came out. The best she could manage with him would be Keeper. There was an unsettlingly high chance at commoner, and even worse, shaduf.

The quill was gently set to rest. "Talo-Toecan will forbid it," he said. Redal-Stan could imagine the hot fallout from that. He hadn't known Alissa long, but it was obvious that telling her she couldn't do a thing would all but guarantee that's what she would do. Whatever Talo-Toecan did, her genetic heritage would be lost. If she joined with her commoner, her children would lack a perfect neural net. If Strell was forbidden to her, she would refuse to join with anyone else.

Talo-Toecan would have to risk allowing her to make the decision herself, hoping she would do the responsible thing by forgoing her desire for Strell for the good of the Hold. If not, the Hold would lose her desperately needed influx of new blood.

"Just as they lost mine," he murmured, wondering if perhaps his rigid pride was why the Hold fell. The Masters counted heavily upon the addition of new genetic material into their dwindling population that their transeunts provided. Centuries ago, upon learning that his conception had been engineered for their benefit, he had resigned himself to a state of bachelorhood, feeling as if he were thought of as only a— brood stallion. His chair creaked as he slumped back. It was exactly what Alissa had accused them of. Perhaps she was right.

If she joined with a Keeper, she would have at least a chance at a raku child. There would have to be lots of Keepers about, even if the Masters were gone. The thought cheered him somewhat, but it would have to be quite a charismatic man to overcome the love she already held for her commoner. Talo-Toecan would have to fly a delicate updraft, appearing to give her a choice of suitors while struggling to find someone worthy of her.

He frowned, thinking. "Though Talo-Toecan is no longer one of my formal students," he said, taking up his quill, "he is bound by ties to respect my wishes, no matter how odd they seem." Redal-Stan bent low, and the sound of his quill scratching lasted for some moments.

It was difficult to decide how best to advise Talo-Toecan in handling the situation without giving away the future too soon. Talo-Toecan was loyal to his beliefs, and if not told otherwise, he would undoubtedly adhere to long-held raku mores that held no place in a Hold that was dying. Perhaps it wouldn't take much convincing. Talo-Toecan was quite the rebel concerning the morality of manipulating the humans' population for their benefit.

He read his letter over twice, made a sharp crease down the center, and propped it up on the mantel to give to Talo-Toecan when he returned. He smiled at the imagined look of bemusement his onetime student would give him after reading it. It was worded so that it would be meaningless until after Alissa got back. His smile faded. If she got back.

Feeling tired and old, he went to his bed and sat on the edge with a heavy sigh. It seemed as if her presence was still here. She had left behind the scent of the wind that ran before a desert storm, lingering among his books and papers. His hand brushed the top sheet as he adjusted his pillows, and he paused, bending close in disbelief. There was grit *under* his sheets! She had left stone chips and sand in his bed! Outraged, he stood, stepping on his writing board. He stiffened as he scooped it up. It was ruined! And his cloak! He shook the sand from it, furious.

Spinning about, he took three long steps to his door. Then he caught himself at his desk. Breath slipping from him in a sigh, he set the board and cloak aside. A smile came over him as he crafted a blanket and eased to his balcony to sleep under the moon.

41

"**G**ood morning, Master Connen-Neute, Keeper Alissa."

"Morning," Alissa stammered, and the unidentified Keeper continued down the hall to the stairs. She recognized him but had no idea as to his name. His footsteps faded to leave the Keepers' hall silent. Taking a deep breath, she turned back to the closed door before them.

"By my Master's Hounds, Alissa," Connen-Neute grumbled. *"You're only asking Nisi to join you for breakfast, not requesting a favor from Redal-Stan."*

Alissa tucked her hair out of her eyes, peeved at the amusement in his thoughts. Nervous, she took a step back. "She probably isn't even in there."

He took her shoulders, stopping her retreat. *"She is."*

"I'd wager she has plans already," Alissa hedged.

"Let's find out." Using his height as an unfair advantage, Connen-Neute picked Alissa up by the elbows and set her firmly before Nisi's door. Grasping her hand, he knocked.

"Stop it!" she hissed, trying to pull away.

"If you're going to run away, you'd better do it now," he said, his eyes dancing.

Nisi flung open her door, and Connen-Neute steeled his face back to a dignified, dispassionate expression. Biting back her cry of outrage, Alissa turned to smile weakly at Nisi.

"Alissa! Hello," Nisi said. "And good morning, Connen-Neute." She flicked a brief glance at him, and he gave her a silent nod.

In a smooth, unhurried motion, Alissa surreptitiously

kicked Connen-Neute. He owed her something. "Good morning, Keeper Nisi," he said aloud, and Nisi blinked in surprise.

"Um, hi," Alissa said into the awkward silence. "I was wondering if you had breakfast yet, and if not, would you like to join me?" Connen-Neute jabbed an unseen finger into her ribs, and she bit back a muffled grunt. "I mean, us."

"I'd love to." Nisi disappeared into her room. "Let me get my coat," she said loudly. "Ashes, but it was cold last night; I had to ward my windows. But at least I don't have Ren's field duties anymore." Nisi joined them in the hall with her coat. "You did know he left?"

"Yes." Alissa dropped her eyes to hide her flush of guilt. His ribbon lay in her pocket like a guilty secret. She had yet to give it to Kally, not wanting to add to the girl's grief.

"No one knows where he went," Nisi said slowly, "but I can't say as I blame him." Her gaze went sad. "Let's get your coat, and we can eat."

Alissa smiled thinly in understanding. "We don't need to eat in the garden. Unless you want to, of course," she added.

Nisi eyed her cautiously. "Redal-Stan said you bruised your tracings at the assembly. That you would be sensitive for a while to the background noise. I tried to visit you, but *he* wouldn't let me." She made a face at Connen-Neute, who didn't look at all apologetic.

"I'm fine," Alissa reassured her. "Redal-Stan gave me a ward to block everything."

"Are you sure? He said it was quite serious."

"It was." Alissa adopted a serious pose and steepled her fingers. "Channeling the mental output of fourteen thousand citizens," she mocked in a low voice, "whipped up to a synchronized frenzy of emotion, could have permanently impaired your ability to communicate."

Nisi laughed, not noticing Connen-Neute struggle to smother his chuckle. "Not bad," Nisi encouraged. "But you need to scowl and harrumph more." She tossed her coat back into the mess she kept her room in, and they started down the hall.

"So," Nisi drawled, giving a nod behind them to where Connen-Neute padded silently along. "Why the shadow?"

Alissa's brow furrowed. "He says Redal-Stan told him to stay with me until he's talking in sentences."

Nisi gave her a doubtful look. "Really?"

"That's what he said." Actually, Alissa knew Connen-Neute was baby-sitting her, and it rankled her to no end.

"Huh." Nisi slowed until Connen-Neute's gray-clothed figure was walking between them. "If I may be so bold," she directed to him. "How many seasons have you?"

"One hundred and sixteen, Keeper Nisi," he whispered.

Alissa smiled at the distress in his voice. Even though Redal-Stan had an ulterior motive for saddling her with him, Connen-Neute would be speaking more today.

"Huh. Thank you," Nisi said, and he inclined his head and retreated. Nisi leaned close. "It's a bit soon, but maybe he's auditing your instruction."

Alissa heard Connen-Neute stumble on the stairs. "Beg your pardon?" she asked.

The smile on Nisi's face was one of an amused delight. "You know," she jostled Alissa's elbow, "learning how to instruct a Keeper. Before going from a student Master to a teaching one, they audit several Keepers' training. Until the novelty wears off, they follow the poor unfortunate about," she nodded behind them, "making a pest of themselves as they try to figure out what's going through our heads." Nisi chuckled. "We aren't supposed to know they're studying us. But like I said," she continued. "It's a shade soon." She turned slightly. "Isn't it, Connen-Neute?"

"Yes," he said with a sigh.

Nisi laughed. "Kind of flattering, though."

"No," Alissa said, scowling. "You had it right the first time."

Together they rounded the base of the stair and entered the dining hall. Connen-Neute winced at the noise of clinking dishes and loud voices. Alissa's head throbbed, and she set up her newest ward. Immediately her headache vanished. Nisi peered about, searching for a spot.

"I've eaten already," came Connen-Neute's thought. *"I'll wait in the kitchen."*

"Sorry," Alissa said, and really meant it. *"I'm a Keeper today. You'll have to verbalize."*

"Kitchen," he muttered, frowning as he realized Redal-Stan's trap, and he slipped away.

"Great," Nisi exclaimed. There's room for two over there."

Alissa followed her, smiling at those she recognized, nodding to those she didn't. The reaction varied from pleased acceptance to wary distrust. Nisi ignored it all, plopping down between an old Keeper who was intently filling his face and a young woman who looked like she was straight from the plains. Alissa sat next to her, thinking she looked like her mother.

"Cups," Nisi muttered. "Where are the blessed cups? Ah, there they are," she said, snagging two and giving Alissa the one not chipped. A Keeper at the end of the table shoved a pot of tea at them, and Alissa smiled at him, relieved she hadn't needed to ask.

"Thanks, Gury," Nisi said, and he went back to his stinky sausage, eyeing Alissa with furtive glances. The tea was cold as she poured it out, and she warmed it with a quick thought.

The sharp clatter of forks hitting the table made her jump. "Hey!" someone shouted. "What was that?" The noise in the Keepers' dining hall cut off, and Alissa shrank into herself, her steaming cup halfway to her lips. Everyone was looking at everyone else, their faces questioning.

"Ashes, Alissa," came Connen-Neute's thought from the kitchen. *"We were saving that ward for a bribe."*

"That was a new resonance," the man who had given Alissa the tea accused. "Anyone else catch it?"

There were nods all around. Beside Alissa, Nisi grinned. Gury leaned halfway across the table. "Nisi? Have you learned something you wish to share with us?"

"Wasn't me," she called gaily, rolling her eyes at Alissa.

Everyone turned, and Alissa flushed. "Um," she hedged.

"What does it do?" someone asked eagerly.

"It's a warming ward," she admitted, hoisting her steaming cup. "You didn't know it?"

Everyone shook their head. Nisi nearly danced in her chair.

"My instructor taught me, but . . ." Alissa stammered. It wasn't her place to impart skills, only acquire them.

Gury leaned back with a sly grin. "We'll ask," he said, confirming Alissa's feeling it would be a mistake to show them. "Don't get yourself in trouble. They'll show us as soon as they get back." He eyed the table knowingly. "Won't they?"

There was a chorus of agreement.

"Here, Alissa." Someone topped off her cup. "It's not often a new ward is discovered."

"And even rarer they tell us," someone else grumbled.

"Alissa?" someone else called. "Try one of Mav's pastries."

"She doesn't want that sticky thing," came a loud voice. "Give the mad, rogue Keeper of the wilds a breakfast worth having. A slab of ham, smothered in gravy."

Alissa looked to find smiling, teasing faces all around. A grin stole over her. "No, thank you," she said over the cheers and jeers at his suggestion, wishing she could bring herself to eat meat just once if only to go along with the fun.

"Alissa's from the foothills," Nisi said. "She has better taste than you, Gury."

"Toast would be fine," Alissa said, scanning the table and finding none.

"Toast! bellowed a masculine voice. "Mav! We need toast!"

"It's fine," she protested. "I'll just have eggs." And she ladled a spoonful on her plate.

"Nonsense." Gury snitched his tablemate's spiced fruit. "You want toast," he mumbled around his full mouth.

It got noisy again as she ate, the conversations taking up where they had left off. To Alissa's thinking there was a new excitement. They had a bone to pick with their respective teachers and were eager for the confrontation. The situation was one she could sympathize with. These were people who would accept her as her own kinsmen would not, and it had taken her a crossed mountain range and almost four hundred years to find them.

"Here, Alissa," whispered a lethargic voice.

It was Kally, and she slid a plate before Alissa and left before Alissa could say thanks. On it was a piece of toast. It was burnt. Alissa's finger went out to turn it over.

Both sides.

She and Nisi stared at it. Slowly Alissa reached for the jam, and Nisi's mouth twisted. "You're not going to eat that, are you?"

Alissa sighed. "After I scrape it." Some things never changed.

"Kally can bring you another," Nisi protested.

As if speaking her name had conjured her, Kally's solemn figure appeared at Alissa's elbow. Her eyes were rimmed in red and her hair was disheveled. "Sorry," the girl mumbled, barely audible over the noise. "I'll get you another."

Not meeting Alissa's gaze, she left, the toast nearly sliding off the plate. Nisi and Alissa watched her disappear into the kitchen. "By the Hounds," Nisi whispered. "She's got it bad."

Alissa swallowed hard. A flush of guilt assailed her, and her fingers went to touch the ribbon carefully wound in her pocket. "Um, Nisi? I'm sorry, but I have to talk to Kally."

Nisi set her cup down. "I should've known you opened the door for him."

"Something like that." She shifted awkwardly. It wasn't nice to leave Nisi like this.

"Go." Nisi gave her a small wave. "If I'm not here, I'll be in my room—cleaning it. Take your time. Kally might need a shoulder to cry on. Or someone to yell at."

Glad Nisi understood, Alissa smiled her good-bye. Halfway to the kitchen she slowed. What had Nisi meant by "someone to yell at"?

Alissa's nose wrinkled at the stench of cooked meat as she entered the kitchen. No wonder Connen-Neute liked it here. She spotted him in the corner, his feet tucked under him as he seriously snitched leftover chicken, ignoring everyone and being ignored in turn. His eyes looked as solemn as an owl's in his long face. He shrugged and continued his pilfering.

"Ah, Alissa!" came Mav's shout. "What can I get for you, dearie?" Her fists slammed into the heavy dough she was working.

Alissa maneuvered through the busy workers. "Hi, Mavoureen." She sat on the edge of the table and swung her legs. Kally was alone by the smallest hearth, stirring a pot.

"It's good to see you taking your breakfast where you ought," Mav said as she thumped the dough again. "Sorry about the toast." The old woman's gaze followed Alissa's to Kally. "She had that bread burnt and out to you before I knew what was what. She's been no use to me these last few days." Mav cut the dough into identical, fist-sized lumps and arranged them in a pan. "She's stirring a pot of water, she is. I told her it was tomorrow's soup. I can't trust her with anything else." Mav draped a linen cloth over her dough and set her hands to rest. "What am I going to do with her? She won't talk to me."

Alissa touched Ren's ribbon, hidden in her pocket. "Maybe I could help."

The old woman turned a sorrowful look to Alissa. "If only you could, but I'm afraid her heart has been wounded to the quick. She won't listen to anyone."

Feeling guilty for having waited, Alissa swung her ankles. "I have a message from Ren."

Mav's wrinkles deepened, and she bit her lip. "Well, go ahead. She can't get worse."

At Mav's encouraging nod, Alissa slid from the table and dodged her way to the relatively empty corner. It was nice having people about, but what she would give to have her quiet kitchen back. Kally looked up, leaning against the hearth as she listlessly stirred a pot.

"Morning, Alissa."

"Kally." She stood there like an idiot, not knowing how to start.

Kally smiled weakly. "Mav has me stirring water, pretending it's soup. Would you like a taste?" She pulled up the spoon and dribbled the water back into the pot. The spoon slipped from her to bob at the surface of the steaming water. "Hounds," she cursed, then slumped down on a stool. "I can't even boil water today."

Alissa dragged a second stool close and sat down as well. Not knowing what to say, she simply pulled out the ribbon. "Um, Ren gave me this to give to you," she said lamely.

Kally stood. Grabbing a new spoon, she violently stirred the pot. Water spilled to hiss on the fire. "Ren? What does he want?" she said a bit too brightly. "Haven't seen him for days."

Miserable, Alissa took the spoon before Kally put the fire out. Turning Kally's hand over, she put the ribbon in it. "I'm sorry."

Anger, followed by hopelessness, flashed over Kally, and she sank down again, her eyes on the length of blue. "He left without saying good-bye," she whispered, pulling it through her fingers. Her eyes grew hard. "Curse him, he owed me that. Why didn't he even say good-bye?"

"Because he loves you." Alissa's gaze dropped.

"I don't care that he didn't make Keeper again," she wailed.

From the corner of her sight, Alissa saw Mav standing motionless, her arms hanging still, helpless. "He knew that," she said. "But he was woefully misled and ill-used. His pride wouldn't tolerate it anymore." Alissa hesitated. "So he left."

Kally's cheeks showed spots of anger. "Just like that," she said bitterly. She threw the ribbon on the floor.

"Yes," Alissa snapped as Kally's anger sparked hers. "And don't think it was easy."

"You're defending him!" Kally shouted, and the kitchen help paused. "He ran away, and you're defending him! You have never lost anyone, have you!" she accused, slamming her spoon to the table. "You have no idea what I feel like."

Alissa's breath caught. *"Um, Alissa?"* Beast whispered, ignored.

The kitchen went silent. "Ren," Alissa said, her back stiff, "asked me to say good-bye for him and that he would miss your breakfasts together. And as for never having lost anyone? I have lost my father, my mother, my teacher, and my—" she stopped, clenching in heartache.

"*Alissa?*" Beast whispered.

Alissa slumped onto the stool, her head in her hands. Wolves. Strell. She had lost Strell.

"I—I need some potatoes for my soup," Kally stammered into the silence. There was a soft breeze, and she was gone.

"*Alissa?*" came Connen-Neute's thought.

"*Go away,*" she thought miserably, and his comforting presence faded.

"Alissa?" It was Mav, putting a bird-light hand upon her shoulder.

"I lost my love," Alissa whispered. The Navigator burn her to ash. She had lost her love.

"Alissa, I'm sorry," Mav said. The kitchen resumed its noise. "Kally didn't know."

"I didn't handle that very well, did I?" Alissa said. Looking up, she was surprised at the guilt on Mav's features. "What?" Alissa whispered. "It wasn't your fault."

The lines on Mav's face deepened. Taking a thick rag, she pushed the pot from the low flames and gazed at nothing. "She would have gone with him but for me," Mav said.

Alissa's depression faltered in understanding. She felt Beast's awareness tighten and was shocked to hear herself say, "Don't lessen your charge's love for you with guilt, old woman." It was Beast speaking through her, and Alissa's first response of fear melted into acceptance. The takeover was inevitable. She would accept it with grace.

Mav looked sharply at Alissa, then lowered herself in stages onto the stool. Her eyes rested on the ribbon, and she picked it up to clean the flour from it. "Yes," the woman said with a sigh, "I'm old. Kally has her entire life ahead of her, and she has exchanged a lifetime of Ren's love for the paltry few more years I can give her."

"Perhaps," Beast admitted, not bothering to apologize to Alissa. "But I think love is measured backwards as well as forwards. The sixteen years you have loved and cared for her are not the quarter of a lifetime that you measure but an entire lifetime for her. She knows no time without your love and can't voluntarily leave it. Ren knew this. Accept his gift in good grace," Beast finished. "Kally will understand in time."

Mav peered into Alissa's eyes. The clatter of bread pans stirred her, and she sighed and straightened. Slowly she stood, and Beast and Alissa gazed up, seeing her emotions shift from guilt to acceptance. "You are wise beyond your years, Alissa."

Alissa felt a ghost of a smile. Slowly Beast settled herself, alert and awake, but silent. Mav tucked Ren's token of love away in a pocket, covering the awkward silence by needlessly wiping her hands on a towel. A sudden cheering from the dining hall drew their attention, and Lodesh all but fell into the room.

"Mav! Quick! Hide me!"

4²

Mav and Alissa looked to find Lodesh's terrified face. From the great hall came a muffled, angry shout, "Warden!"

The kitchen help exploded into cheers. Lodesh absently acknowledged them as he pushed his way closer. "Mav," he pleaded. "I just need a few hours. I'll go back. I promise!"

Mav burst into laughter. "Get to your work!" she bellowed, and everyone became busy. Lodesh danced from foot to foot. Except for his boots, he was dressed all in blue, even down to the overly ornate hat gripped tightly in his hand. He looked miserable. Mav gave him a fierce hug, which he was too spooked to return. "You're too large to hide in my flour cupboard anymore, lad," she cackled. Cocking her head, she appeared to listen. "You'd better run for it."

"Lodesh!" came Breve's indignant voice from the dining hall. "We have an appointment at the hosiery to size you for boots."

Lodesh froze like a startled deer. Alissa jumped as Connen-Neute touched her elbow. "Might I suggest the garden?" he said quietly.

Mav spun the panicked Lodesh about and shoved him to the brightly painted door. "Run!" she said. "We'll hold them as long as we can." She laughed as Connen-Neute and Alissa jostled him out the door. "You there, get the bread pans!" Alissa heard as they fled. "You, sweep the floor. Someone put—" and the door shut with a bang.

A trio of doves sunning themselves burst into flight and swung over the wall.

"Hounds, Alissa," Lodesh gasped. "You're a sight for my tired eyes." Grasping her hand, he tugged her down the path. "They won't let me be! There's always someone talking at me, and they're always so blessedly polite." He glanced furtively behind them. They were nearly running, and Alissa couldn't help her smile as he dragged her along. Connen-Neute paced beside them, not even breathing hard.

"Excuse me, Warden?" Lodesh mocked in a false soprano. "Pardon me, Warden? Oh, Warden, if you have but a moment?" He sighed. "It's got me to my trail's end."

"Good morning, Lodesh," Alissa said breathlessly, reclaiming her hand as it was easier to keep up with him that way.

"Not a moment's peace," he moaned. "They won't even let me choose my stockings."

"It's a wonderfully sunny day, isn't it?" she asked, but he didn't hear. She grinned. He was always so calm and self-possessed. It was nice to know he was human.

"There were three kinds of eggs for breakfast today," he said as they loped past the firepit, "and four pastries. I had to try everything so as not to hurt the cook's feelings."

"Is that a new shirt?" she panted.

Seeing her struggling, Lodesh slowed. "Yes." He picked at the shimmery fabric.

From behind them came Connen-Neute's dark voice, "Keeper Breve is in the garden."

Lodesh paled. "Wolves." He dove off the path. Connen-Neute and Alissa followed. Weaving and darting, Lodesh led them through the garden's back paths as if he had built them. Lungs heaving, they halted in a slight dip in the terrain. Birds scattered as they crouched among the bushes. Connen-Neute and Alissa exchanged amused looks. Lodesh was frantic. His eyes were wide, and his hair was in an unusual disarray. She had to fight to keep from arranging it.

"Warden!" came Breve's distant bellow, echoing off the

walls of the Hold. "This is unseemly. Think of your stand-ing!"

Lodesh sank down, though Breve was clearly far away. "Why won't they leave me alone?" he muttered.

Alissa's hand went out, and he jumped as she tucked a yellow curl behind his ear. "Why are you letting them bully you, Lodesh?"

He blinked, looking at her for the first time. "All I want is the mornings for myself."

"Did you tell them that?"

Lodesh hesitated. Clearly the thought had never occurred to him.

The sound of an aggressive crunching on the path silenced them. Hidden in the bushes, they watched Breve stalk past. His face was red, and he was muttering obscenities. The sound of his steps faded. "Lodesh!" came his muffled shout.

They exhaled as one in a long, noisy breath. Lodesh stood. "Maybe we can slip back out through the kitchen."

Alissa looked at Connen-Neute. A smile hovered about him. At his nod of agreement, they rose and followed Lodesh as he dodged and slunk from cover to cover in the bright, morning sun. Alissa giggled as she tried to keep up with his furtive jumps. Connen-Neute kept to his measured, dignified pace. Together they rounded the last turn before the kitchen door and froze.

A man in citadel livery was waiting, slumped against the wall, idly tossing pebbles. He looked up at the sound of their sliding feet. "Hey!" he cried, bolting upright. "Keeper Breve!"

In an explosion of motion, Lodesh and Alissa turned and ran.

"Keeper Breve! He's over here!"

"Burn me to ash," Lodesh panted. "They have me."

Alissa pulled him to a stop. "Not yet, they don't."

Connen-Neute strode up even with them, his eyes bright and eager. Alissa looked at the tower to place herself. "Come on." Grabbing Lodesh's hand, she ran off the path, laughing as she headed for the hidden door in the wall.

"It's not funny, Alissa," Lodesh muttered.

"Yes, Warden, it is," was Connen-Neute's opinion, exchanging his dignified gait for an effortless run.

The three of them pulled up short at the wall, their gaze traveling up its extensive height. "We can't climb out," Lodesh asserted, dancing from foot to foot.

Connen-Neute adjusted his red sash. "Voice of experience?"

"Yes. I mean, no!" he snapped, watching Alissa run her fingers lightly over the cold stone. "What *are* you doing, Alissa?"

"Got it!" she shouted triumphantly as she found a faint tingle. She turned to see them staring at her as if she had lost her mind. "It's a door!" she cried.

"Warden!" Breve shouted, and Connen-Neute and Lodesh flung themselves at the wall. They all fell through as Breve appeared in a crashing of branches. "Stop!" he shouted. "Connen-Neute, stop him!"

Connen-Neute gave Breve a cold look, took Lodesh's shoulder, and shut the door.

"Lodesh!" filtered faintly over the wall. Together they ran laughing to the nearby woods. Alissa halted against a tree with a hand pressed against her side, doubled over in hilarity.

"Now where?" Lodesh had lost his frantic look, assuming his familiar cocky attitude. A loud boom came from the Hold as the door crashed open. "The Hounds take him," Lodesh cursed. "Doesn't that man ever take a hint?" Putting his fingers to his lips, he whistled.

Connen-Neute and Alissa stared. It would only let Breve know where they were. But then a thumping of hooves came, and Frightful trotted happily into view. Happy, that is, until he caught a whiff of rakus.

Frightened by the flat ears and arched neck, Alissa slid up against Connen-Neute, appreciating his tall height. Lodesh shushed and mollified the ugly horse until he stood calmly. "There now," he murmured. "Connen-Neute won't eat you today. You remember him, yes?"

Lodesh turned, starting at Alissa's wary expression. "I had

no time to stable him," he explained, embarrassed, and he began to rub his mount with handfuls of the long grass that eked out a living at the edge of the woods. Frightful tried to eat the grass, far more eager to fill his belly than have the sweat brushed from his coat.

"Lodesh!" Breve's shout pulled Frightful's head up. His ears flicked back, then forward, listening. "I will marshal the Hold's students and beat you out of the brush like a rabbit!"

Lodesh dropped the grass and swung smoothly up onto the pad he used as a saddle. Leaning down, he held out a hand for her. With thoughts of flashing hooves and snapping teeth, she backed up into Connen-Neute. "Uh-uh."

He wiggled his fingers. "Please, Alissa," he pleaded. "Frightful will allow it if I'm with you. I know it. This is the most fun I've had in two days. Connen-Neute can follow by air. We can meet in the grove."

"No," said Connen-Neute, and Alissa turned in surprise. "You go," he said, his white teeth showing as he grinned. "I'll accompany Keeper Breve."

"Perfect!" Lodesh exclaimed. "Quick. Let's go."

"I don't know," Alissa said, wishing she could just shift and fly.

"Warden!" came Breve's shout, noticeably closer.

Lodesh looked at the cloudless sky. His eyes were pinched and wistful when he looked back. "Please, Alissa. You're the only person who has called me by my name in two days."

She glanced at Frightful, his ears alternately flat and pricked, to Connen-Neute, amusement in his golden eyes, to Lodesh, unashamedly begging. "Oh, Hounds," she muttered as she hiked up her skirt. "I can't believe I'm going to do this."

Lodesh beamed. Frightful shied only the once, and she made it up behind Lodesh in two tries. She settled herself, tugging her skirt back over her legs. "All set?" Lodesh asked, and she nodded nervously, forgetting he couldn't possibly see, but they were so cursedly close he felt her move. Ashes, they were too close.

With no warning, Frightful squealed and rose up on his back feet. Alissa's arms went around Lodesh. The horse's feet returned to the earth with a jaw-rattling thump. It had been Connen-Neute. Ignoring Frightful's quivering attempt to sidestep away, Connen-Neute nearly pulled Lodesh from the saddle. His lips a hand's breath from Lodesh, he whispered, "Keep the beast at bay until I rejoin you."

White-faced, Lodesh nodded, and Connen-Neute released him. Lodesh resettled himself and touched his heels to Frightful. The stupid horse bolted, and Alissa barely kept herself from falling off. "Hold on!" Lodesh shouted too late, but the furious pace quickly subsided into a fast-paced walk. Lodesh angled them through the short grass to the road. "Let's make sure he sees us, eh?" he suggested. "To spice our victory."

"Victory?" she purposely shouted into his ear. She hadn't appreciated that flying start. "He'll know where we're going!"

Lodesh chuckled. "I'm counting on it. But Connen-Neute will be with him."

"What difference will that make?"

"If Connen-Neute accompanies him, Breve will be at the pace Connen-Neute sets."

"Oh. . . ."

"Besides," Lodesh muttered. "I'm sure Connen-Neute has a few words to say to him concerning the wisdom of giving a Master an order." He shuddered. "So," he continued brightly, "we will give Breve wind of us, then take flight like the rabbit he thinks I am."

"But I'll fall off!" Alissa protested.

"Then you'd better hang on."

Alissa whimpered, clasping her hands about him tighter.

"Look," Lodesh whispered, shifting his weight. Frightful stopped and immediately began tugging at the grass. Peeping from around Lodesh, she spied Breve. His fists were on his hips, and he stared at them disapprovingly.

"That's our cue," Lodesh whispered. Frightful turned under some direction Alissa didn't catch. Forewarned, she clutched Lodesh's waist. Frightful lunged forward, and she gasped.

"*I'll join you before sunset, Alissa,*" came Connen-Neute's thought from the edge of the forest. "*Don't let him get into too much trouble.*"

43

Strell stood by the kitchen fire, impatiently turning his scrambled eggs. Alissa's faint presence was headed for Ese'Nawoer. He would have to hurry to catch up as her speed indicated she was on horseback. Eating was the last thing he wanted to do, but without something in his middle, he would drop halfway there.

"They won't cook any faster, stirring them like that," came Talo-Toecan's soft comment.

Strell glanced up. The dignified Master was playing at painter today, kneeling at the threshold of the garden door among his brushes and drop cloths. Yesterday he had been a mason, the day before, a chimney sweep. Strell remembered his father had been like that. When worry hounded him, his father had fixed things. Once, when his eldest sister lay sick for three weeks, he had built a two-story barn of brick by himself.

Pulling the pan from the fire, Strell scraped the egg onto a piece of toast, wondering what had been worrying Talo-Toecan when he had built the Hold.

There was a whisper of boots, and Lodesh appeared in the doorway. He paused, seeming to force himself to enter. "You seem in better spirits today," the tall Keeper said as he cracked several eggs into Strell's still-warm pan and replaced it over the fire.

"No." Strell sat at a table. "Alissa is halfway to the city. I'm in a hurry to catch her up."

By the garden door, Talo-Toecan made a soft grunt.

Lodesh, too, looked up. Strell ignored their incredulity, continuing to put egg into his mouth, chew, and swallow. He was going to the city, even if she turned and headed back as soon as he got there. The chance he might hear her again, that she might hear him, was too strong a pull.

The tightness of Strell's shoulders eased as Talo-Toecan resumed his painting, silently acknowledging that it was his decision, even if it was a fool's errand. Lodesh, though, cleared his throat, and Strell's tension slammed back into him like a wave.

"Strell," Lodesh said, "it will take all morning to get there. By then, she will probably be on her way back. You can't keep up with a horse."

Strell kept his eyes on his food, a part of him surprised at how his fingers trembled. "What do you care what I do with my day?" he said. Then he froze as Lodesh's last words swirled through him. Slowly he raised his head and looked to where Talo-Toecan had paused midbrush. The Master met his eyes, having heard it as well.

Pushing his breakfast away, Strell eyed the back of Lodesh's finely tailored shirt as the Keeper leaned over his cooking eggs. "How do you know she's on horseback?" he said quietly. "I never told you how fast she was moving."

There was the barest stiffening in Lodesh's stance, but it was enough. Talo-Toecan set his brush aside with a small click. Lodesh turned round, his eyes flicking to the open archway, before meeting his solidly. "Everyone rides to Ese'Nawoer. How else would she get there? Do you want my eggs? I'm going to skip breakfast. I have a lot to do." His gaze dropped.

Talo-Toecan stood. "She could fly," he said. "You seem very sure she isn't."

The scrape of Strell's chair as he stood was loud. "You remember her, don't you," he whispered, feeling a bitter satisfaction when Lodesh's face went white. "You know she's on horseback because you're there with her. Right now. You're with her! You knew this was going to happen," he accused. "And you did nothing to prevent it!"

Lodesh stepped from the hearth. His alarm had been rapidly replaced by a look of defiance. "No," he said stiffly. "I
knew it would happen, and I did all I could to encourage it."

"Why?" Strell shouted, closing the gap between them.

Lodesh's jaw clenched as he refused to answer.

Talo-Toecan's face had gone shockingly still. "By my
Master's Wolves," he breathed. "She was the last chance for
my entire species, Lodesh. We are going extinct!" The last
Master stood on the other side of Lodesh, his hands clenched.
"She was to be a fresh infusion of thoughts, ideas and, if noth-
ing more, a new bloodline with which to instigate a rebirth.
Now it's done! It's ended! And you'll tell me why!"

Lodesh turned his back on Strell, clearly knowing he
couldn't relax his guard against Talo-Toecan for even an instant. Strell felt desperate. Lodesh had dismissed him as no
threat. And he was right.

"Do you recall that autumn?" Lodesh asked Talo-Toecan
softly.

The hem of Talo-Toecan's long vest trembled. "The city
lost your uncle and father. You became Warden, though
you're showing a dismal lack of honor to warrant the title."

"There was one other item of note," Lodesh said stiffly,
"though to be quite honest, it meant nothing to anyone but
me."

Talo-Toecan's eyes went distant in thought. "You lost your
heart to a student of Redal-Stan's. The one that disappeared
before I met her." His eyes lit up. "She gets back!"

"Curse you to the ends of time," Strell whispered as
Lodesh shook his head. Lodesh had known. He had betrayed
Alissa. Betrayed them all.

"I don't know if she gets back," Lodesh said. "I only
know . . . I only know she left."

Talo-Toecan clenched his hands at his sides, his face lined
and angry. "You betrayed us in the name of desire?"

Lodesh straightened. "I don't care what you think," he said
in a shockingly even voice. "You won't take my time with her
from me." He tensed in a sudden grief. "I couldn't! And I
won't help you get her back. She's with me now. She'll stay

with me. You can't force me to tell you how she can get back!"

Strell's pulse pounded. Now he knew why Lodesh had never been worried about Alissa. The Keeper knew how to get her back. He as much as said so with his last words. How could he best a Keeper? Strell thought. He was nothing. He didn't deserve Alissa. He couldn't protect her. Couldn't help her. His enemy was more powerful than he, and was his *friend*. But he would be damned if he wouldn't try.

"Lodesh?" he said quietly. As Lodesh turned, Strell swung his left fist with all his frustration. It connected just under Lodesh's eye with a hand-numbing force, jarring him to his feet, sending shivers of pain up his arm and into his own skull.

Lodesh fell like a stone. First onto the table, then the floor. Strell watched, clutching his hand. Wolves, it felt as if he had broken it, but everything moved when he told it to. "Wrong, Lodesh," he whispered as he flexed his hand. "You *will* help me."

Ignoring Talo-Toecan, he bent to check Lodesh's breathing. He glanced up, not caring what he might find in Talo-Toecan's eyes, only to be surprised at his questioning sadness. "Can you make me a rope or something?" Strell asked.

Talo-Toecan shook his head. "What are you doing?"

Strell grimaced. "A scarf? A stocking? Anything?

Saying nothing, Talo-Toecan crafted a long, shimmery scarf. It looked very feminine, and Talo-Toecan shrugged, "It was to have been—" He halted, then steeled his features and handed it to him. "It was to have been a surprise for Keribdis."

Strell nodded, hearing how much the admission cost him. Taking Lodesh's boots off, he tied his ankles together. If the Keeper escaped, it wouldn't be because of his ineptness.

"Strell. What are you doing?"

"Would you help me?" he asked. "My hand hurts too much to make the knots tight." He waited with a stoic patience until the Master silently knelt beside him and knotted the scarf. Finished with his ankles, Strell turned to Lodesh's hands.

"Lodesh is going to accompany me to the city," he said grimly. "He's going to help me get Alissa back."

With a heavy sigh, Talo-Toecan stood. "You can't hold a Keeper against his will. As soon as he wakes up, he'll ward you and escape."

Strell felt a wash of panic. "I know that. But he wouldn't if you warded him first."

The lines in Talo-Toecan's face deepened. "Ward an unconscious man? That's not honorable."

"Do you think he's deserving of any consideration when it comes to honor?" he asked bitterly, not caring if the Master saw his desperation.

"No." It was a quiet admission, full of regret, and Strell's hopes rose when he heard it. "A ward won't do any good, though," Talo-Toecan continued. "He can sunder any I put on him."

But another scarf appeared, and Strell took it without comment. Straining, he propped Lodesh against a table leg. "What about that ward you put between Alissa's tracings and her source last fall so she couldn't use them? The one she burned her tracings with?"

Talo-Toecan crouched to hold Lodesh as Strell bound the Keeper's wrists. "That would work for a time. But it's wrong to use it unless someone is in danger."

Strell arched his eyebrows. "If you don't ward him, I will keep knocking him out."

"That will do," Talo-Toecan said as he nodded.

A wash of delirium came over Strell. "We're going to Ese'Nawoer, the Warden and I," he said. "Lodesh said Alissa disappeared. He said he wouldn't tell us how to get her back. He knows how, and he's going to tell me." Strell eyed his final knot. It was one he learned from the coast. It was to have been a gift for his eldest brother. He would be happy to give it to Lodesh. This one didn't have to be tight. Any movement on Lodesh's part would make it all the stronger.

Strell looked up. "Can you take him to the city for me?"

Talo-Toecan shook his head. "He's too heavy without a

large fall to build momentum. I might get airborne, but without help, I'd probably drop him."

"I don't have any problem with that," Strell said dryly as he stood and looked down at Lodesh. "I'll take him in a handcart from the stables, then. It will be slower, but I'll manage."

"Even if you get him there, what good will it do?"

Strell pushed down his doubts. "Lodesh kept chasing Connen-Neute away. He has been keeping himself scarce as well. I'm going to get both of them together at the city. If Alissa is there, the other Lodesh must be with her. With any luck, Connen-Neute will be there as well." He felt his face turn ugly. "I'll reach Alissa's thoughts. Lodesh will tell me how she can get back, and then I'll tell Alissa." His stomach clenched with an old fear. Talo-Toecan said his tracings were what made it possible to reach her. Septhama points, septhama lines, he would use them if he could, the ghosts he had once seen at Ese'Nawoer be damned.

"What about Connen-Neute?" Talo-Toecan sighed. "You haven't been able to coax him in since that last scare."

He swallowed as his determination faltered. "I'll manage." *Curse Lodesh,* Strell thought. He was a fool. He should have known Lodesh was betraying them all at that point.

"But even if you do lure him in," Talo-Toecan persisted, "Lodesh will make too much noise, scare Connen-Neute away. The ward I can bind him with won't keep his mouth shut."

Strell made a mirthless smile. These Masters were very wise, but they tended to rely upon their mental skills too much. Not saying a word, he took the last scarf and bound it about Lodesh's mouth, tightening it with far too much satisfaction. Perhaps he wasn't so helpless after all.

Talo-Toecan stood and pushed the pan of burning eggs from the fire. "I'll find Connen-Neute and lure him close enough so you may ground him with your music. The smell of blood will probably bring him out of hiding."

Astonished, Strell looked up, and Talo-Toecan added, "I can use more than wards as well, Piper. I'll find a sheep and slaughter it."

Strell took a deep breath. He had a chance. Talo-Toecan had gifted him with a chance. He refused to believe it couldn't be done. He would force Lodesh to tell. Alissa would get home. What happened after that, he didn't care. Slowly his breath slipped from him. "Fine."

44

It was hot in the middle of Ese'Nawoer's field despite the lateness of the day. Alissa and Lodesh were lounging upon the flat rock by the spring. A breeze shifted her hair, and she sat up so as to see the city's green field better. It wasn't truly green but golden. The wind came from the distant mountains to push upon it, and slowly, gently, the field pushed back, making great undulating waves of autumn fragrance.

Lodesh sat up beside her. His curls were tinged red from the setting sun. "Hungry?" he asked around a stem of grass he had slid between his teeth.

"No," she said, ignoring her pained stomach. She was famished, having had nothing but eggs this morning and the apples Lodesh had stolen from his parents' house this afternoon. But if she admitted to being hungry, they would leave, and this was the most at peace she had been with herself since—since she had misplaced herself.

Lodesh made a satisfied noise and went back to his undignified sprawl. The spring reflected the clear, early evening sky, distorted by the ripples of small fish. She looked out to the young geldings that had distantly ringed them. They hadn't seen a mare or foal all day. Alissa clasped her arms about her knees and sighed at how nice a day it had been.

Hearing it, Lodesh propped himself up on an elbow. "What is it?" he asked.

She smiled sheepishly, but the sound of children's laughter turned her head. The horses scattered in a flash of wheeling shades of gray and brown as the tawny grass parted with a tumbled tangle of three dusty, grass-covered children.

"Safe!" the oldest shouted, nearly falling into the spring. "I'm safe!" Spying them, he stopped short, only to be knocked by the other two. In a chorus of cries and shouts, they all went down in a pile of elbows and knees.

"Here! Wait now!" Lodesh admonished as he slid from the rock. His hand flashed into the pile, and he pulled one upright. "Get your foot out of his eye. Watch it. There you are."

Kneeling before the three youngsters, Lodesh brushed them off. They stood like stairsteps, red-faced and dismayed as if they had been caught where they ought not be. "Sorry," the eldest stammered. "We didn't know anyone was at the spring."

"Now." Lodesh finished brushing off the youngest. "What's this all about?"

"Tag, Warden," the smallest piped up, trying to smooth his hair.

Lodesh stood. "Warden! Where?" he shouted, casting about behind him comically.

The middle stairstep giggled and pointed at him.

"Me!" His eyes wide, Lodesh drew back and put a hand to his chest. "Oh, you are a flatterer," he murmured. "Fancy a shabby street urchin such as myself the Warden." He paused. "But I thank you nonetheless. What's your name?"

"Tay." The eldest danced nervously from foot to foot. "But you're the Warden. My mother says only the Warden has such a raggedy beast at his beck and call."

As one they turned to Frightful grazing nearby. Lodesh sighed. "Tay," he said. "Don't you think the Warden would be too busy to sit on a rock and sun himself?"

"I guess." It was a doubtful admission.

"Just so," Lodesh said firmly. "Now make yourselves scarce. And stay out of the grove. Tag is best played in the sun, not under the trees."

The middle child punched his brother in the arm. "You're it!" Giggling, he bolted, the youngest quick behind him. Tay's eyes widened in protest. Then they narrowed, and he darted after them. The grass parted to take them in, whispering as it closed in behind.

"Stay out of the grove!" Lodesh shouted to their bobbing heads.

"Yes, Warden!" Tay called over his shoulder. Alissa watched the boys top a small rise where the grass was stunted. All three stopped to look back. They were dark shadows, outlined against the still-bright sky. The smallest awkwardly scratched his leg. Someone pushed someone else, it didn't matter whom, and they tumbled down the far side. The sound of their laugher pattered over the field like rain. Then they were gone.

Alissa smiled happily as Lodesh sat down beside her. The memory of the children's laughter lingered like a half-remembered song. She felt Beast stir. Her feral consciousness had been awake all day, holding herself silent as if to apologize for the coming ordeal of her reluctant takeover. It was an obvious attempt at giving Alissa a final day to be wholly herself. But with the coming of night, Beast felt the sky call to her. To them. *I like tag,* Beast said wistfully.

"Oh, Lodesh," Alissa said, feeling a touch melancholy. "It's lovely out here. Just feel that west wind pull at you. Smell that air? You can almost taste it." Taking a deep breath, she closed her eyes. "And the sound of the children." She smiled. "Their only care to be home for supper. That's the best part." A tear brimmed. "If only it could stay this way," she whispered.

"It can."

Lodesh's voice was low and compelling. Alissa's eyes flew open at the desire in it. Wolves! What had she said!

"It can, Alissa. It's up to you." Somehow he had her hand in his. His eyes were dark with longing, his face full of solemn expectancy, and hope, and vulnerability.

"I—I have to go," Alissa said, tugging her hand from his. She rose in a flurry of movement, almost falling off the rock.

"Burn it to ash. Don't run off." Lodesh stood, catching her arm and preventing her slip. "Alissa. Please!"

"I can't stay. I have to go," she repeated, afraid if she

stayed, she might say yes to what was coming. She spun away, but Lodesh caught her again.

"Wait! Just hear me out?"

She hesitated, though it might mean her downfall.

"Please?" His eyes were pleading.

She couldn't refuse. Her fate sealed, Alissa nodded, feeling a slow shiver fill her.

Lodesh drooped slightly. His grip on her hands was tight. "It's as if you found me, knowing me already," he said softly. His eyes bright, he smiled in bemusement. "You somehow slipped past my carefully made wall in a twirl of stocking feet. It was as if you didn't even see it."

His hand went out to tuck a wisp of hair behind her ear. She swallowed hard, feeling her pulse pound. "There's no wall about you," she asserted shakily.

Lodesh nodded ruefully. "Yes, there is. I spent the last five years building it." He took her shoulders, and Alissa paled as he took a breath, knowing what was coming.

"I don't want you to leave," he said firmly. "It's that simple. Stay here with me."

A lump formed in her throat, and the breeze tugged at her. She should run—run somewhere—but she couldn't move.

His grip tightened, and his gaze became fierce. "I want you to stay with me," he said. "I want you to be *my* love."

Alissa felt herself go whiter, and her breath came fast.

"Wolves," Lodesh cursed seeing her frantic eyes. "I've scared you again. Listen. I know you're still sorrowing over—over another, but you could be happy with me," he pleaded. "I see the bright shadows of possibilities every time you're with me. But you won't let me show you." Lodesh's brow furrowed with frustration. "Why won't you even let me show you! Please, Alissa," he beseeched, taking her hands again. "Just say you'll let me try, and someday the children you hear playing in the city's fields might be our own."

She stared wide-eyed at him. "I can't forget Strell," she whispered.

His gaze fell. "It's no betrayal to love another when the first is forever out of reach."

"Is he?"

This time Lodesh dropped her hands. He looked over the field to the mirth trees, standing black in the dusk. "All I know is you're here now. And it's the most complete I have felt since Reeve took me in as his own." He turned back, his green eyes pleading. "Why risk your future, your very existence on a thin possibility? Stay with me."

She trembled.

"Be my love."

Lodesh's eyes were hungry. Cupping one hand firmly about hers, he reached into his pocket with the other. The scent of apples and pine blossomed into the twilight-damp air. It was a mirth flower. "You dropped this the other night," he whispered as he placed it in her hand. "I give it to you again, something I promised myself I wouldn't ever do." He chuckled lightly. "That makes two promises I've broken."

Together they gazed at it, his strong hands enfolded about hers. "It's as fresh as if it had just fallen," she said in wonder.

Emotion crossed Lodesh's face, almost seeming to be pain. "When given in love, a mirth flower remains untouched by time until it's returned in kind or refused."

Feeling a flush of panic, Alissa tried to step back, but her feet wouldn't move. "That's magic," she whispered, her voice trembling. "I don't believe in magic."

"I do." Lodesh drew her closer until his warmth tingled through her. "Otherwise I couldn't believe in you." Her pulse quickened as his eyes gathered her in. "I've given this flower to you twice now, Alissa. I need an answer this time."

She was silent, unable to think.

"Alissa?"

She gazed past him over the field, gray in the twilight. From the distance came the sounds of children. They were answered by the squeals of horses. A group of mares with their young nearly as large as they sped by, a disconcerting mix of angry hooves and gently moving grass. Frightful was drawn into their wake, and he ran with them, the herd's stallion in pursuit. Alissa's thoughts went gently to the city, feeling the life, the contentment it sheltered. She knew if she said yes, she would have found a new lodestone and wouldn't go feral.

Home? she thought.

"Alissa." Lodesh took her in his arms, but her eyes were locked upon the field. She could smell mirth wood on him, clean and strong, filling her senses, clouding them, leaving no room for thought or reason. "Stay with me," he breathed against her cheek. "Be my love."

She drew back to see him. Her mind was empty. The herd had scattered, taking the last of her logic with it. "Um . . ." she mumbled, lost in his gaze, and he caught his breath, his eyes hopeful as he ran a gentle finger under her eye. "Uh . . ."

A gust of air assaulted them, sending her hair to blind her. Lodesh looked up. "Burn him to ash," he whispered, releasing her and taking a step back. It was Redal-Stan.

The old raku shifted immediately and strode to them. "The Wolves take you all!" he shouted. "Where is Connen-Neute?"

"Um . . ." Alissa stammered, putting a hand to her head. She could hear a pipe coming over the darkening field. Before her, Redal-Stan glowered. Lodesh stood hunched and angry as his teacher frustrated his plans once again.

An irate finger stabbed toward Alissa. "I charged that winglet with watching you," Redal-Stan shouted. "And when I come with news, I find him gone and Lodesh in his place!"

She shook the numbness from her. "He's with Breve," she said. "Searching for Lodesh."

Redal-Stan's face darkened, and his eyes grew distant. There was a buzz of private conversation. "Not anymore, he isn't."

Lodesh slipped from the rock, clearly distancing himself in the hopes of remaining unnoticed. Alissa spotted a raku winging its way towards them as Redal-Stan held out an impatient hand to help her from her perch. "Talo-Toecan is returning," he growled. "Can't that boy take even a small sabbatical?"

Gasping, Alissa looked at the incoming raku, gold in the sun at the higher altitude.

"No," Redal-Stan snapped. "That's Connen-Neute. Talo-

Toecan is still in the mountains. Our time is up, Alissa. If he truly doesn't know you, something is going to break."

She turned to Lodesh, standing silently. His carefully chosen words still resonated in her thoughts, pulling at her, confusing her. Her mirth flower rested in her hands, a secret still. "I-I," she stammered, not knowing what to say.

"Listen . . ." Beast whispered, and Alissa clenched in sudden heartache.

"Lodesh!" she cried, feeling herself go unreal. "Listen! It's Strell!"

Redal-Stan's eyes went wide in surprise.

"Can you hear him?" Squinting from a gust of wind, she turned to Connen-Neute as the raku landed beside them. "That's Strell's playing. Can't you hear it?"

Not shifting, Connen-Neute nodded his great head, his golden eyes glowing in the dusk.

"I don't hear anything," Redal-Stan said.

"Alissa?" It was as faint as the brush of a moth. *"Wolves. Alissa? Can you hear me?"*

"Strell!" she shrieked, and the faint touch wavered. Immediately she took three quick breaths and slipped into a mild trance. The smell of mirth wood blossomed about her, and she felt Lodesh's steadying hand. *"Yes!"* she sobbed. *"I hear you, Strell."*

"Is Connen-Neute with you," he said urgently, *"and Lodesh?"*

Her eyes cleared long enough to see three anxious faces peering at her. *"Yes."*

She felt Strell heave a ragged sigh. *"Don't let them go anywhere. I know how to get you home. You're in the field, yes? By . . ."*

" . . . the stream," she finished aloud, their thoughts mingling freely.

"Then shift, Alissa! By all that is sacred, set your tracings for tripping the lines, and shift!"

Wild with emotion, she did. The lines glowed, and she disappeared in a swirl of nothing. Alissa fashioned mass about herself, breathless in hope. She winked into existence, her point of view having shifted higher but her situation not changing. It hadn't worked.

"Connen-Neute!" Redal-Stan shouted. "She's going feral!"

"No, she isn't," came the young raku's bemused thought. *"Hear her piper's music?"*

Lodesh backed up in wonder. "Alissa?" he breathed. "You're a—Master?"

"It didn't work!" she wailed, stretching her neck to the sky.

"It didn't work, Lodesh," she heard Strell snarl. He was speaking aloud, but they were linked so tightly, the echo of his voice rang through her thoughts. *"Tell me what she did wrong, or I swear I'll hit you again! I'll hurt you so badly, you'll wish you could die."*

Lodesh? Alissa thought. Her head swiveled to see him. His eyes were wide in shock, but he obviously hadn't heard Strell. *"Lodesh is with you, Strell?"* she asked.

"Wolves," Redal-Stan cursed, looking to the east. "It's Talo-Toecan. Get her hidden, Connen-Neute. I'll try to divert him." In a swirl of gray and black, he shifted and flew.

Connen-Neute was frozen where he was crouched, his vacant stare telling Alissa he, too, was in a slight trance, straining to hear Strell's music if it should start again.

"Strell," she pleaded, beginning to cry. *"It didn't work."*

"She's crying, Warden," Strell said to the Lodesh beside him. *"Can you hear her? Why are you doing this to her? She wants to come home! Tell me how!"*

Alissa gasped as Lodesh's awareness melted into hers. *"It's not right!"* came his thought, ripping through her, stunning in its depth of misery. She looked down through her tears. The Lodesh at her feet was confused, not torn with grief. It had been the Lodesh from her home.

"It's not right," he cried again. *"I shouldn't have to live through this a second time. Wasn't the first penance enough?"*

"Then tell me!" Strell shouted.

Low and beaten, Lodesh's thoughts drifted into hers. *"She should follow your thoughts back,"* he whispered.

Alissa felt Lodesh shudder, both of them. The Lodesh at her feet sat down hard, holding his head, his present and future thoughts mingling in a confusion of paradox.

"You understand, Strell?" came Lodesh's thought, and the Lodesh at her feet moved his lips in tandem with the words. *"She is to follow your thoughts in place of a memory. Oh, Wolves,"* he moaned. *"Why did I do this? Don't do this again,"* he said. *"You hear me, Warden? Don't do this again to her!"*

"Strell. I don't understand!" Alissa exclaimed.

Alissa heard Lodesh groan in mental agony. *"Tell her to shift again,"* he said. *"Tell her to set her neural net to trip the lines using your thoughts in place of a memory."* He paused. *"And tell her I'm sorry,"* he whispered, *"that I never meant for this to happen."*

"That's it?" She stirred in excitement.

"Do it, Alissa," Strell said fervently. *"Now!"*

And Strell gave her a memory of a time she hadn't lived. Thoughts of a cold, black evening, dark clouds pushed by an angry east wind against a washed-out sky, and an empty city, bare of life. Her eyes rose, seeing it over the golden field.

Connen-Neute was there, and Lodesh. Their presence existed in both times. And Strell's music dipped and swooped, pulling her back, filling her senses, taking her home.

And so she shifted. *"Don't forget your clothes,"* Beast admonished, and Alissa thought she heard a chuckle from Connen-Neute as she swirled back into reality, sorry she hadn't had time for a final good-bye.

Alissa clutched her arms about her in a new darkness as she opened her eyes, wondering if it had truly worked. The black shadow of Connen-Neute was crouched nearby, a feral beast lulled into a passive state by Strell's music. Lodesh stood beside him. His clothes were torn and his face bruised. He stood stock-still, anguished and stoic. To her left, his eyes closed, playing his pipe was . . .

"Strell!" she shrieked, flinging herself at him. His eyes flew open. They met in a crushing embrace. She was picked up, swung about in a dizzying swirl, and plunked down hard enough to rattle her teeth. She didn't care. Her head was buried in his shoulder, arms about his neck, exulting in the smell of hot sand that clung to him.

"I tried and tried to get back," she heard herself stutter into his shirt. It was damp. One of them was crying. "Redal-Stan said I couldn't, but I knew I could," she babbled. "And then I heard your music, and—"

"Oh, do shut up," Strell said, and before she knew his intent, he kissed her.

Softer than she expected, his lips met hers, then stronger, pulling a warmth from deep within. Heart pounding, she leaned into him, not wanting it to end. Strell stiffened as he sensed her willingness, as if only now realizing what he was doing. She opened her eyes to see his wide, alarmed stare. Reddening, Strell pulled away but didn't let go.

Alissa blinked as the warmth from his touch seemed to grow, settling to a steady burn.

"He wants to ground you!" Beast hissed, and Alissa mollified her with a bemused thought.

"Hounds," Strell turned even more embarrassed. "I missed you." His eyes pleaded softly. "I thought I'd lost you forever."

Alissa said nothing. Her eyes filled, and she leaned back into him, hiding her smile. Ignoring Beast's outrage, she exerted a slow, tentatively increasing pressure to pull his face back down to hers.

"Ow!" he yelped, then cursed quietly as she let go and backed up to eye him sharply. Her light winked into existence.

"You're hurt," she said in the stark brightness her light made. Her hand went out to run a finger under a swollen eye, and Strell winced. Only now with her light did she see his dirt-stained clothes and the bruises. Alissa reached to pluck a stem of grass from his hair. His hand rose to stop hers. It was bleeding from a skinned knuckle. "Let me fix it?" she asked plaintively.

"No," Strell said grimly. "I don't deserve it. I'll wear my bruises until I heal myself."

Frowning, Alissa took another step back. He and Lodesh had been arguing just before she returned. Her gaze darted to the clearing, empty of all but the feral relic of Connen-Neute. "Where's Lodesh?" she asked. "You were fighting, weren't you!"

Strell's eyes went hard. "He wouldn't tell me how to get you home." He rubbed his hand and straightened his shoulders, a trace of pride and satisfaction seemed to cross him. Then seeing she was upset, he leaned forward, pleading. "Don't be angry. I love you, Alissa. And I would have done far worse than hit him if I had needed to."

Her eyes went wide, and quite abruptly her animosity shifted to something more enduring. "Hounds," she whispered. "I missed you."

Strell slumped. "Me, too." His arms went about to gather her in, when a familiar, much too loud, mental shout nearly split her skull.

"Alissa!"

"Ouch," she said, putting a hand to her head. That bruise still hurt. Pulling away slightly from Strell, she turned to see the gray shadow of Talo-Toecan streak low over the dark field from the east. He braked in a violent backwash of air that laid the grass flat. "Useless!" she shouted, covering her face from the eye-smarting upwelling of grass and dirt.

He shifted before he was even on the ground. Talon was with him, and she landed on Alissa's shoulder, chittering wildly, her eyes whirling.

"Useless! I did it!"

"Useless?" came a confused whisper of thought.

"I really did it!" she shouted, nearly in tears as Useless took her in a fatherly hug smelling of wind and rain. Pushed from her shoulder, Talon hovered over them, squawking.

"So you did," her teacher whispered fiercely. "So you did." Smiling, he put her at arm's length, his gaze running from her head to her stocking feet. "Thank you, Strell," he said, never looking from her.

Alissa felt Strell grin, proud and pleased, and she turned to see him flushing.

"You," Useless gave her a stern shake, "are more adept at the impossible than even my teacher." Talon shifted herself between Strell and Alissa as if unable to decide who deserved her presence more.

"Um, Talo-Toecan?" came a gray thought. *"What happened? You don't look good."*

Alissa's mouth fell open. So did Useless's. Together they turned to the feral beast. The monster sneezed with a huge spasm. "Careful," Strell warned, seeing the direction of their gaze. "He's gotten used to voices, even loud ones, but he's still feral despite his tame looks.

"Tame!" The grass was laid flat by a sweeping tail. *"I don't know how you got here, little man, but I'll teach you the meaning of tame!"*

"Connen-Neute?" Useless breathed, having turned three shades whiter.

The beast vanished in a swirling mist of pearly white. Connen-Neute winked back into existence not looking a day older than when she had last seen him.

With a small sigh, Useless collapsed. Talon started screaming, nearly falling off Strell's shoulder. "Useless!" Alissa gasped, reaching too late for him. "Oh, Hounds, Useless?" On her knees, she gently patted his cheeks. He was out cold. Above her on the rock, Talon squeaked and jumped up and down, ignored as Alissa pulled Useless into a more natural position. Strell bent to help as Connen-Neute stepped forward looking tall and foreboding. Talon continued to scream, hopping on the flat rock as if she had gone insane.

"You're Strell?"

Hearing the danger in his gray voice, Strell rose along with Alissa's gaze. *Oh, for Bone and Ash,* she thought. *Strell had called him tame.* With a last look at Useless, Alissa stood. She had no idea how Connen-Neute had gotten here but had little patience for tender Master sensitivities right now. Lips pursed, she stepped between an angry Connen-Neute and a wide-eyed, white-faced Strell.

"Strell." She cleared her throat loudly. "This is Connen-Neute, a student Master of the Hold who comes before me."

Connen-Neute stopped short, his anger taking pause. Obviously he had never been introduced with such formality. He was the baby of the Hold, a hundred sixteen years old or not.

"Connen-Neute?" Alissa said into the new silence as Talon finally shut up. "This is Strell Hirdune, the last son of a great house of artisans." She bent close and whispered loudly, "He took you for a feral beast his music has charmed in the past." Alissa smiled. "You understand?"

The Master cautiously nodded.

"Could you please make me a paper cup?" she asked him. She could have made her own but this would be a subtle show of feminine dominance. She wouldn't have them fighting like ill-raised children. A bright yellow cone filled her hand, and she gave it to Strell. His eyebrows rose. "Water?" she said, looking at the nearby spring. "For Useless?"

Strell nodded and stepped to the spring. Talon was silently watching her, and upon seeing Alissa's eyes on her, she twittered and hopped to Alissa's shoulder. Alissa's eyes prickled as her fingers caressed Talon's silky feathers. She had missed Talon more than she realized. A sharp pinch on her ear, and Alissa began to change her mind.

Connen-Neute offered his hand to help Strell up from the spring. "It's a pleasure to meet the man who has captured the heart of so strong a flyer," he murmured.

"Uh, thanks." The two clasped hands, and Strell rose. "Likewise, I'm sure." He hesitated, awkwardly. "Sorry about that feral business."

Connen-Neute nodded. "Are you a sibling of Sarken Hirdune, joined to Marga Stryska?"

Strell's eyes widened.

Having exhausted an entire day's worth of words in a matter of moments, Connen-Neute simply smiled. The two returned, and the tension Alissa hadn't known she had, eased. "Thanks, Strell." She accepted the squishy cup, and sprinkled a few drops on Useless to no effect. Strell rocked back-and-forth on his heels, struggling to find something to say. Her light on the grass illuminated everything in a soft, white glow.

Connen-Neute sank into a crouch beside her, frowning as

he took in Useless's lined features. *"I thought the idea was to send you back to your piper."* He warily eyed Talon on her shoulder. *"Not bring your piper to you. What will he do when he realizes what's happened?"*

Feeling a flush of worry, Alissa arranged the hem of Useless's vest. "I—uh—didn't shift Strell," she said slowly. "I shifted me."

"But—" Connen-Neute stiffened.

Alissa sat back on her heels. "Look around. The city is empty. It's colder than the Hold's annexes." She shrugged apologetically. "The clouds are thick, covering the setting sun. It was clear a moment ago. I think somehow your sentience was pulled back with me to slip into your feral skin." She smiled weakly up at his pasty face. "Sorry."

Connen-Neute scrambled to his feet, searching for the absent plumes of smoke from a thousand hearth fires. "The horses," he breathed. "There are no horses." He turned to her, his face drained of color. "But . . . how . . ." His eyes rolled back and he tipped forward.

"Look out, Alissa!" Strell yanked her out of the way as Connen-Neute came crashing down face first onto the cold ground. Together she and Strell tumbled into an awkward pile, coming to a rest with his arms safely about her. "These Masters don't handle surprises very well, do they," Strell said, his words a soft breath in her ear.

Alissa's breath caught, and she turned to him. "Uh-uh," she agreed. It was warmer on the ground in the lee of the stone, and she wasn't going to move for anything.

"You all right?" He smiled, not loosening his grip.

"Uh-huh." She grinned. Her eyes went to Talon, expecting the usual noise and bad temper the bird showed whenever anyone got close to her. Surprisingly enough, she wasn't glaring but was standing stiffly with her feathers raised, turned halfway about as if she didn't want to see but was afraid to ignore them. Strell's gaze followed Alissa's. Never taking his eyes from the small bird, he slowly leaned closer as if to steal another kiss. They both watched as he shifted closer . . . and closer . . .

"Awak!" Sharp eyes and a wicked beak turned to them.

Strell eased back with a forlorn expression. "I guess that's my new limit, now, eh?"

"Yeah," she agreed sourly. *Stupid bird.* She never seemed to get a moment alone with anyone. Someone always interrupted. If it wasn't Talon, it was Useless, or Redal-Stan, or . . .

Her face pinched in worry as she turned to Strell. "Where's Lodesh?"

45

"Stop, Alissa. I'm all right." A long-fingered hand rose to envelop hers. "It's a scratch."

Alissa leaned back on her heels, her lips pursed disapprovingly at her instructor. "Quit fussing," she complained. "If you would just let me see, I'd go away and leave you alone."

His eyes widened. "Don't ever do that. Stay right were you are."

Smiling, she leaned forward again. This time he held still as she parted his short, white hair to find that, yes, the scratch was too small to worry about. Satisfied, she set her light down and tugged the blanket he had made for her closer. It was cold in the field. They hadn't bothered with a fire as they would be leaving as soon as Connen-Neute finished his "nap."

"So," Useless's white eyebrows jumped in delight. "You were Redal-Stan's mysterious Squirrel." His expression soured. "I should have guessed by the trouble he said you were."

Alissa nodded, terribly pleased.

"I'd be willing to wager you were the one who slipped the warming ward to the Keepers."

Her face fell. "No one told me to keep it a secret," she said, and he grinned.

There was a rustle as Strell straightened from his crouch over Connen-Neute. "He's coming around," he said, backing up so Alissa could take his place.

Connen-Neute's golden eyes focused on her. *"Alissa,"* he thought. *"I had the oddest dream."*

From her shoulder came Talon's chitter, sounding like laughter. Connen-Neute's eyes widened, and he sat up in a rush. White-faced, he looked at Useless, then Strell. He fell back with a soft thump. "No dream," he moaned aloud.

Useless extended a hand to help Connen-Neute back to a sitting position.

"What happened?" the young Master whispered into their thoughts.

"Welcome to the aftermath," Useless said. "You missed all the excitement." He seated himself with meticulous care and pulled his light closer. "Alissa tells me you successfully pick-abacked your consciousness upon hers."

Connen-Neute gave Alissa a worried glance, and she shrugged.

"Who," Useless growled, "sanctioned that?"

"Redal-Stan," she offered meekly.

"Harrumph," he grumbled. "That was very ill-advised. You did so again, I gather, in order to hear our most worthy piper's music through Alissa's thoughts?"

Alissa gasped in outrage, and Connen-Neute flushed.

"Unasked, apparently?" Useless added as he put a restraining hand upon her shoulder.

"Pickaback?" Strell looked defensive and confused. "What's that?"

Silently, Alissa fumed. How had he managed that without her knowing? It was almost as if something had been shielding his awareness from hers. Alissa's thoughts went still. *"Beast?"*

"I wanted someone to play tag with," she complained privately.

Horrified at what Beast had done, Alissa covered her mouth. Undoubtedly thinking it was from embarrassment, Useless gave Connen-Neute a severe look. "It would be my guess," he said, "that your mental linkage was so tight, your consciousness was pulled along with hers when she tripped the lines."

Strell touched her shoulder. "What's pickaback?"

"Like when we practiced line tripping with Redal-Stan?" Connen-Neute guessed.

"He was teaching you to trip the lines?" Useless shouted. Talon startled into flight and flew into the dark. "I was almost three hundred before he—" Useless bit his exclamation short, scowling darkly. "Yes. Exactly. Your *recent* experience of line tripping, combined with a precedent of pickabacking your consciousness upon Alissa's, is what's to blame for this."

"See?" Beast simpered so that only Alissa could hear. *"It wasn't my fault."*

"Shut up, Beast. It was, and you know it."

Strell sat down next to Alissa. "What's pickabacking?" he asked again, sounding tired.

Useless nodded sharply. "It's a dangerously tight mental connection. It allowed Alissa to carry his consciousness from the past to the now, leaving him feral in the then." Useless visibly swallowed. "No wonder I couldn't catch you."

A shudder ran through Connen-Neute. "I don't recall being feral." Then his long face went frightened, and he surged to his feet. *"I'll go feral! I have no reference points!"* he shouted frantically, and Alissa winced at the force of his mental cry.

"What's going on?" Strell whispered, having not heard all the conversation.

"He thinks he might go feral again, as I was," Alissa said.

"You went feral again?" Strell's voice was a horrified shout.

"Well, er, not exactly," she began.

"I'm going to go feral!" Connen-Neute exclaimed, terrified.

"Everyone be still!" bellowed Useless. "No one is going feral—I think."

Connen-Neute danced from foot to foot, his smooth, narrow features pinched. He wasn't much older than Alissa in raku years, and he looked scared to death.

Useless sighed heavily as he stood up and leaned against the flat rock. "Finding reference points is something our unconscious does. Your feral self, the baser, more perceptive side, was here all along. You already have your reference points. You never lost them."

Still unsure, Connen-Neute looked a little sick.

"Look," Useless said, clearly exasperated. "If you were going to go feral, it would have happened by now."

"Alissa didn't," he pointed out, and Useless glared until he dropped his eyes.

"Bone and Ash," Alissa heard Useless mutter under his breath. "Now I have two babies to raise by myself." He straightened. "So!" he cried, clapping his hands to make Alissa and Connen-Neute jump. "Now that we are all sane and conscious, shall we return to the Hold?"

No one said anything, and Alissa looked up from the black field. They were waiting for her. "H-m-m? Oh!" Her eyes returned to the grass undulating in the wind. It was from the east, as it should be. "Go on." She pulled her blanket tighter. "I need to—um—I'll catch you up."

Strell settled himself, clearly thinking to stay with her. His eyes narrowed as Connen-Neute pulled him to his feet. He became more angry when the young Master whispered, "Lodesh." Useless, too, was frowning, looking as if he would insist on helping her find him.

Alissa's lips pursed. "I said I'll catch you up."

Useless planted his feet and adjusted his vest, becoming nearly immovable.

"It's her right to confront him first," came Connen-Neute's soft thought.

Useless's eyes grew dark. He snatched his light and spun about to stomp towards the Hold. Connen-Neute took Strell's arm and began leading him forward. "Wait a moment . . ." Strell protested, stumbling into motion.

"She has just traversed three hundred eighty-nine years, Piper!" Useless shouted over his shoulder, his light bobbing in his tight grip. "She can find her way home from here."

"Alissa?" Strell cried.

"I'll see you soon," she whispered into his thoughts, *"my love."* And though she heard no response, a wash of love came back to her, multiplied threefold. Her eyes closed to keep the

tears away. She stood basking in the warmth of his thoughts in the cold of an autumn night. When her eyes opened, Useless's light was gone.

The wind sent her blanket flapping about her ankles. She tensed as she spotted a pair of slippers. She recognized them as having been made by Lodesh. Jaw clenched, she nevertheless put them on and cast about for him. The grove, of course. She extinguished her light and stumbled forward, not wanting him to know she was coming and perhaps slip away.

The moon came out as the cloud cover tore apart in the stiffening wind. It was going to be a cold night. The ground was damp from yesterday's rain, and soon her feet were heavy and slippery with mud. By the time she found the grove, she was decidedly out of sorts.

Her fingers gripping her blanket were stiff with cold as she slipped under the black branches of the trees. Their leaves rattled, not yet willing to part from the tree. Her brow furrowed when she realized only two trees—instead of three—stretched their length upon the ground. It seemed unfair that she could change something as useless at that, and she wondered if she might have made Ren and Kally's future any better.

Alissa slipped on the moss and nearly went down. She caught herself with a hastily outstretched hand, cursing quietly when it found a sharp stick and not the soft moss.

"I'm over here, Alissa."

She spun about at Lodesh's voice. Brushing her hand free of the dirt and pain, she stomped over. By her hastily constructed light, she saw him sitting ramrod straight atop one of the fallen mirth trees. There was a pack beside him.

"You're leaving, then?" she said sharply, and he nodded once. "Where will you go?" Her voice was frighteningly level, betraying her sudden surge of emotion.

"Somewhere else." It was cold and flat.

Alissa was silent, trying to sort out her chaotic feelings and not doing very well. Her hand went up, fingers wiggling, and Lodesh leaned to help her up onto his perch. Not wanting to see the face that went with that distant voice, she let her light go out. The moon hid itself again behind the wind-torn clouds. "You were going to leave without saying good-bye?" she said.

"You did," he accused softly, and she flushed.

Frustration, hurt, and anger ran together until she didn't know what she was feeling. She turned to the easiest emotion, anger. "Why didn't you tell Strell how I could get home right away?"

Lodesh said nothing.

"I was going feral!" she shouted. "Can you imagine what that's like? Watching yourself slowly lose control as the one taking over apologizes profusely!"

Still he sat as if made of stone, a picture of elegance and refinement. "I should hate you for what you put me through," she whispered, and she thought she saw a twitch of an eye. She bit her lip, feeling it go bloodless. "Curse you. Couldn't you see my misery, how I wanted to go home, how much I missed . . ." She faltered, clutching her arms about herself in heartache.

"Yes." A tinge of bitterness stained his perfect control. "I was there, remember? And I already am cursed."

"Damn you then!" she shouted. "You didn't even know if I would make it back!"

"No. I didn't." His voice was empty, distant.

"Then why?" she cried, needing an answer, a reaction, something.

Lodesh took a shaky breath. "I thought you would return to me," he said, the hurt soaking into his words like a red stain. "I thought if you saw Ese'Nawoer and the Hold when they were full of life, you would come back. I hoped if you knew how cold and empty this place is and saw me without the shadow of Strell, you might return," he paused, "in time."

Her anger wheeled, violently shifting. "All you did," she said miserably, "was show me what I don't . . . what I can't have." Her throat tightened, and her eyes stung. "The Hold is empty. The city is dead. Curse you three times over," she whispered, determined not to wipe her eyes as the tears slipped down to make cold trails. "I'm home, Lodesh, but look at me."

He turned away.

"Look at me!" she demanded. "I've come home, but in the doing I have lost Ren, and Kally, and Mavoureen, and Redal-Stan, and . . ." Alissa's breath caught. "And an entire Hold of people. They're dead to me now, Lodesh. All dead in a single shift."

Something that might have been dismay flashed across him.

"You made me go there," she accused, "to see them, to know them, and when I had learned enough to feel their loss, you *let* me come home!" Crying, she sat stiffly as the tears ran. "Well, damn you, Lodesh!" she shouted, "if you think I'll let you walk away. I won't lose you, too, the only one who remembers the way Mavoureen beats her dough into submission, the roar of Ese'Nawoer assembled on the field, the fun of running away from Breve." She wiped her eyes. "And the scent of the mirth trees on an autumn night," she whispered, "as the drums and feet beat out the dance."

Lodesh's eyes were wide in dismay, as if never realizing how deep his betrayal went.

"You're the only one who understands what I've lost," she said, feeling beaten, "and you won't walk away from me.

"Ashes," she swore miserably, turning away. "I'm going to miss Redal-Stan. What . . ." She hesitated, wondering if she wanted to know. "What happened to Kally?"

Lodesh shrank into himself. "Ren came back about a year after Mav died. He stole Kally out from behind the Hold. No one knows how. The doors were locked for the night."

Alissa went cold, glad it was dark enough to hide her guilt.

"Her note said they were going to the plains," he continued, his voice gray and emotionless again. "She came back during—"

"I know the rest," she interrupted. Sick at heart, Alissa pulled her blanket tight. Ren never would have returned if she had let him go to the plains in the first place. Visions of Ren hammering at the gate of Ese'Nawoer rose black and sick from her memory, making her ill.

"How could you not warn me, Alissa?"

She jerked her attention up at the icy control of Lodesh's voice. He was nearly screaming at her in a voice barely above a whisper. "My city shamed and dishonored, its people cursed for nearly four centuries of guilt and humiliation. Why didn't you warn me?"

Alissa stared in alarm. Lodesh was always in control. Suddenly she was afraid. He might do anything. But then his wild eyes dropped, and when he raised them again, the rage was gone, replaced with a haunted abandonment. And she had caused it.

"Why?" he whispered, his misery magnified by the sudden moonlight. "Why didn't you come back to me? At least when it was over and safe? Why did you leave me with no one?"

Alissa felt a stab of anguish. "You told me it wasn't wrong to love another when the first was out of reach," she said, her voice cracking and harsh.

Lodesh took a shaky breath. "I thought you would return." His hand went out to touch her cheek, and he smoothed the damp away. "You never said good-bye. I waited my entire life for you." He turned away with a small moan. "The Wolves of the Navigator should hunt me. I waited four hundred years for you!"

"I was coming back to you," she said, reaching to touch him.

His hand flashed forward, catching her wrist. "Tell that to a twenty-two-year-old in love," he said bitterly and released her. "I lived my entire life with the question of a mirth flower between us, and I died with it haunting my thoughts."

She rubbed at her wrist. His grip seemed to be on her still.

He gave a short bark of laughter. "It wasn't until you woke me, until your voice intruded into my silent grove that I knew you were back," his head dropped, "with another beside you."

She thought she saw a shimmer on his cheeks.

"Poor Lodesh," he mocked bitterly. "His timing is perfect—except where it counts."

Alissa reached out again. He stiffened as she touched him, and her hand dropped, leaving her ashamed. A small spark of anger flickered. "Did it ever occur to you that I might have been trying to get back to more than just Strell?" she said tightly.

Lodesh's head came up. In his green eyes glowed a frightening need and desire, but then it died. "You were pining to feralness over his absence," he said. "Not mine."

"You were next to me!" Alissa exclaimed. "You were keeping me sane!"

"You ran to Strell," he countered. "Not me."

"He was the one trying to get me back!"

His eyes darkened. "And I wasn't," he said flatly.

"No," she agreed. "You weren't."

The moon came out to shift the shadows of the mirth trees. Their black limbs seemed to reach for the wind, to catch it, failing as their leaves succumbed and were torn away.

"Here." Lodesh twisted to his pack. "I was going to leave these where you would find them." The smooth finish of a wooden box filled her hands. "You forgot them—again."

Silently she set her thoughts to make the barest of lights and opened the box. Inside was Redal-Stan's watch, a white seed the size of a pebble, and a single mirth flower. Alissa's heart sank, leaving her empty. It was all she had left.

"We have all been patiently waiting for you." Lodesh stared stoically into the night.

Setting the box aside, she lifted out the flower. The scent of apples and pine pooled about her, bringing with it memories of the dance, of Lodesh and her, and a night filled with music and desire. Her eyes closed, unable to bear the memory. She loved Strell, she reminded herself as her throat tightened and the tears slipped from her. She couldn't give her heart to two men. She couldn't allow herself to love Lodesh.

He took the flower from her numb fingers and considered it. "I have given this particular flower to you twice now. I don't think I'll attempt to give it to you again." His fingers tightened, threatening to crush it.

"Lodesh!" she cried, setting her hand atop his. He gasped,

and his fingers sprang open. "This is mine," she said as she took it back. "You gave it to me, as you say, twice."

His face grew dismayed, panicked. "That's cruel, Alissa."

"So is showing me a beautiful world I can't have," she said, anger seeping into her voice.

"You could have stayed," he shot back.

"You gave me no choice!"

Lodesh sat stiffly, his jaw clenched. "You had all the choice you needed. It was all your choice, never mine." His eyes grew fierce. "What if I had willingly helped Strell? You would have left that much sooner."

Her chin rose. "Maybe." Her eyes dropped. "Probably." Guilt prompted her to add, "All right. I would have."

"I would lose either way, so I *chose*," he hammered the word into submission, "to keep our time together intact. I feared it was going to be my only time with you," he whispered. "No one was going to take that from me. I loved you first. I did."

And with that, Alissa allowed herself to forgive him. "Lodesh," she breathed. "I'm sorry."

He trembled, barely visible in the dark. "So that's it then." His voice was again emotionless, drained. "Give me my flower back and tell me you don't love me."

She felt her face go pale and her mouth become dry. "I can't do that," she whispered.

"Burn you to ash, Alissa," he seethed. "I've waited three lifetimes for you, and you won't even tell me you don't love me?"

Her face twisted, and she turned away in shame. Because she might, she thought silently to herself. Because when she was with him, she couldn't help but forget . . .

But he heard her thoughts, the Wolves help her, she thought he heard, for he gasped and pulled away. "I can't, Alissa," he said hoarsely, grief etched in the lines in his face. "I can't go back to the Hold, to everyone." He gestured weakly. "I broke Talo-Toecan's respect, Strell's friendship, and my honor to win your heart. Now that I have it, I'm not worthy of it."

Her hands went out, and she took his in them. They were cold for the first time. "Please?" she said. "I've lost almost everyone else."

Lodesh sat for a long moment, not looking at her, his face empty. Without a word, he stood and tossed his pack to the ground. He followed it so quickly that they almost hit together. Holding up his hand, he took her box of memories before helping her down. He stared at her, and she felt herself go cold at what she was requesting him to endure.

"What you ask of me is inhuman," he finally said. He picked up his pack and settled it on his shoulder to hide his city's emblem. "Perhaps it's a fitting punishment."

There was a whirl of wings, and Alissa jumped as Talon landed upon her shoulder. The kestrel had been in the trees all this time. "I don't want you to be alone," she protested weakly.

He turned to the Hold, and she fell into step beside him. "It's too late," he said softly. "I already am."

46

"Come on, Strell." Alissa hammered at his door. "I know Connen-Neute had you piping half the night, but it's . . ." she did a quick calculation, ". . . nearly seven o'clock." She stuck her tender knuckle in her mouth. "I think," she added under her breath. That night he'd played verse after embarrassing verse of "Taykell's Adventure," though Strell insisted it was called "Taykell and his Maiden" and always had been. She had left after a particularly lewd verse, ears flaming.

"Strell?" She tried the latch. The door creaked open, and rapping on the doorframe, Alissa peeked in. His bed was empty and neatly made up. An expansive rug spread in soft muted shades of sand across the floor. A carved table had replaced his rickety one. It sat too close to his cold hearth with a cup of forgotten tea upon it. Her eyebrows rose at the tapestry of a tract of desert, but what surprised her most was the crack in the wall, or rather its absence. Someone had fixed it. Strell, apparently, was settling in.

"But where are you?" She retreated into the hall. A mental search of the Hold didn't find him or Lodesh. Either they were out of her range or someone was blocking her search. Useless, though, was in the garden. Curious, she headed downstairs. He might know where they were.

Upon reaching the uppermost landing over the great hall, she paused to gaze down at the pendulum swinging its ponderous cadence, marking time whether anyone noticed or not. It was a quarter after three. Useless hadn't bothered to reset it this morning. She pulled out Redal-Stan's oversized ring from around her neck and dangled it so the sun shone through the tiny hole in the band. Adjusting for the new day, she waited until its slight motions stilled. It was just after seven. Smiling now, she set her watch carefully upon the railing before levering herself to stand upon it. Still struggling for balance, she shifted. As a raku she grabbed her watch and unwisely half fell, half glided down in a tight, thrill-rushing spiral.

The pendulum was now a toy. She easily caught it, shifting it to seven before releasing it to set time back to rights. Alissa watched it swing away and back before returning to her proper form. *Shoes included,* she thought, pleased with herself. Growing more curious, she wandered into the kitchen. The sight of the garden door made her pause. Useless had painted it a bright blue. She had been back nearly a week, and it still startled her.

Talon chittered from the kitchen's crossbeams, dropping to land upon Alissa's shoulder. "Hush," Alissa murmured as she gentled the bird with soft fingers. "Where's everybody?" Talon's feathers were cool and smelled of outside, and Alissa's gaze went to the coat hook. Both Strell and Lodesh's coats were missing. Frowning, she went to find Useless.

The morning sun was warm, as the threatened cold had retreated to allow a return of the last hot days of summer. She walked down the rough path and winced at the weeds. Useless's garden was a mess, looking more so for having run through it last week when it was in all its glory. But that, she vowed, would change: one garden bed at a time.

"Useless?" Her voice broke the silence as she turned the corner and found him at the firepit. A trio of sparrows took flight. He turned, blinking in the morning sun.

"Good morning, Alissa."

She dropped down next to him, pleased he was here, and she was here, and that tomorrow would be the same. "Where is everybody?"

"I can't say," he said guardedly, poking at the fire. "I'm sure they'll be back soon."

"Back? Are they with Connen-Neute?" She felt him at the outskirts of her awareness.

Useless was silent, and Alissa's eyes narrowed. Clearly she was being put off, a feeling that strengthened as he pasted a smile upon his face, deepening his few wrinkles. "I suggest we take the opportunity to discuss something I'd rather not expose Connen-Neute to," he said, and her forthcoming complaint evaporated. Though she and Connen-Neute had been taking instruction together for only a short time, she was already feeling the pinch of competition. Talon seemed to laugh, but she settled meekly at a severe look from Useless.

"Now." Useless laced his fingers together. "Show me again the pattern you use to shift."

A groan escaped her, and her heels thumped against the bench. "We've been over this a hundred times," she moaned.

"Then you should have no problem with it, hm-m-m?"

She made a rude face. "Here's the pattern I use to shift," she said in a monotone as she obediently set it up. "Here's the one for tripping . . ."

"Careful," he warned.

". . . the lines," she finished, hiding a smile. The first ward vanished as she set up the second. Deep in her thoughts the pattern glowed. She squirmed as Useless silently pondered the resonance it made upon his own tracings.

"They don't cross," he grumbled.

"I know," Alissa said tartly, and he gave her a sharp glance.

"Don't take it down, yet," he directed as he continued to check every last synapse.

Alissa slumped. Much to her annoyance, Talon invented a new game involving Alissa's collar and her claws. "Stop it," Alissa whispered, unhooking Talon's tiny weapons, but the bird continued to flap about Alissa's ears, tugging at her neckline. Useless looked up with a questioning bother. "I said stop it! Daft bird." Embarrassed, Alissa plucked the bird up and set her on the bench. Talon fluttered to the ground, continuing her game with Alissa's shoelace.

Useless gave them a dubious look, and Alissa shrugged helplessly. With an insane-sounding screech, Talon rolled on the ground with the lace like it was a deadly viper. Useless sighed and went back to his studies. "We must be missing something," he muttered, then his eyes brightened, and he leaned closer. "What is it you always forget when you shift?"

Alissa felt herself go crimson. "It was only the once."

"Yes, yes. What is it you forget?"

There was a ridiculous screech as Talon clipped off the lace and beat it upon the ground.

She looked up. "My clothes." Her eyes widened. "My clothes!"

Useless grinned. "Careful, now."

Alissa added a new ward to the one already resonating. Her breath caught when the first held firm, the second building off one of the original tracings she used to trip the lines.

"So, careful . . ." Useless warned again as she tried adding the ward to shift.

And there it was. Arching off the ward to make her clothes glowed the pattern she used to shift. The memories she used to make clothes created a short circuit between the two. From her right came Useless's sigh, "Wolves tears and sorrow."

"Uh-huh," she agreed, marveling at the paradox of lines weaving amongst themselves.

"Now, Alissa? Forget it."

"Huh?" She turned in surprise, dropping all three of the wards.

"Alissa?" His voice was thick with smoke, and she shivered. "Forget it. . . ."

There was something very much like a ward, but it was fuzzy, just like her head. She couldn't really see it, and for some reason she didn't want to. Talon screeched and flew away. Her outraged cry brought Alissa back to her senses. "Forget what?" she asked.

Useless settled back, sighing contentedly. "I don't recall. What were we talking about?"

"Um, my shoes?"

"I thought it was tea."

"Tea?" Alissa repeated. "M-m-m. I'll go make some."

"No." Useless caught her arm before she could rise. "Like I said, forget it."

"All right." She resettled herself. Something wasn't quite right. *"Beast?"* Alissa called.

"I don't know," her feral consciousness whispered, clearly unnerved.

"Alissa?" Useless murmured, and she looked up to see him frowning. "Would you explain something to me? It's been bothering me all week."

She waited, more than a little worried.

"Your easy companionship with Lodesh," he said. "How . . . It seems as if—" He took a steadying breath. "How could you forgive him so easily?"

"Oh." Alissa stared into the fire, wanting some tea to hide behind. "Withdrawing my friendship won't punish him nearly so well as he punishes himself."

Useless's face went long. "I don't see him suffering."

Alissa reluctantly turned to him. "I told Lodesh that I loved Strell."

"He knew that," Useless said with a touch of belligerence.

"I also told Lodesh that—that I love him, too." Alissa looked away, wishing she hadn't had to admit it out loud. It had to be wrong; loving two men at once.

"That's not suffering," Useless contended irately. "That was the Warden's goal."

She found the strength to meet his eyes. "Yes, and he achieved his goal at a brutal cost."

Useless placed his hands in his lap. It was a student's position. Clearly he didn't understand. "You will have to speak very plainly, Alissa."

Struggling for words, she bent her attentions to fixing her lace. "Lodesh sets a great store by honor and morality. He uses it to define his worth?" she said slowly, and Useless nodded. "By his standards," she said, "what he did to win my heart made him unworthy to have it."

"Ashes," Useless breathed, his eyes widening in understanding. "He lost what he won by the way he won it. And this is why there's no animosity between the Piper and the Warden?"

Nodding, Alissa tucked the ragged end of her shoelace behind the top of her shoe. "Mostly. Before, Lodesh felt no competition because he was going to outlive Strell, picking up where he left off when Strell was gone. Strell had already won my, er, my affection, and felt confident all he had to do was convince you to let us, uh, to sanction—Ashes, Useless. This is embarrassing."

He gave her a weary look, and she took a breath to continue. "Now Lodesh feels unworthy to pursue his claim; Strell isn't allowed to." She shrugged. "You won't let either one of them wed me, and their friendship has only strengthened over their shared frustrations."

Useless snorted and she flushed. "And Connen-Neute," she rushed to fill in the silence, "is happy just to have two companions who aren't hounding him on proper Master behavior."

"M-m-m . . ." It was a distant, deep-in-thought sound.

"And I'm stuck in the middle," she blathered. "Terribly glad I don't have to make a decision between them anymore—seeing as neither one of them can court me." Biting her tongue, she wondered if she had said too much. She felt Useless's eyes fixed upon her, and she winced. Yes. She had said too much.

It was at that sticky moment that Talon returned, scattering the sparrows like leaves. There was a mangled junco in her grip; winter was coming. Alissa fussed and cooed over Talon's kill, much to the bother of Useless. "What a wonderful catch!" she praised, and the bird puffed in pride. "But you know, I'm not particularly hungry."

Useless harrumphed. Alissa's empty middle had been making itself known since she had joined him. Undeterred by her claims, Talon tossed it at Alissa. "No," she said, picking it up with two careful fingers and placing it before Talon. "Why don't you give it to—to Strell." Strell was always a good distraction, even when he wasn't about.

Talon snatched the carcass up and leapt into the air. Alissa watched the bird dart over the garden wall, holding her breath as she realized Talon was taking it to Strell!

"Uh, excuse me, Useless?" Alissa stood and edged out of the firepit. "I think I know how to find Strell at least."

"What?" Useless's golden eyes went wide. "Wouldn't you rather learn a new ward?"

Her jaw dropped as it occurred to her that she had been tricked. "You're distracting me. They're out with Connen-Neute!" she exclaimed, tearing her eyes from Talon. Not wanting to lose the bird, Alissa shifted. The thump of Redal-Stan's watch hitting the ground sounded loud, and she snatched it up, placing it on her ridiculously long raku finger as a ring.

"Alissa. Wait!"

"Is it a surprise for me?" Excited, she hesitated.

"Ah . . ."

"Bye, Useless," she said as she leapt into the air. Beast slipped into control, as welcoming as the warmth of the sun.

"Burn you to ash, student! Wait!"

Alissa felt Useless shift, but she wasn't about to wait. She continued to circle, gaining altitude. Once she was high enough, she spotted a plume of smoke. Not smoke really, but a tiny updraft caused by a small fire using dry wood. A mental search showed only Connen-Neute.

"She's coming, Connen-Neute," she heard Useless mutter in her thoughts. *"I tried."*

Alissa's breath came faster. It was a surprise! Angling sharply, she dived into a good-sized clearing. She shifted, barely seeing the three men frantically shove unidentified lumps out of sight under blankets and into baskets. By the time she completed her shift, Connen-Neute had seated himself, looking as if he had never moved. Talon chittered a welcome from his shoulder, and Lodesh and Strell stood about looking guilty. "Hello!" she cried cheerfully, slipping her watch into her pocket. "What are you doing?"

Connen-Neute shut his eyes, pretending to nap. Lodesh jostled Strell's elbow. "Uh, hey, Alissa." Strell rocked back and forth on his heels. "What brings you out here?"

"Talon."

Lodesh frowned. "I told you we should have locked it up."

Talon squawked, and Connen-Neute reached to soothe her.

There was a whoosh of air as Useless alighted with far more grace than she had shown. Keeping to the outskirts, he shifted to his human form. His eyes upon Lodesh, he reached up with a long finger and rubbed the corner of his mouth. Alissa turned to see Lodesh mimicking him, wiping whatever it was off on the hem of his sleeve. Her eyes narrowed. "So . . ." She leaned to see the blanket-covered lump behind Strell. "Whatcha doing?"

"Nothing," Lodesh said. "Would you like a drop of tea? I just brewed it. Nice and hot."

She eyed Strell sharply as Lodesh poured tea into one of his oversized cups.

"Have some," Strell offered too quickly. Ignoring the proffered cup, Alissa sniffed the air. Something had been burning. Nothing was over the fire now. In fact, it was all coals. Wary, she circled the camp, walking heel-to-toe, her new shoes crunching on the leaves. By the looks of it, they had spent the night out here—without her. "All right. What's going on?"

"Really, Alissa," Strell pleaded, stepping away from the bump under his blanket. "I can promise it's nothing you would—"

Darting around him, Alissa flicked the blanket up to find—

"Oh, how awful!" she cried, appalled as she stared down at the dripping spit of roasted meat. From behind Connen-Neute came the tiny, plaintive, ba-a-a-a-a of an out-of-season lamb. Her hands found her hips, and she glared. "You *cooked* its *mother?*"

Lodesh and Strell exchanged looks. "Um, we have a present for you," Strell said. "Alas," he said with an unconvincing sigh, "you found us out." Cringing at her look of disbelief, he knelt by Connen-Neute. "Give me the baby sheep," he whispered, and Connen-Neute frowned. "Give me the stinkin' baby sheep!" Strell growled.

From the corner of her sight, Alissa could see Useless struggling to keep from laughing. She didn't see anything funny. Connen-Neute pursed his lips, and with death practically shooting from his eyes, he reached behind him and pulled the lamb from a basket.

Strell rose, cradling the squirming sheep close. It swung its head to hit him in the chest. Its tiny black hooves kicked ineffectively. Despite her efforts, her anger softened, driven away by the sight of the helpless thing.

"We found this wee youngster in the hills last night." Lodesh stepped forward. "His soft gentleness and mild countenance brought you instantly to mind."

Alissa's eyebrows rose, and Useless coughed to cover a guffaw. Undeterred, Lodesh continued. "And as its mother had tragically been struck down by—who knows what?—we all thought who better than you to raise it?"

"Tragically struck down?" Alissa said sourly, and Strell edged his tall frame to block her view of the steaming carcass.

"That," Lodesh said grandly, "is my tale, milady, and I am holding myself to it."

She pointed at the carcass. "And what is *that?*"

"A funeral pyre," Strell blurted, and Useless turned away, shaking in silent laughter.

The lamb continued to squirm, nearly escaping Strell as he wasn't holding it properly. "Oh, here," she said, taking it from him impatiently. "You have it all wrong." The tiny thing gave a final lunge for freedom, then settled in her arms. The scent of sheep dung, asters, and mud rose to fill her world, bringing with it memories of long afternoons of sun, and wind, and open fields—and home. Tears welled up as she buried her nose in the prickly warm wool.

"Oh, Alissa." Strell touched her shoulder, and she shook her head, sealing her emotions away.

"I can't believe you were going to eat this little bit of a thing," she said indignantly.

"We weren't going to eat him," Connen-Neute said. "Not until we fattened him up first."

The palm of Lodesh's hand hit his head with a resounding smack and he turned away. Strell shifted uncomfortably. Talon abandoned Connen-Neute for Useless.

Alissa cuddled Connen-Neute's snack closer. "I have only

one thing to say about this." Her foot nudged the charred carcass. "Go ahead," she said, and Strell and Lodesh exchanged a worried glance. "Eat it," she continued. "Eat a flock of them. Just don't cook it in *my* kitchen."

Lodesh's breath eased from him in contentment as he crouched beside it. "Thanks, Alissa," he said, taking up his knife to cut a slice. Strell watched from unsure eyes, not moving.

"But believe me," she said, and everyone froze. "I will not allow anyone's lips to touch mine that have touched anything remotely similar to—to this!" She gave the roasted meat a final push with her toe and turned away, her cheeks burning for having put it so brazenly.

"Great!" Connen-Neute rose to plunk himself down in front of the headless, charred body, expertly slicing off a dripping portion and stuffing his face. "I told you," he said cheerfully around his full mouth. "She's a grand, fine, young woman. Very understanding."

Strell collapsed where he stood, his head in his hands. Lodesh didn't look any better. Tucking his knife away, he snuck envious glances at Connen-Neute.

Head shaking in amusement, Useless entered the camp. "May I join you?" he asked Connen-Neute, and starting at the respect in his tone, Connen-Neute shifted to make room.

Alissa sat at the edge of camp and tried not to gag. Realizing Useless wasn't going to commandeer the meat, Connen-Neute slowed his pace and began cutting small pieces for Talon as well as for himself. The small bird was coaxed back to his shoulder, no doubt appreciating the switch from cold junco. Lodesh and Strell watched jealously. "That bird eats better than we do," Lodesh whispered.

Useless chose his portion with care, delicately dabbing the excess juice with a quickly crafted bit of cloth. "It has occurred to me," he said casually, "that a reckoning is due. Thanks should be extended and punishments meted out."

Connen-Neute looked up in sudden concern, and Alissa, her fingers busy taming Connen-Neute's snack, went still.

"This is very good," Useless said, all attention focused on him. "Who did the braising?"

"I did," Strell said quickly.

Useless nodded. "Tastes like plainsman's fare. Spare on amenities but rich in natural substance."

"Thank you." Strell shifted nervously.

"But I digress." Useless wiped the tip of one of his fingers clean. "As you recently pointed out, Strell, I have been remiss in the sincerity of my offer of shelter." He paused. "Consider yourself welcome, Strell Hirdune, Piper of the Hold."

Lodesh gasped. Alissa turned to Connen-Neute, reading in his wide, golden eyes, the honor that title held.

"Your room is inadequate," Useless said, feigning ignorance of the effects of his words. "Find one in the tower."

"My room is fine," Strell whispered.

Useless looked at him, his brow furrowing. "You will move to the tower."

"Thank you," Strell said, clearly shocked.

"No. Thank you." Useless inclined his head and poured himself a cup of Lodesh's tea.

"A commoner permanently granted shelter in the Hold?" Connen-Neute blurted.

"There's a precedent." Useless frowned to hide his unease. "Redal-Stan once allowed an elderly woman to stay. She was too aged to comfortably make the daily journey from the city."

Alissa couldn't let that go without comment. "Mavoureen wasn't granted anything," she said dryly. "She won it in a wager."

Useless stared, his face slack. "No. Redal-Stan told me—" Connen-Neute nodded, and Useless sighed. For a moment, she thought it was going to end there, but Useless turned a sharp eye to Lodesh. "Now," he said, and she tensed. "For you, Lodesh, Warden of Ese'Nawoer, I have disappointment."

Lodesh held his head level; no expression crossed his features.

"You have been callous, selfish, and found lacking in

honor. Reeve would be shamed," Useless intoned, and Lodesh paled. "What have to you say in your defense?"

"I have none." It was softly spoken, even toned.

"Useless . . ." Alissa pleaded.

"Hush," he said, then turned to Lodesh. "It's my decision that your title of Warden be struck from you, Lodesh Stryska, and that you be allowed to wear the mirth flower as a family honor only, *not* as token of the city's affections."

Lodesh went paler still, his green eyes turning frightened for the first time.

"You will not be allowed entry to the citadel," Useless continued, "until such time as you recover your title or the grace of one who holds court there."

"Useless!" Alissa cried. Lodesh was being exiled!

"Furthermore," he continued, "you will be reduced to probationary Keeper status."

Lodesh's head came up, a fire in his eyes Alissa didn't understand.

"And as such, you shall be confined to the Hold and its environs unless accompanied by an appropriate escort. You will resume your moral studies under my guidance until such time as I deem you have fully comprehended the ramifications of your—choices."

"What?" Alissa said to Connen-Neute. *"What does that mean?"*

Connen-Neute grinned. *"He's a student Keeper again."*

"He's been forgiven?" she asked.

"No. But his debt to the Hold for his betrayal has been paid by the loss of his title."

"That is," Useless interjected into their private conversation, *"if you agree to it."*

"Yes!" Alissa exclaimed. *"I do!"*

"Fine," Useless said. "So it is." He drained his cup and reached for the pot.

"You can stay?" Strell asked in disbelief

Lodesh nodded. "But I'm a lowly Keeper," he said, smiling, "ranking only a cell in the Keepers' hall. Wolves!" He pushed on Strell's shoulder. "A room in the tower!"

Strell eyed Alissa with an unspoken longing. "I'd rather stay where I am."

Brow furrowed, Alissa glared at Useless. The "honor" had moved Strell farther away from her, putting Lodesh that much closer in his room down the hall. Didn't he trust her?

Useless rose, excusing himself from the cloud of male exuberance to bring Alissa a cup of tea. He sank down beside her, never spilling a drop. The lamb squirmed from her and trotted happily to Strell. Clearly he had been the one caring for the little ram even as Strell seasoned his mother. The lamb frolicked about his feet, butting him in the shins. Talon jumped to the ground to vie for some of the attention.

Alissa raised her cup, and Lodesh's tea was in her mouth before she realized what she was doing. She held it there, trying to decide if she really wanted to swallow when she stopped short. The tea was good. Really good! "This is good!" she exclaimed, earning a curious look from Useless. "No, really," she protested. "It is."

"Well, yes. Lodesh said he made it." Useless settled himself. "He has always made excellent tea. Ever since becoming Warden."

Dumbfounded, Alissa set the cup down and eyed at it as if it were a snake. Slowly she picked it back up and took a careful sip. She glanced at Lodesh, and when he wasn't looking, checked the finish of the cup. There was no blemish under the handle. None at all. She had changed something else, something small, something worthless, and no one but she knew it.

Useless cleared his throat. "You do realize you have a problem, don't you?"

Alissa turned to him. "What's that?"

Taking a slow, measured sip, Useless nodded to Strell and Lodesh. "They're on equal footing." He sat back rather smugly. "You will have to choose."

Alarm trickled through her. "But you won't sanction a Master/commoner union."

Useless nodded. "Ordinarily." Setting his cup down, he pulled out from his sash a tube stopped at both ends. The fragrance of mirth wood bloomed, and she watched in surprise as he twisted open one end and shook out a piece of rolled parchment. Silently he handed it to her.

The paper crackled as she unrolled it, slowly reading the tight, cramped penmanship. It was from Redal-Stan. She couldn't make out the last bit, not because her eyes had filled and the writing had become blurry, but because it was written in Strell's script. The first half, however, was plain enough. "What does the last part say?" she asked, her throat tight. She missed Redal-Stan more than she wanted to admit.

Useless took the letter from her and rolled it up. "If he wanted you to know, he would have written it so you could read it."

She was too miserable to argue. Strell's laugh drew her eyes up to see the lamb charge at Talon, stopping dead in his tracks when his playmate disappeared up into the air. Alissa snuffled back a tear. "Then you'll give your blessing for me to wed either of them?"

"No," he said, and she turned in surprise. "If you read it carefully, you will see Redal-Stan only requested I allow them to freely court you."

"And that means . . ." she prompted.

He leaned to place her cup into her slack fingers. "You were raised foothills, right?" She nodded, and he smiled, clearly pleased. "Marriage isn't anything I've a say in, is it?"

Alissa thought about that. "My mother must show favor," she breathed in dismay.

"Yes," Useless agreed smugly. "Your mother, or a reasonable facsimile thereof."

"But I don't know where she is!" Alissa protested. "The farm's abandoned! She's gone back to the plains! You know that!"

Lodesh and Strell looked up at her cry. Their brows rose in thought, and something she couldn't name passed between them.

"I suppose things will have to wait until she meets them, then, eh?" Useless said, and Alissa scrubbed a hand over her face, trying to find the justice in this new wrinkle. Strell and Lodesh would have to come with her. The trip would be on foot. The earliest she could start would be spring. Months of travel through hostile territory. And that was assuming she could find her mother's thought signature. Alissa sighed and tucked her hair behind an ear. She would work all winter on it, then shove her accomplishment in Useless's face.

Useless chuckled. "I won't have my student bare of choices or taking the easy path when there's a harder one available."

Connen-Neute shook his head in sympathy and went back to his breakfast. Lodesh gave Strell a challenging look, then rose to join the young Master. Her eyes widened as he cut a portion of the carcass and took a mocking bite, never moving his gaze from Strell. "I have eight hundred years to make this up to her," he said, the dare heavy in his voice as he wiped his chin.

Strell's eyes narrowed as he sat with his jaw clenched. The hard anger of perseverance the plains taught fell over him, almost frightening in its intensity. She watched in alarm as he leaned to cut a portion of meat. He chewed methodically, his eyes riveted to Lodesh's. "I only need a night," he said.

Alissa's jaw dropped. She had lost control. Somehow she had become a prize in an asinine man contest. That was going to change. Right now. Lips pursed, she started to rise.

"Alissa?" Useless stopped her with a single hand. He grinned knowingly as she fell back. "I have to ask. Did you really break Earan's arm over a pair of slippers?"

She closed her eyes to gather her strength. It was going to be a long winter.